THE
PERIPHERAL

BY THE SAME AUTHOR

Neuromancer

Count Zero

Burning Chrome

Mona Lisa Overdrive

Virtual Light

Idoru

All Tomorrow's Parties

Pattern Recognition

Spook Country

Zero History

Distrust That Particular Flavor

THE PERIPHERAL

WILLIAM GIBSON

VIKING

an imprint of

PENGUIN BOOKS

VIKING

Published by the Penguin Group

Penguin Books Ltd, 80 Strand, London WC2R 0RL, England

Penguin Group (USA) Inc., 375 Hudson Street, New York, New York 10014, USA

Penguin Group (Canada), 90 Eglinton Avenue East, Suite 700, Toronto, Ontario, Canada M4P 2Y3
(a division of Pearson Penguin Canada Inc.)

Penguin Ireland, 25 St Stephen's Green, Dublin 2, Ireland (a division of Penguin Books Ltd)

Penguin Group (Australia), 707 Collins Street, Melbourne, Victoria 3008, Australia
(a division of Pearson Australia Group Pty Ltd)

Penguin Books India Pvt Ltd, 11 Community Centre, Panchsheel Park, New Delhi – 110 017, India

Penguin Group (NZ), 67 Apollo Drive, Rosedale, Auckland 0632, New Zealand
(a division of Pearson New Zealand Ltd)

Penguin Books (South Africa) (Pty) Ltd, Block D, Rosebank Office Park,
181 Jan Smuts Avenue, Parktown North, Gauteng 2193, South Africa

Penguin Books Ltd, Registered Offices: 80 Strand, London WC2R 0RL, England

www.penguin.com

First published in the United States of America by G. P. Putnam's Sons,
a member of Penguin Group (USA) LLC 2014
Published in Great Britain by Viking 2014
001

Printed in Great Britain by Clays Ltd, St Ives plc

A CIP catalogue record for this book is available from the British Library

HARDBACK ISBN: 978–0–670–92155–3
TRADE PAPERBACK ISBN: 978–0–670–92156–0

www.greenpenguin.co.uk

MIX
Paper from
responsible sources
FSC® C018179

Penguin Books is committed to a sustainable
future for our business, our readers and our planet.
This book is made from Forest Stewardship
Council™ certified paper.

To Shannie

I have already told you of the sickness and confusion that comes with time travelling.

—H. G. WELLS

1.

THE HAPTICS

hey didn't think Flynne's brother had PTSD, but that sometimes the haptics glitched him. They said it was like phantom limb, ghosts of the tattoos he'd worn in the war, put there to tell him when to run, when to be still, when to do the bad-ass dance, which direction and what range. So they allowed him some disability for that, and he lived in the trailer down by the creek. An alcoholic uncle lived there when they were little, veteran of some other war, their father's older brother. She and Burton and Leon used it for a fort, the summer she was ten. Leon tried to take girls there, later on, but it smelled too bad. When Burton got his discharge, it was empty, except for the biggest wasp nest any of them had ever seen. Most valuable thing on their property, Leon said. Airstream, 1977. He showed her ones on eBay that looked like blunt rifle slugs, went for crazy money in any condition at all. The uncle had gooped this one over with white expansion foam, gone gray and dirty now, to stop it leaking and for insulation. Leon said that had saved it from pickers. She thought it looked like a big old grub, but with tunnels back through it to the windows.

Coming down the path, she saw stray crumbs of that foam, packed down hard in the dark earth. He had the trailer's lights turned up, and closer, through a window, she partly saw him stand, turn, and on his spine and side the marks where they took the haptics off, like the skin was dusted with something dead-fish silver. They said they could get that off too, but he didn't want to keep going back.

"Hey, Burton," she called.

"Easy Ice," he answered, her gamer tag, one hand bumping the door open, the other tugging a new white t-shirt down, over that chest the Corps gave him, covering the silvered patch above his navel, size and shape of a playing card.

Inside, the trailer was the color of Vaseline, LEDs buried in it, bedded in Hefty Mart amber. She'd helped him sweep it out, before he moved in. He hadn't bothered to bring the shop vac down from the garage, just bombed the inside a good inch thick with this Chinese polymer, dried glassy and flexible. You could see stubs of burnt matches down inside that, or the cork-patterned paper on the squashed filter of a legally sold cigarette, older than she was. She knew where to find a rusty jeweler's screwdriver, and somewhere else a 2009 quarter.

Now he just got his stuff out before he hosed the inside, every week or two, like washing out Tupperware. Leon said the polymer was curatorial, how you could peel it all out before you put your American classic up on eBay. Let it take the dirt with it.

Burton took her hand, squeezed, pulling her up and in.

"You going to Davisville?" she asked.

"Leon's picking me up."

"Luke 4:5's protesting there. Shaylene said."

He shrugged, moving a lot of muscle but not by much.

"That was you, Burton. Last month. On the news. That funeral, in Carolina."

He didn't quite smile.

"You might've killed that boy."

He shook his head, just a fraction, eyes narrowed.

"Scares me, you do that shit."

"You still walking point, for that lawyer in Tulsa?"

"He isn't playing. Busy lawyering, I guess."

"You're the best he had. Showed him that."

"Just a game." Telling herself, more than him.

"Might as well been getting himself a Marine."

She thought she saw that thing the haptics did, then, that shiver, then gone.

2

"Need you to sub for me," he said, like nothing had happened. "Five-hour shift. Fly a quadcopter."

She looked past him to his display. Some Danish supermodel's legs, retracting into some brand of car nobody she knew would ever drive, or likely even see on the road. "You're on disability," she said. "Aren't supposed to work."

He looked at her.

"Where's the job?" she asked.

"No idea."

"Outsourced? VA'll catch you."

"Game," he said. "Beta of some game."

"Shooter?"

"Nothing to shoot. Work a perimeter around three floors of this tower, fifty-fifth to fifty-seventh. See what turns up."

"What does?"

"Paparazzi." He showed her the length of his index finger. "Little things. You get in their way. Edge 'em back. That's all you do."

"When?"

"Tonight. Get you set up before Leon comes."

"Supposed to help Shaylene, later."

"Give you two fives." He took his wallet from his jeans, edged out a pair of new bills, the little windows unscratched, holograms bright.

Folded, they went into the right front pocket of her cutoffs. "Turn the lights down," she said, "hurts my eyes."

He did, swinging his hand through the display, but then the place looked like a seventeen-year-old boy's bedroom. She reached over, flicked it up a little.

She sat in his chair. It was Chinese, reconfiguring to her height and weight as he pulled himself up an old metal stool, almost no paint left on it, waving a screen into view.

MILAGROS COLDIRON SA

"What's that?" she asked.

"Who we're working for."

"How do they pay you?"

"Hefty Pal."

"You'll get caught for sure."

"Goes to an account of Leon's," he said. Leon's Army service had been about the same time as Burton's in the Marines, but Leon wasn't due any disability. Wasn't, their mother said, like he could claim to have caught the dumbfuck there. Not that Flynne had ever thought Leon was anything but sly, under it all, and lazy. "Need my log-in and the password. Hat trick." How they both pronounced his tag, Hapt-Rec, to keep it private. He took an envelope from his back pocket, unfolded and opened it. The paper looked thick, creamy.

"That from Fab?"

He drew out a long slip of the same paper, printed with what looked to be a full paragraph of characters and symbols. "You scan it, or type it outside that window, we're out a job."

She picked up the envelope, from where it lay on what she guessed had been a fold-down dining table. It was one of Shaylene's top-shelf stationery items, kept literally on a top shelf. When letter orders came in from big companies, or lawyers, you went up there. She ran her thumb across the logo in the upper left corner. "Medellín?"

"Security firm."

"You said it's a game."

"That's ten thousand dollars, in your pocket."

"How long you been doing this?"

"Two weeks now. Sundays off."

"How much you get?"

"Twenty-five thousand per."

"Make it twenty, then. Short notice and I'm stiffing Shaylene."

He gave her another two fives.

2.

DEATH COOKIE

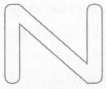etherton woke to Rainey's sigil, pulsing behind his lids at the rate of a resting heartbeat. He opened his eyes. Knowing better than to move his head, he confirmed that he was in bed, alone. Both positive, under current circumstances. Slowly, he lifted his head from the pillow, until he could see that his clothes weren't where he assumed he would have dropped them. Cleaners, he knew, would have come from their nest beneath the bed, to drag them away, flense them of whatever invisible quanta of sebum, skin-flakes, atmospheric particulates, food residue, other.

"Soiled," he pronounced, thickly, having briefly imagined such cleaners for the psyche, and let his head fall back.

Rainey's sigil began to strobe, demandingly.

He sat up cautiously. Standing would be the real test. "Yes?"

Strobing ceased. "Un petit problème," Rainey said.

He closed his eyes, but then there was only her sigil. He opened them.

"She's your fucking problem, Wilf."

He winced, the amount of pain this caused startling him. "Have you always had this puritanical streak? I hadn't noticed."

"You're a publicist," she said. "She's a celebrity. That's interspecies."

His eyes, a size too large for their sockets, felt gritty. "She must be nearing the patch," he said, reflexively attempting to suggest that he was alert, in control, as opposed to disastrously and quite expectedly hungover.

"They're almost above it now," she said. "With your problem."

"What's she done?"

"One of her stylists," she said, "is also, evidently, a tattooist."

Again, the sigil dominated his private pain-filled dark. "She didn't," he said, opening his eyes. "She did?"

"She did."

"We had an extremely specific verbal on that."

"Fix it," she said. "Now. The world's watching, Wilf. As much of it as we've been able to scrape together, anyway. Will Daedra West make peace with the patchers, they wonder? Should they decide to back our project, they ask? We want yes, and yes."

"They ate the last two envoys," he said. "Hallucinating in synch with a forest of code, convinced their visitors were shamanic spirit beasts. I spent three entire days, last month, having her briefed at the Connaught. Two anthropologists, three neoprimitivist curators. No tattoos. A brand-new, perfectly blank epidermis. Now this."

"Talk her out of it, Wilf."

He stood, experimentally. Hobbled, naked, into the bathroom. Urinated as loudly as possible. "Out of what, exactly?"

"Parafoiling in—"

"That's been the plan—"

"In nothing but her new tattoos."

"Seriously? No."

"Seriously," she said.

"Their aesthetic, if you haven't noticed, is about benign skin cancers, supernumerary nipples. Conventional tattoos belong firmly among the iconics of the hegemon. It's like wearing your cock ring to meet the pope, and making sure he sees it. Actually, it's worse than that. What are they like?"

"Posthuman filth, according to you."

"The tattoos!"

"Something to do with the Gyre," she said. "Abstract."

"Cultural appropriation. Lovely. Couldn't be worse. On her face? Neck?"

"No, fortunately. If you can talk her into the jumpsuit we're print-ing on the moby, we may still have a project."

He looked at the ceiling. Imagined it opening. Himself ascending. Into he knew not what.

"Then there's the matter of our Saudi backing," she said, "which is considerable. Visible tattoos would be a stretch, there. Nudity's non-negotiable."

"They might take it as a signal of sexual availability," he said, hav-ing done so himself.

"The Saudis?"

"The patchers."

"They might take it as her offer to be lunch," she said. "Their last, either way. She's a death cookie, Wilf, for the next week or so. Anyone so much as steals a kiss goes into anaphylactic shock. Something with her thumbnails, too, but we're less clear about that."

He wrapped his waist in a thick white towel. Considered the carafe of water on the marble countertop. His stomach spasmed.

"Lorenzo," she said, as an unfamiliar sigil appeared, "Wilf Nether-ton has your feed, in London."

He almost vomited, then, at the sudden input: bright saline light above the Garbage Patch, the sense of forward motion.

3.
PUSHING BUGS

She managed to get off the phone with Shaylene without mentioning Burton. Shaylene had gone out with him a few times in high school, but she'd gotten more interested when he'd come back from the Marines, with that chest and the stories around town about Haptic Recon 1. Flynne figured Shaylene was basically doing what the relationship shows called romanticizing pathology. Not that there was a whole lot better available locally.

She and Shaylene both worried about Burton getting in trouble over Luke 4:5, but that was about all they agreed on, when it came to him. Nobody liked Luke 4:5, but Burton had a bad thing about them. She had a feeling they were just convenient, but it still scared her. They'd started out as a church, or in a church, not liking anyone being gay or getting abortions or using birth control. Protesting military funerals, which was a thing. Basically they were just assholes, though, and took it as the measure of God's satisfaction with them that everybody else thought they were assholes. For Burton, they were a way around whatever kept him in line the rest of the time.

She leaned forward now, to squint under the table for the black nylon case he kept his tomahawk in. Wouldn't want him going up to Davisville with that. He called it an axe, not a tomahawk, but an axe was something you chopped wood with. She reached under, hooked it out, relieved to feel the weight. Didn't need to open it, but she did. Case was widest at the top, allowing for the part you'd have chopped wood with. More like the blade of a chisel, but hawk-billed. Where the back of an axe would've been flat, like the face of a hammer, it was spiked, like a miniature of the blade but curved the other way. Either one thick as your little finger, but ground to edges you wouldn't feel as you cut yourself. Handle was graceful, a little recurved, the wood soaked in something that made it tougher, springy. The maker had a forge in Tennessee, and everyone in Haptic Recon 1 got one. It looked used. Careful of her fingers, she closed the case and put it back under the table.

She swung her phone through the display, checking Badger's map of the county. Shaylene's badge was in Forever Fab, an anxious segment of purple in its emo ring. Nobody looked to be up to much, which wasn't exactly a surprise. Madison and Janice were gaming, Sukhoi Flankers, vintage flight sims being Madison's main earner. They both had their rings beige, for bored shitless, but then they always had them that way. Made four people she knew working tonight, counting her.

She bent her phone the way she liked it for gaming, thumbed Hapt-Rec into the log-in window, entered the long-ass password. Flicked GO. Nothing happened. Then the whole display popped, like the flash of a camera in an old movie, silvered like the marks of the haptics. She blinked.

And then she was rising, out of what Burton said would be a launch bay in the roof of a van. Like she was in an elevator. No control yet. And all around her, and he hadn't told her this, were whispers, urgent as they were faint, like a cloud of invisible fairy police dispatchers.

And this other evening light, rainy, rose and silver, and to her left a river the color of cold lead. Dark tumble of city, towers in the distance, few lights.

Camera down giving her the white rectangle of the van, shrinking in the street below. Camera up, the building towered away forever, a cliff the size of the world.

4.

SOMETHING SO DEEPLY EARNED

L orenzo, Rainey's cameraperson, with the professional's deliberate gaze, steady and unhurried, found Daedra through windows overlooking the moby's uppermost forward deck.

Netherton wouldn't have admitted it to Rainey, or indeed to anyone, but he did regret the involvement. He'd let himself be swept up, into someone else's far more durable, more brutally simple concept of self.

He saw her now, or rather Lorenzo did, in her sheepskin flying jacket, sunglasses, nothing more. Noted, wishing he hadn't, a mons freshly mohawked since he'd last encountered it. The tattoos, he guessed, were stylized representations of the currents that fed and maintained the North Pacific Gyre. Raw and shiny, beneath some silicone-based unguent. Makeup would have calculated that to a nicety.

Part of a window slid aside. Lorenzo stepped out. "I have Wilf Netherton," Netherton heard him say. Then Lorenzo's sigil vanished, Daedra's replacing it.

Her hands came up, clutched the lapels of her open jacket. "Wilf. How are you?"

"Glad to see you," he said.

She smiled, displaying teeth whose form and placement might well have been decided by committee. She tugged the jacket closer, fists sternum-high. "You're angry, about the tattoos," she said.

"We did agree, that you wouldn't do that."

"I have to do what I love, Wilf. I wasn't loving not doing it."

"I'd be the last to question your process," he said, channeling intense annoyance into what he hoped would pass for sincerity, if not understanding. It was a peculiar alchemy of his, the ability to do that, though now the hangover was in the way. "Do you remember Annie, the brightest of our neoprimitivist curators?"

Her eyes narrowed. "The cute one?"

"Yes," he said, though he hadn't particularly thought so. "We'd a drink together, Annie and I, after that final session at the Connaught, when you'd had to go."

"What about her?"

"She'd been dumbstruck with admiration, I realized. It all came out, once you were gone. Her devastation at having been too overawed to speak with you, about your art."

"She's an artist?"

"Academic. Mad for everything you've done, since her early teens. Subscriber to the full set of miniatures, which she literally can't afford. Listening to her, I understood your career as if for the first time."

Her head tilted, hair swung. The jacket must have opened as she raised one hand to remove the sunglasses, but Lorenzo wasn't having any.

Netherton's eyes widened, preparing to pitch something he hadn't yet invented, none of what he'd said so far having been true. Then he remembered that she couldn't see him. That she was looking at someone called Lorenzo, on the upper deck of a moby, halfway around the world. "She'd particularly wanted to convey an idea she'd had, as the result of meeting you in person. About a new sense of timing in your work. She sees timing as the key to your maturation as an artist."

Lorenzo refocused. Suddenly it was as if Netherton were centimeters from her lips. He recalled their peculiarly brisk nonanimal tang.

"Timing?" she asked, flatly.

"I wish I'd recorded her. Impossible to paraphrase." What had he said previously? "That you're more secure, now? That you've always been brave, fearless really, but that this new confidence is something else again. Something, she put it, so deeply earned. I'd planned on discussing her ideas with you over dinner, that last time, but it didn't turn out to be that sort of evening."

Her head was perfectly still, eyes unblinking. He imagined her ego swimming up behind them, to peer at him suspiciously, something eel-like, larval, transparently boned. He had its full attention. "If things had gone differently," he heard himself say, "I don't think we'd be having this conversation."

"Why not?"

"Because Annie would tell you that the entrance you're considering is the result of a retrograde impulse, something dating from the start of your career. Not informed by that new sense of timing."

She was staring at him, or rather at whoever Lorenzo was. And then she smiled. Reflexive pleasure of the thing behind her eyes.

Rainey's sigil privacy-dimmed. "I'd want to have your baby now," she said, from Toronto, "except I know it would always lie."

5.
DRAGONFLIES

She'd forgotten to pee. Had to leave the copter autopiloting a perimeter, fifteen feet out from the client building, and run out to Burton's new composting toilet. Now she tugged up the zip on her cutoffs, fastened the button, tossed a scoopful of cedar sawdust down the hole, and bashed out through the door, making the big tube of government hand sanitizer he'd slung on the outside thump and slosh. Smacked its white plastic, catching some, rubbed it across her palms and wondered if he'd lifted the tube from the VA hospital.

Back inside, she opened the fridge, grabbed a piece of Leon's homemade jerky and a Red Bull. Stuck the lopsided strip of dried beef in her mouth as she sat down, reaching for her phone.

Paparazzi were back. Looked like double-decker dragonflies, wings or rotors transparent with speed, little clear bulb on the front end. She'd tried counting them, but they were fast, moved constantly. Maybe six, maybe ten. They were interested in the building. Like AI emulating bugs, but she knew how to do that herself. They didn't seem to be trying to do anything, other than dart and hover, heads toward the building. She edged a couple, saw them dart away, gone. They'd be back. It felt like they were waiting for something, evidently on the fifty-sixth floor.

Building was black from some angles, but really a very dark bronzy brown. If it had windows, the floors she was working didn't, or else they were shuttered. There were big flat rectangles on the face, some vertical, some horizontal, no order to them.

The fairies had gone quiet as she'd passed twenty, according to the display's floor indicator. Some level of stricter protocol? She wouldn't have minded having them back. It wasn't that interesting up here, swatting at dragonflies. On her own time, she'd have been checking out views of the city, but she wasn't being paid to enjoy the scenery.

Seemed to be at least one street that was transparent, down there, lit from below, like it was paved with glass. Hardly any traffic. Maybe they hadn't designed that yet. She thought she'd seen something walking, two-legged, at the edge of woods, or a park, too big to be human. Some of the vehicles hadn't had any lights. And something huge had sailed slowly past, out beyond the receding towers, like a whale, or a whale-sized shark. Lights on it, like a plane.

Tested the jerky for chewability. Not yet.

Went hard at a dragonfly, front camera. Didn't matter how fast she went, they were just gone. Then a horizontal rectangle folded out and down, becoming a ledge, showing her a wall of frosted glass, glowing.

Took the jerky out of her mouth, put it on the table. The bugs were back, jockeying for position in front of the window, if that was what it was. Her free hand found the Red Bull, popped it. She sipped.

Then the shadow of a woman's slim butt appeared, against the frosted glass. Then shoulder blades, above. Just shadows. Then hands, a man's by their size, on either side, above the shadows of the woman's shoulder blades, his fingers spread wide.

Swallowed, the drink like thin cold cough syrup. "Scoot," she said, and swept through the bugs, scattering them.

One of the man's hands left the glass, its shadow vanishing. Then the woman stepped away, the man's other hand staying where it was. Flynne imagined him leaning there, against the glass, and that there hadn't been the kiss he'd expected, or if there had been, not the hoped-for result.

Moody, for a game. You could open a serious relationship show with that. Then his remaining hand was gone. She imagined an impatient gesture.

Her phone rang. Put it on speaker.

"You good?" It was Burton.

"I'm in," she said. "You in Davisville?"

"Just got here."

"Luke show?"

"They're here," he said.

"Don't mess with them, Burton."

"Not a chance."

Sure. "Anything ever happen, in this game?"

"Those cams," he said. "You edging them back?"

"Yeah. And sort of a balcony's folded out. Long frosted glass window, lights on inside. Saw shadows of people."

"More than I've seen."

"Saw a blimp or something. Where's it supposed to be?"

"Nowhere. Just keep those cams back."

"Feels more like working security than a game."

"Maybe it's a game about working security. Got to go."

"Why?"

"Leon's back. Kimchi dogs. Wishes you were here."

"Tell him I've got to fucking work. For my fucking brother."

"Do that," he said, was gone.

She lunged at the bugs.

6.

PATCHERS

Lorenzo captured the moby's approach to the city. His hands, on the railing, and Netherton's, on the upholstered arms of the room's most comfortable chair, seemed momentarily to merge, a sensation nameless as the patchers' city.

Not a city, the curators had insisted, but an incremental sculpture. More properly a ritual object. Grayly translucent, slightly yellowed, its substance recovered as suspended particulates from the upper water column of the Great Pacific Garbage Patch. With an estimated weight of three million tons and growing, it was perfectly buoyant, kept afloat by segmented bladders, each one the size of a major airport of the previous century.

It had less than a hundred known inhabitants, but as whatever continually assembled it seemed also to eat cams, relatively little was known about them.

The service cart edged fractionally closer to the arm of his chair, reminding him of the coffee.

"Get this now, Lorenzo," Rainey ordered, and Lorenzo turned to focus on Daedra, amid a scrum of specialists. A white china Michikoid knelt, in a Victorian sailor outfit, lacing Daedra's artfully scuffed leather high-tops. A variety of cams hovered, one of them equipped with a fan to flutter her bangs. He assumed the wind test indicated she was going in without a helmet.

"Not bad," he said, admiring the cut of the new jumpsuit in spite of himself, "if we can keep her in it." As if she'd heard him, Daedra reached up, tugged the zip slightly, then a bit more, exposing a greasy arc of abstracted Gyre-current.

"Went clever on the print file for the zip," Rainey said. "Hope she doesn't try it lower, not until she's down there."

"She won't like that," he said, "when she does."

"She won't like it that you lied to her about the curator."

"The curator may have had remarkably similar thoughts. We won't know until I speak with her." He picked up the cup without looking at it, raised it to his lips. Very hot. Black. He might survive. The analgesics were starting to work. "If she earns her percentage, she won't care about a stuck zip."

"That's assuming the powwow's productive," Rainey said.

"She has every reason to want this to be successful."

"Lorenzo's put a couple of larger cams over the side," she said. "They'll be there soon. Ringside."

He was watching the costumers, makeup technicians, assorted fluffers and documentarians. "How many of these people are ours?"

"Six, including Lorenzo. He thinks that Michikoid is her real security."

He nodded, forgetting she couldn't see him, then spilled coffee on the white linen robe as feed from two speeding cams irised into his field, to either side of Daedra.

Feed from their island always made him itch.

"About a kilometer apart now, heading west northwest, converging," Rainey said.

"You couldn't pay me."

"You don't have to go there," she said, "but we do both need to watch."

The cams were descending through tall, sail-like structures. Everything simultaneously cyclopean and worryingly insubstantial. Vast empty squares and plazas, pointless avenues down which hundreds might have marched abreast.

Continuing to descend, over dried crusts of seaweed, bleached bones, drifts of salt. The patchers, their prime directive to cleanse the fouled water column, had assembled this place from recovered polymers. What shape it had taken was afterthought, offhand gesture, however remarkably unattractive. It made him want to shower. Coffee was starting to seep through the front of his robe.

Now Daedra was being helped to don her parafoil, which in its furled state resembled a bilobed scarlet backpack, bearing the white logo of its makers. "Is the 'foil her placement," he asked, "or ours?"

"Her government's."

The cams halted abruptly, simultaneously finding one another over the chosen square. Descended, above diagonally opposite corners, each capturing the other's identical image. They were skeletal oblongs, the size of a tea tray, matte gray, around a bulbous little fuselage.

Either Lorenzo or Rainey brought the audio up.

The square filled with a low moaning, the island's hallmark soundscape. The patchers had wormed hollow tubes through every structure. Wind blew across their open tops, generating a shifting, composite tonality he'd hated from the moment he'd first heard it. "Do we need that?" he asked.

"It's so much of the feel of the place. I want our audience to have that."

Something was moving in the distance, to his left. "What's that?"

"Wind-powered walker."

Four meters tall, headless, with some indeterminate number of legs, it was that same hollow milky plastic. Like the discarded carapace of something else, moving as if animated by an awkward puppetry. It rocked from side to side as it advanced, a garden of tubes atop its length no doubt contributing to the song of the plastic island.

"Have they sent it here?"

"No," she said. "They set them free, to wander with the wind."

"I don't want it in the frame."

"Now you're the director?"

"You don't want it in the frame," he said.

"The wind's taking care of that."

The thing went stiffly on, swaying, on its hollow translucent legs.

On the upper deck of the moby, he saw, her support staff had been withdrawn. The white china Michikoid remained, checking the parafoil, hands and fingers moving with inhuman speed and precision. The ribbon on its sailor cap fluttered in the breeze. A real one, the cam with the fan absent now.

"And here we are," said Rainey, and he saw the first of the patchers, one cam shifting focus.

A child. Or something the size of one. Hunched over the handlebars of a ghostly little bike, the bike's frame the same salt-crusted translucence as the city and the wind-walker. Unpowered, it seemed to lack pedals as well. The patcher progressed by repeatedly scuffing at the avenue's surface.

The patchers repelled Netherton even more than their island. Their skin was overgrown with a tweaked variant on actinic keratosis, paradoxically protecting them from UV cancers. "There's only the one?"

"Satellite shows them converging on the square. One dozen, counting this one. As agreed."

He watched the patcher, gender indeterminate, advancing on its kick-bike, its eyes, or possibly goggles, a single lateral smudge.

7.

SURVEILLANT

They were prepping for a party, behind the frosted glass. She knew because it was clear now, like that trick Burton taught her with two pairs of sunglasses.

The bugs were right on it, so she was right on them, doing what she could to vary the angle of attack. She'd found a pull-down for hotdogging, so she could make the copter behave in ways they were less ready for. She'd almost gotten one that way, dropping on it. Proximity had triggered image-capture, bug in extreme close, but that was gone right away, no way of calling it up. Looked like something Shaylene might print at Forever Fab. A toy, or a really ugly piece of jewelry.

She was supposed to chase bugs, not catch them. They'd have a record of everything she did anyway. So she'd just shoo bugs, but while she did that, she was getting more than a glimpse of what was going on inside.

The couple who'd been up against the window weren't there. Nobody human was. Robots, little low beige things that moved almost too fast to see, were vacuuming the floor, while three almost identical robot girls were arranging food on a long table. Classic anime robot babes, white china faces almost featureless. They'd built three big flower arrangements and now they were transferring food from carts to trays on the table. When the carts came in, rolling themselves to the table, the blur of beige parted just enough to let them through. Flowed around them like mechanical water, perfectly tight right-angle turns.

She was enjoying this a lot more than Burton would have. She wanted to see the party.

There were shows where you watched people prep for weddings, funerals, the end of the world. She'd never liked any of them. But they hadn't had robot girls, or super-fast Roombas. She'd seen videos of factory robots assembling things, almost that fast, but nothing the kids had Shaylene print out for them ever moved that way.

She dropped toward two bugs, hovered, scoping one of the robot girls without changing focus. This one was wearing a quilted vest with lots of pockets, little shiny tools sticking up in them. She was using something like a dental pick to individually arrange things, too small to see, on top of sushi. Round black eyes in the china face, wider apart than human eyes, but they hadn't been there before.

She bent her phone a little more, to give her fingers a rest. Scattering the bugs.

The whirling beige on the floor vanished, like a light turned off, all except for one poor thing, looking like a starfish, that had to hump itself out of sight on what seemed to be wheels in the tips of its five points. Broken, she guessed.

A woman entered the room. Brunette, beautiful. Not boy-game hot. Realer. Like Flynne's favorite AI character in Operation Northwind, the French girl, heroine of the Resistance. Simple dress, like a long t-shirt, a dark gray that went to black where her body touched it, reminding Flynne of the shadows on the window. It migrated down, of its own accord, off her left shoulder entirely, as she walked the length of the table.

Robot girls stopped what they were doing, raised their heads, all eyeless now, shallow sockets smooth as their cheekbones. The woman walked around the end of the table. Cam bugs surged.

Heard her fingers on her phone, whipping the copter side to side, up, down, back. "Fuck off," she told them.

The woman stood at the window, looking out, left shoulder bare.

Then the dress climbed smoothly back, covering her shoulder, neckline rising in a V, then rounding.

"Fuck off!" Lunging at the bugs.

Window polarized again, or whatever that was. "Fuck you," she said to the bugs, though it probably wasn't their fault.

Ran a quick perimeter check, in case another window might have opened and she'd miss something. Nothing. Not a single bug, either.

Back around, the bugs were already bobbing, waiting. She flew through them, making them vanish.

Tongued the cud of jerky away from her cheek and chewed. Scratched her nose.

Smelled hand sanitizer.

Went after the bugs.

8.

DOUBLE DICKAGE

he boss patcher, unless he wore some carnival hel-
met fashioned from keratotic skin, had no neck,
the approximate features of a bullfrog, and two
penises.

"Nauseating," Netherton said, expecting no reply from Rainey.

Perhaps a little over two meters tall, with disproportionately long
arms, the boss had arrived atop a transparent penny farthing, the large
wheel's hollow spokes patterned after the bones of an albatross.
He wore a ragged tutu of UV-frayed sheet-plastic flotsam, through
whose crumbling frills could be glimpsed what Rainey called his
double dickage. The upper and smaller of the two, if in fact it was a
penis, was erect, perhaps perpetually, and topped with what looked to
be a party hat of rough gray horn. The other, seemingly more conventional, though supersized, depended slackly below.

"Okay," Rainey said, "they're all here."

Between the oculi of the twin feeds, Lorenzo was studying Daedra
in profile as she faced the five folding steps to the top of the moby's
railing. Head bowed, eyes lowered, she stood as if in prayer or
meditation.

"What's she doing?" asked Rainey.

"Visualization."

"Of what?"

"Herself, I'd imagine."

"You cost me a bet," she said, "getting together with her. Someone
thought you might. I said you wouldn't."

"It wasn't for long."

"Like being a little bit pregnant."

"Briefly pregnant."

Daedra raised her chin then, and touched, almost absently, the color-suppressed American flag patch over her right bicep.

"Money shot," said Rainey.

Daedra took the steps, dove smoothly over the railing.

A third feed irised into place between the other two, this one from below.

"Micro. We sent in a few yesterday," said Rainey, as Daedra's parafoil unfurled, red and white, above the island. "The patchers let us know they knew, but nothing's eaten any yet."

Netherton swiped his tongue from right to left, across the roof of his mouth, blanking his phone. Saw the unmade bed.

"How does she look to you?" Rainey asked.

"Fine," he said, getting up.

He walked to the vertically concave corner window. It depolarized. He looked down on the intersection, its wholly predictable absence of movement. Free of crusted salt, drama, atonal windsong. Across Bloomsbury Street, a meter-long mantis in shiny British racing green, with yellow decals, clung to a Queen Anne façade, performing minor maintenance. Some hobbyist was operating it telepresently, he assumed. Something better done by an invisible swarm of assemblers.

"She seriously proposed to do this naked," Rainey said, "and covered in tattoos."

"Hardly covered. You've seen the miniatures of her previous skins. That's covered."

"I've managed not to, thank you."

He double-tapped the roof of his mouth, causing the feeds, left and right, from their respective corners of the square, to show him the boss patcher and his cohort of eleven, looking up, unmoving.

"Look at them," he said.

"You really hate them, don't you?"

"Why shouldn't I? Look at them."

"We're not supposed to like their looks, obviously. The cannibalism's problematic, if those stories are true, but they did clear the water column, and for virtually no capital outlay on anyone's part. And they now arguably own the world's single largest chunk of recycled polymer. Which feels like a country, to me, if not yet a nation-state."

The patchers had shuffled into a rough circle, with their scooters and kick-bikes, around their boss, who'd left his penny farthing on its side at the edge of the square. The others were as small as the boss was large, compactly disgusting cartoons of rough gray flesh. They wore layers of rags, gray with sun and salt. Modification had run rampant, of course. The more obviously female among them were six-breasted, their exposed flesh marked not with tattoos but intricately meaningless patterns expressed in pseudo-ichthyotic scaling. They all had the same bare, toeless, shoe-like feet. Their rags fluttered in the wind, nothing else in the square moving.

On the central feed, Daedra soared down, swinging out wide, up again. The parafoil was altering its width, profile.

"Here she comes," said Rainey.

Daedra came in low, along the widest of the intersecting avenues, the parafoil morphing rhythmically now, braking, like speeded-up footage of a jellyfish. She scarcely stumbled, as her feet found the polymer, throwing up puffs of salt.

The parafoil released her, instantly shrinking, to land on four unlikely legs, but only for a second or two. Then it lay there, bilobed again, logo uppermost. It would never have fallen logo-down, he knew. Another money shot. The feed from the micro closed.

On the two feeds from the cams above the square, from their opposing angles, Daedra spent momentum, running, keeping impressively upright, into the circle of small figures.

The boss patcher shifted his feet, turning. His eyes, set on the corners of his vast, entirely inhuman head, looked like something a child had scribbled, then erased.

"This is it," said Rainey.

Daedra raised her right hand in what might either have been a gesture of greeting, or evidence that she came unarmed.

Her left, Netherton saw, was beginning to unzip the jumpsuit. The zipper jammed, a palm's width beneath her sternum.

"Bitch," said Rainey, almost cheerfully, as a micro-expression, curdled fury, crossed Daedra's face.

The boss patcher's left hand, like a piece of sporting equipment fashioned from salt-stained gray leather, closed around her right wrist. He lifted her, her carefully scuffed shoes parting with the translucent pavement. She kicked him, hard, in his slack stomach, just above the ragged plastic tutu, salt jumping from the point of impact.

He drew her closer, so that she dangled above the horn-tipped pseudo-phallus. Her left hand touched his side then, just below the ribs. Her fingers were curled, but loosely, her thumb against gray flesh.

He shivered, for an instant. Swayed.

She raised both feet, planted them against his stomach, and pushed. As her fist came away, it looked as though she were extracting a length of scarlet measuring tape. A thumbnail. As long, when it fully emerged, as her forearm. His blood very bright, against a world of gray.

He released her. She landed on her back, instantly rolling, the nail shorter by half. He opened his vast maw, in which Netherton saw only darkness, and toppled forward.

Daedra was already on her feet, turning slowly, each of her thumbnails concave and slightly curving, the left slick with the patcher's blood.

"Hypersonic," said an unfamiliar voice on Rainey's feed, ungendered, utterly serene. "Incoming. Deceleration. Shockwave."

He'd never heard thunder here, before.

Six spotless, white, upright cylinders, perfectly evenly spaced, had appeared above and slightly outside the circle of patchers, all of whom had dropped their bikes and scooters and taken a first step toward Daedra. A vertical line of tiny orange needles danced up and down each one, as the patchers, in some way Netherton was unable to grasp, were shredded, flung. The oculi of Lorenzo's feeds froze: on one the perfect, impossible, utterly black silhouette of a severed hand, almost filling the frame.

"We are so fucked," said Rainey, her amazement total, childlike.

Netherton, seeing the Michikoid, on the deck of the moby, sprout multiple spider-eyes and muzzle-slits, in the instant before it vaulted the railing, could only agree.

9.
PROTECTIVE CUSTODY

Londonn.

She'd turned the LEDs down, finding that made it easier to spot the bugs. She left them that way now. She'd been hoping to get the ride down the side of the building, back to the van, because she'd be off duty then, free to look at things, but they'd just bumped her straight out.

Unbent her phone, cracked her knuckles, then sat in tacky twilight, image-searching cities. Hadn't taken long. Curve in the river, texture of the older, lower buildings, contrast between that and the tall ones. Real London didn't have as many tall ones, and in real London tall ones were more clustered together, came in more shapes and sizes. Game London, they were megastacks, evenly spaced but further apart, like on a grid. Their own grid, she knew, London never having had one.

She wondered where to leave the paper with the log-in. Decided on the tomahawk case. As she was putting it back under the table, her phone rang. Leon. "Where is he?" she asked.

"Homes," he said, "protective custody."

"Arrested?"

"No. Locked up."

"What did he do?"

"Acted out. Homes were all grinning and shit, after. They'd liked it. Gave him a Chinese tailor-made cigarette."

"He doesn't smoke."

"He can swap it for something."

"Took his phone?"

"Homes take everybody's phone."

Looked at hers. Macon had only just printed it for her the week before. She hoped he'd gotten everything right, now Homeland computers would be looking at it. "They say how long he'll be in for?"

"Never do," said Leon. "Make more sense if it's till Luke's gone."

"How's that looking?"

"'Bout the same as when we got here."

"What happened?"

"Big old boy, holding up one end of a God-hates-everything sign. Burton says tell you same time, same place. What you're doing for him. Till he's back. Says an extra five for every other one."

"Tell him they're all an extra five. What they'd be paying him."

"You make me glad I don't have a sister."

"You got a cousin, dickbag."

"No shit."

"Keep track of Burton, Leon."

"'Kay."

She checked Shaylene on Badger. Still there, still ringing purple. She'd ride over there. Maybe see Macon, ask him about Burton's phone, and hers.

10.
THE MAENADS' CRUSH

The place was a drinking closet for tourists, Netherton supposed, a walled-in 1830s archway in a corner of the lower level of Covent Garden, staffed by a lone Michikoid he kept expecting to erupt in targeting devices. There was a full-sized, vigorously authentic-looking pub sign, depicting what he took to be maenads, a number of them, mounted above a bar long enough for four stools, and the curtained snug where he now sat, awaiting Rainey. He'd never seen another customer in the place, which was why he'd suggested it.

The curtain, thick burgundy velour, moved. A child's eye appeared, hazel, under pale bangs. "Rainey?" he asked, though certain it was her.

"Sorry," the child said, slipping in. "They didn't have anything in adult. Something popular at the opera tonight, so everything in the neighborhood's taken."

He imagined her now, stretched on a couch in her elongated Toronto apartment, a bridge across an avenue, diagonally connecting two older towers. She'd be wearing a headband, to trick her nervous system into believing the rented peripheral's movements were hers in a dream.

"I'm right off Michikoids," she said, looking ten, perhaps younger, and in the way of many such rentals, like no one in particular. "Watched the one from the moby, while it was guarding Daedra. Nasty. Move like spiders, when they need to." She took the chair opposite his, regarded him glumly.

"Where is she?"

"No telling. Her government sent in some kind of aircraft, but of course they blanked the extraction. Ordered the moby away."

"But you could still watch?"

"Not the extraction, but everything else. Big guy down on his face, the rest of them sliced and diced. No more of them turned up, so no more casualties. Good for us, in theory, assuming the project in any way continues."

"Would your friend care for something, sir?" the Michikoid asked, from beyond the curtain.

"No," he said, as there was no point in putting good liquor into a peripheral. Not that this place had any.

"He's my uncle," she said, loudly, "really."

"You suggested we meet this way," Netherton reminded her. He took a sip of their least expensive whiskey, identical to their most expensive, which he'd sampled while waiting for her.

"Shit," she said, small hand gesturing to encompass their situation. "Lots of it. Now. Hitting many fans. Large ones."

Rainey was employed, as he understood it, by the Canadian government, though they were no doubt hermetically walled off from any responsibility for her actions. He considered this to be an arrangement of quite startlingly naked simplicity, in that she probably did know, at least approximately, who her superiors were. "Can you be more specific?" he asked her.

"Saudis are out," she said.

He'd been expecting it.

"Singapore's out," she continued. "Our half-dozen largest NGOs."

"Out?"

The child's head nodded. "France, Denmark—"

"Who's left?"

"The United States," she said. "And a faction in the government of New Zealand."

He sipped the whiskey. Its small tongue of fire on his.

She tilted her head. "Considered to have been an assassination."

"That's absurd."

"What we hear."

"We who?"

"Don't ask."

"I don't believe it."

"Wilf," said the child, leaning forward, "that was a hit. Someone used us to help kill him, not to mention his entourage."

"Daedra had a significant percentage in any successful outcome. Aside from that, what's happened can't be good for her."

"Self-defense, Wilf. Easiest spin on earth. You and I know that she wanted to provoke them. She needed an excuse, to make it self-defense."

"But she was always going to be the contact figure, wasn't she? She was already part of the package when you signed on. Wasn't she?"

She nodded.

"Then you hired me. Who brought her in in the first place?"

"These questions," she said, the child's diction growing more precise, "suggest that you don't understand our situation. Neither of us can afford any interest in the answers to questions like those. We're going to take a hit on this one, Wilf, professionally. But that—" She left it unfinished.

He looked into the rental's still eyes. "Is better than being the object of another one?"

"We neither know," the child said, firmly, "nor desire to know."

He looked at the whiskey. "They had her covered with a hypersonic weapons-delivery system, didn't they? Something orbital, ready to drop in."

"But they would, her government. It's what they do. But we shouldn't even be discussing this now. It's over. We both need it to be over. Now."

He looked at her.

"It could be worse," she said.

"It could?"

"You're still sitting here," the child said. "I'm home, all warm in my jammies. We're alive. And about to be looking for work, I imagine. Let's keep it that way, shall we?"

He nodded.

"This would probably be a little less complicated if you hadn't had a sexual relationship with her. But that was brief. And is over. It is over, isn't it, Wilf?"

"Of course"

"No loose ends?" she asked. "Didn't leave your shaving kit? Because we need it over, Wilf. Really. We need there to be no reason at all that you ever have to communicate with her again."

And then he remembered.

But he could fix it. No need to tell Rainey.

He reached for the whiskey.

11.

TARANTULA

Locked her bike in the alley and used her phone to let herself into the back of Forever Fab, smelling pancakes and the shrimp rice bowl special from Sushi Barn. Pancakes meant they were printing with that plastic you could compost. Shrimp special was Shaylene's midnight snack.

Edward was on a stool in the middle of the room, monitoring. He wore sunglasses against the flashes of UV, with his Viz behind the glasses, on one side. In the low light the glasses looked the same color as his face, but shinier. "Seen Macon?" she asked.

"No Macon." Near comatose with boredom and the hour.

"You want a break, Edward?"

"I'm okay."

She glanced at the long worktable, stacked with jobs needing removal of afterbirth, smoothing, assembly. She'd spent a lot of hours at that table. Shaylene was a solid source of casual employment, if you got along with her and were quick with your hands. Looked like they were printing toys tonight, or maybe decorations for the Fourth.

She went into the front, found Shaylene watching the news: ugly-spirited sign-carriers. Shaylene looked up. "Hear from Burton?"

"No," Flynne lied. "What's happening?" Didn't want to have the Burton conversation. Odds of avoiding it were zero.

"Homeland took some vets away. I'm worried about him. Got Edward to sub for you."

"Saw him," Flynne said. "Breakfast?"

"You're up early."

"Haven't slept." She hadn't said what it was she'd needed to do, wouldn't now. "Seen Macon?"

Shaylene flicked through the display with a fancy resin nail, Luke 4:5 tumbling back into the green of some imaginary savannah. "Wasn't that kind of night." Meaning she'd pitched the all-nighter because there was excess work to be done, not because Macon needed peace and quiet to fab his funnies. Flynne wasn't sure how much of Fab's income was funny, but assumed a good part of it was. There was a Fabbit franchise a mile down the highway, with bigger printers, more kinds, but you didn't do anything funny at Fabbit. "I'm dieting," Shaylene said. Flamingoes rose from the savannah.

"That the purple?"

"Burton," Shaylene said, standing, slipping in a finger to tug at the waist of her jeans.

"Burton can take care of himself."

"VA aren't doing shit, to help him recover."

What Shaylene saw as Burton's primary symptom of traumatic stress, Flynne thought, was his ongoing failure to ask her out.

Shaylene sighed, that Flynne didn't get it, how her brother was. Shaylene had big hair without actually having it, Flynne's mother had once said. Something that came up through any remake, like marker ink through latex paint. Flynne liked her, except for the Burton thing.

"You see Macon, ask him to get in touch with me. Need some help with my phone." Starting to turn to go.

"Sorry I'm a bitch," Shaylene said.

Flynne squeezed her shoulder. "Let you know as soon as I hear from him."

Let herself out the back, with a nod to Edward.

Conner Penske blew past on his Tarantula, as she was turning out of the alley behind Fab, what was left of him a jagged black scrawl behind the two front wheels. Janet sewed him these multizippered socklike things, out of black Polartec. They looked, as Janet worked on them, like fitted cases for something you couldn't imagine, which Flynne guessed they were. Town's only other HaptRec vet, he'd come back in one of the ways she'd been scared Burton would: minus a leg, the foot of the other one, the arm on the opposite side, and the thumb and two fingers of the remaining hand. Handsome face unscarred, which made it weirder. She smelled recycled fried chicken fat hanging in the trike's exhaust trail, as the single huge rear slick vanished down Baker Way. Rode at night, mostly county roads, this county and the next two or three over, steering with a servo rig the VA paid for. She figured he got loose, that way. Basically didn't stop until the fuel was running out, hooked up to a Texas catheter and high on something wakey. Slept all day if he could. Burton helped him out at home, sometimes. He made her sad. A sweet boy in high school, for all he'd been that good-looking. Neither he nor Burton ever said anything to anyone, that she knew of, about what had happened to him.

She rode to Jimmy's, letting the hub do most of the work. Went in and sat at the counter, ordered eggs and bacon and toast, no coffee. In the Red Bull mirror behind the counter, the cartoon bull noticed her, winked. She dodged eye contact. She hated it when they spoke to you, called you by your name.

That mirror was the newest thing in Jimmy's, a place that had been old when her mother had gone to high school. Everything old in Jimmy's had at some point been painted in one or another generation of dark shiny brown, including the floor. The onions were starting to sizzle for the lunch dogs. Stung her eyes. She'd have the smell in her hair.

Hefty Mart would be open. She'd walk up and down the aisles, while forklifts brought in shrink-wrapped pallets. She liked it in there, early. She'd spend one of the shiny new fives on two bags of groceries, things that would keep in the cupboard. The neighbors had all grown more vegetables than they knew what to do with, out of a random stretch of rain. Then she'd go by Pharma Jon and put another

five against her mother's prescriptions. Then ride home, get the pan-
niers unloaded, contents into the pantry, lucky if she didn't wake anybody but the cat.

The edge of the counter was trimmed with LEDs like the ones in
Burton's trailer, under a sloppier application of polymer. She'd never
seen them on, but it had been at least a year since she'd been in here
with the place in bar mode. She pressed the polymer with her thumb,
feeling it give.

Burton and Leon, before they enlisted, learned you could use a
syringe to inject this same stuff, still liquid, into the part of a shotgun
shell that held the shot, then quickly epoxy over the hole you'd made.
The polymer stayed wet in there, most of the time anyway, between
the little lead balls, so it didn't expand. When you fired one, it solidi-
fied as the shot left the barrel, producing a weird, potato-shaped lump
of polymer and lead, so slow that you could almost see it tumble out
of the barrel. Heavy, elastic, they'd bounce these off the concrete walls
and ceilings, in the county storm shelter, trying to hit things around
corners. Leon had gotten keys to the place. Looked weird when you
weren't in there with everybody else, hiding from a tornado. Burton,
after a while, actually could hit things around corners, but the sound
of the Mossberg hurt her ears, even with earplugs.

Burton had been different then. Not just thinner, gangly, which
seemed impossible now, but messy. She'd noticed, the night before,
how everything she hadn't touched, in the trailer, was perfectly
squared up with the edge of something else. Leon said the Corps had
turned Burton into a neatfreak, but she hadn't really thought about it
before. She reminded herself to take that empty Red Bull can out to
the recyc bin, spend some time straightening things up.

Girl brought her eggs.

She heard Conner's trike pass again, out beyond the parking lot.
Nothing else on the road sounded like that. Police pretty much gave
him a pass, because he ran mostly late at night.

She hoped he was on his way home.

12.

THYLACINE

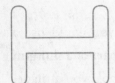e'd wanted to impress her, and what better way than to offer her something money couldn't buy? Something that had felt to him like a ghost story, when Lev had first explained it.

He'd told her about it in bed. "And they're dead?" she'd asked.

"Probably."

"A long time ago?"

"Before the jackpot."

"But alive, in the past?"

"Not the past. When the initial connection's made, that didn't happen, in our past. It all forks, there. They're no longer headed for this, so nothing changes, here."

"My bed?" She spread her arms and legs, smiled.

"Our world. History. Everything."

"And he hires them?"

"Yes."

"What does he pay them with?"

"Money. Coin of their realm."

"How does he get it? Does he go there?"

"You can't go there. Nobody can. But information can be exchanged, so money can be made there."

"Who did you say this is?"

"Lev Zubov. We were at school together."

"Russian."

"Family's old klept. Lev's the youngest. Man-child of leisure. Has hobbies, Lev. This is his latest."

"Why haven't I heard of it before?"

"It's new. It's quiet. Lev looks for new things, things his family might invest in. He thinks this one may be out of Shanghai. Something to do with quantum tunneling."

"How far back can they go?"

"Twenty twenty-three, earliest. He thinks something changed, then; reached a certain level of complexity. Something nobody there had any reason to notice."

"Remind me of it later." She reached for him.

On the walls, the framed flayed hides of three of her most recent selves. Her newest skin beneath him, unwritten.

Ten at night now, in the kitchen of Lev's father's Notting Hill house, his house of art.

Netherton knew there was a house of love as well, in Kensington Gore, several houses of business, plus the family home in Richmond Hill. The Notting Hill house had been Lev's grandfather's first London real estate, acquired midcentury, just as the jackpot really got going. It reeked of the connections allowing it to quietly decay. There were no cleaners here, no assemblers, no cams, nothing controlled from outside. You couldn't buy permission for that. Lev's father simply had it, and likely Lev would too, though his two brothers, whom Netherton avoided if at all possible, seemed better suited to exercise the muscular connectedness needed to retain it.

He was watching one of Lev's two thylacine analogs through the kitchen window, as it did its stiff-tailed business beside an illuminated bed of hostas. He wondered what its droppings might be worth. There were competing schools of thylacinery, warring genomes, another of Lev's hobbies. Now it turned, in its uncanine fashion, its vertically striped flank quite heraldic, and seemed to stare at him. The regard of a mammalian predator neither canid nor felid was a peculiar thing, Lev had said. Or perhaps Dominika had a feed from its eyes. She didn't like him. Had disappeared when he'd arrived, upstairs, or perhaps down into the traditionally deep iceberg of oligarchic subbasements.

"It's not that simple," Lev said now, placing a bright red mug of coffee on the scarred pine table in front of Netherton, beside a yellow bit of his son's Lego. "Sugar?" He was tall, brownly bearded, archaically bespectacled, ostentatiously unkempt.

"It is," Netherton said. "Tell her it stopped working." He looked up at Lev. "You told me it might."

"I told you that none of us have any idea when or why it started, whose server it might be, let alone how long it might continue to be available."

"Then tell her it stopped. Is there any brandy?"

"No," said Lev. "You need coffee. Have you met her sister, Aelita?" He took a seat opposite Netherton.

"No. I was going to. Before. They didn't seem to be that close."

"Close enough. Daedra didn't want it. Neither would I, frankly. We don't do that sort of thing, if we're serious about continua."

"Didn't want it?"

"Had me give it to Aelita."

"To her sister?"

"He's part of Aelita's security now. A very minor part, but she knows he's there."

"Fire him. End it."

"Sorry, Wilf. She finds it interesting. We're having lunch on Thursday, and I hope to explain that polts aren't really what continua are about. I think she may get it. Seems bright."

"Why didn't you tell me?"

"I thought you had your hands full. And frankly you weren't making a great deal of sense, at that point. Daedra rang, told me you were sweet, that she didn't want to hurt your feelings, but why didn't I give it to her sister, who likes odd things. It didn't feel to me as if you were slated to be a very permanent part of her life, so I didn't think it would matter. And then Aelita rang, and she seemed genuinely curious, so I gave it to her."

Netherton raised the coffee with both hands, drank, considered.

Decided that what Lev had just told him actually solved the problem. He no longer had a connection with Daedra. He'd indirectly introduced a friend to the sister of someone he'd been involved with. He didn't know that much about Aelita, other than that she was named after a Soviet silent film. There hadn't been much mention of her in Rainey's briefing material, and he'd been distracted. "What does she do? Some sort of honorary diplomatic position?"

"Their father was ambassador-at-large for crisis resolution. I think she inherited a sliver of that, though some might say Daedra's more the contemporary version."

"Thumbnails and all?"

Lev wrinkled his nose. "Are you sacked?"

"Apparently. Not formally, yet."

"What are you going to do?"

"Fail forward. Now that you've explained things, I see no reason for Daedra's sister not to keep her polt." He drank more coffee. "Why do you call them that?"

"Ghosts that move things, I suppose. Hello, Gordon. Pretty boy."

Following Lev's gaze, Netherton found the thylacine, upright on its hind legs on the small patio, gazing in at them. He really badly wanted a drink, and now he remembered where he thought he might likely find one. Just the one, though. "I need to think," he said, standing. "Mind if I go and stroll the collection?"

"You don't like cars."

"I like history," Netherton said. "I don't fancy walking the streets of Notting Hill."

"Would you like company?"

"No," Netherton said, "I need to ponder."

"You know where the elevator is," said Lev, getting up to let the thylacine in.

13.

EASY ICE

Unstuck her in time, day-sleeping in her bedroom. How old was she? Seven, seventeen, twenty-seven? Dusk or dawn? Couldn't tell by the light outside. Checked her phone. Evening. The house silent, her mother probably asleep. Out through the smell of her grandfather's fifty years of *National Geographic*, shelved in the hall. Downstairs, she found lukewarm coffee in the pot on the stove, then went out back for a shower, in the fading light. Sun had warmed the water just right. Came out of the stall wrapped in Burton's old bathrobe, rubbing her hair with a towel, ready to dress for the job.

Something she'd gotten from Burton and the Corps, that you didn't do things in the clothes you sat around in. You got yourself squared away, then your intent did too. When she'd been Dwight's recon point, she'd made sure she got cleaned up. Doubted she'd be doing that again, even though it was the best money she'd made. She didn't like gaming, not the way Madison and Janice did. She'd done it for the money, got so good at one particular rank and mission in Operation Northwind that Dwight wouldn't have anybody else. Except that he would, by now.

She wanted to be sharp tonight, not just for the job. She wanted to see as much as she could of that London. Maybe it was a game she could get into. Burton said it wasn't a shooter. She wanted to know more about the woman, see more of how she lived.

She went back upstairs, dug through the clothes piled on the armchair. Found her newest black jeans, which were still really black, and the short-sleeved black shirt from when she'd worked at Coffee Jones.

Sort of military, patch pockets and those strap things on the shoulders. She'd taken the Coffee Jones embroidery off, left the FLYNNE in red script over the left pocket. Her sneakers didn't work with black, but they were all she had. She was planning on having Macon fab her some funny ones, but she hadn't found any she really liked, for him to copy.

Back in the kitchen, she made herself a ham and cheese sandwich, snapped it into Tupperware, bent her phone around her left wrist, and headed down to the trailer in the dark, listening to a new Kissing Cranes track. Leon rang her before the chorus. She left it on her wrist. "Hey," she said. "Get him out yet?"

"Homes getting ready to let 'em all go. Luke's decided the Lord's work's about done, for now."

"So what have you been doing?"

"Fucking the dog. Shot a bunch of pool, slept in the car, kept my ass off the street."

"Talk to Burton again?"

"No," he said, "they put 'em all in the center of the track at West Davis High. I could go up in the bleachers and watch him playing cards, or eating MREs, or sleeping. Not much point."

Maybe dull enough to keep Burton from going up there next time, but she doubted it. "When they let him out, you get him to call me."

"Will do," Leon said.

As Kissing Cranes came back on, she saw the tube of hand sanitizer on the door of the composting toilet. It was covered with QRs and requisition numbers, their ink starting to fade. But she'd already used the toilet in the house.

As she opened the trailer's door, it struck her that Burton never locked it, didn't even have a lock. Nobody was coming in without him asking.

She'd forgotten how hot it would get, sitting closed all day. Leon wanted to AC it, but Burton wasn't interested. He usually wasn't there in the daytime. Maybe her shirt and jeans hadn't been a good idea.

She put the sandwich in the fridge, got the windows open as far as she could. A gold and black spider had started spinning a web across one of the foam tunnels, outside.

She tidied up a little, straightening things. As she moved around, the Chinese chair tried to adjust itself for her. She wasn't sure she'd want to live with that, but when she finally sat down on it, it was just right.

Took her phone off, bent it to her preferred controller angle, waved it above his display. Checked Badger. Shaylene was already back at Fab, still showing anxiety, and Burton was now indicated off-map. Which turned out to be the Hefty Mart parking lot in Davisville, which she guessed would be filled with big white Homeland trucks, one of them with Burton's phone locked up in it. She frowned. Homes would know that she'd just checked that, which was okay. What wasn't okay would be if they noticed that her phone was funny. Nothing to be done about it, though. She got out of Badger and back into the searches she'd run for London the night before.

She kept hoping Burton would phone, that they'd already let him out, but really it felt like they would, from what Leon said, so she kept clicking, deeper into random London. City in the game was London for sure, but with something bigger and harder-looking grown up out of it.

When it was time, she got the log-in out of the tomahawk case, waved a finger for Milagros Coldiron SA, and entered the string.

This time, she'd planned what she'd look at, going up.

She got a closer look at the van as the copter emerged. More like an armored car than a van. Sort of heavy shouldered, like Conner's trike. The bay she'd come out of was square, dark. She heard the voices, urgent still and just as impossible to understand.

Same time of day she'd arrived before, late dusk. Wetter clouds, the building's black-bronze face dull with condensation.

Next she located the street she'd noticed before, the one that seemed to be paved with something like glass, lit from underneath. Water under there, moving?

Looked for vehicles, seeing three.

As the counter at ten o'clock ticked off the twentieth floor, the voices were gone.

She first noticed it, the gray thing, as she passed the twenty-third. A dry gray, against the wet dark metal. Color of dead skin pulled from a blister. Size of a child's backpack.

Then she was past it, giving her full attention to a check in three directions, point recon style. Big dark towers, same height, far apart, in their grid across the older city, hers most likely one of them. No whale-thing in the sky.

Gaming having taught her to pay attention to anything that didn't fit, she tried to get a quick second look, down-cam, at the backpack. Couldn't find it.

It overtook and passed her as she reached the thirty-seventh floor. Moving that way, it no longer reminded her of a backpack, but of the black egg case of an almost-extinct animal called a skate, that she'd seen on a beach in South Carolina, an alien-looking rectangle with a single twisted horn at each corner. Tumbling straight up the building now, in a smooth sequence of sticky-footed somersaults. Caught itself with the two tips of whichever pair of horns, or legs, was leading, flipped over, then propelled itself higher with the pair it had just used to grip the surface.

Following it up-cam, she tried to rise more quickly, but that still wasn't under her control. Lost sight of it again. Maybe there had been a way for it to enter the building. She'd watched Macon print little pneumatic bots, like big leeches, that moved something like that, but slower.

Her mother called the skate case a mermaid's purse, but Burton said the local people had called them devil's handbags. It had looked like it ought to be dangerous, poisonous, but it wasn't.

Kept an eye out for the thing, the rest of the way up to the fifty-sixth floor, where she found the same balcony folded down but the window frosted, disappointing. Guessed she'd missed the party, but maybe she could get an idea how it had gone. Bugs didn't seem to be around. Whatever had kept the ride up like an elevator was gone now. She ran a quick perimeter check, hoping for another window, but nothing had changed. No bugs, either.

Back to the frosted glass. Gave it five minutes there, five more, then ran another perimeter. On the far side, a grate she hadn't noticed before was steaming.

Starting to miss the bugs.

Down-camera, a very large vehicle with a single headlight went by, fast.

She'd just gotten around to the window again when it depolarized, and there was the woman, saying something to someone she couldn't see.

Flynne stopped, let the gyros hold her there.

No sign there had ever even been a party. Room didn't look the same at all, like the little bots had been moving serious furniture. The long table was gone. Now there were armchairs, a couch, rugs, softer lighting.

The woman wore striped pajama bottoms and a black t-shirt. Flynne guessed she'd only recently gotten out of bed, because she had the bedhead you could have with hair that good.

Check for bugs, she reminded herself, but they still weren't there.

The woman laughed, as if the person Flynne couldn't see had said something. Had that been her ass against the window, the time before? Was she talking to the man who'd kissed her, or tried to? Had that worked out after all, the party great, and then they'd spent the night together?

She forced herself to do another perimeter, a slow one, watching for bugs, the runaway backpack, anything. The steam had gone, and now she couldn't see where the grate had been. That gave her the feeling that the building was alive, maybe conscious, with the woman inside it laughing, high up in the bugless night. Thinking that, she felt close heat in the trailer, sweat trickling.

Darker now. So few lights in the city, and none at all on the big blank towers.

Coming back around, she found them standing at the window, looking out, his arm around her. Just that much taller than she was, like a model from an ad where they didn't want to stress ethnicity, dark hair and the start of a beard to match, expression cold. The woman spoke, he answered, and the coldness Flynne had seen was gone. The woman beside him wouldn't have seen it at all.

He wore a dark brown robe. You smile a lot, she thought.

Part of the glass in front of them was sliding sideways, and as it did, a skinny horizontal rod rose from the forward edge of the ledge, bringing up a quivering soap bubble. The rod stopped rising. Bubble became greenish glass.

She remembered the SS officer, when she'd worked for Dwight. Face of the man at the window reminded her.

She'd crouched for three days on Janice and Madison's couch, taking her old phone when she ran to the bathroom and back, so as not to miss her chance to kill him.

Janice brought her the herbal tea Burton made her have with the wakey he'd left, white pills, built two counties over. No coffee, he said.

The SS officer was really an accountant in Florida, the man Dwight played against, and nobody had ever killed him. Dwight never fought, himself, just relayed orders from the tacticians he hired. The Florida accountant was his own tactician, and a stone killer to boot. When he won a campaign, which he usually did, Dwight lost money. That kind of gambling was illegal, and federally, but there were ways around that. Neither Dwight nor the accountant needed the money they won, or cared about what they lost, not really. Players like Flynne were paid on the basis of kills, and on how long they could survive in a given campaign.

She'd gotten to feeling that what the accountant most liked, about killing them, was that it really cost them. Not just that he was better at it than they were, but that it actually hurt them to lose. People on her squad were feeding their children with what they earned playing, and maybe that was all they had, like she was paying Pharma Jon for her mother's prescriptions. Now he'd gone and done it again, killed everyone on her squad, one after another, taking his time, enjoying it. He was hunting her now, while she circled, alone, deeper into that French forest and the flying snow.

But then Madison called Burton, and Burton came over, sat on the couch beside her, watching her play, and told her how he saw it.

How the SS officer, convinced he was hunting her, wasn't seeing it right. Because really, now, Burton said, she was hunting him. Or would be, as soon as she realized she was, while his failure to see it was a done deal, fully underway, growing, a wrong path. He said he'd show her how to see it, but he'd need her not to sleep. He gave Janice the white pills, drew a dosing schedule on a napkin. The accountant would sleep, in Florida, leaving his character on some very good AI, but Flynne wouldn't.

So Janice had given her the pills according to the napkin, and Burton had kept coming around, on some schedule of his own, to sit with her and watch, and tell her how he saw it. And sometimes she felt him jerk, haptic misfire, while he was helping her find her own way of seeing it. Not to learn it, he said, because it couldn't be taught, but to spiral in with it, each turn tighter, further into the forest, each turn closer to seeing it exactly right. Down into that one shot across the clearing she found there, where the sudden mist of airborne blood, blown with the snow, was like the term balancing an equation.

She'd been alone on the couch, then. Janice heard her scream.

Got up, walked out on their porch, puked up tea, shaking. Cried while Janice washed her face. And Dwight gave her so much money. But she never once walked point for him again, or ever saw that ragged France.

So why was this all up in her now, watching this guy with the little beard squeeze the woman beside him closer? Why, when she'd run her perimeter around the corner, did she take it up to fifty-seven and double back?

Why was she all Easy Ice now, if this wasn't a shooter?

14.

MOURNING JET

sh, flesh white as paper, was pulling down the lower lid of Netherton's left eye. Her hand quite black with tattoos, a riot of wings and horns, every bird and beast of the Anthropocene extinction, overlapping line drawings of a simple yet touching precision. He knew who she was, but not where he was.

She was leaning over him, peering close. He lay on something flat, very hard, cold. Her neck was wrapped in black lace, a black that ate light, fixed with a cameo death's head.

"Why are you in Zubov's grandfather's land-yacht?" Her gray eyes had dual pupils, one above the other, little black figure eights, affectation of the sort he most detested.

"Stealing Mr. Zubov's oldest whiskey," said Ossian, behind her, "which I'd myself secured against oxidation, with an inert gas." Netherton quite distinctly heard Ossian's knuckles crack. "A pint of plain's your only man, Mr. Netherton. I've told you that, haven't I?" This was indeed something the Irishman sometimes said, though at the moment Netherton was entirely unclear as to what it might mean.

Thuggishly butler-like, Ossian had very large thighs and upper arms, black hair braided at the nape and blackly ribboned. Like Ash, a technical. They were partners, but not a couple. They minded Lev's hobbies for him, kept his polt-world sorted. They'd know about Daedra then, and Aelita.

Ossian was right, about the whiskey. The congeners, in brown liquors. Trace amounts only, but their effects could be terrible. Were, now.

Her thumb withdrew, brusquely, releasing his lower lid. The drawings of animals, startled, fled up her arm, over a pale shoulder, gone. Her thumbnail, he saw, was painted a childish crayon green, chipped at the edges. She said something to Ossian, in a momentary tongue sounding vaguely Italian. Ossian replied in kind.

"That's rude," Netherton protested.

"Encryption isn't optional, when we address one another," she said. It altered constantly, their encryption, something sounding Spanish morphing into a faux German in the course of a simple statement, perhaps by way of something more like birdsong than speech. The birdsong was Netherton's least favorite. Whatever randomly synthetic language the one spoke, the other understood. Never the one thing long enough to provide a sufficient sample for decryption.

The ceiling was pale wood, sealed beneath glassy varnish. Where was he? Rolling his head to the side, he saw he lay on polished black marble, thickly veined with gold. This began to rise now, beneath him, taking him with it, then stopped. Ossian's hard hands seized his shoulders, lifting him to an approximate sitting position on what seemed to have become the edge of a low table. "Hold yourself upright, man," the Irishman ordered. "Flop and you'll crack your skull."

Netherton blinked, still not recognizing the place. Was he in Notting Hill? He hadn't known Lev's house to have a room this small, and particularly not in its basements. The walls were the color of the ceiling, blond veneer. Ash took something from her reticule, a triangular lozenge of plastic, pale green, translucent, frosted like driftglass. Like all of her things, it looked slightly grubby. She slapped its softness against the inside of his right wrist. He frowned as he felt it move, bloodlessly settling incomprehensibly thin tendrils between the cells of his skin. He watched her doubled pupils flick, reading data only she could see. "It's giving you something," she said. "But you mustn't drink on top of that, not at all. You mustn't take liquor from the vehicles again, either."

Netherton was watching the intricate texture of her bustier, which resembled a microminiature model of some Victorian cast-iron station roof, its countless tiny panes filmed as by the coal smoke of fingerling locomotives, yet flexing as she breathed and spoke. Or rather was observing his vision sharpen, brighten, as the Medici had its increasingly welcome way with him.

"Mr. Zubov," said Ossian, meaning Lev's father, and coughed once, into a fist, "may at any time require his father's land-yacht." Not inclined to let Netherton off, but really what was the problem? Lev wouldn't be concerned with a single bottle, regardless of its age.

Ash's Medici released his wrist. She tucked it into her reticule, which he saw was worked with beads of mourning jet.

Netherton stood, briskly, his surroundings now making perfect sense. A Mercedes land-yacht, something Lev's grandfather had commissioned for a tour of Mongolian deserts. There was no place for it, at the house in Richmond Hill, so Lev's father kept it here. The empty bottle, he now remembered, was in a toilet, somewhere to the right. But they obviously knew that. Perhaps he should look into getting one of these things, these hangover alleviators.

"Don't even think about it," Ash said, gravely, as if reading his mind. "You'd be dead in a month, two at most."

"You're awfully grim," he said to her. Then smiled, because, really, she was. Elaborately so. Hair the nano-black of the lace at her throat, the bustier of perpetually rain-streaked iron and glass, as if viewed through the wrong end of a telescope, the layered skirts below it like a longer, darker version of the boss patcher's tutu. And now the line drawing of a lone albatross, slowly and as if in distant flight, circling her white neck.

He looked back at the table he'd slept on, when it had been retracted, flush, into a recess in the floor. Now it was ready to serve as breakfast nook or gaming table, or a place to spread one's maps of Mongolia. He wondered if Lev's grandfather had ever made the journey. He remembered laughing at the vulgarity of what Lev called the Gobiwagen, the one time he'd been shown through, but he'd noted the bar, with its very handsome stock of liquor.

"Keeping it locked from now on," said Ossian, demonstrating his own degree of telepathy.

"Where were you two?" He looked from Ossian to Ash, as if implying some impropriety. "I came down to find you."

Ossian raised his eyebrows. "Did you expect to find us here?"

"I was exhausted," Netherton said, "in need of refreshment."

"Tired," said Ossian, "emotional."

Lev's sigil appeared. "I thought sixteen hours was long enough for you to be unconscious," he said. "Come to the kitchen. Now." The sigil disappeared.

Ash and Ossian, who'd heard nothing Lev had said, were staring at him, unpleasantly.

"Thanks for the pick-me-up," he said to Ash, and left, down the gangway. Into the submarine squidlight of the garage's broad shallow arches, receding down a line of vehicles. Sensing his movement, living tissue coating the arch directly above him brightened. He looked back, and up, at the vehicle's bulging flank. Ossian was watching, from an observation bay, smugly.

As he walked to the distant elevator, past one vehicle after another, light followed him, the skin of one arch dimming as the next fluoresced.

15.

ANYTHING NICE

Leon, the Halloween before, carved a pumpkin to look like President Gonzales. Flynne hadn't thought it looked like her, but that it wasn't racist either, so she left it out on the porch. Second day it was out there, she saw something had nibbled the inside of it, and pooped in it a little. She figured either a rat or a squirrel. Meant to take it around to the garden compost then, but forgot, and next day she found the president's face caved in, pumpkin flesh behind it all eaten away, leaving the orange skin sagging, wrinkled. Plus there was fresh poop inside. She got the rubber gloves she wore for plumbing chores and carried it out back to the compost, where the wrinkled orange face gradually got uglier until it was gone.

She wasn't thinking of that as she hung in the cradle of the gyros, watching the gray thing breathe.

It wasn't gray now, but bronze-black. It had made itself straight, flat, with sharp right angles, but everything else on the face of the fifty-seventh floor, those flat squares and rectangles, was misted, sweating, running with condensation. The thing was perfectly dry, standing out a hand's breadth from the surface behind it. The twisty legs had become brackets. Centered above the floor of the fold-out balcony directly beneath her.

It was breathing.

Sweat broke from her hairline, in the hot dark of the trailer. She wiped it with the back of her forearm, but some ran into her eyes, stung.

She nudged the copter closer. Saw the thing bulge, then flatten.

She had only a vague idea of what she was flying. A quadcopter, but were the four rotors caged, or exposed? If she'd seen herself reflected in a window, she'd know, but she hadn't. She wanted to get closer, see if she could trigger an image, the way proximity had done when she'd dropped on that bug. But if her rotors were exposed, and she touched the thing with one, she'd go down.

It swelled again, along a central vertical line, paler than the rest.

Below her, they were at the railing, the woman's hands on the rod along the top, the man behind her, close, maybe holding her waist.

It flattened. She nudged herself a little closer.

It opened, narrowly, along that vertical line, paler edges curling slightly back, and something small arced out, vanishing. Something scored the forward-cam then, a fuzzy gray comma. Again. Like a gnat with a microscopic chainsaw, or a diamond scribe. Three, four more scratches, insect-quick, flicking like a scorpion's tail. Trying to blind her.

She pulled herself back, fast, then up, whatever it was still slashing at her forward-cam. Found the pull-down and dead-dropped, tumbling three floors before she let the gyros catch and cup her.

It seemed to be gone. Cam damaged but still functional.

Fast, left.

Up, fast. Passing fifty-six, with the cam on her right she saw him take the woman's hands, place them over her eyes. From fifty-seven, she saw him kiss her ear, say something. Surprise, she imagined him saying, as she saw him step back, turn.

"No," she said, as the thing split open. A blur, around the slit. More of them. He glanced up, found it there. Expecting it. Never paused, never looked back. He was about to step back inside.

She went for his head.

She was half up out of the chair, as he saw the copter, ducked, catching himself on his hands.

He must have made a sound then, the woman turning, lowering her hands, opening her mouth. Something flew into her mouth. She froze. Like seeing Burton glitched by the haptics.

He came up off his hands, a track star off blocks. Through the opening, the door in the window, which simply vanished as soon as he was inside, became a smooth sheet of glass, then polarized.

The woman never moved, as something tiny punched out through her cheek, leaving a bead of blood, her mouth still open, more of them darting in, almost invisible, streaming over from the pale-edged slit. Her forehead caved in, like stop-motion of Leon's pumpkin of the president, on top of the compost in her mother's bin, over days, weeks. As the brushed-steel railing lowered, behind her, on the soap-bubble stuff that was no longer glass. Without it to stop her, the woman toppled backward, limbs at angles that made no sense. Flynne went after her.

She was never able to remember any more blood, just the tumbling form in its black t-shirt and striped pants, less a body every inch it fell, so that by the time they passed the thirty-seventh, where she'd first noticed the thing, there were only two fluttering rags, one striped, one black.

She pulled up before the twentieth, remembering the voices. Hung there in the gyros' slack, full of sorrow and disgust.

"Just a game," she said, in the trailer's hot dark, her cheeks slick with tears.

She took it back up, then, feeling blank, miserable. Watching dark bronze sweep past, not bothering to try to see the city. Fuck it. Just fuck it.

When she got to fifty-six, the window was gone, the balcony folded back up over it. The bugs were back, though, the transparent bubbles on their business ends facing where the window had been. She didn't bother shooing them.

"That's why we can't have anything nice," she heard herself say, in the trailer.

16.

LEGO

ifteen minutes," said Lev, scrambling eggs on the kitchen's vast French stove, bigger than either of the ATVs slung from davits on the stern of his grandfather's Mercedes. "Most of that is reading their terms-of-service agreement. They're in Putney."

Netherton at the table, exactly where he'd been earlier. The windows looking onto the garden were dark. "You can't be serious," he said.

"Anton had it done."

The scarier of Lev's two older brothers. "Good for him."

"He had no choice," Lev said. "Our father organized the intervention."

"Never thought of Anton as having a drinking problem," Netherton said, as if this were something he was quite accustomed to being objective about. He was watching two Lego pieces, one red, one yellow, as they morphed into two small spheres, between the Starck pepper grinder and a bowl of oranges.

"He no longer does." Lev transferred scrambled eggs, flecked with chives, to two white plates, each with its half of a broiled tomato, which had been warming on the stovetop. "It wasn't only for drinking. He had an anger management problem. Aggravated by the disinhibition."

"But haven't I seen him drinking," Netherton asked, "here, and recently?" He was fairly certain that he had, in spite of having a firm policy of flight if either brother appeared. Fully spherical now, the two Legos began to roll slowly toward him, across worn pine.

"Of course," said Lev, adjusting the presentation of the eggs with a clean steel spatula. "We're not in the dark ages. But never to excess. Never to the point of intoxication. The laminates see to that. They metabolize it differently. Between that and the cognitive therapy module, he's doing very well." He came to the table, a white plate in either hand. "Ash's Medici says you're not doing well, Wilf. Not at all." He put one plate in front of Netherton, the other opposite, and took a seat.

"Dominika," Netherton said, reflexively trying to change the subject. "She's not joining us?" The two Legos had stopped moving. Still spherical, side by side, they were directly in front of his plate.

"My father would have disowned Anton, if he'd refused treatment," Lev said, ignoring the question. "He made that absolutely clear."

"Gordon wants in," Netherton said, having just noticed the thylacine at the glass door, darkness behind it.

"Tyenna," corrected Lev, glancing at the animal. "She's not allowed in the kitchen when we're eating."

Netherton quickly flicked the red Lego off the table. He heard it click against something, roll. "Hyena?"

"Medici doesn't like the look of your liver."

"Eggs look wonderful—"

"Laminates," Lev said, evenly, looking Netherton in the eye, the heavy black frames of his glasses accentuating his seriousness, "and a cognitive therapy module. Otherwise, I'm afraid this will have to be your last visit."

Fucking Dominika. This was about her. Had to be. Lev had never been like this. The yellow Lego was brick-shaped again. Pretending innocence.

Lev looked up, then, and to the side. "Excuse me," he said, to Wilf. "I have to take this. Yes?" He gestured at Netherton's eggs: eat. He asked something, briefly, in Russian.

Netherton unrolled his knife and fork from the cool heavy napkin. He would eat the eggs and tomato in exactly the way a healthy, relaxed, responsible individual would eat them. He had never felt less like eating eggs, or broiled tomato.

Lev was frowning now. He spoke again in Russian. At the end of it, "Aelita." Had he really said her name, or only something in Russian that had sounded like it? Then a question, also in Russian, which, yes, definitely culminated in her name. "Yes," he said, "it is. Very." His hand came up, to scratch the skin just above his left nostril with the nail of his index finger, something Netherton knew he did when he was concentrating. Another question in Russian. Netherton dutifully tried the eggs. Tasteless. The thylacine was gone now. You almost never saw them leaving.

"That's odd," said Lev.

"Who was it?"

"My secretary, with one of our security modules."

"What about?" Please, Netherton begged the uncaring universe, let Lev be more interested in this, now, than in any behavioral modification in Putney.

"Aelita West's secretary just canceled lunch. Tomorrow, in the Strand. I'd reservations for Indian. She'd wanted to know more about her polt. Your gift."

Netherton forced himself to take another half-fork of eggs.

"The Met was listening in, when her secretary spoke with mine. We were surveilled."

"The police? Seriously? How did it know?"

"She didn't," said Lev, annoyingly personalizing a program. "The security module did, though."

Klept as established as the Zubov family's, Netherton assumed, was layered in byzantine tediousness. He refrained from saying so.

"The security module interpreted it as being related to a very recent event," Lev said, adjusting his black frames to peer at Netherton.

"How could it know that?"

"Any listener necessarily assumes a particular stance, informed by intention. Our module's more sophisticated than that which was listening. The shape of their listening suggested what they were listening for."

So unexpectedly welcome was this distraction that Netherton had scarcely been paying attention, but now he realized that it fell to him to keep the conversation going, and as far away from Putney as possible. "What would that be, then?"

"Serious crime, it assumed. Abduction, possibly. Even homicide."

"Aelita?" It struck Netherton as absurd.

"Nothing so clear as that. We're having a look. She held a reception, just this evening. While you were sleeping it off."

"You've been watching her?"

"The security module's done a retrospective, since her secretary's call."

"What sort of reception?"

"Cultural. Semigovernmental. It would originally have been about your project, in fact. One would assume celebratory, if Daedra hadn't killed your man and had the cavalry in. Rather than cancel, it seems, Aelita reframed it. No idea what as. Security was excellent."

"Where was it held?"

"Her residence. Edenmere Mansions." Lev's pupils moved as he read something. "She has the fifty-fifth through fifty-seventh floors. Daedra attended."

"She did? Did you have someone there?"

"No," said Lev, "but our modules tend to be a bit sharper than theirs. Eat." His fork, neatly loaded with both eggs and tomato now, was almost to his mouth when he stopped, frowned. "Yes?" He lowered the fork. "Well," he said, "it isn't as though there hasn't been the odd rumor that it's possible. I'll be down shortly."

"Secretary?" Netherton asked.

"Ash," Lev said. "She says that someone else is accessing our stub. Seems as though it has to do with your polt."

"Who?"

"No idea. We'll go down and see." He began to eat his eggs and tomato.

Netherton did the same, finding that with the distancing of Putney and liver lamination, and possibly the aftereffects of Ash's Medici, they'd acquired flavor.

The red Lego, spherical, now rolled slowly from behind the bowl of oranges, to join, becoming rectilinear again, with the tiniest of clicks, its yellow companion. He wondered what shape it had taken to get back up the table leg.

17.

COTTONWOOD

oing back to Jimmy's was a bad idea. Knew it soon as she'd walked into the dark and the dancing, the smell of beer and state weed and homegrown tobacco. The bull was leaning out of the mirror, eyeing a girl who might have been fourteen. The LEDs were pulsing to a song Flynne had never heard before and wouldn't have wanted to again, and she was the oldest living thing in the building. Still wearing her improv security guard outfit. And she hadn't even found Macon, over on the side of the lot where mostly black kids hung, where he did his funny business. She'd come because she still needed to ask him what Homes might have thought of the phone he'd made for her, but maybe she'd really just been hoping for someone to talk to. She hadn't felt like the sandwich she'd made to eat after the shift, and she didn't feel like she'd ever be hungry.

That shit in the game. She hated that shit. Hated games. Why did they all have to be so fucking ugly?

She got a beer, her phone dinging as Jimmy's ran a tab. Took the bottle to a little round corner table, unwiped but mercifully empty, sat down, tried to look like the meanest old lady she could. Girl who'd passed her the beer had a Viz, like Macon and Edward had, a tangle like silver cobweb filling one eye socket, but you could still see the eye behind it, watching whatever the little units strung in the tangle were projecting. Hefty Mart had to scan your socket before they fabbed you one, so it would fit, and there weren't any funny ones yet. Looked better on a black face, she thought, but most every kid here had one and it made her feel old, and more so that she thought they looked kind of stupid. It was something every year.

"Look like you've come up short on the number of fucks you need to not give," Janice said, appearing out of the crowd with a beer of her own.

"Short a few," Flynne agreed, but no longer the oldest thing in Jimmy's. She'd always liked Janice. She automatically looked around, because Janice and Madison weren't usually very far apart. He was at a table with two boys, each one with a silver-tangled eye. He looked like Teddy Roosevelt, Madison, and most of what she knew about Teddy Roosevelt was that Madison looked like him. He had a mustache he trimmed but never shaved off, round titanium-wire glasses, and a moth-eaten wool cruiser vest, olive green, complicated breast pockets bristling with pens and little flashlights.

"Want some company with it?"

"Long as it's you," Flynne said.

Janice sat down. She and Madison had that thing going, that some married people did, where they'd started to look like each other. Janice had the same round glasses but no mustache. They could have swapped outfits without attracting any attention. She was wearing cammies that were probably his. "You really don't look too happy."

"I'm not. Worried about Burton. Homes had him for going up to Davisville and beating on Luke 4:5. No charges, just a public safety detention."

"I know," Janice said. "Leon told Madison."

"He's doing something on the side," Flynne said, glad of the music, looking around, knowing Janice would understand about the disability money. "I filled in for him."

Janice raised an eyebrow. "You don't give the impression you liked it much."

"Beta testing some kind of creepy-ass game. Serial killers or something."

"You played anything, since that time at our place?" Janice was watching her.

"Just this. Twice." Flynne felt differently uncomfortable. "You seen Macon?"

"He was here. Madison was talking to him."

"In here much, you and Madison?"

"Do we look like it?"

"So fucking young."

"It was young when we were here before, remember? You were, anyway. Burton's kid sister." She smiled, looked around.

As the song ended, there was a blast of deep-throated exhaust from out in the parking lot.

"Conner," said Janice. "Not good. Fucking with those boys."

Flynne, feeling like they were back in high school, followed Janice's gaze. Five big boys with bleached hair, at a table covered with beer bottles. They'd be on the football team. Too thick for basketball. None wore a Viz. Two of them stood, each taking an empty green beer bottle in either hand, by the neck, and headed out to the porch.

"He was here about an hour ago," Janice said. "Drinking in the lot. Not good when he drinks, on top of the other. One of them said something. Madison backed 'em off. Conner left."

Flynne heard the sound of an impact, glass breaking. The next song started. She got up and went out onto the porch, thinking as she did that she liked this song even less than the last one.

The two football players were there, and she saw how drunk they were. Conner's Tarantula, in the center of the gravel, bathed in harsh light from tall poles, was shaking with its exhaust, scenting the lot with recycled fat. His shaven head was propped up at the front, at that painful angle, one of his eyes behind a sort of monocle.

"Fuck you, Penske!" bellowed one of the football players, drunk enough to sound half cheerful, and flung his remaining bottle, hard. It caught the front of the trike, shattering, but off to the side, away from Conner's head.

Conner smiled. Moved his head a little, and Flynne saw something move with it, above the Tarantula and what was left of his body, higher than the three big tires.

She marched past the football players then, down the steps, and out across the gravel, the kids on the porch falling silent behind her. She was older than they were, nobody knew her, and she was all in black. Conner saw her coming. Moved his head again. She could hear her sneakers in the gravel, and she could hear the bugs ticking against the lights, up on their poles, but with Conner's engine throttled down low, drumming, how could she?

Stopped before she was close enough that he'd have had to crane to see her face. "Flynne, Conner. Burton's sister."

Looked up at her, through the monocle. Smiled. "Cute sister."

She raised her eyes and saw, above him, the skinny, spinal-looking scorpion-tail thing the monocle controlled. Looked like he'd daubed black paint on it, to make it harder to see. She couldn't make out what was on its tip. Something small. "Conner, this is some bad bullshit here. You need to go home."

He did something with his chin, on a control surface. The monocle popped up, like a little trapdoor. "You going to get out of my way, Burton's cute sister?"

"Nope."

He twisted around, to rub his eyes with what was left of the one hand. "I'm a tiresome asshole, huh?"

"It's a tiresome asshole town. Least you got an excuse. Go home. Burton's on his way back from Davisville. He'll come see you." And it was like she could see herself there, on the gray gravel in front of Jimmy's, and the tall old cottonwoods on either side of the lot, trees older than her mother, older than anybody, and she was talking to a boy who was half a machine, like a centaur made out of a motorcycle, and maybe he'd been just about to kill another boy, or a few of them, and maybe he still would. She looked back and saw Madison was on the porch, bracing the football player who'd thrown the bottles, titanium glasses up against the boy's eyeballs, boy backing to keep from being poked in the chest with the rows of pens and flashlights in Madison's Teddy Roosevelt vest. She turned back to Conner. "Not worth it, Conner. You go home."

"Fuck-all ever is," he said, and grinned, then punched something with his chin. The Tarantula revved, wheeled around, and took off, but he'd been careful not to spray her with gravel.

A drunken cheer went up from Jimmy's porch.

She dropped her beer on the gravel and walked to where she'd locked her bike, not looking back.

18.

THE GOD CLUB

etherton was fully as annoyed with the bohemian nonsense of Ash's workspace as he would have expected to be. It wasn't that it was pointlessly tiny, Ash having used scaffolding and tarps to wall off the furthest, smallest possible triangular corner of Lev's grandfather's garage, or that she'd decorated it to resemble some more eccentric version of the Maenads' Crush, but that her display went to such pains not to resemble any other display, though whatever she was about to show them could as easily have been viewed as a feed.

Polished spheres of variously occluded crystal, agate perhaps, were supported in corroded chemistry apparatus she boasted of having bought from the mudlarks who'd pulled it from the Thames. And she'd prepared exceptionally horrible tea, in eggshell-thin china cups, without handles, cups that had cruelly suggested the possible offer of some wormwood-based liqueur, but no. It was like meeting in an antique phone box in which a psychic had set up shop, crammed in beside Lev at the ridiculously ornate little table.

Now she was selecting rings from a black suede pouch: interface devices, the sort of thing a less precious person would have permanently and invisibly buried in her fingertips. But here were Ash's, gotten up like the rusty magic iron of imaginary kings, set with dull pebbles that lit and died as her white fingers brushed them.

The tea tasted burnt. Not as if anything in particular had burned, but like the ghost of the taste of something burnt. The walls, such as they were, were heavy curtains, like the ones in the Maenads' Crush, but stained with tallow drippings, distressed to reveal bald fabric. The floor was covered with a faded, barely legible carpet, its traditional pattern of tanks and helicopters worn to colorless patterns of weft.

A drawing of a gecko whirled excitedly on the back of Ash's left hand, as she seated an angular brown lump around the index finger of her right. Her animals weren't to scale, or rather they appeared as if rendered at various distances. He didn't think you'd see a gecko and an elephant at the same time, for reasons of scale. She had, evidently, no direct control over them.

Having donned four rings and two tarnished silver thimbles, she interlaced her fingers, causing the gecko to flee. "They put up a want ad, as soon as they came in," she said.

"Who did?" Netherton asked, not bothering to suppress his irritation.

"I've no idea." She made a steeple of her index fingers. "The server is the platonic black box. In the visualization, they appear to emerge directly beside us, but that's oversimplification."

Netherton was relieved that she hadn't yet called the display a shewstone.

"Wanting what?" asked Lev, beside Netherton.

"To hire someone willing to undertake an unspecified task, likely involving violence. The board where they chose to place their ad is on a darknet, hence a market for criminal services. We have access to everything, in all of their nets, given the slower processing speeds. They offered eight million, so murder's assumed."

"Is that a reasonable amount?" Lev asked.

"Ossian thinks it is," Ash said. "Not too much to be unusual in terms of the economy of this particular board, or to attract the attention of informers, or of their various governments' agents, who no doubt are present. Not too little, either, to avoid attracting amateurs. They had an applicant almost immediately. Then the ad was taken down."

"Someone answered an ad, to murder a stranger?" He saw Lev and

Ash exchange a look. "If it's all so transparent to you," he asked, "why don't we know more?"

"Some very traditional modes of encryption remain highly effective," Lev said. "My family's security could probably manage it, but they know nothing of any of this. We'll keep it that way."

Ash unlaced her fingers, flicked her rings and thimbles among the spheres, exactly the sort of pantomime Netherton had expected. The spheres glowed, expanded, grew transparent. Two hair-thin arcs of lightning shot down, through miniature nebulae of darker stuff, froze. "Here, you see. We're blue, they're red." A fine jagged line of blue had emerged, as from a cloud of ink, a scarlet jag beside it, following one another down into a jumble of less dynamic-looking clouds, faintly luminous.

"Perhaps it's all just the Chinese having a bit of fun at your expense, with superior processing," Netherton said, which had in fact been Daedra's immediate supposition.

"Not unfeasible," said Lev, "but that sort of humor doesn't suit them."

"You've heard," Netherton asked, "of this happening before? Stubs being infiltrated?"

"Rumors," said Lev. "Since we don't know where the server is, or what it is, let alone whose it might be, that's been a minor mystery by comparison."

"All word of mouth," said Ash. "Gossip among enthusiasts."

"How did you get involved in this?" Netherton asked.

"A relative," said Lev. "In Los Angeles. It's by invitation, to the extent that you need someone to tell you about it, explain how it works."

"Why don't more people know about it?"

"Once you're in," Lev said, "you don't want just anyone involved."

"Why?" asked Netherton.

"The God club," Ash said, meeting Netherton's eye with her figure-eight pupils.

Lev frowned, but said nothing.

"In each instance in which we interact with the stub," Ash said, "we ultimately change all of it, the long outcomes." A still image swam into focus, within one of the spheres of her display, steadied. A dark-haired young man, against what Netherton took to be a metric grid. "Burton Fisher."

"Who is he?" Netherton asked.

"Your polt," said Lev.

"Our visitors have hired someone to find him," Ash said. "To kill him, Ossian assumes."

Lev scratched his nose. "He was on duty, during that reception of Aelita's."

"No," she said. "After. Your module estimates the event, whatever it may have been, to have occurred the evening after the reception. He would have gone on duty afterward."

"They want to kill a dead man in a past that effectively doesn't exist?" Netherton asked. "Why? You've always said that nothing that happens there can affect us."

"Information," Lev said, "flows both ways. Someone must believe he knows something. Which, were it available here, would pose a danger to them."

Netherton looked at Lev, in that moment seeing the klept in him, the klept within the dilettante youngest son, within the loving father, the keeper of thylacine analogs. Something hard and clear as glass. As simple. Though in truth, he sensed, there wasn't much of it.

"A witness, perhaps," Ash said. "I've tried phoning him, but he isn't picking up."

"You've tried phoning him?" Netherton asked.

"Messaging as well," Ash said, looking at her rings and thimbles. "He hasn't responded."

19.

AQUAMARINE DUCT TAPE

The drone, the size of a robin, had a single rotor. As it matched her speed, under a streetlight on that level stretch of Porter Road, she'd spotted a one-inch square of aquamarine duct tape on its side.

Leon came home from a swap meet with a big roll of the stuff, about the time Burton moved into the trailer, a shade none of them had seen before in duct tape. He and Burton used it as a sort of team badge for their toys, when they played drone games. She didn't think they were playing one now, but they seemed to be seeing her home from Jimmy's, which meant they were back from Davisville.

She had a headache, but getting Conner Penske out of Jimmy's parking lot seemed to have lightened her shitty mood. She wouldn't fill in for Burton on the game anymore; she'd help Shaylene fab things, or find something else to do.

Burton was going to have to find out what that was that Conner had mounted on the back of the Tarantula, though. That wasn't good. She hoped it was just a laser, but she doubted it.

She was pedaling fast, helping the hub build up the battery, but also because she wanted to tire herself out, get a good night's sleep. Looked up, under the next light, and saw the drone again. Not that much bigger than the paparazzi in the game, but probably printed at Fab.

She swung into the curving downhill stretch of Porter, and there was Burton, and Leon, under the next light, waiting beside a cardboard Chinese car they must have rented for the trip to Davisville. Burton in his white t-shirt and Leon in an old jean jacket most people wouldn't wear to mow the lawn. Leon wasn't a believer in Burton's idea of getting dressed for work, or for anything else. She saw him reach up, plucking the drone out of the air, as she braked in front of them.

"Hey," she said.

"Hey yourself," said Burton. "Get in. Leon'll bring your bike."

"Why? He won't pedal. I need the juice."

"It's serious," said Burton.

"Not Mom—"

"She's fine. Sleeping. We need to talk."

"I'll pedal some," Leon promised.

She got off the bike, Leon holding it up with one hand on the bars.

"Tell you in the car," Burton said. "Come on."

She got into the two-seater their mother would have called an egg box, its paper shell nanoproofed against water and oil. It smelled of buttered popcorn. The floor on the passenger side was littered with food wrappers.

"What happened?" Burton asked, as soon as he'd closed his door.

"At Jimmy's?" Leon had mounted her bike, was wobbling, the drone in one hand, then finding his balance.

"On the goddamn job, Flynne. They called me."

"Who?"

"Coldiron. What happened?"

"What happened is it's just another shitty game. Saw somebody murder a woman. Some kind of nanotech chainsaw fantasy. You can have it, Burton. I'm done."

He was looking at her. "Somebody killed?"

"Eaten alive. From inside out."

"You saw who did it?"

"Burton, it's a game."

"Leon doesn't know," he said.

"Doesn't know what? You said he was getting the Hefty Pal for you."

"Doesn't know what it is, exactly. Just that I'm making some money."

"Why'd they call?"

"Because they want to know what happened, on the shift. But I didn't know."

"Why don't they know? Don't they capture it all?"

"Don't seem to, do they?" He drummed his fingers on the wheel. "I had to tell them about you."

"They going to fire you?"

"They say somebody took out a hit on me tonight, on a snuff board, out of Memphis. Eight million."

"Bullshit. Who?"

"Say they don't know."

"Why?"

"Somebody thinks I saw whatever you saw. You see who did it? Who did you see, Flynne?"

"How would I know? Some asshole, Burton. In a game. Set her up for it. He knew."

"The money's real."

"What money?"

"Ten million. In Leon's Hefty Pal."

"If Leon has ten million dollars in his Hefty Pal, he's going to hear from the IRS tomorrow."

"Doesn't have it yet. He'll win a state lottery, next draw. Has to buy a ticket, then I give them the number."

"I don't know what Homes did to you, but I know you're crazy now."

"They need to talk to you," he said, starting the car.

"Homes?" And now she was frightened, not just confused.

"Coldiron. It's all set up." And they were headed down Porter, Burton driving with the headlights off, his big shoulders hunched over the fragile-looking wheel.

20.
POLT

It was Ash who'd suggested using Lev's grandfather's land-yacht as the set for the office. She knew that the table Netherton had slept on also converted to a very pretentious desk. Then Lev had pointed out that the vehicle's camera system would lend a vintage, or from the polt's sister's point of view, a somewhat contemporary look. How Netherton himself had been selected to play the human resources officer was somewhat mysterious to him.

The grandfather's displays, which Ossian had located in storage on some lower level, then brought up on an electric cart, were rectangular black mirrors, framed in matte titanium. Netherton knew the look from media of the period, but imagined they'd be unconvincing. Of course they hadn't looked like that when they were in use. Ash, whose enthusiasm for theater came as no surprise, had taped a single blue LED to the one he'd be facing, just for that bit of infill on his face, to disguise the fact of the dead screen.

He checked his reflection in that one now. He was wearing his suit, the one he'd slept in, though Ossian had hung it in the bathroom while Netherton showered, which had taken out most of the wrinkles, and a black turtleneck, Ossian's, too large in the shoulders and upper arms. Netherton's shirt had acquired what he supposed were Scotch stains, and was being laundered. He regretted Ash's having refused to reacquaint him with her Medici. He would have looked better, with a bit of that. Waiting, he tapped his fingertips on Lev's grandfather's multipurpose slab of gold-flecked black marble.

He was about to present himself as an executive of Milagros Cold-iron, SA, of Medellín, Colombia, a largely imaginary company in a country he knew little about. Lev had registered Milagros Coldiron in both the Colombia and Panama of his stub; shell corporations, consisting of a few documents and several bank accounts each, both of them managed through a Panama City law firm.

Actually seeing the polt had been surprisingly interesting. That was a lot of why he was here now. It had been a bit too interesting. The tedium of Ash's workspace had probably contributed to that: a matter of heightened contrast. But there the polt had been, driving, eyes on whatever motorway, seventy-some years earlier, on the far side of the jackpot, his phone something clamped to the dashboard of his car. The polt had had a very broad chest, in a thin white singlet, and was, or so it had struck Netherton in the moment, entirely human. Gloriously pre-posthuman. In a state of nature. And hustling, Netherton had soon seen, eye on the money. Improvising, and with utterly unfamiliar material.

Ash had placed the call, speaking with the polt first. No attempt to present herself as anything other than an elective freak with four pupils. Demanding to know what he'd seen on his most recent shift. The polt had been evasive, and Ash, after a nod from Lev, had put Lev on. Lev, without introducing himself, had gotten right to it. The polt was about to be terminated, no pay for his two previous shifts, unless he could explain himself. The polt, then, had promptly admitted to having hired his sister, who he described as "qualified and reliable," to substitute for him, his cousin Luke having been critically injured in a fight. "I had to get up there. They didn't think he was going to make it."

"What does he do, your cousin?" Lev had asked.

"He's religious," the polt had said. Netherton had thought he'd heard a laugh, just then, and the polt had quickly taken one of his hands off the wheel.

The polt had said that he was on his way home now, from visiting his injured cousin, and hadn't spoken with his sister. Lev had advised him not to, until he could speak with her in person. And then he'd told the polt about the ad.

At which point Netherton had decided that Lev, whatever small degree of klepty cultural essence he might possess, was out of his depth here. The polt hadn't needed to know that. It would have been less wise to tell the polt that they were phoning from a future that wasn't his, one in which he was part of a wealthy obsessive's hobby set, but hardly more unnecessary. Netherton had been about to type Lev a note, his phone's keyboard appearing unevenly on the table's carved top, but then he'd considered the dynamics of his own relationship with Lev. Better to sit and listen, watching as the polt carved himself a new and potentially more lucrative position. The polt had tactical skills, Netherton saw, ones that Lev, bright as he was and in spite of familial predisposition, had never had cause to fully develop.

The polt had told Lev that he was not, as it happened, a particularly easy target for a hired assassin. That he had resources to draw on, in a situation of that sort, but that his sister being potentially a target was "unacceptable." The word had fallen on the air in Ash's narrow tent with a surprising weight. And what, the polt had asked, did Lev intend to do about that?

"We'll give you money," Lev had said. "You'll be able to hire protection."

Netherton had been aware of Ash trying to catch his eye. He'd known that she got it, that the polt was on top now, Lev outmaneuvered. He'd met her eye, but neutrally, without giving her what she wanted.

Lev had told the polt that he needed to speak with the polt's sister, but the polt had wanted to hear a figure, a specific sum of money. Lev had offered ten million, a bit more than the fee for the supposed murder contract. The polt had said that that was too much for his cousin to receive by something called Hefty Pal.

Lev had explained that they could arrange for the cousin to win that amount in their state's next lottery. The payment would be entirely legitimate. At that, Netherton had been unable to resist looking at Ash again.

"You don't think that that lottery business casts the whole thing as a Faustian bargain?" Netherton had asked, when the call was done.

"Faustian?" Lev looked blank.

"As if you have powers one would associate with Lucifer," said Ash.

"Oh. Well, yes, I see what you mean. But it's something a friend stumbled across, in his stub. I have detailed instructions for it. I'd been meaning to bring it up with you."

"It's close in here," Netherton had said, standing, distressed velour heavy against his shoulder. "If we're going to chat, let's do it in the Mercedes. It's more comfortable."

And that had been that, really, except that now he was sitting here, waiting for the polt's sister to call.

21.

GRIFTER

They never caught up with Leon. Maybe he actually did some pedaling, or more likely did some and used the hub at the same time. Her bike was propped against the oak in the front yard, Leon nowhere in sight, but a buddy of Burton's, Reece, was sitting in the wooden lawn chair there, with a mandolin across his lap. As she and Burton got closer, after they left the car by the gate, she saw it wasn't a mandolin but an Army rifle that looked like it had been telescoped back into itself, squashed front to back. A bullpup, they called that. Reece had a ball cap pulled down level with his eyebrows, the kind that continually altered its pattern. Reece had been something in the Army, special something but less special than HaptRec, and admired Burton in a way that she found unhealthy, though whether for Reece or Burton she wasn't sure.

"Hey, Reece," Burton said.

"Burton," Reece said, touching the bill of his ball cap, close to a salute, but staying put in the chair. He had a Viz in his left socket, and now she was close enough to see moving light from it, reflected in his eye.

"Who else is here?" Burton asked, looking up at the dark house, white clapboard starting to lighten with the dawn.

"Duval's up the hill," Reece said, as Flynne watched a pixelated blob of tan migrate a little closer to where the button would have been on a regular ball cap. They didn't have a button, Marine caps, because if someone hit you on top of your head, they could drive the button into your skull. "Carter's around the back, Carlos down by the trailer.

Got a net up, twenty units, twenty in reserve." Twenty drones over the property, she understood, flying synchronously in repeating pattern, each of the three men monitoring a third of it. That was a lot of drones.

"We're going to the trailer," Burton said. "Tell Carlos."

The bill of the ball cap bobbed. "Luke after you? Duval said he heard."

"Luke's not the problem," Burton said. "Need to be expecting scarier company than that." He put his hand on Reece's shoulder for a second, then started down the hill.

"Night, Flynne," said Reece.

"Morning," she said, then caught up with Burton. "What did they look like," she asked him, "the people who phoned you?"

"Remember the Sacrificial Anodes?"

She barely did. From Omaha or something. "Before my time."

"She looked like the singer in the Anodes, Cat Blackstock, but with Halloween contact lenses. Other one was maybe my age, big boy, sloppy, some beard, antique eyeglasses. Used to people agreeing with him."

"Were they Colombian? Latino?"

"English. From England."

Remembering the city, the curve in the river. "Why did you believe them?"

He stopped, and she almost bumped into him. "I never said I believed them. Believe in the money they've been paying me, I can spend that. They put ten million in Leon's Hefty Pal, I'll believe in that too."

"You believe somebody's been hired to kill you?"

"I think Coldiron might believe it."

"Enough to get Reece and them over here, with guns?"

"Can't hurt. They like an excuse. Leon wins the lottery, he can spread a little around."

"The lottery's rigged?"

"Surprise you if it was?"

"You think they're the government, Coldiron?"

"It's money. Anybody offer you any, lately, aside from me?" He turned, starting down the path again. Birds were beginning to sing.

"What if it's some kind of Homeland sting?"

Over his shoulder: "Told them you'd talk to them. Need you to do that, Flynne."

"But you don't know who they are. Why don't they have video of everything? They were paying us to fly cameras."

He stopped again, turned back. "There's a reason there's a website to sign up to kill people you never heard of. Same reason nobody in this county's making a decent living, unless they're building drugs." He looked at her.

"Okay," she said. "Not like I said I wouldn't. It just feels crazy."

"Homeland Security officer was telling me I should apply to get on with them. Guys working under him were rolling their eyes, behind his back. Hard times."

They were almost to the unlit trailer now, its soft-looking paleness starting to show in the dark between the trees. It felt like she hadn't been there for a long time.

A figure turned, barely visible past the trailer, beside the trail. Carlos, she guessed. He gave them a thumbs-up sign.

"Where's the log-in?" he asked.

"Under the table. In your tomahawk case."

"Axe," he corrected, opening the door and climbing in. The lights came on. He looked down at her. "I know you think this is crazy, but this just might be a way out of our basic financial situation. Ways are thin on the ground, in case you hadn't noticed."

"I'll talk to them."

The Chinese chair got larger, for Burton. She got the slip of Fab paper out of the case, read Burton the log-in as he typed.

He was about to flick GO, when they had it entered, but she put her hand over his. "I'll do it, but I can't if you're here. If anybody's here. You want to listen from outside, that's okay."

He flipped his hand over, squeezed hers. Got up. The chair tried to find him. "Sit down before it has a breakdown," he said, picking up the tomahawk, and then he was out the door, closing it behind him.

She sat down, the chair audibly contracting, a series of sighs and clicks. She felt the way she had at Coffee Jones, every time she'd had to go in the office in back and get shit from Byron Burchardt, the night manager.

She took her phone off, straightened it, used it as a mirror. Hair wasn't doing so good, but she had lip gloss that Janice had brought a case of home from Hefty Mart when she'd worked there. Most of the writing was worn off the tube, just a nub left inside, but she got it out of her jeans and used it. Whoever she was going to talk to now, it wouldn't be poor Byron, whose car had been run over by an autopiloted eighteen-wheeler on Valentine's Day, about three months after he'd fired her.

She flicked go.

"Miss Fisher?" Just like that. Guy maybe her age, short brown hair, brushed back, expression neutral. He was in a room with a lot of very light-colored wood, or maybe plastic that looked like wood, shiny as nail polish.

"Flynne," she told him, reminding herself to be polite.

"Flynne," he said, then just looked at her, from behind an old-fashioned monitor. He was wearing a high black turtleneck, something she wasn't sure she'd ever seen in real life before, and now she saw the desk was made of marble-look stuff, shot through with big veins of fake gold. Like the loan office in a grifter bank ad. Maybe that was Colombian. He didn't look Latino to her, but neither did he have a beard or glasses, like the one Burton had described.

"How about you?" she said, sounding more testy than intended.

"Me?" He sounded startled, like he'd been lost, thinking.

"I just told you my name."

The way he was looking at her now made her want to check over her shoulder. "Netherton," he said, and coughed, "Wilf Netherton." He sounded surprised.

"Burton says you want to talk to me."

"Yes. I do."

Like the ones Burton said he'd talked to, he sounded English.

"Why?"

"We understand that you were substituting for your brother, on his last two shifts—"

"Is it a game?" Hadn't known what she was going to say. It just came out.

He started to open his mouth.

"Tell me if it's a fucking game." Whatever this was talking, she knew, was what she'd had going on since she'd quit playing Operation Northwind. Sometimes it felt like she'd caught Burton's PTSD, sitting there on Madison and Janice's couch.

He closed his mouth. Frowned slightly. Pursed his lips. Relaxed them. "It's an extremely complex construct," he said, "part of some much larger system. Milagros Coldiron provide it security. It isn't our business to understand it."

"So it's a game?"

"If you like."

"The fuck does that shit mean?" Desperate to know something but she didn't know what. No way that that wasn't a game.

"It's a gamelike environment," he said. "It isn't real in the sense that you—"

"Are you for real?"

He tilted his head to the side.

"How would I know?" she asked. "If that was a game, how would I know you aren't just AI?"

"Do I look like a metaphysician?"

"You look like a guy in an office. What exactly do you do there, Wilf?"

"Human resources," he said, eyes narrowing.

If he was AI, she thought, somebody quirky had done the design. "Burton says you claim you can fix—"

"Please," he interrupted, quickly, "this is hardly secure. We'll find a better way to discuss that. Later."

"What's that blue light, on your face?"

"It's the monitor," he said. "Malfunctioning." He frowned. "You took a total of two shifts for your brother?"

"Yes."

"Will you describe them to me, please?"

"What do you want to know?"

"All you remember."

"Why don't you just look at the capture."

"The capture?"

"If nobody was capturing that, what's the point of me flying your camera?"

"That would be up to the client." He leaned forward. "Will you help us out, here, please?" He actually looked worried.

He didn't seem like someone she should trust, particularly, but at least he seemed like someone. "I started the first one in the back of a van or something," she began. "Came up out of this hatch, controls on override . . ."

22.

ARCHAISM

L istening to her, Netherton found he lost himself, not unpleasantly. Her accent fascinated him, a voice out of pre-jackpot America.

There had been a Flynne Fisher in the world's actual past. If she were alive now, she'd be much older. Though given the jackpot, and whatever odds of survival, that seemed unlikely. But since Lev had only touched her continuum for the first time a few months earlier, this Flynne would still be very like the real Flynne, the now old or dead Flynne, who'd been this young woman before the jackpot, then lived into it, or died in it as so many had. She wouldn't yet have been changed by Lev's intervention and whatever that would bring her.

"Those voices," she said, having finished her account of the first shift, "before the twentieth floor. Couldn't make them out. What were they?"

"I'm not familiar with the particulars of your brother's assignment," he said, "at all." She was wearing what he took to be a rather severe black military shirt, unbuttoned at the neck, with epaulets, and something in scarlet, possibly cursive, above the left pocket. She had dark eyes, dark brown hair that might as well have been cut by a Michikoid. He wondered if she'd been in the same unit Lev had mentioned her brother having been in.

Ash was giving him the girl's feed, and had centered it in his field of vision to facilitate eye contact. He was supposed to keep his head down, pretend to be viewing her on the dead monitor, but he kept forgetting to.

"Burton said they were paparazzi," she said. "Little drones."

"Do you have those?" She made him conscious of how vague his sense of her day actually was. History had its fascinations, but could be burdensome. Too much of it and you became Ash, obsessed with a catalog of vanished species, addicted to nostalgia for things you'd never known.

"You don't have drones, in Colombia?"

"We do," he said. Why, he wondered, did she appear to be seated in a submarine, or perhaps some kind of aircraft, its interior coated with self-illuminated honey?

"Ask her," said Lev, "about what she witnessed."

"You've described your first shift," said Netherton. "But I understand there was an event, during your second. Can you describe that?"

"The backpack," she said.

"Excuse me?"

"Like a little kid's knapsack, but made out of some shitty-looking gray plastic. Tentacle thing at four corners. Sort of legs."

"And when did you first encounter this?"

"Came out of the hatch in the van, same deal, straight up. Past twenty, those voices were gone, like before. Then I spotted it, climbing."

"Climbing?"

"Somersaulting, like backflips. Moving right along. Passed it, lost track. Thirty-seventh, it caught up with me, passed me. Lost it again. Got to fifty-six, got control of the copter, there's no bugs. Did the perimeter, no paparazzi, no sign of the gray thing. Then the window defrosted."

"Depolarized."

"What I thought," she said. "Saw the woman I saw before the party. Party's over, different furniture, she's in pj's. Somebody else there, but I couldn't see. Saw her make eye contact, laugh. Did another perimeter. They were at the window, when I got back."

"Who?"

"The woman," she said. "Guy beside her, early thirties maybe, dark hair, some beard. Kind of racially nonspecific. Brown bathrobe." Her expression had changed. She was looking in his direction, or in the direction of his image on her phone, but she was seeing something else. "She couldn't see the look on his face, because she was beside him, had his arm around her. He knew."

"Knew what?"

"That it was about to kill her."

"What was?"

"Backpack. I knew they'd see the copter. A door was opening, in the glass. A kind of railing was rolling up, for the balcony. They were going to step out. I had to move. I went like I was making another perimeter, but I stopped around the corner. Took it up to fifty-seven, doubled back."

"Why?"

"Look on his face. Just wrong." Her face still, utterly serious. "It was over the window, on the front of fifty-seven. Morphed so it looked like the rest of the shit on the building, same kind of shape, same color, but everything else was wet. It was dry. Sort of breathing."

"Breathing?"

"Swelling, going flat, swelling. Just a little."

"You were above them?"

"They were at the railing, looking out. Toward the river. I wanted to get an image, didn't know how. I'd managed it by accident, with a bug, first shift. Figured there was a proximity trigger, but I didn't know exactly what I was flying. When I got a little closer, it spit something. Fast, too small to see. Started hitting the camera I had on it. Taking a bite out each time. I killed the props before it could spit any more, dropped about three floors, caught myself. Biter's gone, I took it left, then straight up. He was behind her. Putting her hands over her eyes. Kissing her fucking ear. Whispering something. 'Surprise.' I bet he said 'surprise.' He was stepping back, turning, headed in. And those things are coming out of it, lots of them. Saw him look up. He knew. Knew it would be there." She looked down, as if at her hands. Back up at him. "I tried to ram his head. But he was fast. Went down on his knees. Then they were inside her, eating her. And he was up and in and the door was gone and the window went gray. I think the first one killed her. Hope it did."

"This is horrible," said Ash.

"Hush," ordered Lev.

"She was leaning back against the railing," she said, "and it started to roll down, retract. She went over. Fell. I followed her down. They ate her up. Almost to the ground. Just what she was wearing. That was all that was left."

"Is this the woman you saw?" asked Netherton, raising Ash's matte print of a headshot from Aelita's site.

She looked at it, from seventy-some years before, in a past that was no longer quite the one that had produced his world, and nodded.

23.

CELTIC KNOT

She lay in bed, the curtains closed, not sure what she felt. Sick sad shit in the game that looked like London, Conner and his Tarantula in the parking lot at Jimmy's, Burton telling her about Coldiron, about somebody taking a contract out on him because of what she'd seen, then getting home with him to his posse of other vets.

And finally telling her story to Wilf Netherton, who'd looked like a low-key infomercial for an unnamed product. Burton hadn't been around, when that was finished, so she'd walked up the hill alone, wondering why, if the thing she'd been in was a game of some kind, somebody would want to kill Burton, thinking he'd been there instead of her. For having seen a kill in a game? When she'd asked Netherton about that, he'd said he didn't know, like he didn't know why there was no capture, wasn't anxious to know, and that she shouldn't be either. Which had felt to her like when he was realest.

Her mother, up early, had been making coffee in the kitchen, in her bathrobe older than Flynne was, with the oxygen tube under her nose. Flynne had kissed her, declined coffee, been asked where she'd been, said Jimmy's. "Older than dirt, Jimmy's," her mother had said.

She'd taken a banana and a glass of filtered water upstairs. Saved some of the water for brushing her teeth. Noticed, as she always did when she brushed them, that the brass fittings on the sink had once been plated, but now there were only little flecks of chrome left, mostly near the porcelain.

She'd gone back into her room, closed the door, taken off her debadged Coffee Jones shirt, her bra and jeans, put on a big USMC sweatshirt of Burton's and gotten into bed.

To sort of vibrate, exhausted but far from sleep. Then she remembered that she had an app for Burton and Leon's drone games on her old phone, and that Macon would have moved it to her new one along with the rest of her stuff. She got the phone from beneath the pillow and checked. There it was. She launched it, selected a top-down view, and saw a low satellite image of their property, the roof she lay under a gray rectangle, while above it moved, in a complicated dance, the twenty drones, each one shown as a point of light, weaving something she knew to call, if only from tattoos, a Celtic knot. Each one to be replaced by one of the twenty spares, then recharged, in rotation.

Burton won a lot of drone games, was really good at them, Haptic Recon 1 having been about them, so many ways. Even, she'd heard someone say, that Burton himself had been a sort of drone, or partially one, when he'd still had the tattoos.

Watching the drones weave their knot above her house seemed to help. Soon she thought she might be able to sleep. She closed the app, shoved her phone under the pillow, closed her eyes.

But just before she did sleep, she saw the woman's t-shirt and striped pajama pants, fluttering and turning, down into the street.

Fuckers.

24.

ANATHEMA

The thylacine preceded Lev into the Mercedes, its claws ticking dryly on pale wood. It regarded Netherton beadily and yawned, dropping a jaw of quite noticeably undoglike length, like a small crocodile's but opening in the opposite direction.

"Hyena," Netherton greeted it unenthusiastically. He'd spent the night in the master cabin, which made the gold-veined desk seem austere.

Lev frowned, Ash behind him.

Ash wore what he'd come to think of as her sincerity suit, a long-sleeved one-piece cut from dull gray felt, an antique aluminum zip running from crotch to throat. It was covered with a multitude of patch pockets, some of them stapled on. Wearing it, he'd noted before, seemed to dampen her more florid gestural tendencies, as well as hiding her animals. It signified, he assumed, that she wished to be taken more seriously.

"So you've slept on it," Lev said, absently bending to stroke Tyenna's flanks.

"Have you brought coffee?"

"The bar will make you whatever you like."

"It's locked."

"What would you like?"

"An Americano, black."

Lev went to the bar, applied his thumb to the oval. It opened instantly. "An Americano, black," he said. It produced one, almost silently. Lev brought it to him, steaming. "What did you make of her story?" Passing him the cup and saucer.

"Assuming she told me the truth," Netherton said, watching as Tyenna closed her mouth and swallowed, "and if that was Aelita she saw . . ." He caught Lev's eye. "Not an abduction." He sipped his coffee, which was painfully hot but quite good.

"We'd hoped to find out what her building says happened," Lev said.

"I hadn't," Ash said, "rumor having it that it doesn't."

"Doesn't what?" Netherton asked.

"Say," said Ash. "Or know."

"How could her building not know?" Netherton asked.

"In the sense that this house doesn't know," said Lev. "That can also be arranged on a temporary basis, but it requires . . ." He made a small, quick, multifingered, pianist-like, iconically Russian gesture: klept, but of some degree not to be spoken of.

"I see," said Netherton, who didn't.

"We're going to need capital, in the stub," said Ash. "Ossian is reaching the end of what he can improvise. If you wish to maintain a presence—"

"Not a presence," said Lev. "It's mine."

"Not exclusively," said Ash. "Our visitors didn't hesitate to book themselves an assassination, on coming through the door. If they out-capitalize us, we'll be helpless. Your family's quants, however . . ." Netherton decided that she'd donned the felt suit before attempting to convince Lev to allow his family's financial modules access to the stub. He looked at Lev. It was not, he decided, going to be easy.

"Ossian," Lev said, "can optimize manipulation of virtual currencies in their online games. He's working on it."

"If our visitors were to buy a politician," said Ash, "or the head of an American federal agency, we'd find ourselves playing catch-up. And possibly losing."

"I'm not interested in creating a mess more baroque than the one they're historically in," said Lev. "That's what happens, with too much interference. As it is, I've let Wilf talk me into letting someone use polts like some ludicrous form of artisanal AI."

"Best get used to it, Lev." Ash almost never used his name. "Someone else has access. It stands to reason that whoever it is is better connected than we are, since we've absolutely no idea how to get into anyone else's stub."

"Can't you," asked Netherton, "just jump forward and see what happens? Look in on them a year later, then correct for that?"

"No," said Ash. "That's time travel. This is real. When we sent our first e-mail to their Panama, we entered into a fixed ratio of duration with their continuum: one to one. A given interval in the stub is the same interval here, from first instant of contact. We can no more know their future than we can know our own, except to assume that it ultimately isn't going to be history as we know it. And, no, we don't know why. It's simply the way the server works, as far as we know."

"The idea of bringing in family resources," said Lev, "is anathema."

"My middle name," Ash was unable to resist pointing out.

"I know that," said Lev.

"I suppose," Netherton said to Lev, putting his empty cup down on its saucer, "that it's been one of a very few places in your life where there've been none. Family resources."

"Exactly."

"In that case," Ash said, "plan B."

"Which is?" Lev asked.

"We feed a combination of historical, social, and market data to freelance quants, plus information we obtain in the stub, and they game us a share of the economy there. They won't grind as finely, as powerfully, as quickly, as your family's finance operation, but it may be enough. And you'll have to pay them. Here, with real money."

"Do it," said Lev.

"Formal notice, then," she said, "that my first recommendation was use of your family's quants. These children at the LSE are bright, but they aren't that."

"Children?" asked Netherton.

"If we find ourselves undercapitalized," Ash said to Lev, "you won't be able to blame me."

Netherton decided then that really she'd wanted Lev to do what he'd just agreed to, which surprised him. He hadn't thought of her as that effectively manipulative. Probably it had been Ossian's idea. "Well, then," he said, "this has been fascinating. I hope you'll remember to keep me up-to-date. Delighted to have been able to help."

They both stared at him.

"Sorry," he said, "I have a lunch date."

"Where?" asked Ash.

"Bermondsey."

She raised an eyebrow. A drawing of a chameleon flicked its head up, out of her collar band of stiff gray felt, and withdrew as quickly, as if seeing them there.

"Wilf," said Lev, "we need you here."

"You can always reach me."

"We need you," said Lev, "because we've called the police."

"The Met," said Ash.

"On the basis of the polt's sister's story," said Lev, "and given what we know of the situation here, we'd no choice but to alert legal." That would be his family's solicitors, whom Netherton assumed would constitute something of an industry unto themselves. "They've arranged a meeting. Of course you'll have to be there."

"Detective Inspector Lowbeer will be expecting you," said Ash. "Very senior. You wouldn't want to disappoint her."

"If Anathema's your middle name," Netherton asked her, "is Ash your first?"

"That would be Maria," she said. "Ash is my surname. There was a final *e*, but my mother had it amputated."

25.

KYDEX

From between her bedroom curtains she saw Burton come around the corner of the house, walking fast in bright sunlight, swinging the handle of the tomahawk. He held it as if the head were the T-shaped top of a walking stick, which meant its edges were clipped into a Kydex mini-sheath he or one of the others had made. Making thermoplastic sheaths and holsters was a hobby of theirs, like macramé or quilting. Leon teased them about merit badges.

One of those big retro-looking Russian motorcycles, shiny and red, with matching sidecar, was waiting by the front gate. Rider and passenger wore round black helmets. The passenger was Leon, she saw, the jacket unmistakable.

She'd slept through again. Remembered no dreams. Angle of sun said early afternoon. Leon removed his helmet as Burton came up to the red motorcycle, but stayed put in the sidecar. Took something from a jacket pocket, passed it up to Burton, who glanced at it, then put it in his back pocket.

She stepped back from the curtains, put on her bathrobe, gathered up clothes for after the shower.

But first she needed to tell Burton about Conner. She headed downstairs, in robe and flip-flops, clothes under her arm in a towel. Heard the Russian bike heading out.

Burton was on the porch. She saw that the sheath on the tomahawk was that flesh tone, like orthopedic devices. That was the shade they all preferred, black being considered too dressy. Maybe if somebody saw that orthopedic shade, under the hem of your shirt, they'd just think you'd had an operation. "Seen Conner lately?" she asked him.

"No. Just pinged him, though."

"What for?"

"See if he wants to help us out."

"I saw him last night," she said, "in the parking lot at Jimmy's. Seriously not good. Like he was that close to doing something to a couple of football players. Right in front of everybody."

"Need somebody to watch the road, nights. He'd stay straight for that. He's getting fucked up out of boredom."

"What was that," she asked, "on the back of the trike?"

"Probably just a .22."

"Shouldn't somebody be trying to help him, he gets that fucked up?"

"Way less fucked up than he has every right to be. And I'm trying. The VA isn't going to."

"I was scared."

"He'd never hurt you."

"Scared for him. What was Leon here for?"

"This." He pulled a state lottery ticket, bright and stiff, out of his back pocket, showed it to her.

Leon stared at her out of a blurry foil hologram, to the left of a retinal scan. "Looks like it should have his genome on it," she said. It had been a while since she'd seen one, their mother having taught them both never to pay what she called the stupidity tax. "You think he'll win ten million?"

"It's not that much, but if he does, we're onto something."

"You weren't here last night, after I talked to Milagros Coldiron."

"Carlos needed some help, tightening the pattern. Who was it?"

"Neither of the ones you talked to. Name's Netherton. Said he was human resources."

"And?"

"Wanted to hear what happened. Told him, same as I told you."

"And?"

"He said they'd be in touch. Burton?"

"Yeah?"

"If it's a game, why would anybody want to kill you, just for seeing something happen in a game?"

"Games cost, to build. That's some kind of beta version. They keep all that shit secret."

"There wasn't anything that special about it," she said. "Plenty of kills that ugly, in lots of games." Though she wasn't so sure about that.

"We don't know what it was, about what you saw, that they'd think was special."

"Okay," she said, handing him the ticket. "I'm taking a shower."

She went back into the house, through the kitchen, and out to the shower.

She was taking off her bathrobe when her phone buzzed on her wrist. "Hey," she said.

"Macon. How you doing?"

"Okay. How're you?"

"Shaylene says you're looking for me. Hope it's not a user satisfaction issue." He didn't sound worried.

"More like tech support, but it'll have to wait till I can see you."

"I am just now holding a little salon, as it happens, in the snack bar here. We have Hefty's famous pork nubbins. Pretty much all of them."

"Confidential."

"Absolutely."

"I'll be over on my bike. Don't leave."

"You got it."

She showered, then dressed in the jeans she'd worn the day before and a loose gray t-shirt. Left the robe and towel and flip-flops on the shelf outside. Headed around the house to her bike.

Didn't see any of Burton's posse, but assumed they were there, more settled in. And the drones would be up too. None of that seemed very real to her. Neither did the gaudy ticket with Leon's hologram and retina on it. Maybe Conner wasn't the only one batshit, she thought.

She unlocked her bike, got on it, seeing that Leon had somehow managed to not actually deplete her battery, and pedaled away, smelling the roadside pines in the warm afternoon.

She was about a third of the way along Porter, when the Tarantula passed her in the opposite direction, engine whining, too fast for her to get even a glimpse of Conner.

She rode on, through the fried-chicken smell, until that thinned and was gone, and forty-five minutes later was locking her bike outside of Hefty Mart.

Macon had his own table in the snack bar, furthest from where you paid. It was because he could troubleshoot for the local management, handle things the chain's headquarters in Delhi didn't have a handle on. When things went wrong with inventory tracking, or with the shoplifter blimps, Macon could fix it on-site. He wasn't on any payroll, but part of the deal was that he got to use the table in the snack bar as his office, with an open tab on snacks and drinks.

He wouldn't do anything, for anybody, that had to do with building drugs, not the usual position for someone in his line of work. It could make things tricky for him, if people who built drugs had something that needed fixing, but it could make other things easier. Deputy Tommy Constantine, in Flynne's opinion the closest thing in town to an attractive single man, had told her the Sheriff's Department called on Macon if they couldn't get their shit fixed otherwise

The snack bar smelled of nubbins, the pork ones. The chicken ones didn't smell as much, maybe because they lacked the traditional red dye. Macon was working his way through a plate of the pork ones as she came up to the table. His back was to the wall, as always, and Edward, to his left, was fixing something that wasn't there.

Edward had a Viz in either eye, she assumed for the depth perception, and a lavender satin sleep mask over them both, to block out the light. He wore a pair of tight flu-orange gloves, with what looked like black Egyptian writing all over them. She could almost see the thing he was working on, but of course she couldn't, because it wasn't there. It might be in the manager's office upstairs, or for that matter in Delhi, but Edward could see it, and control the pair of plastic hands that held it, wherever that was.

"Hey," said Macon, looking up from his nubbins.

"Hey," she said, pulling up a chair. The chairs here all looked like they were molded from the stuff Burton had coated the inside of the trailer with, but less flexy.

Edward frowned, carefully placed the invisible object six inches above the tabletop, and reached up to raise the sleep mask to his forehead. He looked out at her through the silver webbing of the two Vizs, grinned. A grin was a lot, from him.

"Nubbins?" Macon asked.

"No thanks," she said.

"They're fresh!"

"All the way from China."

"Nobody grows pork nubbins juicy as China." Macon, lighter skinned than Edward, sort of freckled, had very beautiful eyes, irises mottled greenish brown. The left one, now, was behind his Viz. "Phone's bricked, huh?"

"Don't you worry about those things?" she asked, meaning the Viz. "Seeing everything."

"Ours have been pretty thoroughly fiddled with," he said. "Right out the box, you'd be wise to worry."

"Mine hasn't bricked," she said, knowing he knew perfectly well that it hadn't. "Thing is, Homes stuck Burton out on the athletic field at Davisville High, to keep him from beating on Luke 4:5."

"Sorry to hear," he said. "He didn't get to beat on them at all?"

"Enough to get taken into protective custody. So they had his phone overnight. What worries me is that they might have looked at mine while they had his."

"In that case," he said, "they'd have looked at mine as well. Your brother and I pretty much in a way of business."

"You tell, if they had?"

"Maybe. Some bored Homes in a big white truck, looking for porn, I could probably tell. To be frank, if they did, I'd know. But some panoptic motherfucker federal AI? Fuck only knows."

"Would they see my phone was funny?"

"They could," said Edward, "but something would have to be looking at you, something that really specially wanted to know about certain people's phones."

"Actually," said Macon, "we did you quite the job. Manufacturer in China hasn't spotted one of ours yet."

"That we know of," said Edward.

"True," said Macon, "but usually we hear if they do."

"Basically, you don't know?"

"Basically, no. But I'll give you permission not to worry about it. Free."

"You get anything for Conner Penske lately?"

Macon and Edward gave each other a look. Edward lowered the sleep shade over his Vizs and picked up the thing that wasn't there. Turned it over. Prodded it with an orange and black forefinger. "What sorta anything you thinking of?" Macon asked.

"I was over at Jimmy's last night. Looking for you."

"Sorry I missed you."

"Conner was there, getting into it with a couple of high school dicks. Had something on the back of his trike."

"Yellow ribbon?"

"Kinda robot snake-spine? Hooked up to a monocle-looking thing."

"We didn't fab him that," Macon said. "Surplus off eBay. Legal. We got him a servo interface and circuitry, is all."

"What's on the business end?"

"Nothing we know of," he said. "Arm's length."

"He could wind up in some serious trouble. You know that?"

Macon nodded. "Conner, he's a compelling motherfucker, you know? Hard to say no to. That trike and shit's all he got now."

"That and wakey and drinking. If it was just the trike and some toys, it maybe wouldn't be so bad."

Macon looked at her, sadly. "Little manipulator on the end," he said, "like Edward's using, but fewer degrees of freedom."

"Macon, I've seen you do guns."

Macon shook his head. "Not for him, Flynne. No way for him."

"He could still get one."

"You could walk through this town, fall down 'most anywhere, you'd land on a fabbed gun. Not like they're hard to get. I stay out of Conner's way, then his shit stops working, then the VA can't fix it for him, so his quality of life falls off, fast. If I don't, and we keep his shit up and running, he's grinning up at me asking for whatever he knows he shouldn't have. It is, honestly, very hard. Understand me?"

"Burton might be hiring him."

"I like your brother, Flynne. Like you. You sure you don't want a plate of nubbins?" He grinned.

"I'll pass. Thanks for the tech support." She stood up. "Be seeing you, Edward."

The lavender sleep mask nodded. "Flynne," he said.

She went out and unlocked her bike.

One of the blimps was hanging over the lot, pretending to just be advertising next season's Viz. But the banner with the big close-up of an eye behind a Viz made it look like it was watching everybody, which of course she knew it was.

26.
VERY SENIOR

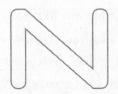etherton had never been in Lev's grandfather's drawing room before. He found it simultaneously gloomy and gaudy, foreign by virtue of being somehow too vehemently British. The woodwork, of which there was a great deal, was painted a deep mossy green, gloss enamel highlighted with gilt. The furniture was dark and heavy, the armchairs tall and similarly green.

He was grateful that Ash had specified a gender for Detective Inspector Ainsley Lowbeer, the first law enforcement officer to have set foot in this house since its purchase by Lev's grandfather.

Her face and hands were a uniformly pale pink, as though she were lightly inflated with something not quite so dark as blood. Her hair, short and businesslike at the back and sides, was thick and perfectly white, like sugary cream, and swept up in a sort of buoyant forelock. Her eyes, too brightly periwinkle, were sharply watchful. She wore a suit as ambiguous as she was, either Savile Row or Jermyn Street, not one stitch placed by robot or peripheral. The jacket's cut accommodated broad shoulders. Her trousers, ending above a banker's very precise black oxfords, revealed slender ankles in sheer black hose.

"Extremely kind of you to see me on such short notice, Mr. Zubov," she said, from her armchair. "And most particularly in your own home." She smiled, revealing expensively imperfect teeth. In recognition of the historic nature of her visit today, Netherton knew, two large vehicles were even now circling through Notting Hill, each bearing a battle-ready contingent of Zubov family solicitors. He himself avoided the hyperfunctionally ancient whenever possible. They were entirely too knowing, and invariably powerful. They were quite few, though, and that was by far the best thing about them.

"Not at all," replied Lev, as Ossian, looking even more butler-like than usual, brought in the tea.

"Mr. Murphy," Lowbeer said, evidently delighted to see him.

"Yes, mum," said Ossian, freezing, silver tray in hand.

"Forgive me," she said. "We haven't been introduced. Someone my age is all feeds, Mr. Murphy. For my sins, I've continual access to most things, resulting in a terrible habit of behaving as if I already know everyone I meet."

"Not in the least, mum," Ossian said, staying in character, eyes downcast, "no offense taken."

"Which," she said, to the others, as if she hadn't heard him, "in a sense, of course, I do."

Ossian, carefully expressionless, placed the heavy service on the sideboard and prepared to offer small sandwiches.

"You may also understand," Lowbeer said, "that I am looking into the recent disappearance of one Aelita West, United States citizen resident in London. It would be helpful if you would each explain your relationship to the missing party, and to each other. Perhaps you would like to begin, Mr. Zubov? Everything, of course, becoming a matter of record."

"I understood," said Lev, "that there were to be no recording devices of any kind."

"None," she agreed. "I, however, possess court-certified recall, fully admissible as evidence."

"I don't know where I should begin," said Lev, after considering her narrowly.

"The salmon, thank you," Lowbeer said to Ossian. "You might begin by explaining this hobby of yours, Mr. Zubov. Your solicitors described you to me as a 'continua enthusiast.'"

"That's never entirely easy," said Lev. "You know about the server?"

"The great mystery, yes. Assumed to be Chinese, and as with so many aspects of China today, quite beyond us. You use it to communicate with the past, or rather *a* past, since in our actual past, you didn't. That rather hurts my head, Mr. Zubov. I gather it doesn't hurt yours?"

"Far less than the sort of paradox we're accustomed to culturally, in discussing imaginary transtemporal affairs," said Lev. "It's actually quite simple. The act of connection produces a fork in causality, the new branch causally unique. A stub, as we call them."

"But why do you?" she asked, as Ossian poured her tea. "Call them that. It sounds short. Nasty. Brutish. Wouldn't one expect the fork's new branch to continue to grow?"

"We do," said Lev, "assume exactly that. Actually I'm not sure why enthusiasts settled on that expression."

"Imperialism," said Ash. "We're third-worlding alternate continua. Calling them stubs makes that a bit easier."

Lowbeer regarded Ash, who now wore a slightly more staid version of her Victorian station-roof outfit. Fewer animals visible. "Maria Anathema," Lowbeer said, "lovely. And you facilitate Mr. Zubov in this colonialism, do you? You and Mr. Murphy?"

"We do," said Ash.

"And this would be Mr. Zubov's first continuum? First stub?"

"It is," said Lev.

"I see," said Lowbeer. "And you, Mr. Netherton?"

"Me?" Ossian was offering him the sandwiches. He took one blindly. "A friend. A friend of Lev's."

"That's the part I find confusing," said Lowbeer. "You are a publicist, a public relations person, complexly employed through a rather impressive series of blinds. Or were, rather, I should say."

"Were?"

"Sorry," said Lowbeer, "but yes, you've been let go. You've unread mail to that effect. I also see that you and your former associate, Clarisse Rainey, of Toronto, were witness to the recent killing of one Hamed al-Habib, by an American attack system." She looked around the table, as if curious to see reactions to the name, though there seemed to be none.

It had never occurred to Netherton that the boss patcher would have a name. "That was his name?"

"It is," said Lowbeer, "though not very generally known."

"There were many witnesses," Netherton said, "unfortunately."

"You and Miss Rainey were notable in your virtually localized views of the event. In any case, you seem to be having quite a full week."

"Yes," said Netherton.

"Could you explain the circumstances of your being here now, Mr. Netherton?" She raised her teacup and sipped.

"I came to see Lev. I was upset. Over the patcher business, seeing them killed that way. And I thought I'd probably be sacked."

"You desired company?"

"Exactly. And in the course of speaking with Lev—"

"Yes?"

"It's rather complicated . . ."

"I'm rather good at complications, Mr. Netherton."

"You know that Aelita's sister is, or was, a client of mine? Daedra West."

"I was so hoping we'd get to that," said Lowbeer.

"I had arranged for Lev to give Daedra a gift. On my behalf."

"A gift. Which was?"

"I'd arranged for her to have the services of one of the inhabitants of Lev's stub."

"What services, exactly?"

"As a security guard. He's ex-military. A drone operator, among other things."

"Was security something you thought she was in need of, particularly?"

"No."

"Then why, if I may ask, did it occur to you?"

"Lev was interested in this one particular military unit in his stub, the one this fellow had belonged to. Transitional technology, slightly pre-jackpot." He looked at Lev.

"Haptics," said Lev.

"I thought it might amuse Daedra," Netherton said, "the oddness of it. Not that imagination's her forte, by any means."

"You wanted to impress her?"

"I suppose so, yes."

"Were you having a sexual relationship with her?"

Netherton looked at Lev again. "Yes," he said. "But Daedra wasn't interested."

"In the relationship?"

"In having a polt as a security guard. Or in the relationship, it soon turned out." It was, he was discovering, somehow unnaturally likely that one would tell Lowbeer the truth. He had no idea how she managed that, but he didn't like it at all. "So she asked him to give it to her sister instead."

"You've met Aelita, Mr. Netherton?"

"No."

"Did you, Mr. Zubov?"

Lev swallowed the last of his sandwich. "No. We'd arranged a lunch. It would have been today, actually. She was quite interested in the idea. Of the continuum, the stub"—he looked at Ash—"as you will."

"So this person," Lowbeer said, "from the stub, the ex-soldier, would have been on duty in the period of time during which Aelita West is assumed to have vanished from her residence?"

"It wasn't him," Netherton said, then resisted the urge to bite his lower lip, "but his sister."

"His sister?"

"He was called away," said Lev. "His sister was his substitute, for the past two shifts."

"His name?"

"Burton Fisher," said Lev.

"Hers?"

"Flynne Fisher," said Netherton.

Lowbeer put her cup and saucer down on the table beside her. "And who has spoken with her, about this?"

"I have," said Netherton.

"Can you describe what she told you she saw?"

"As she was going up for her second shift—"

"Going up? How?"

"In a quadcopter. As a quadcopter? Piloting one. She saw something climbing the side of the building. Rectangular, four arms, or legs. It turned out to contain what sounds like a swarm weapon. The woman who came out on the balcony, whom she identified as Aelita from an image file we showed her, was killed with that. Then destroyed. Eaten, she said. Entirely."

"I see," said Lowbeer, unsmiling now.

"She said he knew."

"Who knew?"

"The man Aelita was with."

"Your witness saw a man?"

Netherton, no longer certain what he might say if he spoke, nodded.

"And where is she now, this Flynne Fisher?"

"In the past," said Netherton.

"The stub," said Lev.

"This is all most interesting," said Lowbeer. "Really very peculiar, which isn't something one can honestly say about the majority of investigations." She rose unexpectedly, from the green armchair. "You've all been so helpful."

"Is that it?" asked Netherton.

"I beg your pardon?"

"You've no more questions?"

"Many more, Mr. Netherton. But I prefer to wait for still more of them to arrive."

Lev and Ash rose then, so Netherton stood as well. Ossian, already standing, by the dark, mirrored sideboard, came to attention in his chalk-striped apron.

"Thank you for your hospitality, Mr. Zubov, as well as your assistance." Lowbeer shook Lev's hand briskly. "Thank you for your assistance, Miss Ash." She shook Ash's hand. "And you, Mr. Netherton. Thank you." Her palm was soft, dry, and of a neutral temperature.

"You're welcome," said Netherton.

"Should you wish to contact Daedra West, Mr. Netherton, don't do it from these premises, or from any other of Mr. Zubov's. There's a potential for excess complexity there. Unnecessary messiness. Go elsewhere for that."

"I had no such intention."

"Very well, then. And you, Mr. Murphy," stepping to Ossian, "thank you." She shook his hand. "You seem to have done very well for yourself, considering the frequency of your youthful encounters with the law."

Ossian said nothing.

"I'll see you out," said Lev.

"You needn't bother," said Lowbeer.

"We do have pets," said Lev. "I'm afraid they're rather territorial. Best if I accompany you."

Netherton had never had any sense of Gordon and Tyenna being anything more than existentially creepy, and in any case he'd assumed they were behaviorally modified.

"Very well," said Lowbeer, "thank you." She turned, taking them all in. "I'll be in touch with you individually, should that be necessary. Should you need to reach me, you'll find you have me in your contacts."

Lev closed the door behind them as they left the room.

"Sampled our fucking DNA," said Ossian, examining the palm of the hand that had shaken Lowbeer's.

"Of course she did," said Ash, to Netherton, else she encrypt. "How could she be positive we're who we claim to be?"

"We could bloody sample hers," said Ossian, frowning down at the teacup Lowbeer had used.

"And be renditioned," said Ash, again to Netherton.

"Gets right up me," said Ossian.

"Murphy?" asked Netherton.

"Don't push it," said Ossian, briefly but powerfully wringing the white cloth in his large hands. Then he flung the strangled tea towel onto the sideboard, picked up two of the small sandwiches, put both into his mouth, and began to chew, forcefully, his features regaining their usual impassivity.

Ash's sigil appeared. Netherton met her eyes, caught her very slight nod. She opened a feed.

He saw, as from a bird's point of view, one able to hover in complete stillness, Lowbeer. She was getting into the rear door of a car, a very ugly one, bulbous and heavy looking, the color of graphite. Lev said something, stepped back, and the car cloaked itself, jigsaw pixels of reflected streetscape scrawling swiftly up the subdued gloss of its bodywork.

Cloaked, it pulled away, seeming to bend the street around it as it went, and then was gone. Lev turned back, toward the house. The feed closed.

Ossian was still chewing, but now he swallowed, poured tea into a crystal tumbler, drank it off. "So," he said, but not particularly to Ash, else it encrypt, "we're using student quants at the London School of Economics?"

"Lev's agreed," said Ash, to Netherton.

"County's economy is entirely about manufacturing drugs," said Ossian, to Netherton. "We might well have all we need there."

Lev opened the door, smiling.

"How was that?" Ash asked. Netherton saw a flight of birds cross the backs of her hands. She didn't notice them.

"What an extraordinary person," Lev said. "Hadn't met a senior police officer before. Or, for that matter, any police officer."

"They aren't all like that," said Ossian, "thank Christ."

"I don't imagine they are," said Lev.

You, thought Netherton, have just now been sold something. Very thoroughly and a good quick job of it. He saw no reason to doubt that Inspector Ainsley Lowbeer was capable of that.

27.
DEAD OLD BOYS

She woke in the dark, to the sound of men's voices, close by, one of them Burton's.

She'd gone to Pharma Jon, picked up her mother's meds, ridden back, helped her make dinner. She and Leon and her mother ate in the kitchen, then she and Leon did the dishes and watched some news with her mother. Then she'd gone up to bed.

Now she looked out the window and saw the rectangular bulk of the white Sheriff's Department car by the gate. "Four?" she heard her brother ask, just below her window, on the walk to the front porch.

"Plenty for this jurisdiction, Burton, believe me," said Deputy Tommy Constantine. "Hoping you won't mind coming along with me and having a look, just in case you might know them."

"Because they wound up dead on Porter, and I live out on the end of Porter?"

"It's a long shot," said Tommy, "but I'd appreciate it. My week's just gone seriously sideways, with these dead old boys."

"What do they look like?"

"Two pistols, a brand-new set of steak knives, zip ties. No ID at all. Car was stolen yesterday."

Flynne was getting dressed as fast and as quietly as she could.

"How were they killed?" Burton asked, like he'd ask about an inning in a baseball game.

"Shot in the head, with what I'd take to be a .22, from the size of the holes. Plus there's no exit wound, so anyway we'll get bullets."

"Made to sit still for it?"

Flynne was pulling a clean t-shirt over her head.

"Where it gets complicated," Tommy said. "Chinese four-seater, they were shot from outside. Driver got it through the windshield, one beside him got his through the door window on his side, one behind him through the rear door window, one behind the driver through the rear window, back of the head. Like somebody walked around the car, popped 'em one at a time. But it looks like two of them were holding pistols when they were shot, so why weren't they shooting back?"

Flynne was scrubbing her face with a wet wipe. She used yesterday's t-shirt as a towel. Then she dug her lip gloss out of her jeans and put some on.

"Got a locked-room mystery on your hands, Tommy," Burton said.

"What I got on my hands is State Police," she heard Tommy say, as she went out into the hall, touching the *National Geographic*s for luck, and down the stairs.

She didn't see her mother as she went through the house, but this time of night the medication tended to keep her asleep.

"Tommy," she said, through the screen door, "how are you?"

"Flynne," Tommy said, smiling, taking off his deputy hat in a way she knew was only half a joke.

"You two woke me up." She opened the screen door, came out. "Don't wake Mom. There's dead people?"

"Sorry," said Tommy, lowering his voice. "Multiple homicide, assassination-style, about midway between here and town."

"That's builders settling scores?"

"Probably is. But these boys stole themselves a car outside of Memphis, so they'd come a ways."

Memphis brought her up short.

"I'll go look at them for you, Tommy," said Burton, watching her.

"Thanks," said Tommy, putting his hat back on. "Nice to see you, Flynne. Sorry we woke you."

"I'll go with you," she said.

He looked at her. "Dead people with holes in their heads?"

"State Police and stuff. Come on, Tommy. It's not like much ever happens around here."

"If it was up to me," he said, "I'd get a backhoe, dig a hole big enough, shove the car in, them in it, and cover it up. Weren't nice people. At all. But then I'd be left wondering if whoever did it might not be worse. But we got a new coffeemaker for the car. Coffee Jones. Choice of French or Colombian." He stepped down off the porch.

They followed him to the big white car and got in.

She was finishing her little paper shot of Coffee Jones French espresso as the lights and the tent and the State Police car and the ambulance came into view, Tommy slowing. She was up front with him, passenger side, the Coffee Jones unit squatting on the transmission hump between them. There were two of those stumpy bullpup guns racked below the dashboard, above her feet.

The tent was white and modular. They'd sized it to fit the vehicle, which wasn't very large. Bigger than the rental car Burton and Leon had taken to Davisville, but not by much. The State Police car was a standard black Prius Interceptor with that origami-looking bodywork that Leon called go-faster folds. The ambulance was the same one she'd ridden in when they'd had to take her mother to the hospital in Clanton. They had big lights up on tall skinny orange poles, their feet weighted with sandbags.

"Okay," Tommy said, pulling over, to someone who wasn't there. "Got a resident to try for an ID, but I doubt he'll know 'em. Still dead, are they?"

"What are they doing there?" she asked, pointing. Two biggish white quadcopters were hovering about nine feet above the road, beside the white tent, making those small plotting movements, mostly still but with the odd precise twitch in one direction or another. They were probably about the size of the one she'd flown in the game, which she never had seen. They were making a lot of noise between them, and she was glad it hadn't happened any closer to the house.

"The big ones are mapping data off the little ones," Tommy said, and then she saw the little ones, pale gray and swarmy, a lot of them, flitting a few inches above the surface. "Sniffing for tire molecules."

"Plenty on that road, I guess," she said.

"Map enough, something recent might show."

"Who called you?" Burton asked, seated behind Tommy, in the Faraday cage where they put prisoners.

"State AI. Satellite noticed the vehicle hadn't moved for two hours. Also flagged your property for unusual drone activity, but I told 'em that was you and your friends playing games."

"Appreciate it."

"How long you intend to be playing?"

"Hard to say," said Burton.

"Kind of a special tournament?"

"Kind of," said Burton.

"Ready to have a look, then?" Tommy asked.

"Sure," said Burton.

"You can stay in the car, Flynne. Want another coffee?"

"No," she said, "and no thank you. I'm going with you." She got out, noticing how clean the car was. Department's pride and joy, she knew, only a year old.

Tommy and Burton got out, Tommy putting his hat on and checking the screen of his phone.

There was Queen Anne's lace grown up flat and level, a carpet of flowers, from the bottom of the roadside ditch, hiding the fact that there was a ditch at all. She must have walked past this spot hundreds of times, going to school, then coming back, but it hadn't been a place. Now, she thought, looking at the lights, the square white tent, it looked like they were making a commercial, but really it was a murder scene.

A policewoman, State, in a white paper hazmat suit, half unzipped, was standing in the middle of Porter, eating a pulled-pork sandwich. Flynne liked her haircut. Wondered if Tommy did. Then she wondered where you got a pulled-pork sandwich, this time of night.

Two figures in hazmat suits emerged from the tent, one of them dangling, in either hand, a pistol in a large zip-top freezer bag. One pistol was black, the other a multicolored fab job, ghetto-style, yellow and bright blue.

"Hey, Tommy," said the one with the guns, muffled by the suit.

"Hey, Jeffers," said Tommy. "This is Burton Fisher. Family's lived up the road since about World War One. He's kindly agreed to see if he's ever laid eyes on our customers before, much as I assume he hasn't."

"Mr. Fisher," said the hazmat suit, and then its goggles looked at her.

"His sister, Flynne," Tommy said. "She doesn't need to see the customers."

The hazmat suit passed the freezer bags to the other one, then undid zips on the goggled hood. A pink, closely shaved head, blinking. "Prints came back on all four customers, Tommy. Nashville, not Memphis. Lots of prior. About what you'd expect. Muscle for builders: grievous bodily harm, plenty of suspicion of homicide but nothing that's stuck."

"Burton can have a look anyway," said Tommy.

"We appreciate your time, Mr. Fisher," said Jeffers.

"I need to suit up?" Burton asked.

"No," said Jeffers, "these were for before we did the yucky parts. So we wouldn't contaminate them."

Burton and Tommy ducked into the white tent, leaving her with Jeffers, as the other cop was carrying the pistols away.

"What do you think happened?" she asked Jeffers.

"They were driving along the road," said Jeffers, "headed in the direction you came from. Tooled up to kill somebody. No ID on any of 'em, so they left that somewhere, to pick up later. Then, we don't know. Front wheel's in the ditch, hit it pretty fast, and they're all dead, shot in the head from outside the vehicle."

She watched the little molecule-hunters darting close to the road. Under the lights, they cast shadows like bugs.

"So if he ran off the road, say somebody blocked it," Jeffers said, "ambush, shot the driver first, he went into the ditch, then maybe a couple of ambushers ran over and shot the other three before they could respond." He looked at her, glumly pop-eyed. "Or," he said, "anybody around here drive a trike?"

"A trike?"

He shrugged in the hazmat suit, in the direction of the drones. "We're getting some tire tracks out of particulate collection. Looks like three wheels, but it's just borderline so far, too faint."

"Can they do that?" Flynne asked.

"When it works," Jeffers said, unenthusiastically.

Burton emerged from the tent, Tommy behind him. "Anonymous-ass strangers," Burton said, to her. "Ugly ones. Wanna see?"

"Take your word for it."

Tommy removed his hat, fanned his face with it, put it back on. "I'll drive you back now."

28.
THE HOUSE OF LOVE

ev's father's house of love, a corner property but otherwise undistinguished, was in Kensington Gore.

The car that had driven them was piloted by a small peripheral, a homunculus seated in a cockpit rather like an elaborate ashtray, embedded in the top of the dash. Netherton assumed it was controlled by some aspect of Lev's family's security. It irritated him, as pointless in its way as Ash's theatricalities. Or, he supposed, it was intended to amuse Lev's children, in which case he doubted it did.

Neither he nor Lev had spoken, on the way from Notting Hill. It felt good to be out of Lev's house. He'd wished his shirt could have been pressed, though at least it had been laundered, the best such bot-free premises could offer. An antique unit called a Valetor needed repair, Ossian said.

"You don't, I suppose," Netherton asked, looking up at the polarized windows of the house of love, "use this yourself?"

"My brothers do," said Lev. "I loathe the place. A source of pain for my mother."

"I'm sorry," said Netherton, "I'd no idea." He now remembered that he had, actually, Lev once having told him all too much about it, drinking. He looked back at their car, in time to see their driver, the homunculus, hands on its hips, apparently watching them from atop the dash. Then windows and windshield polarized.

"I don't think my father was ever that enthusiastic about this sort of thing," said Lev. "There was something pro forma about it all, as if it were expected of him. I think my mother saw that too, and that made it worse."

"But they're together now," Netherton observed.

Lev shrugged. He wore a battered black horsehide jacket with a Cossack collar. When he shrugged, it moved like a single piece of armor. "What did you think of her?"

"Your mother?" Netherton had only seen her once, in Richmond Hill, at some particularly Russian function.

"Lowbeer."

Netherton glanced both ways, up and down Kensington Gore. Not a pedestrian or vehicle in sight. London's vast quiet seemed suddenly to press in. "Should we be talking, here?" he asked.

"Better here than in the house," said Lev. "More than one person's been set up for extortion, there. What did you think of her?"

"Intimidating," said Netherton.

"She offered me help with something," Lev said. "That's why we're here."

"I was afraid of that."

"You were?"

"When you came back from escorting her to her car, you seemed taken with her."

"I sometimes find my family oppressive," Lev said. "It's interesting, to meet someone with a countervailing degree of agency."

"Isn't she basically doing the City's will, though? And aren't your family and the Guilds quite deeply in one another's pockets?"

"We all do the City's will, Wilf. Don't imagine otherwise."

"What was her suggestion, then?" Netherton asked.

"You're about to see," said Lev. He mounted the steps to the entrance of the house of love. "I'm here," he said to the door, "with my friend Netherton."

The door made a low whistling sound, seemed to ripple slightly, then swung smoothly and silently inward. Netherton followed Lev up the steps and through it, into a foyer of variegated pinks and corals.

"Labial," said Lev. "So crushingly obvious."

"Majora," agreed Netherton, craning his neck at a fretwork archway carved from some glossy and particularly juicy-looking rose stone. Or deposited, rather, piecemeal, by bots, the whole place having that look of never having been touched by human hands.

"Mr. Lev. So good to see you, Mr. Lev." Not young, the woman was otherwise of no particular age, possibly Malaysian, her cheekbones etched in graceful arcs of tiny triangular laser scars. "It's been too long."

"Hello, Anna," said Lev. Netherton wondered if she'd been calling him Mr. Lev since his childhood. It seemed possible. "This is Wilf Netherton."

"Mr. Netherton," said the woman, ducking her head.

"They're here?" Lev asked.

"Upstairs, first floor. The escort satisfied herself that we were legitimate prospective buyers, then left. Should you choose to purchase, the nutrient equipment and other service modules will be delivered to Notting Hill. If not, they'll send someone to collect her."

"Who will?" Netherton asked.

"A firm in Mayfair," said Lev, starting up a curving coral stairway. "Estate sales, mainly. Pre-owned."

"Pre-owned what?" Netherton followed, the woman a few steps behind.

"Peripherals. Quite high end. Some early collectibles. We haven't time to have something printed up."

"Is this about Lowbeer helping you?"

"It's about my helping her. Reciprocally," said Lev.

"I was afraid of that."

"The blue salon," said the woman, behind them. "Would you care for drinks?"

"Gin tonic," said Netherton, so quickly that he was afraid she mightn't have been able to understand him.

"No, thanks," said Lev.

Netherton turned on the stairs, catching the woman's eye and nodding, as he held up two fingers.

"This way," Lev said, taking his arm, as the stairs ended. He led Netherton into a depthless, deeply blue room, its walls seemingly at some great but indeterminate distance. A fantastically cheesy twilight, a gloaming of second-rate nightclubs, seaside casinos, illusorily extended in a room that could scarcely have been the size of Lev's drawing room.

"This is truly foul," said Netherton, impressed.

"Least repulsive room," said Lev. "The bedrooms are hideous beyond belief. I gave Lowbeer your conversation with the polt's sister."

"You did?"

"It was quickest. She needed to make a match, source something locally. How did she do?"

"Do?"

"Stand," ordered Lev, and a young woman Netherton hadn't noticed rose from one of the bulbous blue armchairs. She wore a pale blouse and a dark skirt, both quite neutral as to period. Her hair and eyes were brown. She looked at Lev, then at Netherton, then back to Lev, her expression one of mild interest. "She said that she found two others who were nearer matches by facial recognition, but that this one felt better, to her."

Netherton stared at the girl. "A peripheral?"

"Ten years old. One owner. Bespoke. Estate sale. From Paris."

"Who's operating it?"

"No one. Basic AI. Does she look like the polt's sister?"

"Not remarkably. Why would it matter?"

"Lowbeer says it will, the first time she looks in a mirror." Lev stepped closer to the peripheral, which looked up at him. "We want to minimize the shock, speed her acclimatization."

The woman with the laser-etched cheeks appeared with a tray: two highball glasses, bubbles rising in iced tonic. Lev was still looking at the peripheral. Netherton picked up one of the glasses, drank off the contents, returned it quickly to the tray, picked up the other, and turned his back on her.

"We'll need to buy specialized printers in the stub," Lev said. "This will be beyond what they usually work with."

"Printers?"

"We're sending files for printing an autonomic cutout," said Lev.

"Flynne? When?"

"As soon as possible. This one will do?"

"I suppose," said Netherton.

"She's coming with us, then. They'll deliver the support equipment."

"Equipment?"

"She doesn't have a digestive tract. Neither eats nor excretes. Has to be infused with nutrient every twelve hours. And Dominika wouldn't like her at all, so she'll be staying with you, in grandfather's yacht."

"Infused?"

"Ash can deal with that. She likes outmoded technology."

Netherton took a drink of gin, regretting the addition of tonic and ice.

The peripheral was looking at him.

29.

ATRIUM

etherton, the man from Milagros Coldiron, looked like he was standing in the back of something's throat, all pink and shiny.

She heard plates rattling in the kitchen, from where she'd stepped out on the porch to answer her phone. She'd regretted that Coffee Jones French espresso, trying to get back to sleep, but then she had, for a while.

Tommy had let them off at the gate, and they'd walked to the house, neither of them wanting to say anything about Conner until Tommy had driven away. "That was him," she'd said, but Burton had just nodded, told her to get some sleep, and headed down to the trailer.

Leon woke everybody up at seven thirty, to tell them he'd just won ten million dollars in the state lottery, and now their mother was cooking breakfast. She could hear him now, from back in the kitchen.

"Drones," said Wilf Netherton's little pink-framed face, when she answered her phone.

"Hey," she said, "Wilf."

"You mentioned having them, when we spoke before."

"You asked me if we had any, and I told you we did. What's all that pink, behind you?"

"Our atrium," he said. "Do you print your own? Drones?"

"Does a bear shit in the woods?"

He looked blank, then up and to his right. Appeared to read something. "You do. The circuitry as well?"

"Most of it. Somebody does it for us. The engines are off the shelf."

"You contract out the printing?"

"Yes."

"The contractor is reliable?"

"Yes."

"Skilled?"

"Yes."

"We need you to arrange some printing. The work will have to be done quickly, competently, and confidentially. Your contractor may find it challenging, but we'll provide technical support."

"You'd have to talk with my brother."

"Of course. This is quite urgent, though, so you and I need to have this conversation now."

"You aren't builders, are you?"

"Builders?"

"Making drugs."

"No," he said.

"Person does our printing won't work for builders. Neither will I."

"It's nothing to do with drugs. We're sending you files."

"Of what?"

"A piece of hardware."

"What does it do?"

"I wouldn't know how to explain it. You'll be paid handsomely for arranging it."

"My cousin just won the lottery. You know that?"

"I didn't," he said, "but we'll find a better way. It's being worked on."

"You want to talk to my brother now? We're about to have breakfast."

"No, thank you. Please go ahead. We'll be in touch with him. But contact your contractor. We need to move on this."

"I will. That's one ugly-ass atrium."

"It is," he said, smiling for a second. "Goodbye, then."

"Bye." Her screen went black.

"Got biscuits," Leon called from the kitchen, "gravy."

She opened the screen door, into the shadowy morning cool of the front hall. A fly buzzed past her head, and she thought of the lights, the white tent, the four dead men she hadn't seen.

30.
HERMÈS

She could stay with Ash," Netherton said, glancing at the peripheral in the squidlight. He reminded himself again that she, it, wasn't sentient.

She didn't look like an it, though. And she did look sentient, if disinterested, walking between them now, controlled by some sort of AI. Not, he supposed, unlike the period figures that populated tourist attractions he scrupulously avoided.

"Ash doesn't live here," Lev said.

"Ossian then."

"Neither does he."

"She can stay in Ash's fortune-telling tent."

"Sitting upright at the table?"

"Why not?"

"She needs to sleep," said Lev. "Well, not literally, but she needs to recline, be relaxed. She also needs to exercise."

"Why can't you put her upstairs?"

"Dominika wouldn't have it. Put her in the yacht's rear cabin," Lev said. "Cover her with a sheet, if that helps."

"A sheet?"

"My father had dust covers, for his. Two or three of them on chairs, in a back bedroom, covered with sheets. I pretended they were ghosts."

"Not remotely human."

"At the cellular level, as human as we are. Which is fairly approximate, depending on who you're speaking to."

The peripheral looked at whichever of them was currently speaking.

"She doesn't look like Flynne," said Netherton. "Particularly."

"Similar enough." Lev had both served as camera and monitored the call, in the foyer of the house of love. "Ash is having some clothing run up, based on what she wore in the first interview. Familiar."

Netherton saw, then, as for the first time, imagining how she might see it, the ranks of Lev's father's excess vehicle collection, under the arches of their purpose-built cave. The majority were pre-jackpot, fully restored. Chrome, enamel, stainless steel, hex-celled laminates, enough Italian leather to cover a pair of tennis courts. He couldn't imagine her being impressed.

They were nearing the Gobiwagen now. Beside its gangway, as the arch above brightened, was a treadmill, near which stood, to Netherton's unease, a white, headless, simian figure, arms at its sides. "What's that?" he asked.

"Resistance-training exoskeleton. Dominika has one. Take her hand."

"Why?"

"Because I'm going upstairs. She's staying with you."

Netherton extended his hand. The peripheral took it. Its hand was warm, entirely handlike.

"Ash will be along to discuss plans, and to see to her."

"Fine," said Netherton, indicating that it wasn't, led the peripheral up the gangway and into the yacht, then into the smallest of the three sleeping cabins, the lighting sensing them as they entered. He studied the fitted hardware in the pale veneer, succeeded in allowing a narrow bunk to lower itself from the wall. "Here," he said, "sit." It sat. "Lie down." It did. "Sleep," not sure this last would work. It closed its eyes.

Rainey's sigil appeared, pulsing.

"Hello?" he said, quickly stepping back, out of the cabin, closing its centrally hinged door.

"You haven't been checking messages."

"No," he said, rattled. "Nor reading mail. I understand I'm sacked." Back through the short narrow passageway, to the master cabin.

"People here didn't believe me," Rainey said, "when I told them you prided yourself on not knowing who you worked for. When you were fired, they all looked you up. Couldn't tell who'd fired you. Where are you?"

"At a friend's."

"Can't you show me?"

He did.

"What are those old screens for?"

"He's a collector. How are you?"

"I'm a public servant, technically, so it's different for me. And I blamed you."

"You did?"

"Of course. You aren't likely to be spreading résumés around our government, are you?"

"I should hope not."

"Your friend has odd taste. A very small place?"

"The interior of a large Mercedes."

"A what?"

"A land-yacht, built to tour a Russian oligarch around the Gobi desert."

"You're riding in it?"

"No," he said, "it's in a garage. No idea how they brought it in. May have had to take it apart." He sat down at the desk, facing the black mirrors that must once have shone with the data of Lev's grandfather's exponentially expanding empire.

"Claustro," she said.

"Someone told me your given name is Clarisse," he said. "Struck me, that I hadn't known."

"Only because you're so utterly self-centered," she said.

"Rainey," he said. "That's a lovely name."

"What have you got listening in, Wilf? It's enormous. It's giving my security the cold grue."

"That would be the family of the friend I'm staying with."

"He lives in a garage?"

"He has one. Or rather his father does. It goes down and down. And so does their security, evidently."

"It profiles like a medium-sized nation."

"That would be them."

"Is that a problem?" she asked.

"Not so far."

"Daedra," she said, after a pause. "You know she had a sister?"

"Had?"

"There's chatter," she said. "Back channel. The patchers. Retaliation."

"The patchers?" That disgusting recovered plastic. Flynne Fisher's description of the thing that had scaled Edenmere Mansions, to murder Aelita. "Who's suggesting that?"

"Chinese whispers. Ghosts of the Commonwealth."

"New Zealand?" He imagined everything they were saying swirling down a citywide funnel, into whatever unimaginable consciousness Lev's family's security module might possess. He was suddenly aware of valuing this pretentious, overvarnished space, finite and dull and comforting.

"Never told you that."

"Of course not. But they were the last ones left, last we spoke, along with the Americans."

"Still are," she said, "in theory. But it's all back to square one. We, or rather they, as I'm no longer officially involved, need to regroup, rebrand, reassess everything. See who emerges to replace the boss patcher."

Lowbeer had used a name, too foreign to recall. "Rainey," he asked, "why are you calling, exactly?"

"Your friend's family is making me self-conscious."

"Why don't we meet, then? Same place."

"When?"

"I'll have to see—"

"Hello," said Ash, from the door. She had a matte aluminum attaché in either hand, trimmed with pale leather.

"Have to go," he said. "Call you back." Rainey's sigil vanished.

"Where is she?" Ash asked.

"Rear cabin. What are those bags?"

"Hermès," said Ash. "Her factory-original kit."

"Hermès?"

"Vuitton are always blond," she said.

31.

FUNNY

Shaylene had a box of cronuts for them, the salted caramel ones from Coffee Jones. When Flynne worked there, one of her jobs had been shifting the trays of freshly printed cronuts to the oven. If you didn't do it right, the lattice of the salted caramel caved in, and you got a flatter, less special cronut, one where the topping might pull your fillings out if you chewed too fast. Still, it was nice of Shaylene to have gotten them for the meeting. She'd also gotten Lithonia, a woman who worked for Macon sometimes, to mind the front counter so they wouldn't be interrupted.

"First question," Shaylene said, looking from Macon to Edward to Flynne, "is how funny is this?" The four of them were sitting around a card table that had been used as a cutting board, its top frayed with repeated scoring.

"Agreed," said Macon.

"And?" Shaylene opened the Coffee Jones box. Flynne smelled warm caramel.

"We can't find patents that match up," said Edward, "let alone products, so we're not going to be counterfeiting. Looks like the thing we're printing is for doing something that something a lot more evolved could do a lot better."

"How can you tell that?" Flynne asked.

"Lotta redundancies. Obvious workarounds. We're being paid to build something they have the real plans for, but we're building it out of available parts that approximate that, plus other parts we print. Plus some other available parts we modify, print on." He'd taken his Viz out and put it in his pocket, as had Macon. Professional courtesy.

Shaylene offered Edward the cronuts. He shook his head. Macon took one. "So?" she asked. "How funny is that? And if it's not funny, why is somebody willing to buy me a pair of very high-end printers, just to run one off?"

"Run off four," Macon corrected. "One and three backups."

"Homes," Shaylene said, "they set people up." She looked at Flynne.

"It's Burton's deal," Flynne said, to Shaylene.

"Then why isn't he here?"

"Because Leon went and won the lottery this morning. Needs help dealing with the media." Which had a top layer of truth to it, but latticed, like the caramel on the cronuts.

"Heard he did," said Macon. "Money flooding into the Fisher clan?"

"Not that much. Ten mil, with taxes on it. This fabbing's a job, though. These are people Burton's been working for, on the side. I've done a little for them too."

"Doing what?" Shaylene asked.

"Gaming. They won't say what it is. Like we're beta testing something."

"A gaming company?" Macon asked.

"Security," said Flynne, "working for a gaming company."

"That would fit," said Edward. "We're printing hands-free interface hardware."

"Sort of thing the VA might hook Conner up with, if they had the money," Macon said, looking at Flynne. "Lets you operate things by thinking about it. Closest patent matches are medical, neurological." He pulled his cronut apart, the caramel stretching, sagging. "Even the haptics Burton used in the Marines."

"What's it look like?" Flynne asked, taking a cronut as Shaylene offered them.

"Headband with a box on it," Edward said. "Too heavy for comfort. Have to print a special cable for it. One of the two printers is just for doing that, the cable. That printer'll only be the thirty-third in this state."

"And fully registered," Shaylene said.

"If we're not fabbing funny," Macon said, "registered is fine. And no way to get one, unregistered. We looked."

"Both those machines'll be here tomorrow," said Shaylene, "if the goth's telling the truth."

"Goth?" Flynne asked.

"Wait up," said Macon. "You agree to the job already?"

"I figure I've still got the option to not take delivery," said Shaylene. Then, to Flynne, "English woman, dumb-ass contact lenses. You gave her my number."

"Burton must have. I deal with a guy."

"Said they're in Colombia," said Shaylene. "Printer order came out of Panama. Those printers each cost way over what I gross annually, both sides of the business. Once they're delivered, they're mine, and she didn't seem to give a shit about the fee on top of that. Sounds like builders to me."

"There's a game," said Flynne, "I've seen it, and the guy I've talked with says they're security, working for the game company. Asked him if they were builders. Said no. They've got money, seem to not mind spending it. I know you're particular about this, Macon, and so am I, but this isn't like we're taking money from people we know are builders." She wasn't doing that great a job of convincing herself, so she doubted she was convincing Macon. "That's Burton's take on it too."

Nobody said anything. Flynne took a first bite of her cronut. They'd gotten the lattice just right.

"Colombia was a drug place before there were builders," said Edward. "Now it's a money place. Like Switzerland."

Flynne swallowed. "You want to do it?"

Edward looked at Macon.

"Good money," said Macon, "our cut of Shaylene's fee."

"You're careful, Macon," Flynne said. "So why take it on?"

"Careful," said Macon, "but curious. Got to be a balance."

"I don't want you blaming me," said Flynne. "Why would you take this on?"

"The files they sent," Edward said. "We're being asked to fab something that we can't find any record of having been built before."

"Could be corporate espionage," said Macon. "That would be interesting. Haven't gone there before. That has our attention."

Edward nodded.

"If you could figure out what it was for," Flynne said, "you could make more of them?"

"We could make more of them anyway," Macon said, "but we'd have to figure out what it does whatever it does to. There isn't anything we know of, exactly, for that thing to control."

"But," said Edward, shyly reaching for a cronut, "we probably could. Reverse engineering."

Shaylene was staring down the last three cronuts, locked in inner battle with her diet. "Then you're on," she said, not looking up. Then she looked at Flynne. "We're doing this," she said.

Flynne took another bite of cronut. Nodded.

32.

TIPSTAFF

Lev's sigil appeared, strobing, as Netherton was getting out of the cab in Henrietta Street. "Yes?" Netherton asked.

"How long is this going to take, do you think?"

"I have no idea," said Netherton. "I don't know what we'll be discussing. I told you that."

"I'll send Ossian, when you're done."

"I don't need Ossian, thank you. No Ossian."

"I haven't done this since I was a teenager," said a slender young man, stopping on the pavement beside Netherton. Pale, with paler hair. A fairy prince in a flat tweed cap. Netherton dismissed Lev's sigil with a tongue-tap. The young man's eyes were a startling green.

"I beg your pardon?" said Netherton.

"Opera again. The rental place is busy. They had the little girl, but I thought I'd give you a break. Be more fun if they'd had something really strapping."

"Rainey?" Her sigil appeared, then faded.

"Hello," the young man said. "Shall we?"

"You lead the way," said Netherton.

"Cautious of you," observed the rental, its tone unimpressed. It adjusted the angle of its cap. "Look," it said, pointing across Henrietta Street, "that's where George Orwell had his first publisher." That annoying thing that tourists did, opening a feed into London's sea of blue plaques.

Netherton ignored the otherwise unremarkable building, dismissing the text with another tongue-tap. "Let's go," he said. The rental started for Covent Garden. Netherton wondered if it had been infused with nutrients from a matte aluminum case.

The streets here were busy, or relatively so. Couples going to the opera, he supposed. He wondered how many were peripherals, rented or otherwise. A light rain began to fall. He turned up the collar of his jacket. He'd asked the rental to lead because he had no way, really, of knowing that it was Rainey. Sigils, he knew, could be spoofed. For that matter, he supposed, he had no way of knowing that this was a peripheral. On the other hand, it sounded like her. Not the voice, of course, but it had her manner.

Streetlights were coming on. Goods were on offer, in the windows of shops staffed by automata, by homunculi, by the odd person either present or peripheral. He'd known a girl who'd worked in a shop near here, though he couldn't recall the street, or her name. "I've been worried about you," said the rental. "Things are getting strange, here." They were passing a shop in which a Michikoid in riding habit was folding scarves. "How do you stand having a beard?" the rental asked, running fingertips up its pale cheek.

"I don't," said Netherton.

"After it's been shaved, I mean. It makes me want to scream."

"I take it that's not what you're worried about, on my behalf," Netherton said. The rental said nothing, walked on. It wore brown demiboots with elastic side gores.

Then they were entering the market proper, the building itself. Netherton saw that it was leading them toward stairs to the lower level. He decided that it was her, not that he'd ever seriously doubted that.

"We'll have a little privacy, even if it's purely symbolic," it said. They'd reached the bottom of the stairs. He saw the Maenads' Crush in its narrow archway, devoid of clientele, its Michikoid behind the bar, polishing glasses.

"Very good," said Netherton, taking the lead. "We'll have the snug," he told the Michikoid. "Double whiskey. House. My friend isn't drinking."

"Yes, sir."

The burgundy drapes reminded him of Ash's fortune-telling booth. As soon as the Michikoid brought his whiskey, he drew them closed.

"They're saying you did it," the rental said.

"Did what?" The whiskey was halfway to his mouth.

"Killed Aelita."

"Who is?"

"Americans, I'm assuming."

"Does anyone have any proof that she's dead? Missing, evidently, but dead?" He drank some of his whiskey.

"It's that fuzzy sort of malignant publicity. You're starting to surface in gossip feeds. Highly orchestrated."

"You really don't know who?"

"Daedra? Maybe she's mad at you."

"Us. Mad at us."

"This is serious, Wilf."

"It's also ridiculous. Daedra ruined everything. Deliberately. You were there. You saw what happened. She killed him."

"And please, don't get drunk."

"Actually," he said, "I've been drinking considerably less. Why would Daedra be angry with me?"

"I've no idea. But it's the sort of ongoing complication I was hoping to avoid."

"Pardon me, sir," said the Michikoid, from beyond the curtain, "but there's someone here for you."

"You told someone we were meeting?" The green eyes widening.

"No," said Netherton.

"Sir?" said the Michikoid.

"If someone puts a hole in this thing," the rental tapped its chest through the waxed-cotton jacket, "I wake up on the sofa. You aren't in that position."

Netherton took a preparatory drink and pushed the curtain aside.

"Forgive my interruption," said Lowbeer, "but I'm afraid I've no choice." She wore a hairy tweed jacket and matching skirt. It occurred to Netherton that that went quite well with Rainey's peripheral's outfit. "Please allow me to join you." The Michikoid, Netherton saw, was bringing a chair. "Miss Rainey," said Lowbeer, "I am Inspector Ainsley Lowbeer, of the Metropolitan Police. You do understand that you are present here, legally, under the Android Avatar Act?"

"I do," said the rental, unenthusiastically.

"Canadian law makes certain distinctions, around physically manifested telepresence, which we do not." Lowbeer took her seat. "Still water," she said, to the Michikoid. "Best we keep the curtain open," she said to Netherton, glancing out into the lower level of the market.

"Why?" asked Netherton.

"Someone may wish you harm, Mr. Netherton."

The rental raised its eyebrows.

"Who?" asked Netherton, wishing he'd ordered a treble.

"We've no idea," said Lowbeer. "Our attention has been drawn to the recent rental of a peripheral, one with potential as a weapon. The public isn't aware of how closely such transactions are monitored. We know it to be nearby, and we believe you to be its target."

"Told you," said the rental, to Netherton.

"And why would you assume Mr. Netherton to be in danger, may I ask?" asked Lowbeer, as the Michikoid placed her glass of water on the table.

"You may, obviously," said the rental, quite effectively managing to convey Rainey's unhappiness. "The police, Wilf. You didn't tell me."

"I was about to."

"You were Mr. Netherton's colleague, in the business with the Garbage Patch," said Lowbeer. "Have you been let go as well?" She took a drink of water.

"I was permitted to resign," the rental said. "But merely from the project. I'm a career bureaucrat."

"As am I," said Lowbeer. "At the moment, on official business. Would that be true of you?"

The green eyes considered Lowbeer. "No," it said, "I'm here privately."

"Are you now involved," Lowbeer asked, "in what the former project may be becoming?"

"I'm not at liberty to discuss that," the rental said.

"But here you are, meeting privately with Mr. Netherton. Expressing concerns over his safety."

"She says," said Netherton, surprising himself, "that the Americans are spreading a rumor that I had Aelita killed."

"No," said the rental. "I said that they seemed the most likely suspects, in spreading it."

"You said you thought it might be Daedra," said Netherton, and finished his whiskey. He looked around for the Michikoid.

"We are aware of a whispering campaign," said Lowbeer, "while uncertain as to its origins." She glanced out again. "Oh dear," she said, and rose, reaching under the flap of her brown satchel. "I'm afraid we'll have to be going now." She drew out a business card, passing it to the Michikoid, which had just then arrived, as if summoned. It accepted the card with two hands, bowed, smartly retreated. Lowbeer reached back into her satchel, producing what at first appeared to be a fussily ornate, gold-and-ivory lipstick, or perhaps atomizer, but which promptly morphed into a short, ceremonial-looking baton, its staff of fluted ivory topped with a gilt coronet. A tipstaff, evidently. Netherton had never actually seen one before. "Come with me, please," she said.

Rainey's peripheral stood. Netherton looked down at his empty glass, started to stand, saw the tipstaff morph again, becoming a baroque, long-barreled gilt pistol, with fluted ivory grips, which Lowbeer lifted, aimed, and fired. There was an explosion, painfully loud, but from somewhere across the lower level, the pistol having made no sound at all. Then a ringing silence, in which could be heard an apparent rain of small objects, striking walls and flagstones. Someone began to scream.

"Bloody hell," said Lowbeer, her tone one of concerned surprise, the pistol having become the tipstaff again. "Come along, then."

She shooed them out of the Maenads' Crush, as the screaming continued.

33.

STUPIDITY TAX

Leon was finishing a second breakfast, at the counter in Jimmy's. Flynne sat beside him. He'd had to come into town to do contractually obligated promo media with a crew from the lottery, with, he said, the douchebag he'd bought the ticket from. Burton had driven them.

"If he's a douchebag," Flynne asked, "why'd you buy the ticket from him?"

"'Cause I knew it would burn his ass so bad, when I won," Leon said.

"How much did you get, after taxes and the Hefty Pal fees?"

"About six million five."

"I guess it's proof of concept."

"What concept?"

"Wish I knew. Nobody's supposed to be able to do that. Some security company in Colombia?"

"All this shit's like a movie to me," Leon said, and belched softly.

"You put anything down on Mom's meds?"

"Eighty grand," letting his belt out a notch. "That latest biological she's on does burn through it."

"Thanks, Leon."

"When you're rich as me, everybody's always after your money."

Flynne gave him the side eye, saw him keeping a straight face. Then noticed, in the mirror behind the bar, way back in it, in the glare of the gravel lot, the cartoon bull. It winked at her. She resisted the urge to give it the finger, because it would just add that to whatever little profile it kept on her.

Being here was making her think of Conner, of the square white tent out on Porter, the drone swarm sucking up molecules of tires. She still hadn't had the face time she needed to talk to Burton about that. Conner, she figured, his first night on the job, had killed those four men.

He'd done it with speed, intensity, and violence of action. That was the Corps' fighting ethos, and maybe more so for Haptic Recon. As she understood it, it meant that your intel might not be great, your plan iffy, your hardware not the best, but you made up for it by just going for it, every time, that hard and that fast. In Burton, that coexisted with his idea of there being a right way of seeing, but she guessed that might at least partly come from hunting to put food on the table, something he'd always been good at. Conner, on the other hand, would be purely the other.

"What were you doing over at Fab?" asked Leon.

"Meeting with Shaylene and Macon."

"Don't do anything funny," he said.

"You're telling me that, today?"

"All I've done, today," he said, "is help get people around here to pay their damn stupidity tax, next lottery." He slid off his stool, hitched up his jeans.

"Where's Burton now?" she asked.

"Over at Conner's, if his to-do list went okay."

"Rent a car and drive me over there," she said. "I'll hang my bike on the back."

"Leon can rent the car, he's got money."

"Burton's hoping you'll have to get used to that."

"I don't know about that," said Leon, suddenly serious. "Those people you and him talk to sound made up. That story that went viral, about the pediatrician who gave all his money to his imaginary girlfriend in Florida? Like that."

"Know what's worse than imaginary, Leon?"

"What?"

"Half imaginary."

"What's that mean?"

"Wish I knew."

After she'd called for the car, they waited outside while it drove itself over.

34.
HEADLESS

ould you mind my lighting a scented candle?"
Lowbeer asked. "I've an unfortunate reaction to
bombings." She looked from Netherton to the
rental. "I've had memories muted, but certain
things continue to be triggers. Pure beeswax, essential oils, low-soot
wick. Nothing at all toxic."

"This unit doesn't seem to have a sense of smell," said Rainey. "Not
that high end."

Ash, Netherton thought, might make a point here, about beeswax
in a world devoid of bees. "Please do," he said, unable to stop seeing
the tall, exceptionally graceful man's shaven black head explode,
repeatedly, in slow motion, from all those different angles and distances. It had happened as he'd descended the stairs, in front of the
Maenads' Crush. Where he still lay, for all Netherton knew, sprawled
back, entirely headless. Lowbeer had shown them feeds from a variety
of cams, and he wished she hadn't.

There were four small, bulbous, swivel-mounted leather armchairs
in the seemingly windowless passenger compartment of Lowbeer's
car, arranged around a low round table. Netherton and the rental had
the two rearmost, facing forward, with Lowbeer seated facing them.
The upholstery was slightly worn, scuffed at the beading along its
edges, oddly cozy.

"It was rented as a sparring partner, from a martial arts studio in
Shoreditch," Lowbeer said, taking a short, wax-filled glass tumbler
from her purse. It lit as she placed it on the table. "Rented the moment

you told your cab to take you to Covent Garden, Mr. Netherton. When I targeted it, I assumed you were about to be physically assaulted. A matter of blows, likely, with hands or feet, but easily fatal, as it was optimized for unarmed combat."

Netherton looked from Lowbeer to the candle flame and back. They had emerged from the Maenads' Crush to find the air thick, relatively speaking, with a variety of aerial devices. Four yellow-and-black diagonally striped Met units, each with two brightly blinking blue lights, had been hovering, unmoving, above the decapitated figure, on its back, on the stairs he and Rainey had themselves so recently descended. Many smaller units had darted, buzzing, some no bigger than houseflies.

What blood there was had seemed localized on the stonework adjacent the stairway. The screaming had turned to racking sobs, emanating from a woman seated, knees up, on the flagstones at the foot of the stairs. "See to her," he'd heard Lowbeer say, to someone unseen, "immediately." Lowbeer had lifted the tipstaff briefly then, shoulder high, and turned, displaying it. Netherton had seen people glance away, fearing to be marked by the sight of it, though of course they already were.

Bystanders had continued to avert their gaze, as Lowbeer led Netherton and the rental to the opposite end of the building, and up another open flight of stairs. Her car uncloaked before them as they'd emerged, its passenger door open. He had no idea, now, of where they were parked. Not far from Covent Garden. In the direction of Shaftesbury Avenue, perhaps.

"That poor woman," Lowbeer said.

"Didn't appear to have been physically injured," said the rental, slouched in its club chair, tweed cap low on its forehead.

"Traumatized," Lowbeer said, and looked at her candle. "Neroli. Girly, but I've always loved it."

"You blew its head off," Netherton said.

"Not intentionally," said Lowbeer. "It left Shoreditch in a car leased by the martial arts studio. Alone, supposedly. But it can't have been alone, because someone opened its cranium."

"Its cranium?"

"The skulls are modular. Printed bone, assembled with biological adhesives. The structural strength of an average skull, but capable of disassembly."

"Why is that?" asked Netherton, who just then found peripherals steadily less pleasant the more he learned of them.

"The brainpan of a sparring model ordinarily contains a printed cellular replica of a brain. A trainer, nothing cognitively functional. Registers levels of concussion, indicates less subtle trauma. The user can determine the exact efficiency of blows delivered. But the trainer, and for that matter the modular cranium, aren't user-serviceable. A person or persons unknown voided the studio's warranty, on the drive from Shoreditch. They removed the trainer, replacing it with an explosive charge. It would have approached you, then detonated. Unaware of that, I called in flashbots. The four nearest responded when my request cleared. They positioned themselves around its head and simultaneously detonated. A mere fraction of a gram of explosive each, but correctly distanced, precisely spaced, sufficient to immobilize virtually anything. Instead, we're very fortunate my actions didn't result in at least one death."

"But otherwise," said the rental, "it would have killed Wilf."

"Indeed," said Lowbeer. "The use of explosives is unusual, and we prefer to keep it so. Too much like asymmetric warfare."

"Terrorism," said the rental.

"We prefer not to use that term," said Lowbeer, studying her candle flame with something that looked to Netherton to be regret, "if only because terror should remain the sole prerogative of the state." She looked up at him. "Someone has made an attempt on your life. It may also have been intended to intimidate any associates who might survive you."

"Wilf and I are only former associates," the rental said.

"I was thinking of Mr. Zubov, actually," said Lowbeer. "Though anyone intending to intimidate him must either be singularly unfamiliar with his family, extremely powerful, or entirely reckless."

"How did you know," Netherton asked, "that it would be on its way here?"

"The aunties," said Lowbeer.

"Aunties?"

"We call them that. Algorithms. We have a great many, built up over decades. I doubt anyone today knows quite how they work, in any given instance." She looked at the rental now, her expression changing. "Someone modeled that peripheral, rather romantically, after Fitz-David Wu. I doubt you'd know him. Arguably the best Shakespearean actor of his day. His mother was quite a good friend of mine. Those eyes were an afterthought, of course, later regretted. Not so easily reversible, in those days."

Netherton, wishing he had another whiskey, wondered if she felt that way about her own periwinkle blues.

35.

THE STUFF IN HIS YARD

onner lived on Gravely Road, off Porter past Jimmy's. A gravel road, so growing up there'd been jokes about that, even though you pronounced it like grave, not gravel. Gravely had been a make-out spot in high school, somewhere to park on a date. As Leon pulled into what she supposed was Conner's driveway, she wondered if she'd ever had any cause to come this far out Gravely before. The last stretch hadn't felt familiar, though there was nothing about it that she would have particularly remembered. But she didn't think she'd known that there were any houses out this far. Mostly it was posted woods here, or subdivided lots, overgrown now, that nobody had built on.

Conner's house wasn't as old as theirs, but it was in worse shape. It hadn't been painted for a long time, so the wood had turned gray where the paint had come off. Its single story sat back from the road on what had once been a lawn, but now was a collection of junk overgrown with morning glory. A tall old tractor, all rust, not a fleck of paint left on it, a trailer smaller than Burton's, down on its axle on flat tires, the standard history lesson of stoves and refrigerators, and a big old Army quadcopter, the size of Conner's Tarantula, up on four concrete blocks. You'd need a license to fly that, if they'd let you fly it at all.

The Tarantula was at the far end of the driveway, beside the house, with Macon and Edward busy at the back of it, by the big lone slick. They had a pale blue tarp spread beside it, with their toolkits lined up on that.

She got out, as soon as Leon had stopped, and walked over to them.

She wanted to see what was on the spiny tentacle arm she'd seen at Jimmy's.

"Afternoon," said Macon, straightening up. Like Edward, he wore blue latex gloves. Neither he nor Edward had a Viz in.

"What's up?" Looking at the arm. It ended in some random-looking mechanism, moving parts but she had no idea what for.

"Troubleshooting for Conner," said Macon. "This," and he pointed at the thing, "is a grapple, for a fueling nozzle. Big help for him, at a gas station."

"You're just now putting it on?"

"No," said Macon, giving her a look. "We put it on back when we mounted the arm. He's been having trouble with it."

"Should be okay now," said Edward, neutrally.

They both knew she knew this was bullshit, but she guessed that was the way it went, when somebody you knew killed some people and you didn't want them to get caught for it. They were teaching her the story as it needed to be told, and telling it to her in a way that wouldn't require her to tell anything but the truth about what they'd told her. "What's that black stuff on it?" The grapple lacked it, whatever it was, but she bet they'd fix that.

"Looks like bed liner," said Edward, "rubber truck-paint."

They'd removed the gun, or whatever had held the gun, and replaced it with this thing. Maybe it was in one of the toolkits, or maybe one of Burton's boys had already taken it away.

"Hope it works for him," she said. "Burton here?"

"Inside," said Macon. "Actually we need to get a scan of your head. With a laser."

"Do what?"

"Measure your head," said Edward. "Headpiece we're printing isn't flexible. Contact's critical. Depends on fit."

"Comfort too," added Macon, encouragingly.

"Me?"

"It's for you," Macon said. "Ask Ash."

"Who's Ash?"

"Lady at Coldiron. Tech liaison. Keeps calling us up. She's a details person."

"So are you," said Flynne.

"We get along."

"Okay," she said, not feeling that anything particularly was.

"Leon," Macon said, as Leon joined them, "congratulations. We hearin' you a multimillionaire."

"Admire you not showing how impressed you are." Leon dragged a sun-bleached wooden box out of a tangle of morning glory. Faded black lettering on the side read DITCHING DYNAMITE and more. "Oughta put this on eBay," he said, considering its markings before sitting on it. "Collectible. I like to watch working men."

"Why do you?" Macon asked.

"It's your work ethic," said Leon. "Beautiful thing."

She went up the steps and into the house, through a screened side door with wooden trim older than the dynamite box. Into the kitchen, cleaner than she expected but she guessed it wasn't used for much. Went into the living room and found Burton, sitting on a broken-down sofa with brown-and-beige floral slipcovers, and Conner, who was sitting up very straight in a chair. Then Conner stood, and she saw there'd been no chair.

He was Velcro'd into a prosthetic the VA bought for him. Made him look like a character from an old anime, its ankles wider than its thighs. Dynamic, until he moved, and then she saw why he didn't like wearing it.

"Little sister," he said, grinning at her, freshly shaved and remarkably uncrazy looking.

"Hey, Conner," she said, then looked at Burton, wondering whether this was going to be like her conversation with Macon and Edward. "Saw Macon in the driveway," she said.

"Got them over to fix the bike," Burton said. "Conner's been having trouble fueling up."

"You weren't so happy," she said to Conner, "last time I saw you."

Conner's grin sharpened. "Worried Homes might keep your bro in Davisville. Beer?" Gestured toward the kitchen, left arm and two remaining fingers. "Red Bull?"

"I'm good, thanks." VA would have transplanted a toe, she knew, to use as a thumb, if he'd had a few. He could still get a donor thumb, if he'd just sign up and be ready to give it the time. Maybe a right foot that way, too. But there wouldn't be any transplants for his right arm or left leg, because the stumps weren't long enough. Something about needing a certain minimum length of the transplantee's own nerves to splice. But whatever had happened to his mind, she suddenly knew in some different way, had been the worst. Because right now he seemed all smoothed out, could even pass for happy, and she guessed it was because he'd just killed four total strangers. She felt tears starting. Sat down fast, on the opposite end of the sofa from Burton.

"They're seriously good for the money," Burton said.

"I know," she said. "Came over here with a lottery winner."

"Not just that. They put something better together."

"What do you mean?"

"Sent a man over from Clanton today, with cash."

"How do you know they aren't builders, Burton?"

"He's a lawyer."

"Builders all have lawyers."

"I'll have a beer," Burton said.

Conner's prosthetic locomoted him into the kitchen and up to the fridge, which was new and shiny. When she saw him snag the door handle with his two fingers, she heard the quick gnat-whine of a small servo. The prosthetic, she now saw, had its own thumb. He opened the door, fished out a beer, swung the prosthetic's shoulder enough to nudge the door shut, and clumped back out to Burton. It was like the thing had only the one gait. Then he stuck the bottle cap against what would have been the front of the bicep of his right arm, if he'd had one, and popped it off. She saw he had a rusty old opener glued there, on the black plastic. The cap bounced on the bare vinyl floor, rolled under the sofa. He grinned at her, handed Burton the beer.

"It's okay," Burton said, and took a swallow from the bottle. "I don't think they're builders and I don't think they're Homes. I think it's about their game. And they want to get you back in their game. They want them some Easy Ice. That's why they've got Macon building some kind of interface gear."

"Fuck their game," she said.

"Your gaming assets have gotten very expensive. That's what brought that man over from Clanton." He drank some more, looked at the level of beer in the bottle, seemed about to say something more, but didn't.

"So you agreed on my behalf?"

"Deal breaker, otherwise. Has to be you."

"You could've asked me, Burton."

"We need the money for Pharma Jon. Whatever this is, we don't know how long the money'll last. So we do the work, stack up what we can, and see. I figured you'd agree to that."

"I guess," she said.

Conner's prosthetic squatted down again, becoming a chair for him. "Scoot the sofa. Sit with me," he said.

"Ready to measure your head," said Macon, from the kitchen door. He held up something in flu orange, complicated, skinny sticks and a ring. It looked more like some Hefty Mart bow-hunting accessory than a laser. "You want to sit on the couch?"

"Let's do it on the front porch," she said to Macon. She'd seen there was a faded red plastic chair out there, as Leon had driven in, and she needed to get away. "I'll sit with you sometime, Conner, but right now my brother's being a dickhead."

Conner grinned.

She went out the front door, onto the porch, swept a dry brown mulch of last year's leaves out of the butt-shaped depression molded into the seat of the chair, and sat down, looking out at the tall rusty tractor. Macon handed her something, like the funny eye protector they gave you in a tanning joint, but made of polished stainless. "How strong's this laser?" she asked.

"Not strong enough to need that, but we'll play it safe."

"How long'll this take?"

"A minute or so, once we get it adjusted. Put 'em on."

The protector had a thin white elastic cord. She pulled it on, settled the eye-shaped steel cups over her eyes, and sat in pitch darkness, while Macon positioned the soft tips of the thing's legs on her shoulders. "When do you start printing?" she asked him.

"Printing the circuitry already. Do this headset stuff tonight. We pitch an all-nighter, might have it together tomorrow. Now hold really still. Don't talk."

Something began to tick around the ring-shaped track, headed to the right. She pictured the stuff in Conner's yard, humped over with morning glory vines, and imagined him never joining the Marines. Failing the medical, for something harmless but never noticed before. So that he'd stayed here, found some unfunny way to make a living, met a girl, gotten married. Not to her, definitely, or to Shaylene either, but somebody. Maybe from Clanton. Had kids. And his wife getting all the morning glory cleared away, and everything hauled off, and planting grass for a real front yard. But she couldn't make it stick, couldn't quite believe it, and she wished she could.

And then the laser was right behind her head, still softly clicking, and then beside her left ear, and when it was back around the front, it quit clicking. Macon lifted it away and removed the eye shield.

The stuff in his yard was still there.

36.
IN SPITE OF EVERYTHING

nton had one," Lev said, when Netherton had finished telling him about what had happened in Covent Garden. "He tore its jaw off at a garden party, in a drunken rage."

They were standing together at the top of the Gobiwagen's gangway, watching the peripheral run the treadmill. "Impossible to deny that it has a certain beauty," Netherton said, hoping to change the subject, else it somehow lead to Putney. Though he did find it beautiful. Ash, standing near the treadmill, had the look of someone reading data on a feed, which she likely was.

"Dominika was furious," Lev said. "Our children might have seen him do it. He sent it back to the factory. Then he shot it. Repeatedly. On the dance floor, at Club Volokh. I wasn't there. Hushed up, of course. That was the turning point, for our father."

Netherton saw Ash say something to the peripheral. It began to slow its pace. Running, he saw its beauty differently, the grace it brought to the repetitive act somehow substituting for personality.

"Why did Anton do that?" Netherton asked, as he watched the muscles working, exquisitely, in the thing's thighs.

"He refused to adjust its level of difficulty. Sparred with it at the highest setting. It always won. And was far the better dancer."

The peripheral had slowed to a trot. Now it leapt off the treadmill and began jogging in place, in loose black shorts and a sleeveless black top. Two closets in the yacht had now been filled with clothing Ash had had made up for it, which meant quite a lot of black.

It looked up now, seeming to see him.

Lev turned then, going back inside. Netherton followed, unsettled by the peripheral's gaze. The space felt more inhabited now, or perhaps simply cluttered, with the antique monitor array and the peripheral's support kit.

"Lager," said Lev. Netherton blinked. Lev pressed his thumb against a small steel oval set into the bar's door. The door slid up, out of sight, the counter silently extruding an opened bottle. Lev took it, then noticed Netherton. He passed Netherton the chilled bottle. "Lager," he repeated. The bar produced another. "That will do," he said, and the door slid down. Lev clinked the base of his bottle against the base of Netherton's, raised his, and drank. He lowered it. "What did she have to say, on the way back, after you'd returned your friend's rental?"

"She told me about Wu."

"Who?"

"Fitz-David Wu. An actor. She and his mother were friends."

"Wu," said Lev. "Hamlet. Grandfather's favorite still. Forty years ago, at least."

"How old is she, do you think?"

"A hundred, more," said Lev. "Is that really all you discussed?"

"She seemed unsettled. Off-task. She'd lit a scented candle."

"Candles, essences. I've seen them do that. Something to do with memory."

"She said she's had some muted. Something to do with bombing, I supposed."

"They go in for that," said Lev. "Grandfather views it as a sin. Getting on himself, but he's quite Orthodox. I could do with more of an idea of what she's up to."

"You were the one who made a deal with her," Netherton reminded him. "And you've rather pointedly not shared what that was."

"True," said Lev, "but it's not to be shared. If I didn't adhere to her terms, I imagine she might find out."

"She might ask you," said Netherton, "and you might find yourself telling her."

Lev frowned. "You're right about that." He drank off the rest of his lager, put the empty bottle down on the marble desktop. "Meanwhile, though, there's progress in the stub. The technicals you sourced through the polt's sister have impressed Ash. They're readying their best approximation of a neural cutout. And Ash's quants at the LSE have abundantly solved any in-stub financial worries. Though if they keep it up, we'll be noticed. More than noticed."

"What are they doing?" asked Netherton, after finishing his own lager. He wished he had several more.

"Herding trading algorithms, basically. The stub doesn't quite have the capacity to do that, though they're aware that it sometimes happens naturally. They would have started to do it soon enough themselves. But we're definitely funded to deal with contingencies now. Which has already proven necessary."

"It has?"

"Assassins turned up to fulfill that contract, four of them. Who were disposed of, prior to doing so, by one of the polt's associates."

"Requiring money?"

"It was illegal," said Lev. "He'd been set to watch for anyone who looked as though they might be coming to do that. He didn't like their look, killed them. Cost something to make it go away. Their immediate political unit is a county. The head of law enforcement is the sheriff. The county's most viable economy is the molecular synthesis of illicit drugs. The sheriff is in the pay of the most successful local synthesist."

"How do you know that?"

"Ossian."

"You had the polt and his sister pay off the police?"

"No," said Lev, "he paid off the drug manufacturer. Ossian judged that to be the appropriate channel, and the polt agreed. But someone tried to kill you, earlier today. Aren't you concerned?"

"I haven't really thought about it," said Netherton, discovering that this was true. "Lowbeer said that if they had done, it might have been meant to serve as a warning to you."

Lev looked at him. "I know I don't seem like a gangster," he said, "and I'm delighted that I don't, but I wouldn't have been frightened. Sad, and I suppose angry, but not frightened."

Netherton imagined Lev being sad that he was dead, or tried to. It didn't seem real. But neither did what had happened in Covent Garden. He wished Lev's grandfather's bar would give him a cold German lager whenever he asked.

37.

COUNTY

She hadn't decided to tell Janice everything that had been going on, she just did. Janice had been starting to make them coffee, in the kitchen, with one of Madison's bandanas on her head, a black one with white skulls and crossbones. Macon had once said that Janice and Madison looked like schoolteachers with biker DNA, and Flynne guessed that that was close enough. She could tell Janice anything, and not worry about her telling anybody, except probably Madison, and Madison wasn't going to tell anybody anything.

Janice had brought up the scene at Jimmy's with Conner and the football players, said that Flynne had saved Conner's ass. Flynne said that that was a major exaggeration.

"Those fuckers," Janice said, meaning the football players, "they get me doing hate Kegels. Always have. New crop of them every four years."

"It's Conner," Flynne said now, as Janice finished cranking the grinder, which she'd done with a practiced lack of hurry. "He gets them going. He's the one bullying them."

"I know that," Janice said, dumping the ground beans into a jelly jar and weighing it on a scale like a drink coaster, "but they fucking don't. They think they're bullying him. I'm supposed to give them points for being stupid? Seen him since?"

"Over at his place. Just now."

"Not that he's crazy," Janice said, transferring some exact number of grams of coffee to the beige paper filter in the ceramic funnel, which she'd already wetted down to get the chemical taste out, "but that he's tedious with it. I know he's got reason, but I'm tired of it." She checked the temperature of the water in the kettle, then poured a little on the coffee, to let it sit awhile. "But you don't look very happy, and I don't think that's much to do with Conner."

"It's not."

"What is it, then?"

So Flynne told her, starting from Burton hiring her to sub for him while he went up to Davisville. Janice listened, continuing her ritual, which shortly produced two cups of very good strong coffee. Flynne had hers with milk and sugar, Janice took hers black, and Janice hardly asked her a question, just listened and nodded at the right times, and widened her eyes at the weirder parts, then nodded again. When Flynne got to the part about going out on Porter with Tommy and Burton, to the tent around the car she'd never seen, the four dead guys, Janice raised her hand, said, "Whoa."

"Whoa?"

"Conner," Janice said.

Flynne nodded.

Janice frowned, shook her head slightly, then said, "Go on."

So Flynne told her the rest, not being specific about what she thought Macon and Edward had been up to at Conner's, but seeing Janice got that too, and right up to Leon driving her over here, and how there'd been a pair of small drones, each with its square of aquamarine duct tape, spelling each other, watching them all the way from Conner's.

They moved to the couch in the living room, the one where she'd played her last game of Operation Northwind.

"The man from Clanton," Janice said, "the one who brought the bag of money. You know who he was?"

"No. A lawyer?"

"Name's Beatty. Lawyers in Clanton."

"How do you know?"

"Because Reece was over here a couple of hours ago to see Madison about some work. And now we've got our own piece of that money, down in the basement, in a hole behind the furnace."

"You do?"

"Not into wishful thinking. Not that much, anyway."

"What for?"

"Help with a drone. Big one. Conner's got an Army quadcopter he wants Madison to fly for him."

Flynne remembered the thing in Conner's yard. "I saw it," she said. "Looked like a gun platform."

"That money in the basement is more than Madison and I'd make out of a year of Sukhoi Flankers." This obviously not making Janice happy.

"What did Reece say?"

"Too much, from Burton and Conner's point of view. Not enough, from mine. He's a groupie, Reece. Loves a secret, has to tell it or you won't know he has it. So impressed with Burton and Conner that he's got to tell you their business. Impressed with Pickett too."

The only Pickett Flynne could think of was the one who'd owned Corbell Pickett Tesla, which had been the last new-car dealership in the county to shut down. He was assumed to still be the richest man in the county, although you didn't see him much. She'd seen him a couple of times in town parades, but not for a few years now. He'd sent a daughter her age to school in Europe, and as far as Flynne knew she'd never come back. "Corbell Pickett?"

"Corbell fucking Pickett."

"What's he got to do with Burton and Conner?"

"Where it gets funny," Janice said.

"You think the money comes from Corbell Pickett?"

"Shit no," said Janice. "Burton's paying a lot of that Clanton money to Corbell. Reece was all jacked up from getting to take it over there with Carlos. Needed two shopping bags, he kept saying."

"Why was Burton paying Pickett?"

"Those four dead men, on Porter. Get 'em lost track of. They'd be lost track of pretty fast anyway, here in the county. State Police have a little longer attention span, but Corbell has the statehouse juice to get that span shortened too, for a price."

"He used to own the Tesla dealership and ride with the mayor in the Christmas parade. When we were kids."

"In a brand-new Tesla," said Janice. "I hate to do the tooth fairy thing to you, honey, but nobody builds so much as a gram of drugs in this county without Corbell's getting his."

"No way. I'd have heard before now."

"Thing is, you don't know your family and friends have all been taking care of you, basically by never so much as mentioning the fucker's name. Which is how you forget about him so easy."

"You don't like him," said Flynne.

"No shit."

"But if they're paying off the Sheriff's Department, that means Tommy knows."

Janice looked at her. "Not so much."

"He either knows or he doesn't."

"Tommy," Janice said, "is a good person, like Madison is a good person. Trust me on that. Okay?"

"Okay."

"Like you're a good person. But here you are, up to your tits in some deal with people who say they're in Colombia, but can fix the state lottery for Leon? That's seriously funny, Flynne, but does it make you less of a good person?"

"I don't know." And she realized that she didn't.

"Girl, you are not doing this crazy shit, whatever it is, in order to make yourself rich. You're paying the cancer rent for your mom, down at Pharma Jon. Just like a lot of people. Most people, it can feel like."

"It's not cancer."

"I know it's not. But you know what I mean. And Tommy, he's keeping this county together the best he can. He's honest, believes in the rule of law. Sheriff Jackman, that's another story. Jackman does whatever he does, keeps getting reelected, and Tommy's the law here. The county needs Tommy the way your mother needs you and Burton, and maybe sometimes that means he has to work a little harder not to notice things."

"Why didn't I know this before tonight?"

"People do you a kindness, keeping their mouths shut about that shit. Economy here's been based on building since before we were in high school."

"I did know, kind of. I guess."

"Welcome to the county, hon. You want more coffee?"

"I think I might've had too much."

38.
STUB GIRL

fter Dominika phoned Lev to come upstairs, Nether-
ton returned to the doorway, to watch the peripheral
doing resistance exercises in the exoskeleton. The
muscles of the peripheral's bare arms and thighs were
really very highly defined. He wondered if they'd been printed
that way.

Ash was out of his line of sight, having an argument with Ossian,
who must be elsewhere. He knew that because he could only hear her
side of it, which was in whatever current faux-Slavic iteration of their
mutual crypto-language. He went to the closed bar, tried pressing his
thumb against the steel oval. Nothing happened.

But now Ash appeared, carrying a large white ceramic vase of
flowers past the silently straining peripheral and up the gangway.
"You shouldn't have," he said, as she reached the top.

"She deserves a welcome," she said, the pallor of her face contrasting
with the bright flowers. "You can't offer her a drink."

Netherton felt an unexpected pang of empathy for the not quite
graspable construct of Flynne inhabiting the peripheral. She wouldn't
be offered a drink either.

"Water, within hourly limits," Ash said, mistaking his expression
for one of concern for the peripheral. "There's a dehydration alarm.
But no alcohol." She pushed past him with her flowers.

"When do we expect her?"

"Two hours, now," said Ash, behind him.

"Two hours?" He turned. Ash was trying the vase of flowers in different positions on his desk.

"Macon's very good," she said.

"Make who?"

"Macon. Her printer, in the stub. He's fast."

"What sort of name is that?"

"A city. In Georgia. The American Georgia." She was rearranging the flowers in their vase, a flock of distant beasts stampeding across the back of her left hand. "I'll be here with you."

"You will?"

"How long since you've used a peripheral?"

"I was ten," said Netherton. "A homunculi party, on Hampstead Heath. A schoolmate's birthday."

"Exactly," said Ash, swinging to face him, hands on hips. She was in her sincerity suit again. He remembered the stance of the homunculus, on the dashboard of Lev's car.

"That was you," he said, "wasn't it, driving, to and from the other house?"

"Of course. And what will you tell her, when she arrives?"

"About what?"

"What this is," she said. "Where it is. When it is. Isn't that what we pay you for?"

"No one's paying me anything, thank you."

"Discuss that with Lev," she said.

"I don't regard this as a job. I'm here to support Lev."

"She'll have no idea what any of this is about. She's never experienced a peripheral. You scarcely have yourself. All the more reason for me to be here."

"Lev didn't tell me she'd be here in two hours."

"He doesn't know," she said. "Ossian only just learned. Lev is upstairs with his lady wife. We're forbidden to phone him while he's with her. When we do tell him, he'll inform Lowbeer. I imagine she'll advise us then. In the meantime, we'd best decide what to tell her if Lowbeer hasn't weighed in."

"Do you know what he's up to, with Lowbeer? He won't tell me."

"Then he isn't a complete idiot. Yet."

"But this was her idea, bringing Flynne here, wasn't it?"

"Yes," she said.

"Why?"

"Whatever it is, she's in a hurry." She touched a section of veneer. It opened. She adjusted controls. Netherton felt a slight breeze. "Stuffy," she said.

"The office is supposed to be in Colombia."

"They've air con in their Colombia, surely. Lowbeer wanted a variety of outfits for both of you. Some of them definitely aren't for sitting in here. She'll be seeing London. So will you."

"She ordered me clothing?"

"Not a bad idea. You're looking less than professional."

"When I first spoke with Flynne," Netherton said, "she thought I might be just another part of the game she'd assumed the job to be."

"We told her brother that it was a game."

"It would be better to tell her the truth."

Ash said nothing. Simply looked at him.

"What are you looking at?"

"I was wondering if you've ever said that before," she said.

"Why try to mislead her? She's bright. She'll guess."

"I'm not sure it would be best, strategically," Ash said.

"Then give her more money," he said. "You've all the money in their world, or you could have, and you can't spend it on anything here. Tell her the truth and double the money. We're her generous future."

Ash glanced up, and to the left. Trilled something in a synthetic tongue that hadn't existed a moment before. Looked at him. "Take a shower," she said. "You look sticky. Your clothes are in the closet to the left, at the very back."

"Did Lowbeer choose them?"

"I did, from her suggestions."

Black, he guessed, unless Lowbeer had had something more festive in mind. "I'm starting to feel institutionalized," he said.

"I know what I'd call that."

"What?"

"Realism," she said. "We'll be needing you for the foreseeable future."

39.
THE FAIRY SHOEMAKERS

acon's rented car smelled of freshly printed electronics. Her phone had smelled like that, back when he'd first passed it over to her, brand-new, in the Hefty snack bar. The smell had gone in an hour or two. "You didn't think it would be ready until tomorrow," she said to Macon.

"We got some help. Fabbit did some of it. We loaned them the printer."

"You got Fabbit to do funny printing?"

"It's not funny," said Edward, seated sideways in the back, "just unusual."

"Fabbit's all chain," she said. "Hefty owns them."

"Cousin of mine's part-time floor manager," said Macon. "And, yeah, ordinarily not a chance, but your brother made him an offer, and he saw fit. The only polymer they had that would work for this looks like sugar frosting, though. Usually only use it at Christmas, but it bonds perfectly with the skin-conduction stuff, so you've got Snow White's crown. That was also good because nobody at Fabbit had any idea what it was they were printing."

"What skin-conduction stuff?"

"Across your forehead. First design we roughed out, we would've had to shave a two-inch band clear around the back of your head."

"Fuck that."

"Figured you'd feel that way. Got this Japanese stuff instead. Just needs the forehead, use a dab of saline for good measure."

"You said it was a game controller."

"Telepresent interface, no hands."

"You try it?"

"Can't. Nothing to try it on. Your friends have something they want you to operate, but they didn't want us trying it first. You lie down for it. Otherwise, you might drool."

"What's that mean?"

"If this works, and it should, you'll be controlling their unit full-body, full range of motion, but your body won't move as you do it. Interesting, how it does that."

"Why?"

"Because we still can't find any patents for most of it, and we imagine if there were, they'd be valuable. Very."

"Could be military," said Edward, behind them. They were about midway along Porter now, and already she was losing her sense of where the white tent had been, where the swarm of drones had scoured the road for molecules from Conner's tires.

To the right, fields she hardly ever really looked at, stands of stunted, storm-broken pine. To the left the ground sloped down, toward what became the course of the creek below their house, beside Burton's trailer. Soon, where Porter narrowed in the distance, there'd be just enough light to make out the tops of the tallest trees, near their house. "Have they said what it is they need me to do?"

"No," Macon said. "We're just the fairy shoemakers. You're the one gets to go to the ball."

"I doubt it," she said.

"You haven't seen the crown we made you," he said.

She left it at that, and thought about Corbell Pickett and what Janice had told her, and Tommy. It still said CORBELL PICKETT TESLA on the side of the building that had housed his dealership, but it said it in unpainted concrete, where the aluminum and carbon-fiber letters had come off.

Carlos was waiting for them, by the gate. "Your mom's having dinner with Leon and Reece," he told her, as she was getting out. "Eaten anything lately?"

"No," she said, "what is there?"

"They don't want you to eat," Carlos said, the "they" already understood to be whoever was paying, not that he knew. "Say you could throw up, first time you do this. Aspirate." He was, she remembered, a volunteer EMT.

"Okay."

Macon and Edward were unloading the back of the car. A pair of blue Dyneema duffels the color of surgical gloves, three crisp new cardboard cartons with the Fabbit logo.

"Want help with that? I can get somebody. I need two hands free for this." He indicated the bullpup slung beneath his arm, in the hollow of his waist, its muzzle spiky with accessories whose functions she could never keep straight.

"Nope," said Macon. He and Edward both had a crinkly duffel shoulder-strapped now. Edward held two of the cartons, Macon only one, but larger. They didn't look heavy at all. "It's the trailer, right?"

"Burton's down there," Carlos said, and gestured for Flynne to go ahead.

It reminded her of that night he'd gone up to Davisville. Same light, sun almost gone, moon unrisen.

The lights were on in the trailer. As she got closer, she could see Burton by the closed door, smoking a pipe. Its bowl glowed red, showing her the upper half of his face. She smelled tobacco.

"If you were smoking in there, I'll fucking kill you."

He grinned, around the bowl. It was one of those cheap white clay pipes, from Holland, the ones the long stem broke off of the first few days you had it, until it was stumpy, like a cartoon sailor's pipe. He took it out of his mouth. "I didn't. And I'm not starting."

"You just did. Now start quitting."

He stood on one leg, the other across his thigh, and knocked the pipe against the sole of his boot, loosening a little eye of hot red home-grown. It fell on the trail. He put his foot down and ground it out.

"Give us a minute to get set up," Macon said. Edward put his cartons down, opened the door, and went in. Macon passed him up his own carton, then Edward's two, then stepped up himself, his hand guarding his duffel from the doorframe. He pulled the door shut behind him.

"Nobody told me I should be fasting," she said.

"Came together quicker than we thought," Burton said.

"You know what the meeting's about?"

"Want you to meet the human relations guy you talked to, and Ash, the tech liaison."

"In a game?"

"Somewhere."

"Corbell Pickett." She saw him frown, in the dark. "We need to have a talk."

"Who's been talking?"

"Janice."

"Had to pay him. Conner."

"They know it was him?"

"Nobody does, now."

"They fucking do. They're just being paid to pretend they don't."

"Close enough."

"Tommy know?"

"Tommy," he said, "has to work pretty hard to not know a lot of things."

"That's what Janice said."

"Didn't make it that way, did I?"

"You part of it, now?"

"Not how I look at it."

"How do you look at it?"

The door opened. "Ready for Snow White," Macon announced. He held up something for her to see. She thought it looked like a drone's fuselage, the single-rotor kind, but bigger. Except someone had bent it into an oval, to fit her head, with the forward bulge of the fuselage over the center of her forehead. It didn't look like any crown she'd ever seen, but it was made of something that glittered, white as the snowman in a plastic Christmas globe.

40.

BULLSHIT ARTIST

fter showering, Netherton put on gray trousers, a black pullover free of any turtle's neck, and a black jacket, chosen from the clothing Ash had provided.

It was the peripheral's turn to shower. He could hear the pumps, and wondered what percentage of that was the same water he'd just used. The vehicle's water management regime had been designed for desert exploration. Ash had warned him not to swallow any, in the shower. At least two pumps were running, whenever the shower was in use, one sucking every fallen drop away for recycling.

The sound of the shower stopped. After several minutes Ash emerged, followed by the peripheral, which looked, after showering, radiant, as though freshly created. Ash herself was still in her sincerity suit, but the peripheral wore the black shirt and jeans that Ash had based on the clothing Flynne had worn when he'd first spoken with her.

"Did you cut its hair?" he asked.

"We borrowed Dominika's hairdresser. Showed him the files of your conversation. He was impressed, actually."

"It doesn't look like her. Well, the hair, a bit. Has this been done before? Someone from a stub using a peripheral?"

"The more I think of it, the more it seems a natural, but no, not that I know of. But continua enthusiasts are generally secretive, while peripherals of this grade tend to be very private possessions. Owners don't often advertise the fact."

"How will we do this, then, with Flynne?" The peripheral was looking at him. Or wasn't, but seemed to be. He frowned. It looked away. He resisted an urge to apologize.

"We'll have her on a bunk," Ash said, "in the rear cabin. There can be initial balance issues, nausea. I'll greet her when she arrives, help her orient. Then I'll bring her out to meet you. You can be at the desk, the way she's seen you before. Continuity of experience."

"No. I want to see her. Arrive."

"Why?"

"I feel a certain responsibility," he said.

"You're our bullshit artist. Stick with that."

"I don't expect you to like me—"

"If I didn't at all, you'd know it."

"Have you heard from Lowbeer yet?"

"No," she said.

Lowbeer's sigil appeared, pulsing softly, gilt and ivory.

41.
ZERO

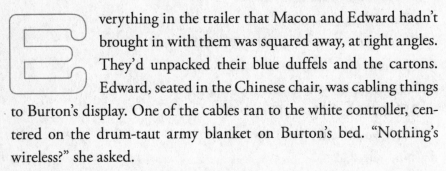verything in the trailer that Macon and Edward hadn't brought in with them was squared away, at right angles. They'd unpacked their blue duffels and the cartons. Edward, seated in the Chinese chair, was cabling things to Burton's display. One of the cables ran to the white controller, centered on the drum-taut army blanket on Burton's bed. "Nothing's wireless?" she asked.

"These aren't just cables. They're about a third of the device. Give me your phone."

She handed him her phone, which he passed to Edward.

"Password?"

"Easy Ice," she said, "lowercase, no space."

"That's such a shit password, it's not even a password."

"I'm a just normal fucking person, Macon."

"Normal fucking people never do whatever it is you're about to." He smiled.

"Ready," said Edward, who'd already cabled her phone, rolling the chair back from the table.

"Can we get the lights down?" asked Macon. "You'll have your eyes closed, but this is still too bright. Otherwise, there's an eyeshade for you."

She went to the display, waved through it, turning the LEDs down to teen-boy sex pit. "Okay?"

"Perfect," said Macon.

"How's this going to work?" she asked him.

"You lay on the bunk here, head at a comfortable angle, wearing this." Indicating the controller. "Close your eyes. We'll be here for you if you need us."

"For what?"

He indicated a yellow plastic bucket with Hefty Mart stickers still on it. "Nausea's a possibility. Inner ear thing. Phantom inner ear, she said, but I think that was shorthand for our benefit. You fast?"

"By accident," she said. "I'm starving."

"Use the toilet now," said Macon. "Then we go."

"I go."

"I know. Pisses me off."

"Jealous of the crown?"

"Curious. As I've ever been."

"Whatever it is, I'll tell you."

"Not while it's happening, you won't. This thing works, you'll be in an induced version of sleep paralysis."

"Like how we don't hurt ourselves when we're dreaming we do things?" She'd seen an episode of *Ciencia Loca* about that, plus lucid dreaming and being hagridden.

"That's it. Go use the ladies' now. It's time."

When she came out of the trailer, she saw Burton and Carlos standing there, about fifteen feet away. She gave them the finger, went into the toilet, where there was no light at all, peed, hoped she didn't get the cedar sawdust on the seat in the dark, came back out, used sanitizer, and stepped up into the trailer, ignoring Burton and Carlos. Closed the door behind her.

Macon and Edward were looking at her. "Take off your shoes," said Macon.

She sat down on the bed, Macon carefully moving the controller aside for her. She got a closer look at it as she took her sneakers off. It looked tight as all of Macon's top-end printing, tight as her phone, except for the sugarplum fairy stuff he'd fabbed it from. Edward was positioning Burton's pillow. "Have any more pillows?" he asked.

"No," she said. "Bunch it in half. You have their log-in?"

"We do." Macon produced a little plastic tube, showed her the Pharma Jon logo. "This'll be cool."

"That's what they all say," she said.

Macon put saline paste on his fingertip.

"Don't get any in my eyes."

He spread a line of chill wetness across her forehead, like some weird and possibly unwelcome blessing. Then he picked up the controller. "Pull your hair back." She did, and he settled it on her head. "Fit?"

"I guess. It's heavy. In front."

"Our hunch is that the real deal weighs about as much as a pair of throwaway sunglasses, but this is the best we can do, short notice, on our printers. Pinch anywhere?"

"No."

"Okay. So it's heavy, right? I'm going to hold on to it while you lay back, slow, and Edward'll position the pillow. Okay? Now."

She lay back, straightened her legs.

"Because of the cable," Macon said, "you need to keep your hands away from your head, your face, okay?"

"Okay."

"We're running off our own batteries here, just in case."

"Of what?"

"More doctor's orders."

She looked from him to Edward, just moving her eyes, then back to him. "So?"

He reached down, took her right wrist in his hand, squeezed it. "We're here. Anything looks too funny, we get you out. We built in some very basic monitors, on our own. Vital signs." He released her wrist.

"Thanks. What do I do?"

"Close your eyes. Count down from fifteen. About ten, should be a wobble."

"Wobble?"

"What she called it. Keep your eyes closed, keep counting down to zero. Then open 'em. We see you open 'em, it hasn't worked."

"Okay," she said, "but not until I say go." Holding her head still, she looked up and to the right: the window, in the wall beside her. Up: the ceiling, tubes of lights glowing in polymer. Toward her feet: Burton's display, Edward. To her left: Macon, the closed door behind him. "Go," she said, closing her eyes. "Fifteen. Fourteen. Thirteen. Twelve. Eleven. Ten."

Pop.

That color like Burton's haptics scar, but she could taste it inside her teeth. "Nine. Eight. Seven. Six." It hadn't worked. Nothing had happened. "Five. Four. Three." She should tell them. "Two. One. Zero." She opened her eyes. A flat ceiling sprang away, polished, six feet higher than the one in the trailer, as the room reversed, was backward, was other, weight of the crown gone, her stomach upside down. A woman's eyes, close, weirdly blurred.

She didn't remember sitting up but then she saw her own hands and they weren't. Hers.

"If you need this," the woman said, holding out a steel canister. "There's nothing in you but some water." Flynne leaned over, saw a face not hers reflected in the round, mirror-polished bottom. Froze. "Fuck." The lips there forming the word as she spoke it. "What the fuck is this?" She came up off the bed fast. Not a bed. A padded ledge. She was taller. "Something's wrong," she heard herself say, but the voice wasn't hers. "Colors—"

"You're accessing input from an anthropomorphic drone," the woman said. "A telepresence avatar. You needn't consciously control it. Don't try. We're recalibrating it now. Macon's device isn't perfect, but it works."

"You know Macon?"

"Virtually," said the woman. "I'm Ash."

"Your eyes—"

"Contact lenses."

"Too many colors—" She meant her own vision.

"I'm sorry," the woman said. "We'd missed that. Your peripheral is a tetrachromat."

"A what?"

"It has a wider range of color vision than you do. But we've found the settings for that and are including them in the recalibration. Touch your face."

"Macon told me not to."

"This is different."

Flynne raised her hand, touched her face, not thinking. "Shit—"

"Good. The recalibration is taking effect."

Again, with both hands. Like touching herself through something that wasn't quite there.

She looked up. The ceiling was pale polished wood, shiny, inset with round flat little metal light fixtures, glowing softly. Tiny room, higher than it was wide. Narrower than the Airstream. The walls were that same wood. A man stood at the far end, by a skinny open door. Dark shirt and jacket. "Hello, Flynne," he said.

"Human resources," she said, recognizing him.

"You don't look like you're going to need this," the woman called Ash said, putting the canister down on the cushioned ledge Flynne had awakened on. Awakened? Arrived? "Would you mind speaking to Macon now?"

"How?"

"By phone. He's concerned. I've reassured him, but it would help if he could speak with you."

"You have a phone?"

"Yes," said the woman, "but so do you."

"Where?"

"I'm not sure. It doesn't matter. Watch."

Flynne saw a small circle appear. Like a badge in Badger. It was white, with a gif of a line drawing of an antelope or something, running. She moved her eyes. The circle with the gif moved with them. "What's that?"

"My phone. You have one too. I have Macon. Now I open a feed—"

A second circle expanded, to the right of the gif and larger. She saw Macon, seated in front of Burton's display. "Flynne?" he asked. "That you?"

"Macon! This is crazy!"

"What did you do, here, just before we did the thing?" He looked serious.

"Had a pee?"

He grinned. "Wow . . ." He shook his head, grinned. "This is mission control shit!"

"He can see what I'm seeing," said Ash.

"You okay?" Macon asked.

"Guess so."

"You're okay here," he said.

"We'll get her back to you, Macon," Ash said, "but we need to speak with her now."

"Send somebody up to the house to get me a sandwich," she said to Macon, "I'll be starving."

Macon grinned, nodded, shrank to nothing, was gone.

"We could move to my office," said the man.

"Not yet," said Ash. She touched the pale wall and a section slid aside, out of sight.

A toilet, sink, shower, all steel. A mirror. Flynne moved toward it. "Holy shit," she said, staring. "Who is she?"

"We don't know."

"This is a . . . machine?" She touched . . . someone. Stomach. Breasts. She looked in the mirror. The French girl in Operation Northwind? No. "That's got to be somebody," she said.

"Yes," said Ash, "though we don't know who. How do you feel now?"

Flynne touched the steel basin. Someone else's hand. Her hand. "I can feel that."

"Nausea?"

"No."

"Vertigo?"

"No. Why is she wearing a shirt like mine, but silk or something? Has my name on it."

"We wanted you to feel at home."

"Where is this? Colombia?" She heard how little she thought this last might be true.

"That's my department, so to speak," said the human resources man, behind her. Netherton, she remembered. Wilf Netherton. "Come out to my office. It's a bit roomier. I'll try to answer your questions."

She turned and saw him standing there, eyes wider than she remembered. Like someone seeing a ghost.

"Yes," said Ash, putting her hand on Flynne's shoulder, "let's."

Her hand, thought Flynne, but whose shoulder?

She let Ash guide her.

42.
BODY LANGUAGE

Flynne completely altered the peripheral's body language, Netherton realized, as Ash directed her toward him. Inhabited, its face became not hers but somehow her.

He found himself backing down the corridor, barely shoulder-wide, away from that smallest of the Gobiwagen's cabins. Unwilling to lose sight of her, out of something that felt at least partially like terror, he couldn't turn his back.

Ash, earlier, had explained that peripherals, when under AI control, looked human because their faces, programmed to constantly register changing micro-expressions, were never truly still. In the absence of that, she'd said, they became uniquely disturbing objects. Flynne was now providing the peripheral with her own micro-expressions, a very different effect. "It's fine," he heard himself say, though whether to himself or to her he didn't know. This was all much stranger than he'd anticipated, like some unthinkable birth or advent.

He backed into the scent of Ash's flowers. Ash had had Ossian remove Lev's grandfather's displays, and the luggage as well, deeming them unnecessary, not conducive to "flow" in the space, so the flowers were at the end of the desk nearest two compact armchairs she'd raised from hidden wells in the floor. They'd reminded him of the seats in Lowbeer's car, but slicker, unworn.

"They're for you," Ash said, indicating the flowers. "We can't offer you anything to eat, or drink."

"I'm fucking starving," Flynne said, accent her own but the voice not as he recalled it. She looked at Ash. "I'm not? I—"

"Autonomic bleed-over," Ash said. "That's your own body's hunger.

Your peripheral doesn't experience it. It doesn't eat, has no digestive tract. Can you smell them, the flowers?"

Flynne nodded.

"Colors more normal?"

Flynne hesitated. Took two deep, slow breaths. "They hurt, before. Not now. I'm sweating."

"You've flooded its adrenal system. You won't find the transition this unsettling again. There was no way we could cushion it for you, as a first-time user, other than have you prone, eyes closed, on an empty stomach."

Flynne turned, slowly, taking in the room. "I saw you here," she said to Netherton. "Looked this tacky, but I thought it was bigger. Where's that atrium?"

"Elsewhere. Take a seat?"

She ignored his suggestion, went to the window instead. He and Ash had argued over whether or not to have the blinds closed. In the end, Ash had ordered Ossian into her workspace in the garage's corner, leaving the blinds open. With no motion in the garage, the arches had faded to their faintest luminosity. Flynne bent slightly, peering out, but now the nearest arch sensed her movement, pulsed faintly, greenly. "A parking lot?" She must have seen Lev's father's cars. "Are we in an RV?"

"A what?" asked Netherton.

"Camper. Recreational vehicle." She was moving her head, trying to see more. "Your office is in an RV?"

"Yes." He wasn't sure how that would strike her.

"Came here from a trailer," she said.

A short promotional video précis, he recalled. "Pardon me?"

"A caravan," said Ash. "Please sit down, both of you. We'll try to answer your questions, Flynne." She took a seat, leaving Flynne the one nearest the flowers.

Netherton seated himself at the gold-marbled desk, regretting its gangster pomp.

Flynne took a last look out the window, scratching the back of her neck, something he couldn't imagine the peripheral doing on its own, then went to the remaining chair. She folded herself into it, knees high, wide apart. She leaned forward, raised her hands, studying the nails closely, then shook her head. She looked up at him, lowering her hands. "I used to play in a game," she said, "for a man who had money. Did it because I needed the money. Man he had us play against was a total shit, but that was just sort of an accident. It wasn't about making money, for either of them. Not like it was for us. It was a hobby, for them. Rich fucks. They bet on who'd win." She was staring at him.

All his glibness, all his faithful machinery of convincing language, somehow spun silently against this, finding no traction whatever.

"You say you're not builders." She looked to Ash. "Some kind of security, for a game. But if it's a game, why did someone send those men to kill us? Not just Burton, but all of us. My mother too." She looked to him again. "How'd you know the winning number in the lottery, Mr. Netherton?"

"Wilf," he said, thinking it sounded less like a name than an awkward cough.

"We didn't," said Ash. "That was why your cousin had to purchase a ticket. Your brother gave us the number of the ticket. We then interfered with the mechanism of selection, making his the winning number. No predictive magic. Superior processing speed, nothing more."

"You sent that lawyer over from Clanton, with bags full of money? Make him win a lottery too?"

"No," said Ash, who then looked irritably at Netherton, as if to say that he was supposed to be the one handling this. Which he was.

"This isn't," he said, "your world."

"So what is it?" asked Flynne. "A game?"

"The future," said Netherton, feeling utterly ridiculous. On impulse, he added the year.

"No way."

"But it isn't your future," he said. "When we made contact, we set your world, your universe, whatever it is—"

"Continuum," said Ash.

"—on a different course," he finished. He'd never in his life said anything that sounded more absurd, though it was, as far as he knew, the truth.

"How?"

"We don't know," he said.

Flynne rolled her eyes.

"We're accessing a server," Ash said. "We know absolutely nothing about it. That sounds ridiculous, or evasive, but what we're doing is something people do here. Perhaps," and she looked at Netherton, "not unlike your two rich fucks."

"Why did you hire my brother?"

"That was Netherton's idea," said Ash. "Perhaps he should explain. He's been curiously silent."

"I thought it might amuse a friend—" he began.

"Amuse?" Flynne frowned.

"I'd no idea any of this would happen," he said.

"That's true, really," said Ash. "He was in a far messier situation than he imagined. Trying to impress a woman he was involved with, by offering her your brother's services."

"But she wasn't impressed," Netherton said. "And so she gave him, his services rather, to her sister." He was in freefall now, all power of persuasion having deserted him.

"You may have witnessed her sister's murder," Ash said to Flynne.

The peripheral's eyes widened. "That was real?"

"'May'?" asked Netherton.

"She witnessed something," Ash said to him, "but we've no evidence as to what, exactly."

"Ate her up," said Flynne. A drop of sweat ran down her forehead, into an eyebrow. She wiped it away with the back of her forearm, something else he couldn't imagine the peripheral doing.

"If you consider how you're able to be here now," Ash said to her, "virtually yet physically, you may begin to understand our inability to know exactly what you saw."

"You're confusing her," Netherton said.

"I'm attempting to acclimatize her, something you're so far utterly failing to do."

"Where are we?" Flynne demanded.

"London," said Netherton.

"The game?" she asked.

"It's never been a game," he said. "It was easiest for us to tell your brother that."

"This thing," she indicated the cabin, "where is it, exactly?"

"An area called Notting Hill," said Ash, "in a garage, beneath a house. Beneath several adjacent houses, actually."

"The London with the towers?"

"Shards," Netherton said. "They're called shards."

She stood, the peripheral unfolding with a slender but suddenly powerful grace from its awkward position in the chair. She pointed. "What's outside that door?"

"A garage," said Ash. "Housing a collection of historic vehicles."

"Door locked?"

"No," said Ash.

"Anything out there that'll convince me this is the future?"

"Let me show you this." Ash stood, the stiff fabric of her suit rumpled. She undid zips, from inner wrist to elbow, on both her sleeves, quickly folding them back. Line drawings fled. "They're in a panic," she said. "They don't know you." She put her thumb through the central zip's aluminum ring, at the hollow of her neck, and drew it down, exposing a complexly cantilevered black lace bra, below which swarmed a terrified tangle of extinct species, their black ink milling against her luminous pallor. As if seeing Flynne, they fled again. To her back, Netherton assumed. Ash zipped up her suit, rezipped the sleeves in turn. "Does that help?"

Flynne stared at her. Nodded slightly. "Can I go out now?"

"Of course," Ash said. "These aren't contact lenses, by the way."

Netherton, realizing that he hadn't moved, possibly hadn't breathed, since Flynne had stood up, pushed himself up from the desk, palms flat on the gold-veined marble.

"How can I be sure it isn't a game?" Flynne asked. "At least half the games I've ever played were set in some kind of future."

"Were you paid large sums to play them?" Netherton asked.

"Didn't do it for free," Flynne said, stepping to the door, opening it.

He managed to beat Ash there, at the cost of bruising his thigh on the corner of the desk. Flynne was at the top of the gangway, looking up at the arch nearest them, as its cells, sensing her there, luminesced.

"What's that?" she asked.

"Engineered from marine animals. Motion activated."

"My brother used a squidsuit, in the war. Cuttlefish camo. What's that?" Pointing, down, to the left of the gangway, to the white anthropomorphic bulk of the muscular-resistance exoskeleton.

"That's yours."

"Mine?"

"Your peripheral's. An exercise device. You wear it."

She turned toward him, placing her palm flat on his chest, pushing slightly, as if to test that he was there. "Don't know whether to scream or shit," she said. And smiled.

Breathe, he reminded himself.

43.
'SPLODING

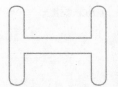er mouth was full of pork tenderloin with garlic mayo, on a big crusty white bun. "Don't choke," Janice advised, seated beside her on Burton's bed. "Be a sad end to whatever you've been up to. Drink?" She offered Flynne her black Sukhoi Flankers water bottle.

Flynne swallowed tenderloin, then some water, and handed the bottle back. "It's a body," she said. "Got a phone built in. Like a Viz, but it's inside, somewhere. On-off and menus on the roof of your mouth, like a keyboard."

"You got a lot pointier tongue than me."

"Really small magnet, just in the tip." She'd counted back to zero again, just a little wobble then and she'd opened her eyes in the Airstream, her neck stiff, looking up at Burton and Macon and Edward and Janice, hungry as she'd ever been in her life.

"You going back?" Janice asked her, now. "Tonight?"

Flynne bit into the sandwich again, nodded.

"Maybe you don't want to eat all of that now. They were worried about you puking, before."

Flynne chewed, swallowed. "That's a first-time thing. People who use them get used to it. I need food. Need to be able to stay there longer."

"Why do they call them that, 'peripherals'?"

"Because they're extensions? Like accessories?"

"Anatomically correct?"

"Didn't think to check."

"Put that in Hefty Mart, there goes the neighborhood. Probably there goes vintage flight sims too, 'cept for old folks and the church people. Could Madison learn to pilot one?"

"Guess he could."

"Nobody's going to kick the one they got you out of bed for eating crackers. Macon showed me a screen-grab." Janice smiled. "Impressed you told Burton and them a lady needed time to collect herself."

"Lady fucking did," Flynne said.

"You don't think that's really the future, do you?" Janice asked, her best game face, no tells.

"Or am I batshit insane, you mean?"

"I guess, yeah."

Flynne put what was left of the sandwich down, on the plastic Janice had brought it in. "Might as well be. We went upstairs, in an elevator, and there was this big fancy old house. Then out onto a kind of walled patio in back, at night, with these two Tasmanian tigers."

"Extinct," said Janice. "Seen 'em CG'd on *Ciencia Loca*."

"These aren't really them. They tweaked Tasmanian devil DNA. I could smell all the different flowers, dirt, hear birds. It was almost dark. Like the birds were going to sleep. Weird."

"What was?"

"Hearing birds. Because we were right in the city. Too quiet."

"Maybe it was too late."

"Quiet as here, at night."

"So what do you think it is?"

"If it's a game, it's not just another game. Maybe a whole new platform. That would explain the money."

"Would it explain how they can fix the state lottery?"

"They aren't telling me it's a game. They're telling me it's a future. Not ours exactly, because now they've messed with us, even just first getting in touch, we're headed somewhere else."

"Where?"

"Say they can't tell. That it's not like time travel in a show. Just information, back and forth. Minute later here is a minute later there. If I waited a week to go back, it would be a week later there."

"What's in it for them?"

"Don't know. Lev, it's his house, but really it's his dad's other house, so doing this is like Dwight gambling on Operation Northwind. Rich man's hobby. He pays Ash and Wilf and another guy to run it for him, handle the details. But Wilf, he fucked up, over some woman, and somebody else got in here, where we are, and hired those dead guys from Tennessee to kill my family."

Janice made her eyes wide as she could. "Brain 'splode."

"Don't have the luxury of 'sploding," Flynne said. "Whatever it is, it's rolling. With a lot of moving parts, and my brother thinks he can steer it. He's making deals with Corbell Pickett, he's setting terms with Lev and them, and it's about me. Not about me, but I'm the one who saw that asshole. I might be the only one who saw him."

"Then the first order of business," Janice said, reaching over to squeeze Flynne's hand, "is you getting a say in what's going on."

44

PERVERSELY DIFFICULT

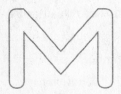inus Flynne, the peripheral seemed to occupy less space. It was seated where she'd sat earlier, looking at Lev, where he leaned on the edge of the desk. "Things went well," he said, looking from Netherton to Ash, who was seated in the other armchair. "She's quite something, isn't she?"

"I'd spoken with Lowbeer earlier," Netherton said, "and she'd agreed that a little time outside might be a good idea." Actually this had been Lowbeer's suggestion, but Flynne's visit had gone so well that he felt he deserved some credit. Flynne herself had insisted on going out, for that matter, but it had been Netherton, happening to glance in the direction of Ash's vase of flowers, who'd suggested the garden. Then they'd found Lev in the garden with Gordon and Tyenna, out to distribute their expensively modified DNA among the hostas.

"Yes," said Lev, giving him a look, "Lowbeer phoned me as you were on the way up."

"She'll be back," said Ash.

"Lowbeer?" Netherton asked.

"Your polt girl. We do have her attention. Though she isn't going to do just anything we suggest." She was looking at Netherton.

"Indeed."

"You're supposed to be good at manipulating people," Ash said. "Frankly, I've never been able to see it."

"I have my moments," said Netherton. "Results aren't always replicable. Actually, I've noticed that you're rather good at it yourself."

"Stop it," said Lev. "Ash is a bit more of a generalist, while you're highly specialized. I'm quite satisfied with that."

"My difficulty," said Netherton, "is a lack of context. Until you tell me what Lowbeer wants done, what she intends to do, I've nothing to work with."

"What did she tell you when she phoned?" asked Lev.

"I told her that I thought it was best to tell Flynne that this isn't a game. She agreed, that I should begin to explain the stub, to the extent that I understand it. Which, I gather, really isn't that much less than your own understanding. Is it true, that you've no idea what or where this server is?"

"None," said Lev. "We assume it's in China, or is in any case Chinese, but that's assumption only. Someone has a device that sends and receives information, to and from the past. The act of doing so, initially, generates continua. Unless those continua are already there, some literally infinite number of them, but that's academic. It's massively encrypted, whatever it is. It took Ash and Ossian months to find their way in, even with the willing help of several experienced enthusiasts."

"Perversely difficult," said Ash.

"But," asked Netherton, with no real expectation of a meaningful answer, "what does Lowbeer want?"

"To learn what happened to Aelita, and why," Lev said, "and who was responsible."

"If your taste runs to perverse difficulty," Netherton said, "getting that out of Daedra and her cohort, assuming they know, should provide it. But that's not something I want any part of."

Lev looked at him, then, and he didn't like it.

45.

UP THERE

'll talk to Burton," Flynne said to Janice. "You talk to Macon. Need the head measurement right away, and printed out."

"What'll you do when you get him there? Seriously, honey. That's a lateral move."

"I won't be alone. And I need a witness, somebody to confirm my version. Then we can double-team Burton, if we have to."

"That why you wouldn't just take Burton in the first place?"

"I guess. I'm winging it, Janice."

"You are that," said Janice.

Flynne turned, reaching for the door handle.

"Hold on a sec," said Janice. "Costume department." She was flipping through Burton's hyper-tidy rod of mostly raggedy clothes, across the front of the Airstream, everything facing in one direction, on identical hangers from Hefty Mart. Janice pulled out something long, shiny, coppery brown. A robe he'd won in a mixed martial arts contest in Davisville, last winter. Ripstop nylon with maroon lapels, a screaming American eagle fabbed across the back. Like a boxer's robe. She was surprised he'd kept it. "Perfect," said Janice, holding it open for her.

"That?"

"You just went to the future, hon. Or somewhere they say's the future. Major event."

"It's too big," Flynne protested, shrugging into it.

Janice wrapped it tight, knotted the maroon belt, readjusted the knot. "Like you just skinned you a Marine combat artist. Best we can do."

"Okay," Flynne said, "but you get Macon on that, right?"

"I will."

Flynne turned, squared shoulders that felt lost in Burton's robe, and opened the door. A burst of applause.

Burton standing there, lit by the open door. Behind him, Macon and Edward, Leon, Carlos. Leon whistled, between two fingers.

"Never much going on around here," she said, and stepped down.

"That could change," Macon said. "Remember how I saw you there?"

"They've got more for you to do," she said to him, hearing Janice step down behind her. "Janice, she'll tell you." She looked at the others. Realized she had no idea what anybody in particular thought was going on, herself included. "Burton and I," she said, "we need to talk. Excuse us." She started up the path, then stopped as he caught up with her.

"You ready now?" he asked, quietly.

"Couldn't talk, before. Forget talking: Couldn't think. It did something to my head."

"Macon says you went somewhere. Says he saw you there on his phone. Where?"

"Not Colombia. They say it's the future. London. What we saw in the game."

"What do you think it is?"

"Don't know."

"If you were in the trailer, how'd Macon see you somewhere else?"

She looked at him, his face in the moonlight. "Kind of robot body. Macon saw it. But it feels human. Like a drone, but you don't have to think about operating it. Thing on my head, in the trailer, they call a neural cutout. Keeps your own body from responding when you do something with the peripheral."

"The what?"

"Peripheral. What they call them. The body things."

"Who are they?"

"Ash, she's the first one you talked to, she works for Lev. That's his name. I think he's Russian, but English Russian? Grew up there."

"When do they say they are?"

She told him.

"Just over seventy years? How different does it look?"

"You saw it yourself," she said. "Different but not that much. Or maybe a lot and it doesn't all show?"

"You believe them?"

"It's something."

"They have a lot of money." It wasn't a question, but she could see he didn't want her to tell him it wasn't true.

"Metric fuck-tons, for all I know, but there's no way any of that's getting here. But they're figuring out ways to game the markets, here."

"Because they know what's going to happen, before it does?"

"Say it doesn't work that way. They can spend money on their side, pay people there to figure out how they can make money here, then have the Coldiron lawyers do things, here. Information from there affects things here. But they don't know our future. They don't need to know our future to kick ass in the market, though, because they can find out whatever they need to know about our present, any day. Their stuff's all seventy years faster than ours."

"Okay," he said, and she wondered if what she was seeing in his eyes was the Corps' speed, intensity, violence of action, or his right way of seeing. Because he just got it. Ignored the crazy, went tactically forward. And she saw how weird that was, and how much it was who he was, and for just that instant she wondered if she didn't somehow have it too.

"Follow the money," he said. "What's in it for them?"

"That's where it gets fucked up."

"You don't think it's already fucked up?" His eyes crinkled, like he was about to laugh at her.

"It was like a game, for Lev. We aren't their past. We go off in some different direction, because they've changed things here. Their world's not affected by what happens here, now or going forward. But shit's gone sideways on them, some other way. Because I saw that woman killed. Whatever that's about. I saw the man who knew she was going to be killed. Who got her out on that balcony for that thing to eat her. And now somebody up there's gotten in here too."

"Here?"

"Now. Our time."

"Who?"

"Whoever hired those men from Memphis, to kill us."

"But why's this Lev in it now? He's the man, right? It's still his show?"

"I don't know. I'm going back there now, to find out."

"Now?"

"Soon as I can use myself a flush toilet, I'm back in the Snow White hat. Janice brought me a sandwich and some water, so I won't starve here, while I'm back up there. Then we'll have more to work with. I don't want you doing anything, okay? Things are complicated enough. Just lock everything down, really tight. Don't let anybody on the property but our closest people. We don't know enough now to make any kind of move at all."

He looked at her. "Easy Ice," he said, and she saw the shiver run through him in the moonlight, the haptic thing, but then it was gone.

"Where's Conner?" she asked.

"At his place."

"That's good," she said. "Keep him there."

"Go use that flush toilet," he said. "Nobody's stopping you."

46.
THE SIGHTS

etherton watched as the peripheral opened its eyes. Ash had had it recline again on the bunk in the back cabin, had readjusted the lights.

"Okay," Flynne said, tentatively. Then: "Not bad."

"Welcome back," said Lev, over Netherton's shoulder.

"How's the tetrachromia?" asked Ash.

"I can't remember what it was like," Flynne said, "except I didn't like it."

"Try sitting up," suggested Ash.

Flynne sat up, shook her hair to the side, then touched it, froze. "My haircut. Saw it before, in the mirror here, but I couldn't think. You did that?"

"The stylist was impressed," said Ash. "I imagine he'll be copying it."

"That's Carlota," said Flynne. "She's the best. She's in the Marianas, has a bot chair in our Hefty Clips. Keeps up with the styles."

"You're used to telepresence, then," Lev said.

"We call it getting a haircut," Flynne said, giving him a look as she got to her feet, "back in frontier days."

"We have something you might like to see," said Lev. He turned, behind Netherton, and walked back along the corridor. Netherton smiled at her, self-consciously, and followed Lev, Ash behind him.

"Where's your dogs?" Flynne asked, behind them, loud in the veneered narrowness.

"Upstairs," Lev said, turning, as she emerged.

Netherton watched her touching things. Running a finger across the glassy veneer. Lightly tapping a knuckle on a steel handle. Testing the peripheral's sensoria, he guessed.

"I liked them," she said. "I could see how they weren't dogs, but in a dog ballpark." She touched her black trousers. "Why do these clothes all feel like yoga pants?"

"They have no seams," said Ash. "The seams on the outside are decorative, traditional. They were made for you by assemblers. All of a piece."

"Fabbed," said Flynne. "Don't mean to be rude, but if you aren't wearing contacts, like you said, is that some kind of condition?"

"A modification," said Ash. "A species of visual pun, on a likely mythical condition called pupula duplex. Which is usually depicted as dual irises, but I chose to make it literal."

"How do things look?"

"I seldom use the lower pair. They register infrared, which can be interesting in the dark."

"You don't mind if I ask questions? I'm not sure what anything is, here. You could've been born that way. Or have a religion or something. How would I know? But tattoos that run around, I sort of get that."

"Please," Ash said, "ask questions."

"Where's the phone, in this?" Flynne asked, holding up her hands. "I was trying to tell my friend about it."

"I could check with Hermès," said Lev. "The components are very small, though, and distributed. Some are biological. I couldn't tell you where my own are, without accessing medical history. Part of my cousin's became inflamed, had to be replaced. Base of the skull. But they can put them anywhere." He propped himself against the edge of the desk. "May we show you London now? We've a helicopter above the house, like the one you flew for us. You'll want to take a seat."

"Can I fly it?"

"Let us show you the sights," said Lev. He smiled.

She looked from Lev to Ash, then to Netherton. "Okay," she said, and sat.

Ash took the other chair. Netherton joined Lev on the edge of the desk, glad to not be behind it, so less associated with its psychological functions of hierarchy and intimidation. "It wasn't such a shock for you, this time," he said to Flynne.

"I couldn't wait to get back here," she said. "But I'm not necessarily going to believe you about any of this, okay?"

"Of course," said Lev.

Netherton was suddenly aware of smiling in a particularly stupid fashion, while Ash smirked at him, her gray eyes doubly gimleted. But then she turned, and spoke to Flynne. "You're seeing my sigil now," she said, and Flynne nodded, Netherton seeing it too. Now Lev's was there, and Flynne's, which was featureless. "Now I'll open a feed," Ash said, "full binocular."

The room vanished, replaced by a foggy midmorning aerial vista of London, the angular uprights of the shards set regularly out across the city's compacted intricacy, a density relieved by greenways he'd hiked as a child, by systematic erasures of alleged mediocrities, by new forests grown thick and deep. The glass roofing some of the cleansed and excavated rivers dully reflected what sun there was, and in the Thames he saw the floating islands, rearranged yet again, the revolving blades beneath them better positioned to gather the river's strength.

"Damn," said Flynne, evidently impressed.

Ash piloted them toward Hampstead, where Netherton's parents had taken him to a schoolmate's party, when he was ten, to spend the afternoon within a length of clay drainpipe, buried under a cast-iron bench, a space strung with tiny colored lanterns, where costumed mice had sung and danced and staged mock duels. The hands of his homunculus had been crude and translucent, not unlike those of the patchers. As he remembered this, Ash was telling Flynne of the water-wheels turned by the rescued rivers, but nothing of any preceding history, times prior, darkness.

He crossed the roof of his mouth with his tongue tip, blanking the feed, returning to the Gobiwagen, preferring to watch Flynne's face.

"But where is everybody?" she asked. "There's no people."

"That's complicated," said Ash, evenly, "but at this altitude you wouldn't notice anyone."

"Hardly any traffic, either," Flynne said. "Noticed that before."

"We're almost in the City now," said Ash. "Cheapside. Here's your crowd."

But those aren't people, thought Netherton, watching Flynne's expression as she took it all in.

"Cosplay zone," said Lev, "Eighteen sixty-seven. We'd be fined for the helicopter, if it didn't have cloaking, or if it made a sound."

Netherton tapped the requisite quadrant of palate, returning to Ash's feed, to find them stationary over morning traffic, already so thick as to be almost unmoving. Cabs, carts, drays, all drawn by horses. Lev's father and grandfather owned actual horses, apparently. Were said to sometimes ride them, though certainly never in Cheapside. His mother had shown him the shops here as a child. Silver-plated tableware, perfumes, fringed shawls, implements for ingesting tobacco, fat watches cased in silver or gold, men's hats. He'd been amazed at how copiously the horses shat in the street, their droppings swept up by darting children, younger than he was, who he'd understood were no more real than the horses, but who seemed as real, entirely real, and terrifying in the desperation of their employment, cursing vividly as they dodged with crude short brooms between the legs of the animals, as men his mother said were bankers, solicitors, merchants, brokers, or rather their simulacra, hurried along beneath tall hats, past handpainted signs for boots, china, lace, insurance, plate glass. He'd loved those signs, had captured as many as he could while holding his mother's hand, uncomfortable in his stiff and requisite clothing. He'd kept a lookout for fierce-eyed boys hurtling handcarts along, or running, shouting, back into dark courts stinking, he supposed, as realistically as the green dung of the horses. His mother had worn broad dark skirts for such visits, swelling from a narrow waist to brush the pavement, below a very fitted sort of matching jacket, some unlikely hat perched on the side of her head. She hadn't cared for any of it. Had brought him here because she felt she should, and perhaps he'd elaborated on that, later, developing his own sharp distaste for anything of the sort.

"Look at it," Flynne said.

"It isn't real," he said. "Worked up from period media. Scarcely anyone you see is human, and those who are, are tourists, or school-children being taught history. Better at night, the illusion." Less annoying, in any case.

"The horses aren't real?" Flynne asked.

"No," said Ash, "horses are rare now. We've generally done better, with domestic animals."

Please, thought Netherton, don't start. Lev might have thought the same thing, because now he said, "We've brought you here to meet someone. Just to say hello, this time."

They began to descend.

Netherton saw Lowbeer then, looking up, in skirts and a jacket very like the ones his mother had worn.

47.

POWER RELATIONSHIPS

n the middle of a walking forest of black hats stood a white-haired woman with bright blue eyes. The men seemed no more to see her than they saw whatever Ash was flying, which Lev said they couldn't, though they felt the turbulence, each one reaching up to hold his hat as he walked through it. They walked around the woman as she stood there, looking up at what they couldn't see, one gray-gloved hand holding a little hat against the downdraft.

There was a new badge, beside Lev's, Ash's, Wilf's. A sort of simple crown, in profile, gold on cream. The others dimmed now. "We're in privacy mode," the woman said. "The others can't hear us. I am Detective Inspector Ainsley Lowbeer, of the Metropolitan Police." Her voice in Flynne's head, sounds of crowd and traffic muted.

"Flynne Fisher," Flynne said. "Are you why I'm here?"

"You yourself are why you're here. If you hadn't chosen to stand in for your brother, you wouldn't have witnessed the crime I'm investigating."

"Sorry," said Flynne.

"I'm not sorry at all," the woman said. "Without you, I'd have nothing. An annoyingly seamless absence. Are you frightened?"

"Sometimes."

"Normal under the circumstances, insofar as they can be said to be normal. Are you satisfied with your peri?"

"My what?"

"Your peripheral. I chose it myself, I'm afraid on very short notice. I felt it had a certain poetry."

"Why do you want to talk to me?"

"You witnessed a peculiarly unpleasant homicide. Saw the face of someone who may be either the perpetrator or an accomplice."

"I thought that might be why."

"Some person or persons unknown have since attempted to have you murdered, in your native continuum, presumably because they know you to be a witness. Shockingly, in my view, I'm told that arranging your death would in no way constitute a crime here, as you are, according to current best legal opinion, not considered to be real."

"I'm as real as you are."

"You are indeed," said the woman, "but persons of the sort pursuing you now would have no hesitation whatever in killing you, or anyone else, here, now, or elsewhere. Such persons are my concern, of course." Bright blue, her eyes, and cold. "But you are my concern as well. My responsibility, in a different way."

"Why?"

"For my sins, perhaps." She smiled, but not in any way Flynne found comforting. "Zubov, you should understand, will pervert the economy of your world."

"It's pretty fucked anyway," Flynne said, then wished she'd put it another way.

"I'm familiar with it, so yes, it is, though that isn't what I mean. I don't like what these people are doing, these continua hobbyists, Zubov included, though I do find it fascinating. Some might think you more real than I am myself."

"What does that mean?"

"I'm very old, elaborately and artificially so. I don't feel entirely real to myself, frankly. But if you agree to assist me, I shall assist you in return, insofar as I can."

"Got a male version of this? Peripheral?"

The Detective Inspector raised penciled eyebrows. "You would prefer one?"

"No. I don't want to be the only one who's seen this, been here. I need someone who'll back me up, when I go home and tell them what's going on."

"Zubov could arrange it, I'm sure."

"You're after whoever sent that gray knapsack thing to kill her, aren't you? And that asshole who brought her out on the balcony?"

"I am, yes."

"I'll be a witness. When it comes to trial. I would anyway."

"There shall be no trial. Only punishment. But thank you."

"I want that peripheral, though. And fast. Deal?"

"Consider it done," said Lowbeer. The other badges undimmed, the din of Cheapside flooding back, now with an added booming of big church bells. "We've had our chat," Lowbeer called up. "Thank you so much for bringing her by. Goodbye!"

Cheapside was the size of one of the badges then, then smaller, gone. Flynne blinked across at Lev. He was seeing her, she saw, and so was Wilf Netherton, but Ash's weird eyes were fixed on blank veneer.

"Actually, Inspector," Ash said, "I believe we can borrow one. Yes. Of course. I'll speak with Mr. Zubov. Thank you." She turned to Lev, seeing him now. "Your brother's sparring partner," she said. "Your father keeps it in Richmond Hill, brings it out to remind Anton of his folly?"

"More or less," Lev said, glancing at Flynne.

"Have them send it over in a car. Lowbeer wants it here."

"Why?"

"I didn't ask. You wouldn't have either. She said that we need a male peripheral, soonest. I remembered that it was there."

"I suppose it's the easiest way," said Lev. "Who'll be using it?" He looked at Flynne.

"Bathroom's in the back?" she asked.

"Yes," he said.

"Excuse me," she said. Stood.

In the narrow steel toilet-shower room off the little room in the back, its door closed behind her, she looked into the mirror. Unbuttoned the black shirt, finding a bra she hadn't been aware of and breasts slightly larger than her own. Not hers, and that was comforting, and so was the small flat mole over the left collar bone. Which was why she'd looked, she realized, buttoning up the shirt, though she hadn't understood until she'd done it.

She wondered if it needed to pee. She didn't, so she'd assume that it didn't. It drank water, Ash had said, but didn't eat. Whoever had cut its hair had done Carlota proud.

She turned, opened the door, and returned to the room Netherton had pretended was his office at Milagros Coldiron. He and Lev were gone. Ash stood by the window, looking out. "Where did they go?" she asked.

"Up to the house. Netherton and Ossian will wait for it to arrive. I hope you like jaw."

"Jaw?"

"It has a rather prominent jawline. Extremely high cheekbones. A sort of fairy-tale Slav."

"You . . . know it?" Was that the word?

"I've never seen it with a human operator. Only with cloud AI from its manufacturer. It belonged to Lev's brother."

"He's dead, Lev's brother?"

"Unfortunately, no," said Ash.

Okay, Flynne thought. "Is it athletic? Like this one seems to be?"

"Extremely. Quite off the scale, actually."

"Good," said Flynne.

"What are you up to?" asked Ash, her eyes narrowing until Flynne could only see her upper pupils.

"Nothing Lowbeer doesn't know about."

"Quite good at power relationships, are we?"

"How long till it's here?"

"Half an hour?"

"Show me how to call Macon," Flynne said.

48.
PAVEL

Lev's entranceway was cluttered with parenting equipment. Miniature Wellingtons, coatrack clumped with bright rainwear, a push-bike reminding Netherton of the patchers, things to hit balls with, many balls themselves. A few stray bits of Lego edged fitfully about among lower strata, like bright rectilinear beetles.

Netherton and Ossian sat on a wooden bench, facing these things. The end nearest him was smeared with what he assumed was partially dried jam. Anton's sparring partner was expected momentarily, from Richmond Hill. Ossian had rejected his suggestion that they wait outside.

"Had the nannies shitting themselves, that did," Ossian said now, apparently apropos of nothing.

"What did?"

"Your buggy, there." Indicating, Netherton at first thought, the burdened coatrack. "Against the wall." He pointed. "Cloaked."

Netherton now made out the outline of a folded pushchair, currently emulating what happened to be nearest, in this case grubbily off-white wall and the brown tartan lining of a weathered jacket.

"The grandfather had it sent from Moscow," Ossian said, "when the girl was born. Diplomatic bag. Only way to get it in."

"Why was that?"

"Has a weapons system. Pair of guns. Nothing ballistic, though. Projects very short-term assemblers. Disassemblers, really. Go after soft tissue. Take it apart at a molecular level. Seen footage of doing that to a side of beef."

"What happens?"

"Bones. It's autonomous, self-targeting, makes its own call of threat levels."

"Who would pose the threat?"

"Your Russian kidnappers," said Ossian.

"It does that with a baby aboard?"

"Being shown pandas against the trauma, by then. Headed home, nannies or no, in armed evasion mode."

Netherton considered the faintly visible, harmless-looking thing.

"Zubov's missus wouldn't have it. Never gotten on with the grandfather. Sided with the nannies."

"How long have you worked here, Ossian?"

Ossian regarded him narrowly. "Five years, near enough."

"What did you do previously?"

"Much the same. Near enough."

"Did you train for it?"

"I did," Ossian said.

"How?"

"Misspending my youth. How did you train to stand up smart and lie to anyone?"

Netherton looked at him. "Like you. Near enough."

A shadow darkened one sidelight. Chimes sounded.

"That would be itself," said Ossian, standing, tugging down his dark waistcoat. He turned to the door, squared his shoulders, and opened it.

"Good evening." Tall, broad-shouldered, in a dark gray suit. "Pleased to see you, Ossian. You may not remember me. Pavel."

"Quick about it," ordered Ossian, stepping back.

The peripheral entered, Ossian closing the door behind it. "Pavel," it said to Netherton. Pronounced jawline, strong facial bones, eyes pale and somehow mocking.

"Wilf Netherton." Offering his hand. They shook hands, the peripheral's grip warm, careful.

"The garage," said Ossian.

"Of course," said Pavel, and strolled ahead of them, toward the elevator, entirely at home.

49.

THE SOUNDS HE MADE

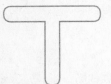his Pavel had cheekbones you could chop ice with, Flynne thought, but his voice was nice.

"Personality's AI," the Irishman said. "We'll have that turned off before your man moves in."

"I'm Flynne," she said.

"Pleased to meet you," said the peripheral, eyeing the Irishman like he had no fucks to give.

"Programmed to take the piss," Ossian said. "Part of the sparring functionality. Makes you want to beat it out of them."

The peripheral shifted its weight. It was well over six feet, taller than Burton, pale hair pushed to one side. It cocked a blond eyebrow at Flynne. "How may I be of service?"

"Go into the back cabin," Ash said. "Lie down. Notify the factory that we won't be needing the cloud."

"Of course," it said. It had to turn its shoulders a little, to clear shiny walls almost the color of its hair.

"I see why Anton kept murdering it," Ossian said. "Mindless, but it's always at you."

Ash said something to him in one of their weird private languages.

"She says that that could be adjusted," Ossian said to Flynne. "True, but Anton couldn't be arsed. Not his way. I always hoped he'd do it sufficient damage that the factory couldn't put it back together."

"Macon has everything ready," Ash said to Flynne. "I have him now. He'd like to speak with you."

"Sure," said Flynne. Ash's badge appeared, then another beside it, yellow with an ugly red lump. Then Macon. "That a nubbin, Macon? Got your own future-folks badge already?"

"Yours is sorry-ass," Macon said. "Just blank. Get her to fix it for you." He grinned.

"Kinda busy," she said.

"Things okay?"

"Not messed up the way I was the first time. Saw a little more of the place. He ready?"

"Too ready, you ask me."

"Burton know?" she asked him.

"As it happens," Macon said, doing a side eye.

"He's there?"

"Uh-huh."

"Shit."

"It's all good. Set to go."

"Let's do this thing."

"Ready when you are," he said. The nubbin badge dimmed.

"Ash and I go in," Flynne said to Netherton and Ossian. "Not sure how he's going to take this. Thing to remember is to cut him slack, okay? He gets excited, you better back off, fast."

Netherton and Ossian looked at each other.

"Okay," Flynne said to Ash, and walked into the corridor, three strides to the back room, where the peripheral lay on the bunk, ankles hanging off the end.

"Pavel," Ash said to it, around Flynne's shoulder, "close your eyes."

It looked at Flynne, then closed its eyes.

"Fifteen," said Ash, Flynne presumed to Macon.

Flynne counted down in her head. At ten, she imagined the wobble. Kept counting.

"Zero," Ash said.

The peripheral's eyes opened wide. "Christ on a corndog," it said, raising large hands until it could see them. It wiggled the fingers of both, then each thumb touched each finger in turn, then back again to the index. Sat up like it was driven by a spring. Flowed to its feet.

"It's me, Conner," Flynne said.

"Know that. Macon showed me a screen-grab. You," he said to Ash, "I saw something like you in a club in Atlanta. Boy there said it was a hyperspace elf, and technically an overdose."

"This is Ash," Flynne said, "be nice. Colors okay?"

"Colors? This better not just be a drug experience."

"It's not tetrachromatic," said Ash, causing Conner to peer at her suspiciously.

"You feel okay?" Flynne asked.

He grinned wolfishly, scary on the former Pavel. "Goddamn. Look at all these fingers."

"This way," Flynne said, "but there's two men out here. They're with us. They're okay. Okay?"

"Fuck yes," said Conner, looking at his hands again. "Jesus."

She took his hand, led him out. Ash was standing beside Ossian, Netherton behind them. "Conner Penske," Flynne said to them, releasing his hand. "Conner was in the Marines with my brother."

The three of them nodded, staring. The peripheral had a different way of standing now. Conner looked from one to the next, seemed to decide handshakes weren't in order, and stuck his hands into the pockets of his gray pants. Looked around the cabin. "Boat? Dry dock?"

"Big fancy RV," Flynne said.

He went to the window, bent, looked out. "My ass, out of here," he said, probably not to them. Flynne was right behind him as he yanked open the door. He didn't bother with the gangway. Did an acrobat's flip, sideways, over the railing, and dropped, a good fifteen feet. Came up running, maybe faster than anyone she'd ever seen run, straight out across the garage, down the long line of what they'd said was Lev's father's car collection. As he ran, each long arch lit up with its glow stuff, so shallow they might almost have been beams, to fade again as he passed below, and she hadn't imagined there were so many, or how big this place was. And as he ran he screamed, maybe how he hadn't screamed when what had happened to him had torn so much of his body off, but between the screams he whooped hoarsely, she guessed out of some unbearable joy or relief, just to run that way, have fingers, and that was harder to hear than the screams.

Then one last arch faded when he ran beneath it, and there was only darkness, and the sounds he made.

50.

WHILE THE GETTING'S GOOD

S hould we go out to him?" Ash asked.

Ossian, Netherton knew, had shut down the elevator, and probably other things as well. Anton's sparring partner, whoever was operating it, would be staying on this level.

"Don't," Flynne said, from where she stood at the top of the gangway, looking out across the darkened garage.

"What's he doing?" Netherton asked Ossian, who seemed to be peering narrowly at the locked bar, but was actually observing the former Pavel via some in-house system.

"Pacing backward," Ossian said, "then forward. Doing something complicated with his hands."

"Integrative workout," Flynne said, coming back in. "Marine thing. Used to do that a lot, before he got disabled."

"What happened to him?" Netherton asked.

"War."

Netherton remembered the headless figure on the stair in Covent Garden.

"Dusting off his jacket," Ossian announced. "Looking at his hands. Has mastered the thing's night-vision toggle, by the way. Starts this way, at a relaxed trot." He looked at Flynne, obviously seeing her now. "Quite the entrance, your man," he said. "Military, was he?"

"Haptic Recon 1," said Flynne. " 'First in, last out.' He's maybe got stuff going on from the embeds, like my brother does. VA tried to figure it out."

"Victoria and Albert?" Ash asked.

"Veterans Administration."

Netherton went to the door, saw the nearest arch pulse as the sparring partner came loping beneath it. He would have preferred cloud AI to whatever this instability might be, that Flynne was suggesting. Why had she brought this person, and not her brother?

Now it was coming up the gangway.

"Maybe dislocated a finger," it said, in the doorway, the accent reminding Netherton of hers. Left hand, little finger extended. "Rest of it's okay. More than okay. They all like this, these things?"

"That one's optimized for martial arts," Netherton said, which caused it to raise an eyebrow. "A training unit. It belongs to our friend's brother."

Ash produced the Medici. "Come here, please."

It crossed to her, finger extended, like a child. She placed the Medici against the finger. "Sprained," she said. "The discomfort will be gone now, but try not to do much with it."

"What's that?" asked the peripheral, looking down at the Medici.

"A hospital," said Ash, tucking it away.

"Thanks," said the peripheral, making a fist of its injured hand, opening it. It went to Flynne, put its hands on her shoulders. "Macon figured this was what it was," it said.

"Told him not to tell you much," she said. "Afraid it might not work."

"It's like I'm okay," it said, taking its hands from her shoulders, "then I decide it's a dream and I'm not okay."

"It's not a dream," Flynne said. "I don't know what it is, but it's not a dream. Don't know that any of us are okay."

"Never sprained anything in a dream," the peripheral said. "Kinda got it, when I was out there, if I wasn't careful I could break its neck."

"You could," said Ash. "Assume it's human. It is, genetically, for the most part. It's also a very considerable piece of property, which we've borrowed in order to have you here."

It came to attention, with an audible click of its heels, massive chin

211

tucked comically in, saluting crisply, then flowed back into that easy, perpetually off-balance stance that hadn't quite been Pavel's. "Macon," it said to Flynne, "thinks this is the future. And Burton, he told me it was."

"He's at your place, now, Burton?" Flynne asked.

"Was when I left. Maybe gone now."

"He pissed with me?"

"Doesn't have time, looks to me. Somebody's bought themselves the next level up, at the statehouse, and they're leaning on the sheriff. Tommy wants to talk to me about some old Memphis boys." Netherton found its grin terrifying. "Burton says they're just doing it to fool with you and him," it continued. "Said to tell you that needs some attention on this end."

"What kind of attention?"

"Says they need to get them the governor now," it said, "while the getting's good. You don't have enough money for that."

"That would be Ossian and Ash," Netherton said, causing Flynne and the peripheral to both turn and look at him. "Sorry. But if it's a matter of any urgency, I suggest you bring it up now. The London School of Economics, at your service. Some unofficial undergraduate aspect of it, at any rate."

Now Ossian and Ash were staring at him.

"It's only money," he said to them.

51.
TANGO HOTEL SOLDIER SHIT

ev's backyard was the same as before, walls too high to see over, stone paving with a few flower beds. She'd come out here with Conner, leaving the others in the kitchen with Lev, who was making them coffee. A tall blonde she figured was Mrs. Lev had been there when they'd come up, but she'd left, fast, giving Wilf a seriously shitty look. They were telling Lev about money to buy the governor, and she'd had a feeling that wasn't going to be a problem for them, but that they were telling Lev like it was. Then they'd get to tell him they'd solved it. She'd done that herself, working. Seemed to her Lev would be happier not having heard about it in the first place.

The sky was duller, out here in the garden, than when they'd taken the copter to that Cheapside. Like a dome of Tupperware.

"This the future, Flynne?" Conner asked.

"Trying not to worry about it. Neither of us is crazy, and we both think we're here."

"Thought I was," he said, "crazy, then Macon came over and put that thing on my head. Opened my eyes and saw you. 'Cept it's not you. That's not crazy?"

"Don't frown. Too scary, on that thing."

"Say you got some guy who's hearing voices," he said, "so you matter-transport his ass to Venus, okay? So would he still be hearing voices, or would he think he was crazy because he was on fucking Venus?"

"Were you hearing voices?"

"Sort of trying to, you know? Just for something different to do?"

"Shit, Conner. Don't be like that."

"I'm not, now," he said. "But who the fuck are those people?" Looking back into the house, through glass doors.

"Big guy's Lev. You're in his brother's peripheral. He borrowed it."

"Four-eyed lady?"

"Ash. She and Ossian are gofers for Lev, or like IT? Other one's Wilf Netherton. Said he was human resources, but the company he works for is mostly imaginary."

"Any idea what they're up to?"

"Not really, even if everything they've told me so far is true."

"How'd it start?" he asked.

"Netherton fucked up."

"Looks like he would," said Conner. He looked at her. "You want me to take them out?"

"No!" She punched him in the arm. Like punching a rock. "Want to go back to your sofa? I can call Macon."

"Don't have a lot to offer you by way of thanks," he said. "Just the first thing came to mind. Owe you."

"You don't have to thank me. I woke up in this, though," and she touched her face, "and thought of you. We both might live to regret it."

"Whatever it is, I've got these fingers. Just tell me what to do, or not to."

Ash's badge. "Edward," Ash said.

Another badge beside Ash's, this one yellow, with two scarlet nubbins, one above the other. "Flynne? Macon put me through." Voice, no image.

"What's up?"

"In the trailer. With you."

"Where's Macon?"

"Over at Conner's. This is kind of embarrassing."

"What is?"

"I think you maybe need to pee."

"What?"

"You're getting restless. Here."

She imagined Edward in Burton's chair, watching her on the bed. "You want me back?"

"Just for a minute?"

"Hold on. Ash?"

"Yes?" Ash said.

"I need to go back for a minute. Can we do that?"

"Of course. Come back into the house, we'll find you a place to sit."

"You hear that, Edward?"

"Okay," he said, "thanks." The two-nubbins badge was gone.

"Come back in," she said to Conner, "I need to go to the trailer for a minute."

"Why?"

"Edward thinks I need to pee."

He looked at her, over the cheekbones. "Guess he can't do it for you." He started toward the house. "I'll keep that in mind, though," he said.

"Why?"

"Next time, I'm using the Texas catheter off the Tarantula."

"This way," said Ash, as they entered the kitchen. "You can do it in the gallery." She put down her coffee. Flynne followed her, Conner taking up the rear. Left down a wide hallway, then right, into a very large room.

"It's too big for the house," Flynne said.

"It extends into the two houses adjacent," Ash said.

"Fake Picassos?" She remembered some of them from high school.

"Someone would be in a very awkward position if they were," Ash said. "Sit here," pointing at an ancient-looking marble bench. "You're more accustomed to transitioning, now, so in theory you should be able to inhale, close your eyes, exhale, open them."

"Why close my eyes?"

"Some find it unpleasant not to. Mr. Penske can wait with you."

"Conner," he said. "Planned to."

Flynne sat. The stone was cold, through the peripheral's jeans. She was facing two large paintings she'd been seeing on screens all her life. "Okay," she said, inhaled, and closed her eyes.

"Now," said Ash.

Flynne exhaled. Opened her eyes. It was like being flipped on her back, but with no actual movement, the Airstream's illuminated Vaseline ceiling way too close.

Edward was right. She needed to go.

"Hold on," he said, as she started to sit up, "got to get this off." He had his Viz in. He lifted the crown off her head.

"Burton here?" she asked, as she sat up the rest of the way, dizzy.

"At Conner's, with Macon."

"Janice?"

"Up at your house, minding your mom."

Flynne stood, unsteady. "Okay," she said, "be right back." She veered slightly, on the way to the door, corrected for it. Heard the shots as she opened the door. Maybe three on automatic, then two more, spaced, like a different gun. Not close, but not that far either. She looked back at Edward. "Shit."

His Vizless eye was wide.

"Who's on duty?"

"Bunch of them," he said. "I can't keep track."

"Find out what it was," she said, and stepped out. Listened. Sound of bugs. Creek rushing. Wind in the trees. Went into the toilet, the spring on the door twanging. Undid her jeans, sat there in the dark, a universe away from Picasso. Remembered to toss some sawdust down into the hole when she was done.

The spring made a different sound, opening the door from the inside. Four drones whipped past, in the light from the trailer, marked with duct tape.

"Who shot?" she asked Edward, stepping up into the Airstream.

"Had somebody on your property," he said.

"Had?"

"I think so, but they talk that tango hotel soldier shit. Your brother's on it, whatever it was. On his way back."

"Bet it's the fucking statehouse," she said, sitting down on the bed. "Do me." Gesturing at the baking sugar crown.

"What are you going to do?"

"Go back. Try to raise some money. Have Burton call me there. Ash can put it through. If you can't reach him, tell Macon."

"Conner okay?"

"Easiest person there to understand. Okay's probably stretching it."

He ran a cold dab of saline across her forehead, lowered the crown into place. Helped her lie back.

She took a breath, closed her eyes.

52.
BOOTS ON THE GROUND

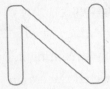etherton stood in the entrance to the gallery. Flynne's peripheral was seated on a bench, three meters away, back to him, apparently viewing Lev's father's two best Picassos. The sparring partner stood nearby, facing the doorway, hands in its trouser pockets. "Good distance right there," it said.

"Yes," said Netherton, who'd been about to step closer.

"This a museum?" asked the sparring partner.

"A private gallery," Netherton said. "In a home."

"They live in a museum?"

"They live with art," Netherton said. "Though the man who actually owns it lives elsewhere."

"Didn't have so much art, he could live here," it said. "As much space as that parking lot downstairs."

"I'm Wilf Netherton."

"Conner," it said.

"If you have questions," Netherton said, "I can try to answer them."

"She said you fucked up," it said.

"Who did?"

"Flynne. Said this was all happening because you fucked up."

"It is, I suppose."

"How?"

"I was less than professional. With a woman. One thing led to another."

"Led to a lot."

"I suppose it did—" said Netherton, forgetting and taking a step forward.

"Stop," it said.

Netherton did. "Do you know Flynne very well?" he asked.

"High school," it said. "Best friend's sister. Smart. She'd have left, gone somewhere, hadn't been for their mother."

Netherton wondered if Flynne's peripheral was taking in visual information, and if so, where it was going. Then it turned.

"Where are they?" Flynne asked. "Something's happening. Need to talk to them. Now."

"Ask him," the peripheral said, meaning Netherton.

"Still in the kitchen," Netherton said.

She stood, turned. "Got the money to buy the governor yet?"

"I imagine they already have quite a lot of money, on your end. It would be more a matter of finding a way to apply it."

"Find them." And she was out the door, headed for the kitchen. The sparring partner swept past him. Netherton followed, noting that it didn't regard him as sufficient threat to not allow him to take up the rear.

"Good evening," said Lowbeer, her voice unmistakable. In the entrance to the kitchen, with Lev and Ash. "And this would be Mr. Penske."

"Problem back home," Flynne said. "Shooting."

"Who's shooting whom?" Lowbeer asked.

"Just went back for a minute. Shots, on the property. Edward heard our guys talking, like they'd engaged somebody. What about buying that governor now?" This last to Lev.

"A matter of acquiring majority stakes in the two firms who most directly enabled his election," Lev said. "Ossian is on it."

"You're understandably concerned," said Lowbeer, to Flynne.

"My mother's in the house. Nobody's supposed to be able to get on the property. Had drones up."

"Can you check on the situation there and report to us, please?" Lowbeer asked Ash. "We'll be in that charming room upstairs. Unfortunately I've only a little time now, but I did want to meet Flynne in her peripheral—" She smiled. "And of course Mr. Penske. And I've a proposal. A course of action."

Ash asked something, briskly, in yet another synthetic language. Listened to the reply they couldn't hear. "Ossian's on the phone, with Edward," she said to Flynne. "The situation there is under control."

"What about my mother?"

Ash asked a shorter question, in what was already a different language, listened. "She wasn't disturbed. Your friend is with her."

"Janice," said Flynne, visibly relieved.

"If you're satisfied for the moment," Lowbeer said to Flynne, "please join us upstairs. You're entirely central to my proposal. You'll join us as well, Conner."

Netherton saw the peripheral silently query Flynne, who nodded. "Don't know shit about any of this," it said, to Lowbeer.

"You're boots on the ground, Mr. Penske, as we said in my youth," Lowbeer said. "We'll need that."

"Never good news," said the peripheral, though it didn't seem particularly displeased.

"Lead the way then, Mr. Netherton," said Lowbeer.

Netherton did, imagining, as he climbed the stairs, a better world, one in which a relaxing drink would be waiting in the sitting room.

53.

SANTA CLAUS'S
HEADQUARTERS

arts of Lev's house, Flynne thought, climbing after Netherton, Lowbeer behind her, were really a lot like any house. The kitchen, for instance, smelled of bacon, even though it had a stove half the size of the Airstream. But then there was the art gallery, which looked to be most of the length of a football field. And the garage below that, and whatever might be further down. But these stairs were just stairs, wooden, polished, a long tongue of what she guessed was Turkish carpet up them, fastened with brass rods and fancy hooks. Looked walked on, like people lived here.

At a square landing, the stairs turned right, then ended on a hallway. Old-fashioned furniture, paintings and mirrors in big frames, incandescent bulbs, frosted glass. And Netherton, ahead of her, walking through open double doors, into the gold-trimmed forest green of the Hefty Mart Santa's Headquarters display.

They always set it up in a window, just after Halloween. The holograms changed every year, but the room had been what she'd loved. This was better, realer, and she wondered why they'd do that, but now Lowbeer was guiding her in, hand on her shoulder, pulling out a chair for her at the long dark table. Dark green curtains hid tall windows. The others coming in behind them, Ash and Ossian and Lev, then Conner. Lev turned to close the doors, Conner watching him.

"Be seated, Mr. Murphy," said Lowbeer, who was wearing a sort of mannish pantsuit. "You aren't playing butler now." Ossian took a seat across from Flynne, Ash beside him. Lowbeer sat in one of two tall green armchairs at the head of the table, Lev in the other. Conner lounged back against a dark green wall, beside something she thought was probably a sideboard, with a silver tray on it, and on that, one of those cut-glass bottles, with matching glasses. Netherton, still standing, seemed to be looking at that, but then he looked around, blinked, sat down beside Flynne.

"Delighted to see you," Lev said, to Lowbeer.

"No solicitors evident," she said. "Most cordial."

"They haven't been convinced that they're entirely unnecessary, but they've agreed to be less obviously present."

"More pleasant in any case," Lowbeer said. She looked around at the rest of them. "I wish to propose a course of action."

"Please," said Lev.

"Thank you. Tuesday evening, in four days' time, Daedra West hosts a gathering, the venue yet to be announced. Possibly one of the guildhalls. Her guest list, so far, is interesting." She looked at Lev. "The Remembrancer himself may be there. Lesser faces from the City. We've been unable to determine even an ostensible purpose. I would suggest, Mr. Netherton," and Flynne saw Netherton's eyes narrow slightly, "that you might, in your way, be able to conjure up some sufficiently vivid rationale for an invitation."

"For whom?" asked Netherton, beside Flynne. He sat close to the table, hunched forward, like someone holding cards.

"You yourself," said Lowbeer, "plus one."

"I don't know that she'd even return my call," said Netherton. "She hasn't tried to get in touch."

"I'm perfectly aware of that," Lowbeer said. "But you could, if I understand your method, find a narrative that leads quite naturally to her inviting you. I'll tell you when I think it best for you to approach her. Recently former lover may be awkward, as entrances go, but not without traction. If you're entirely unwilling, however, I see no way of going forward." Her hair white as the crown Macon had printed in Fabbit. "You'd be taking Flynne, allowing her to survey Daedra's guests." She looked at Flynne. "You'll be looking for the man you saw on Aelita West's balcony."

"These are rich people, right?" Flynne asked.

"Indeed," said Lowbeer.

"So why isn't there footage out the ass, on whoever was at that party?" Flynne asked. "Why isn't there any record of what I saw? What about those paparazzi? Why was I even there?" She noticed how little space Conner was managing to take up, big as his peripheral was, against the wall. He looked like he'd just found himself there, hadn't thought about it yet. He winked at her.

"Yours is a relatively evolved culture of mass surveillance," Lowbeer said. "Ours, much more so. Mr. Zubov's house, here, internally at least, is a rare exception. Not so much a matter of great expense as one of great influence."

"What's that mean?"

"A matter of whom one knows," said Lowbeer, "and of what they consider knowing you to be worth."

"The deal that gets you privacy is funny?"

"Our world itself is funny," said Lowbeer. "Aelita West's soiree was held under a somewhat similar protocol, but temporary, quasi-diplomatic. Nothing, by agreement, was recorded. Not by Aelita's systems, nor Edenmere Mansions', nor by your drone. News agencies and freelancers were kept away. That was the nature of your job, in fact."

"He might be at this party?"

"Possibly," said Lowbeer. "We shan't know, if you can't attend."

"Get us in," Flynne said, to Netherton.

He looked at her, then at Lowbeer. Closed his eyes. Opened them. "Annie Courrèges," he said, "neoprimitivist curator. English, in spite of the name. Daedra met her, with me, at a working lunch in the Connaught. Later, I convinced her that Annie had a flattering theory about the artistic progress of her career. Now Annie is unable to attend her party physically, to her very great regret. But would be delighted to accompany me via," he nodded toward Flynne, "peripheral."

"Thank you, Mr. Netherton," Lowbeer said. "I hadn't the least doubt in you."

"On the other hand," Netherton said, "according to Rainey, she may think I killed her sister. Or have friends spreading the rumor that I did." He stood. "So I think that that calls for a drink." He walked around the end of the table. Flynne saw Conner's peripheral's eyes follow him. "Who else will have one?" Netherton asked, over his shoulder.

"Wouldn't mind," said Lev.

"Nor I," said Ossian.

"Too early for me, thank you," said Lowbeer.

Ash said nothing.

Netherton brought the silver tray, with its bottle and glasses, to the table.

"Mr. Penske will be going along as well," Lowbeer said to Netherton, "as your security. To attend sans security would single you out."

"Up to Flynne," said Conner.

"You're coming," Flynne told him.

He nodded.

Netherton was pouring the whiskey, if that was what it was, into three glasses.

"We need to buy the governor," Flynne said. "Shit's happening. Shooting on our property—"

"In progress," said Ossian, as Netherton passed him a glass, then took the other two to Lev, who took one.

"Cheers," said Netherton. The three of them raised glasses, drank. Netherton put his down, empty, on the table. Lev's joined it there, almost untouched. Ossian swirled the whiskey, smelled it, sipped again.

"Is that it?" Flynne asked Lowbeer. "I need to go back, see Burton. Conner too."

"I have to be going myself," said Lowbeer, standing. "We'll stay in touch." Smiling, nodding to them, looking pleased, she left the room, Lev behind her. Flynne didn't think of tall people as scuttling, ordinarily, but she thought Lev scuttled after Lowbeer, like she was the key to something he wanted bad. They went down the stairs.

"Where do we park these?" Flynne asked, meaning the peripherals. "We'll be a while."

"The Mercedes," said Ash. "Yours is due a nutrient infusion, so we'll do that while you're away." She stood, the Irishman putting down his glass and rising with her.

Flynne started to push her chair back, but then Conner was pulling it back for her. She hadn't seen him come around the table. His peripheral smelled of aftershave or something. Citrusy, metallic. She stood up.

Netherton picked up Lev's glass. "The master cabin has a larger bed," he said to Conner. "You can use that." He took a sip of Lev's whiskey.

Ash led the way out of what Flynne now understood wasn't really meant to be Santa's Headquarters, however much it looked like it. Netherton swallowed the last of Lev's whiskey and they all went downstairs, then into the elevator to the garage.

"You may find your reentry disorienting," said Ash, beside her, in the elevator.

"I didn't, before."

"There's a cumulative effect, aside from jet lag."

"Jet lag?"

"The endocrine equivalent. You're five hours behind London time, where you are, plus there's an inherent six-hour difference between the time here and the time in your continuum."

"Why?"

"Purely accidental. Established when we happened to manage to send our first message to your Colombia. That remains fixed. Do you suffer much, from jet lag?"

"Never had it," Flynne said. "Flying's too expensive. Burton had it in the Marines."

"Aside from that, the more time you spend here, the more likely

225

you are to notice dissonance on returning. Your peripheral's sensorium is less multiplex than your own. You may find your own sensorium seems richer, but not pleasantly so. More meaty, some say. You'll have gotten used to a slightly attenuated perceptual array, though you likely don't notice it now."

"That's a problem?"

"Not really. But best be aware that it happens."

The bronze doors opened.

Ossian drove them to Netherton's RV in a golf cart that made no more noise than the elevator. Netherton had taken the seat beside hers. She could smell the whiskey. Conner sat behind him. Those rafters lit up, one after another, as the cart rolled under them. Past grilles and headlights of all those old cars. She turned, looking back at Conner. "Who've you got at your place, when you get back?"

"Macon, maybe."

"Ash says it might be weird for me. Might be weird for you too. Like jet lag and stuff."

Conner grinned, through the peripheral's bone structure but somehow it was totally him. "I can do that standing on my head. When we coming back?" He widened the peripheral's eyes.

"I don't know, but it won't be that long. You need to eat, sleep if you can."

"What are you doing there?"

"Trying to find out what's going on," she said, as she saw that headless robot exercise thing, standing where they'd left it.

54.

IMPOSTOR SYNDROME

wouldn't have imagined this as your sort of place," Ash said, looking at what Netherton knew to be only the first of several themed environments, this one hyper-lurid dawn in a generic desert. Something vaguely to do with downed airships, it was on the floor above the Kensington High Street showrooms of a designer of bespoke kitchens. She'd driven him here in one of Lev's father's antiques, an open two-seater reeking of fossil fuel.

"I was here once with friends," he said. "Their idea, not mine."

She was enfolded, or encased, depending, in a Napoleonic greatcoat apparently rendered in soot-stained white marble. When she was still, it looked like sculpted stone. When she moved, it flowed like silk. "I thought you hated this sort of thing."

"You're the one telling me Lowbeer wants me to approach Daedra now. She insists I not phone from Lev's."

"She also insists on returning you there herself," she said. "Please be careful. We can't protect you, here. Particularly not from yourself."

"You should stay, really," he said, trusting that she wouldn't, "have a drink."

"You probably shouldn't, but it isn't my decision." She walked away, into a cheesily augmented surround rivaling the one in Lev's father's blue salon.

"Your pleasure, sir?" inquired a Michikoid he hadn't heard approaching. Its face and slender limbs were scoured aluminum, under something resembling the remnants of an ancient flight suit.

"Table for one, cloaked, nearest the entrance." He extended his hand, allowing it to access his credit. "Not to be approached by any-thing other than serving units."

"Of course," it said, and led him toward something aspiring, and failing, to look as though it were constructed from bits of derelict air-ships, roofed with netted bulges of gasbag, within which faint lights leapt and shuddered.

There was music here, of some genre he didn't recognize, but a cloaked table would allow the option of silence. Splintered sections of fuselage, wooden propellers, none of it genuine, though he supposed that that might be the point. A thin crowd, this early in the evening, and relatively inactive. He spotted Rainey's Fitz-David Wu, though almost certainly not the same one. This one wore a retro-proletarian one-piece, one pale cheek artfully daubed with a single smudge of dark grease. It was neutrally eyeing a tall blonde, one emulating, he supposed, some iconic pre-jackpot media asset.

The Michikoid decloaked his table. He took a seat, was cloaked, ordered whiskey. He dialed the silence up, sat watching the peripheral dumb show, waiting for his drink. When a different Michikoid had arrived with his whiskey, he decided that the place did at least offer decent drink. Otherwise, he wasn't sure why he'd chosen it. Possibly because he'd doubted anyone else would be willing to put up with it. Though perhaps he'd also had in mind that it might provide some perspective on the fact of Flynne, in however lateral a way. Not nearly lateral enough, he decided, looking at the peripherals.

He wasn't a peripheral person, something his one prior visit here should have definitively proven. He and the others had had a cloaked table then as well. He remembered wondering why anyone would choose to indulge in such behavior, when they could be almost certain of invisible observers. That was what the clientele paid for, someone had said, an audience, and weren't they themselves, after all, paying to watch? Here, at least, in this first room, it was a purely social exhi-bitionism, and for that he was grateful.

This would be as stimulating, he decided, as sitting alone in Ash's tent. Though he was glad to not be in Lev's basement. And of course there was the whiskey. He signaled a passing Michikoid, who could see him, to bring another.

Whoever the operators of these peripherals were, wherever they were, they were everything he found tedious about his era. And all of them, he supposed, sober, as they were all couched, somewhere, under autonomic cutoff, so unable to drink. People were so fantastically boring.

Flynne, he thought, was the opposite of all of this, whether in her peripheral or not.

Now Lowbeer's sigil appeared, pulsing, as the Michikoid was delivering his drink, momentarily obscuring its artfully weathered nonface. "Yes?" he asked, not having expected the call.

"Courrèges," Lowbeer said.

"What about her?"

"You're definitely proceeding with that?"

"I think so."

"Be certain," she said. "It's someone's life. You'll be sending her on her way."

"Where?"

"To Brazil. The ship departed three days ago."

"She's gone to Brazil?"

"The ship has. We'll send her to catch up with it, retroactively altering the passenger manifest. She'll be entirely unavailable during the voyage. Practicing a form of directed meditation she requires in order to be accepted by the neoprimitives she hopes to study."

"That seems rather elaborate," said Netherton, preferring looser, more readily rejigged deceptions.

"We don't know who Daedra may know," said Lowbeer. "Assume your story will be examined in considerable depth. It's a simple story. She left three days ago, for Brazil. Neoprimitives. Meditation. You don't know the name of the airship, or her exact destination. Please restrain yourself in the invention of extraneous detail."

"You're the one fond of elaboration, I thought," said Netherton, and allowed himself a very small sip of whiskey.

"We won't be monitoring digitally. Too evident a footprint. Someone in the club will be reading your lips."

"So much for cloaking?"

"You might as well be convinced you're invisible when you close your eyes," said Lowbeer. "Call her now, before you finish that drink."

"I will," said Netherton, looking down at his whiskey.

Her sigil was gone.

He looked up, expecting to find someone watching him, in spite of the cloaking, but the peripherals were busy with one another, or with pretending not to be, and the Michikoid waitstaff all smoothly eyeless. He remembered the one on Daedra's moby sprouting at least eight eyes, in pairs of different sizes, black and spherical and blank. He drank some whiskey.

He imagined Annie Courrèges boarding some government craft, whisked out to a moby en route to Brazil. Her own plans, whatever they had been, as suddenly and irrevocably altered as anyone's would be, should someone like Lowbeer decide to alter them. Lowbeer wasn't simply the Met. No one Lowbeer's age was simply anything. He looked up at those lights, dimly flitting within the sagging bladders of an imaginary airship, and noticed for the first time that they were vaguely figural. Captive electrical souls. Who designed these terrible things?

He drank off the very last of his whiskey. Time to phone Daedra. But first he'd have another.

55.
COMPLICATED

yes closed, she didn't recognize the sound of rain on the foam over the Airstream, a dull steady smacking. Eyes open, she saw the polymer-embedded LEDs.

"With us now?" asked Deputy Tommy Constantine.

Turned her head so fast that she almost lost the white crown, managing to catch it with both hands as it tipped off her head.

He was sitting beside the bed, facing her, on that beat-up little metal stool, in a black Sheriff's Department jacket beaded with rain. He held his gray felt hat on his knees, protected by a waterproof cover.

"Tommy," she said.

"Sure am."

"How long have you been here?"

"On your property, about an hour. In here, a little under two minutes. Edward's up to your house to get a sandwich. Didn't want to, but he hadn't eaten since noon and I told him it was the better part of valor."

"Why're you here?"

"Thing is," he said, "strangers keep getting killed out this way."

"Who?"

"Right on your property, this time. Down in the woods, there." He indicated the direction.

"Who?"

"Young men, two of 'em. Your brother figures them to have been pretty much like him, or anyway like these boys he always has around. Who I am by the way increasingly unconvinced are just out here in the pissing rain all night, every night, for some kind of drone competition with their opposite numbers two counties over. Burton figures these two particular veterans to have been operators in the military, specialists, because they got all the way in under your drone cover, just like that, and would have made it the rest of the way if somebody, I'm inclined to guess Carlos and Reece, hadn't been posted down there with rifles, the old-fashioned way."

She was sitting up now, stocking feet on the floor's polymer coating, with the crown on her lap, and it struck her how she and Tommy were sitting there, both holding stupid-looking hats. And how she really did wish, even in whatever this was about, that she had lip gloss on. "What happened?"

"They aren't telling me."

"Who?"

"Burton and them. I'd imagine, one thing being another, Carlos and Reece, with night-vision, took one look at those other two boys, who were also wearing night-vision, and shot 'em both dead."

"Fuck," said Flynne.

"What I thought when I got the call."

"From Burton?"

"Sheriff Jackman. Who I figure your brother did call. Who called me, starting off by reminding me about our new arrangement."

"What new arrangement?"

"That I'm not officially here."

"What's that mean?"

"I'm here to help out Burton. You too, I guess, but Jackman didn't mention you."

She looked at him, stuck for what to say.

"Why," he asked, "if you don't mind my asking, have you been sleeping, if that was sleeping, with some kind of sugarloaf cake on your head? And what, and this is what I've really been wanting to ask somebody for the last little while, the actual fuck is going on out here?"

"Out here?" Her own voice sounded incredibly stupid to her.

"Out here, in town, with Jackman, with Corbell Pickett, over in Clanton, at the statehouse . . ."

"Tommy—" she said, and stopped.

"Yes?"

"It's complicated."

"Are you and Burton building some kind of drugs out here?"

"Have you been working for Pickett, all this time?"

He tilted his hat forward a little, to let a couple of little pools of rain roll off the plastic-covered brim. "Haven't met the man. Haven't had anything directly to do with him before. He gets Jackman reelected, so Jackman has ways of making it clear to me what's Corbell's business and what isn't, and I do my best, around that, to enforce the law in this county. Because somebody's got to. And if we all woke up one day and Corbell and that building economy had been taken up to heaven, after a few weeks most people around here wouldn't have any money for food. So that's complicated too, and sad if you ask me, but there it is. How about you?"

"We aren't builders."

"The basic flow of cash in the county's changed, Flynne, and I mean overnight. Your brother's paying Corbell to fuck with elected officials at the statehouse. There hasn't really been much of any other kind of cash around here, not for quite a while. So pardon my jumping to conclusions."

"I won't lie to you, Tommy."

He looked at her. Tilted his head. "Okay."

"Burton got hired by a security company. In Colombia. Who say they're working for a game company. They hired him to fly a quadcopter in what he figured was a game."

Tommy was looking at her a different way now, but not like he thought she was crazy. Yet.

"Started substituting for him," she said, "when he was up in Davisville. Now we're both working for them. They've got money."

"Must have a lot of it, if you can get Corbell Pickett to hop around."

"I know," she said. "This is all weird, Tommy. It's its whole own level of weird. Better if I don't try to explain much more of it, right now, if you're okay with that."

"Those four boys in the car?"

"Somebody fucked up. In the security company. I saw something, by accident, and I was the only witness."

"Can I ask what?"

"A murder. Whoever sent those boys wants to get rid of Burton, because they figure I was him. Probably our whole family, in case he told somebody."

"That's why Burton's got the drones up, and boys sitting down in the woods."

"Yes."

"And the two tonight?"

"Probably more of the same."

"And all this money coming in?"

"The company in Colombia. They need me to ID the killer, or anyway an accessory, and I saw him and he's guilty as shit."

"In a game, you said?"

"That's too complicated, for now. Believe me?"

"I guess," he said. "What's going on here with the money's unlikely enough, I figured whatever was behind it wouldn't be garden variety." He drummed his fingers, very lightly, on the plastic hat cover. "What's that thing you were sleeping under?" He raised an eyebrow. "Beauty treatment?"

"User interface," she said, and lifted it to show him. "No hands." She carefully put it down, still cabled, on the bed.

"Flying?" he asked.

"Walking around. It's like another body. Wasn't sleeping. Telepresent, somewhere else. Disconnects your body here, when you do it, so you don't hurt yourself."

"You okay, Flynne?"

"Okay how?"

"You seem pretty calm about all this."

"Sounds batshit, you mean?"

"Yep."

"Way crazier than I've told you. But if I get crazy about how crazy it is, then everything's really fucked." She shrugged.

" 'Easy Ice.' "

"Who told you that?"

"Burton. Suits you, though." He smiled.

"That was just games."

"This isn't?"

"The money's real, Tommy. So far."

"Your cousin just won the lottery, too."

She decided not to get into that.

"Ever met Corbell Pickett?" he asked.

"I haven't even seen him, since he did the Christmas parades with the mayor."

"Neither have I, in person," he said, and looked at what was probably his grandfather's wristwatch, the old-fashioned kind that only told the time, "but we're about to. Up at the house."

"Who says?"

"Burton. But I'd guess it's Mr. Corbell Pickett's idea." He carefully put his hat on, using both hands.

56.
THE LIGHT IN HER
VOICE MAIL

t just seemed to happen, as he most liked it to. Lubricated by the
excellent whiskey, his tongue found the laminate on his palate of
its own accord. An unfamiliar sigil appeared, a sort of impacted
spiral, tribal blackwork. Referencing the Gyre, he assumed, which
meant the patchers were now being incorporated into whatever the
narrative of her current skin would become.

On the third ring, the sigil swallowed everything. He was in a
wide, deep, vanishingly high-ceilinged terminal hall, granite and gray.

"Who's calling, please?" asked a young Englishwoman, unseen.

"Wilf Netherton," he said, "for Daedra."

He looked down at his table in the bar, his empty glass. Glancing
to the right, he saw the circle of bar floor, scoured aluminum, that
surrounded the round table, set now, with a jeweler's precision, into
Daedra's granite floor, the demarcation a function of the club's cloaking mechanism. Unable to see the bar, or the Michikoids, he realized
that he was also unable to signal for another drink.

Receding down the length of the dully grandiose hall, like an illus-
tration of perspective, were chest-high plinths of granite, square in
cross-section, supporting the familiar miniatures of her surgically flayed
hides, sandwiched between sheets of glass. Typical self-exaggeration,
as she'd so far only produced sixteen, meaning that the majority were
duplicates. A wintery light found its way down, as from unseen windows. The ambient sound was glum as the light, as calculated to
unsettle. An anteroom, reserved for cold calls. A point was being made.
"Fine," he said, and heard the echoes of the word deflect across granite.

"Netherton?" asked the voice, as if suspecting the name of being an unfamiliar euphemism.

"Wilf Netherton."

"What would this be concerning, exactly?"

"I was her publicist, until recently. A private matter."

"I'm sorry, Mr. Netherton, but we have no record of you."

"Associate Curator Annie Courrèges, of the Tate Postmodern."

"I beg your pardon?"

"Be quiet, darling. Let pattern recognition have its way."

"Wilf?" asked Daedra.

"Thank you," he said. "I've never liked Kafka."

"Who's that?"

"Never mind."

"What do you want?"

"Unfinished business," he said, with a small and entirely unforced sigh that he took as an omen that he was on his game.

"Is it about Aelita?"

"Why would it be?" he asked, as if puzzled.

"You haven't heard?"

"Heard what?"

"She's vanished."

He silently counted to three. "Vanished?"

"She'd hosted a function for me, after the business on the Patch, at Edenmere Mansions. When her security came back on, afterward, she was gone."

"Gone where?"

"She's not tracking, Wilf. At all."

"Why was her security off?"

"Protocol," she said, "for the function. Did you sabotage my costume?"

"I did not."

"You were upset about the tattoos," she said.

"Never to the extent that I'd interfere with your artistic process."

"Someone did," she said. "You made me agree. In those boring meetings."

"It's good that I've called, then."

"Why?" she asked, after slightly too long a pause.

"I wouldn't want to leave it this way."

"I wouldn't want you to imagine you haven't left it," she said, "if that's what you're suggesting."

He sighed again. His body did it for him. It was a quick sigh, propulsive. The regret of a man who knew both what he had lost and that he had well and truly lost it. "You misunderstand me," he said. "But this isn't the time. I'm sorry. Your sister . . ."

"How can you expect me to believe you didn't know?"

"I've been on a media fast. Only recently learned that I've been fired, for that matter. Busy processing."

"Processing what?"

"My feelings. With a therapist. In Putney."

"Feelings?"

"Some horribly novel sort of regret," he said. "May I see you?"

"See me?"

"Your face. Now."

Silence, but then she did open a feed, showing him her face.

"Thank you," he said. "You're easily the most remarkable artist I've ever met, Daedra."

Her eyebrows moved fractionally. Not so much approval as a temporary recognition that he might have the capacity to be correct about something.

"Annie Courrèges," he said. "Her sense of your work. Do you remember me telling you about that, on the moby?"

"Someone jammed the zip on that jumpsuit," she said. "They had to cut me out of it."

"I know nothing about that. I want to arrange for you to have something."

"What?" she asked, with no effort to disguise a routine suspicion.

"Annie's vision of your work. Happenstance, really, that she confided in me, and of course she had no idea about us. Having had that glimpse of her vision, and knowing you as I do, I find I must at least attempt to bring it to you."

"What did she say?"

"I couldn't begin to paraphrase. When you've heard it, you'll understand."

"You're getting this from therapy?"

"It's been a huge help," he said.

"What are you asking me for, Wilf?"

"That you allow me to introduce you to her. Again. That I might contribute, in however small a way, to something whose importance I may never fully comprehend."

She might, he thought, have been looking at a piece of equipment. A parafoil, say, wondering whether to keep or replace it. "They say you did something to her," she said.

"To who?"

"Aelita."

"Who does?" If he gestured now, with the empty glass, there was a chance a Michikoid would bring him another, but Daedra would see him do it.

"Rumors," she said, "media."

"What are they saying about you and the boss patcher? That can't be pretty."

"Sensationalism," she said.

"We're both victims, then."

"You aren't a celebrity," she said. "There's nothing sensational about you being suspected of something."

"I'm your former publicist. She's your sister." He shrugged.

"What is that you're sitting in?" she asked, appearing fully in front of him now, between two plinthed miniatures, no mere headshot. Her legs and feet were bare. She was wrapped in a familiar long cardigan, teal.

"A cloaked table, in the bar of a place in Kensington, Impostor Syndrome."

"Why," she asked, a single comma of suspicion appearing between her brows, "are you in a peri club?"

"Because Annie's away. On a moby bound for Brazil. If you're willing to meet her again, she'd need a peripheral."

"I'm busy." The comma deepened. "Perhaps next month."

"She's going into fieldwork. Embedding with neoprims. Technophobics. She's had to have her phone extracted. If it goes well, she might be with them for a year or more. We'd have to do it soon, before she arrives."

"I've told you I'm busy."

"I'm concerned about her, there. Were we to lose her, her vision goes with her. She's years from publishing. You're her life's work, really."

She took a step toward the table. "It's that special?"

"It's extraordinary. She's in such awe of you, though, that I don't know how we could arrange it even if you weren't so busy. A one-on-one meeting would be too much for her. If we could meet you, seemingly at random, perhaps at a function. Surprise her. She's ordinarily very confident socially, but she could scarcely speak to you, at the Connaught. She's been desolate about that. I suspect this embedding is an attempt at distraction."

"I do have something coming up . . . I don't know how much time I'd have for her."

"That would depend on how interesting you find her," he said. "Perhaps I'm mistaken."

"You can be," she said. "I'll think about it."

And she and her teal cardi and her bare legs were gone, and with them the chill stone light of her voice mail.

He was looking out at the peripherals in Impostor Syndrome again. Their fretful animatronic diorama, viewed in utter silence. He signaled a passing Michikoid. Time for another drink.

57.

GOOD CHINA

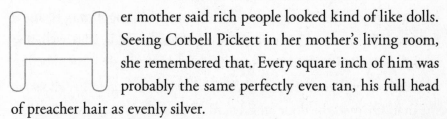er mother said rich people looked kind of like dolls. Seeing Corbell Pickett in her mother's living room, she remembered that. Every square inch of him was probably the same perfectly even tan, his full head of preacher hair as evenly silver.

She'd worn an old fishtail parka of Leon's up from the trailer. He'd used that evil hydrophobic nanopaint on it, because it hadn't been waterproof at all, in the Korean War Leon said it was from. Not the one he and Burton had been two years too young for, but the one before that, ancient history. She'd found it on Burton's clothes rod, after she'd used his shaving mirror to put on some lip gloss, the rain still smacking on the Airstream's cocoon. Tried not to touch the outside when she put it on. They'd shown PSAs about that paint, not touching it, in high school, when the government was first getting the stuff off store shelves. Fit her like a tent, stiff with paint.

"Damn," she'd said, looking down at the white controller on Burton's army blanket, "it's cabled to my phone. Don't like leaving my phone, but I don't know how you disconnect that."

"Leave 'em. Anybody you aren't already on a first-name basis with tries to walk in here, tonight," Tommy had said, zipping up his jacket, "they aren't walking out."

"Okay," she'd said, from beneath the cavelike hood, as he'd opened the door into the rain, wondering if she was getting that "meaty" thing Ash had told her about, from being back in her own body. Like the supersaturated color in an old movie, maybe, and everything with a little more texture?

So she'd followed him out, feet slipping in the mud when she stepped down. Not hydrophobic, her shoes, and not even that comfortable. She'd wished she had her other ones, but then she'd remembered they were in a future that this world didn't even lead to. And maybe weren't even her size. She'd thought of the peripheral on its bunk, then, in the back room of that giant RV. Made her feel some emotion there might not be a name for, but was that just being back in her body too? Her shoes and socks already soaking through, she'd followed Tommy up the trail, thinking the rain made a little sizzling sound, as it tried its fastest to get off the coated cotton.

When they'd gotten up to the backdoor, she'd wiped her shoes on the mat. Opened the door on Edward, Vizless, finishing a sandwich at the kitchen table. He'd nodded to her, mouth full, eyes wide, and she'd seen, through the door into the dining room, that her mother had the good china out. Nodding back at him, slipping out of the parka, which was perfectly, scarily dry, she'd hung it on the rack beside the fridge.

"And here's your pretty daughter, Ella." He was beside the fireplace, with Burton, her mother sitting in the middle of the sofa. "And this must be Deputy Tommy."

"Evening, ma'am," Tommy said. "Mr. Pickett. Burton."

"Hi," said Flynne, almost silenced by how much anybody like Corbell Pickett was never supposed to be in their living room. "Remember you from the Christmas parade, Mr. Pickett," she said.

"Corbell," he said. "Been hearing good things about you. From Ella here, and your brother. And Tommy, by way of Sheriff Jackman. Good to finally meet you, Tommy. Appreciate you coming out."

"Pleased to meet you, Mr. Pickett," said Tommy, behind her, and she turned to see him. He'd hung his black jacket on the rack beside the parka, and now he put his hat on the hook. He turned, in his starched tan uniform shirt with the patches on the sleeves, badge flashing in the light, expression neutral.

What she really wanted, she realized, was to ask Burton if they'd managed to buy the governor yet, but her mother was here, not to mention Pickett.

"Hey," said Burton, how he stood reminding her of Conner in the peripheral: off-centered but just so, ready to swing either way.

"Hey," she said.

"You must be tired."

"Not sure."

"Bring in the coffee, Flynne," her mother said. "Help me up, Burton. I'm past my bedtime." Burton crossed to her, took her hand. Flynne could see her staying on top of her sickness, something she could still do when she needed to. Unwilling for Pickett to see it. The oxygen was nowhere in sight.

She went back into the kitchen and got the pot off the stove. Edward was just sneaking out, under one of those giveaway rain capes with the Hefty logo across the back. He gave her a nervous half wave. The plastic blinds on the door's window clattered as he closed it behind him.

"Eat his sandwich?" her mother asked, from the living room.

"He did," Flynne said, coming back with the coffee.

"Knew his aunt. Reetha. Worked with her. Sorry I have to turn in, Corbell. Pleasure to see you. It's been a long time. Pour Corbell some coffee, Burton. Flynne, you help me to bed, please."

"I will," she said, and put the pot down on the coffee table, on a thing made of big wooden beads that Leon had done in Scouts. She followed her mother through the door beside the fireplace, closed it behind them.

Her mother bent down, plucked up her oxygen, turned the knob, stuck the little clear plastic horns into her nose. "What are you and Burton up to with that man?" she asked, voice down so he wouldn't hear, and Flynne could see her being really careful not to swear, which meant she was seriously angry.

58.

WU

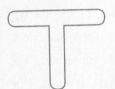he Fitz-David Wu rental, the one with the grease-smeared cheek and the creased boiler suit, was approaching his table, a drink in its hand. It seemed to see him.

"You see me," he said, resentfully.

"I do," it said, putting the drink down in front of him, "though others can't. That's your last. You've been cut off."

"By whom?" he asked, but knew.

The peripheral reached into a pocket at its hip, withdrew something, which it then exposed on its open palm: a small cylinder, wrought in gilt and fluted ivory. It morphed, becoming a gilt-edged ivory locket that opened, revealing Lowbeer in what seemed a hand-tinted image, orange tweed and a green necktie, gazing sternly up. Vanishing as the locket seamlessly became a thumb-tall lion, crowned and rampant, then back into the ornate little cylinder.

"Am I to assume it's genuine? Easily done with assemblers."

It pocketed the thing. "The punishment for emulating a tipstaff is extremely severe, and not at all brief. Drink up. We need to be going."

"Why?" asked Netherton.

"As you reached her voice mail, various individuals, across the entire Thames Valley, began to move in this direction. None connected to her, or to you, in any known way, but evident to the aunties as violating statistical norms. We need you out of here, then, with as little hint as possible of any contrivance of authority. Drink up."

Given such unqualified permission, Netherton tossed back the whiskey. He stood, a bit unsteadily, knocking over his chair.

"This way, please, Mr. Netherton" said the peripheral, rather wearily he thought, and took his wrist, to lead him deeper into Impostor Syndrome.

59.

ADVENTURE CAPITALISTS

eople think the really bad ones are something special, but they're not," her mother said, sitting on the edge of her bed, next to the table crowded with meds. "Psycho killers and rapists, they never ruin as many lives as a man like Corbell does. His daddy was a town councilman. Stuck-up boy, Corbell, selfish, but no more than lots that age. Thirty-some years on, he's ruined more people than he can be bothered to remember, or even know." She was looking at Flynne.

"We took something on," Flynne said. "Took the money. Nothing to do with him, that we knew of. Now he's turned up in it. Not like we asked him to, or asked for him."

"If Burton's moonlighting, and the VA finds out," her mother said, "they'll cut him off."

"Might not matter, if things work out."

"VA's not going out of business any time soon," her mother said.

Flynne heard the door open behind her. Turned.

"Sorry," said Janice, "but that asshole's giving Burton the gears. Didn't want to be standing where he might see me and think I heard."

"Where've you been?"

"On your bed, doing hate Kegels. Went up there after I'd put the coffee on and helped Ella put her hair up, when Burton told us who was coming over. You okay, Ella?"

"Fine, honey," said Flynne's mother, but her sickness was showing.

"You take your meds now," Janice said. "You'd better get back there," she said to Flynne. "Sounded like there was business being done."

Flynne noticed the picture of her very young dad, younger than

Burton, in his dress uniform. The room had been his den, then her mother's sewing room. After she started having trouble with the stairs, they'd moved her bed down here. "Have to go back now," Flynne said to her mother. "I'll look in after. If you're still awake, we'll talk."

Her mother nodded, not looking at her, busy with her pills.

"Thanks, Janice," Flynne said, and went out.

"Not without a better idea who's doing the buying," Pickett was saying, as she entered the living room. He sat in the rocker armchair with the tan slipcover, which she now saw could do with a wash. Burton and Tommy were at either end of the sofa, facing him across the coffee table. Pickett saw her, kept talking. "My people in the state-house won't talk to you. This outfit you've hooked up with will be going through me. The other thing they need to understand is that what they've spent so far was just to get the door open. Maintenance is going to be due, on a regular basis."

She realized, sitting down between Burton and Tommy, that each sentence of what he'd just said had been in a cadence she remembered from his commercials for his dealership, a sort of spoken wedge, narrow on the front end but widening out to a final emphasis. Driven like a nail.

"Now you," Pickett said, looking her in the eye, "you've actually met our Colombian adventure capitalists."

Tommy, on her left, leaned forward, elbows on his knees, one hand around the other, which was curled into a loose fist. From where she sat she could see there was a pistol, smaller than the one in his belt holster, down the front waistband of his pants.

She met Pickett's hard stare. "I have," she said.

"Tell me about them," Pickett said. "Your brother either doesn't know or isn't that eager."

"They have money," she said. "You've had some of it yourself."

"What flavor, though? Chinese? Indian? I'm not even convinced it's offshore. Maybe it starts here, goes out, comes back in."

"I wouldn't know about that. Company's Colombian."

"Columbia S.C., for all I know," Pickett said. "You and Burton in partnership with them?"

"Trying to be," said Burton.

Pickett looked from Burton to Flynne. "Maybe they're government."

"Wouldn't have occurred to me," she said.

"Homes," Pickett said, "on a sting?"

"Not Homes as we know it," she said.

"Milagros Coldiron," Pickett said, as if foreign words tasted bad. "Not even good Spanish, people tell me, 'cold iron.'"

"I don't know why they call it that," she said.

"Your Milagros bought an interest in a Dutch bank. Just while I was driving over here. Spent a lot more than this county's worth, this one and the next three over. What have you and Burton got that they want?"

"They chose us," she said. "So far that's all they've told us. Could you have bought that bank, Mr. Pickett?"

He didn't like her. Maybe didn't like anybody. "You think you can be in partnership with something like that?" he asked her.

Neither she nor Burton answered. She didn't want to look at Tommy.

"I can," said Pickett. "I can right now, and the result, for you, if I do, would be money you don't even know how to dream of. If you don't partner with me, though, you don't have a statehouse connection. As of now."

"You aren't comfortable not knowing where the money's from?" she asked him. "What would you need, to be comfortable?"

"Access to who I'm really dealing with," Pickett said. "That company didn't exist, three months ago. I want somebody with a name to explain to me what they're a shell for."

"Netherton," she said.

"What?"

"That's his name. Netherton."

She saw that Burton was looking at her. His expression hadn't changed.

"Tommy," Pickett said, "nice to meet you. Why don't you go and make sure that business with the two boys has been taken care of. Jackman tells me you're good with the details."

"Yes sir," said Tommy, and stood. "I'll do that. Burton. Flynne." He nodded to both of them, went into the kitchen. She heard him putting on his jacket, zipping it up. Then she heard the blinds on the backdoor rattle, as he went out.

"Got yourself a smart sister, Burton," Pickett said.

Burton didn't say anything.

She found herself looking at the plastic tray propped on the mantelpiece, the one with the aerial-view cartoon map from Clanton's bicentennial year. Her mother had driven the three of them over for the celebrations, when she was eight. She remembered it, but it seemed like somebody else's life.

60.

BROWNING IN

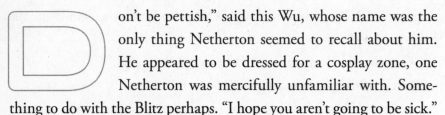on't be pettish," said this Wu, whose name was the only thing Netherton seemed to recall about him. He appeared to be dressed for a cosplay zone, one Netherton was mercifully unfamiliar with. Something to do with the Blitz perhaps. "I hope you aren't going to be sick."

That was a possibility, Netherton thought, as this small windowless room did seem to be moving, though mercifully in a single direction, and smoothly. "You're that actor," he said. He knew that, though not which actor he meant. One of them.

"I'm not Wu," said Wu. "There happened to be one available here. I'd seen your former colleague in one earlier. You must try not to drink so quickly, Mr. Netherton. It impairs your memory of events. I need to discuss your conversation with her, since I only have access to what I could see you say."

Netherton sat up slightly, in his own little armchair, his role in any of this now somewhat identified, if still largely unclear. He remembered being led through narrow, absurdly tidy subterranean corridors of brick. Under squidlight, not the least fleck of dust. That deadening cleanliness of the assemblers, London's microscopic caretakers. "Who?" he asked.

"Daedra West."

Netherton remembered her voice mail then, the oppressive height of it. "We're in your car," he said. "Where are we going?"

"Notting Hill."

"We'll be invited," Netherton said. He remembered hoping that, at any rate.

"It did seem to me that you set the hook. Assuming, that is, that she's so self-centered as to be literally impaired. I don't feel I can afford to be quite so readily convinced of that. Perhaps you shouldn't either, Mr. Netherton."

So deliberately difficult, actors.

61.
TIMESICK

've got to sleep," she said to Burton, in the kitchen, after Corbell had gone with the big man who'd brought in a golf umbrella to walk him back to his car. She was having trouble keeping her eyes open.

"You think Netherton can handle Corbell?"

"Lowbeer and the others can tell him what to say."

"Who's that?"

"Conner's met her. I think we're actually working for her, but getting paid Lev's money. Or Lev's money here, as much as it's his. Damn. I'm about to fall over."

"Okay," he said, squeezed her shoulder, put on his jacket, and went out. The rain had stopped. She put out the kitchen light, went through the living room to check there was no light showing under her mother's door, then up the stairs. They'd seldom been as steep.

Janice was in her room, cross-legged on the bed with half a dozen *Geographics*. "Kills me," Janice said, looking up, "national parks before they privatized. Asshole gone?"

"Burton too," Flynne said, touching her own wrist and then all four pockets of her jeans before she remembered her phone was in the trailer. She pulled her t-shirt off, tossed it on the chair, then had to root under it for the USMC sweatshirt. Put that on, sat on the edge of the bed, and got her wet shoes and socks off. Undid her jeans and managed to get them off without standing up again.

"You looked whacked," Janice said.

"Time difference, they said."

"Ella okay?"

"Didn't look in," Flynne said, "but her light's out."

"I'll sleep on the couch." Picking up the magazines.

"I have seen so much weird shit," Flynne said. "Woman who told me about the time difference has two pupils in each eye, animated tattoos of animals running around on her ass."

"Just on her ass?"

"Arms, neck. On her belly once, but then they all ran off to her back, like cartoons, because they didn't know me. Maybe to her ass. Can't tell."

"Tell what?"

"Whether I'm getting used to it. It's weird, then it's the way it is, then it's weird again."

Janice sat up. She was wearing handknit pink acrylic slippers. "Lay back," she said. "You need to sleep."

"We just bought ourselves the damn governor. That's weird."

"He's a bigger asshole than Pickett."

"Didn't really buy him. Got a deal with Pickett to pay him on a regular basis."

"What's it supposed to get you?"

"Protection. Two of Burton's guys killed a pair of ex-military who were trying to sneak in. Not just thugs. Down past the trailer."

"I wondered what they got all quietly excited about."

"Pickett got Tommy out here to make sure the bodies get disposed of okay." She made a face from childhood, without meaning to. "Where's Madison?"

"Over at Conner's, with Macon, working on an Army copter for Burton. Or he was, last time I checked Badger. Might be home now." Janice stood up, the old *Geographic*s pressed to her stomach. "But I'm keeping Ella company."

"Thank you," Flynne said, and let her head down on the pillow, timesick, or maybe that and that texture thing, her old chambray pillowcase intricate as chess against her face, less familiar.

sh was waiting, when Lowbeer's car's door slid open. She reached in, took his wrist, pressed her Medici's softness against it with her other hand, and drew him out, his feet with difficulty finding Notting Hill pavement.

"Bed rest," advised Lowbeer, briskly, as the door closed, "moderate sedation."

"Goodbye," Netherton said, "goodbye forever."

The door, the only part of the car that had uncloaked, vanished itself in a bilious stir of pixels, moving away, a diminishing whisper of invisible tires.

"Here," Ash said, clamping the Medici against his wrist, leading him. "If you're sick in Lev's house, Ossian will have to clean it up."

"Hates me," said Netherton, peering down the street, vaguely wondering how many of these houses were conjoined with Lev's.

"Hardly," said Ash, "though you're tiresome enough, in your current state."

"State," said Netherton, contemptuously.

"Keep your voice down." Leading him up the steps, into the house, past the entranceway's Wellies and outerwear. The memory of Dominika hushed him.

He felt more secure in the elevator, if less than entirely well. He did feel that the Medici might be helping.

In the silent garage, Ash strapped him firmly into the cart and drove it to the Gobiwagen. "I'm putting you upstairs," she said, when they'd climbed the gangway and entered, releasing his wrist and tucking the

Medici away. "Her peripheral is in the back cabin, Lev's brother's is in the master." She touched something on the wall. A narrow stairway, previously hidden, folded almost silently out of laser-cut veneer, taut support wires gleaming. "After you," she said. He climbed, unsteadily, into a glass-walled crow's nest fitted with gray leather upholstery.

"This is a hydrotherapeutic tub, optionally," she said. "Please don't try it. Medici's given you something for sleep, something else to reduce your hangover. That's a toilet." She indicated a narrow, leather-padded door. "Use it. Then sleep. We'll call you for breakfast." She turned, and descended the complicated stairs, whose design made him think of cheese slicers.

He sat on a leather-cushioned ledge, wondered whether it was part of a tub, removed his shoes, took off his jacket, got to his feet with some difficulty, and pushed the center-hinged door. Behind it was a combination hand basin and urinal, the latter probably a toilet as well. He used the urinal, then shuffled back to the integral couch. He lay down. The lighting dimmed. He closed his eyes and wondered what the Medici had given him. Something agreeable.

He woke, almost immediately it seemed, to sounds from below.

The lights came on, down there, but not here in the gray-padded crow's nest. He sat up, improbably clearheaded and pain-free, to the sound of someone retching, something splashing. He wondered if he himself might be dreaming, while actually vomiting in his sleep, but there seemed no great urgency in the idea.

He stood. Stocking feet. Children's games of stealth. Crept to the dangerous-looking, Germanic edge of the stairway. Heard water running. Tiptoed down, as quietly as he could, until, bending further, he spied Flynne's peripheral, in black jeans and shirt, cupping water from a tap in the open bar. She spat, forcefully, into the round steel sink, then looked up at him, sharply.

"Hello," he said.

She tilted her head, without breaking eye contact, and wiped her mouth with the back of her hand. "Puked," she said.

"Ash thought you might, the first time—"

"Netherton, right?"

"How did you open the bar?"

"Not locked."

It occurred to Netherton, for the first time, that he was the only one who couldn't open it. That they'd specifically set it that way. "You mustn't drink anything but water," he said to the peripheral, coming the rest of the way down the stairs. It seemed peculiar advice to be offering.

"Don't move," she said.

"Is something wrong?"

"Where are we?"

"In Lev's grandfather's Mercedes."

"Conner says it's an RV."

"That's what you called it," he said.

Her eyes narrowed. She took a step forward. He remembered her musculature, in the resistance trainer. "Flynne?" he asked.

Someone came pounding up the gangway.

She was across the cabin in two strides, ready by the door as Ossian rushed in. And seemed to fall, Ossian, as if propelled by his own weight, over and around the ready pivot of her hip, but then somehow she was instantly, fluidly in a position from which to kick him powerfully in the shoulder, from behind, leg exactly reaching full extension. Ossian's forehead struck the floor audibly.

"Stay down," she said, breath unaltered, hands curved slightly in front of her. "Who's our friend?" she asked Netherton, over her shoulder.

"Ossian," said Netherton.

"Dislocated . . . my fucking . . . shoulder," gritted Ossian.

"Probably just the bursal sac," she said.

Ossian glared up at Netherton. "Her fucking brother, isn't he? The boy just phoned Ash." Tears ran suddenly from his eyes.

"Burton?" Netherton asked.

The peripheral turned.

"Burton," Netherton said, seeing it now.

"Mr. Fisher," said Ash, from the doorway. "A pleasure to finally meet you in person, or more relatively so. I see you've met Ossian."

Ossian snarled something, syllables of a translated obscenity never previously voiced.

"Glad to be here," Flynne's peripheral said.

Ash touched the wall, causing an armchair to rise from the floor. "Help me get Ossian up," she said to Netherton. "I'll see to his shoulder." This proved more easily said than done, both because the Irishman was solidly built and because he was in considerable pain, not to mention a foul mood. When he was finally settled, his face slick with tears, Ash produced the Medici. She pressed it against the black fabric of his jacket, above the injured shoulder, and released it. It stayed there, quickly ballooning, then sagging, worryingly scrotal, unevenly translucent, and doing whatever it was doing through the black jacket, which somehow made Netherton particularly queasy. He could see blood and perhaps tissue whirling dimly within it. It was larger than Ossian's head now. He looked away.

"Hey," said the peripheral, from the top of the gangway, just outside, "what's this?"

Netherton crossed to it, careful not to get too close. "What?"

"Down there. Big white."

Netherton craned his neck. "That's a resistance-training exoskeleton," he said. "An exercise device."

"Now I could do that," it said. Glanced down, seemingly at its breasts. "Conner had me expecting weird, but . . ." It shrugged slightly, but that made its breasts move. It looked up at Netherton with a certain desperation.

"That can be easily arranged," said Ash, behind them. "The exo isn't a peripheral, though it does have a full range of movement. But it can be controlled via a homunculus, a miniature peripheral. Until we find you something else, you might prefer it to your sister's. Which happens to be of very immediate strategic importance. You didn't damage it, I hope, when you struck Ossian?"

The peripheral lifted the foot with which it had kicked Ossian, rotated it at the ankle, as if checking for discomfort. "No," it said, putting it down. "Kicks ass."

Ash firmly pronounced some freshly minted monosyllabic negative, her hand on Ossian's injured shoulder, keeping him in the chair.

Netherton watched as the peripheral loped loosely, and, he had to admit, fetchingly, down the gangway, then circled the exo, head to one side, taking its measure.

63.
THREW UP

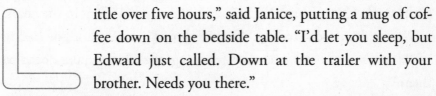

ittle over five hours," said Janice, putting a mug of coffee down on the bedside table. "I'd let you sleep, but Edward just called. Down at the trailer with your brother. Needs you there."

Flynne slid her hand under her pillow for her phone, remembered it wasn't there. Sunlight at the edges of the curtains. Pillowcase felt normal. "What's happening?"

"Said Burton threw up, you should come down."

"Threw up?"

"What he said."

Flynne hitched herself up. Took a sip of coffee. Remembered looking down at the white crown, its cables running off the army blanket to Burton's display and her phone. "Shit," she said, putting the mug down. "He's fucking around with it." Then she was up and pulling on her jeans, the cuffs damp and mud-flecked.

"With what?" Janice asked.

"Everything," said Flynne, getting up and digging for dry socks in the clothes on the chair. She found two that didn't match, but were both black. Sat down on the bed and pulled them on. Her damp laces were a mess.

"You drink that coffee," Janice said. "You aren't rich enough yet to waste Ella's coffee."

Flynne looked up. "How's she doing?"

"Pissed at you and Burton for being involved with Pickett, but it gives her something to do. Seriously, drink that coffee. Doesn't matter if you get there two minutes later."

Flynne picked up the mug, went to the window. Pushed the curtain aside. Bright and clear, everything soaked from the night before. That red Russian bike out by the gate, beside it the Tarantula, scorpion tail tipped with the brand-new fuel-nozzle grapple he was supposed to have had all the while. "Conner's here?"

"'Bout ten minutes ago. Carlos and another guy took him down to the trailer, in kind of a swing, slung between a couple of pieces of plastic pipe."

Flynne drank some coffee. "Tommy gone?"

"Haven't seen him. There's a fresh jug of coffee to take down to them."

A few minutes later, face washed, headed down the hill, big orange Thermos banging against her knee with each step, the path looked like a platoon had been marching up and down, boots churning dark mud, but really it would only have been Burton's posse going back and forth, however many times, plus Tommy and whoever else had been down here. A small drone whipped over from behind, headed downhill, stopped and hovered for a second, then flew on.

Burton was sitting in the Airstream's open door, wearing an old gray sweater, light blue boxer shorts, unlaced boots. His legs seldom got any sun, but now his face was whiter than they were. She stopped in front of him, the jug bumping her knee one last time. "Well?"

"Didn't tell me it makes you puke," he said.

"Didn't ask me. Anything."

He looked up at her. "You were asleep. Saw that thing on the bed, still hooked up, and there was Edward. You know I saw Conner use his. You'd have done the same."

"Hey, Flynne," called Conner, from inside, "wassup?"

"Coffee."

"Bring it. Wounded warrior here."

"What did you do?" she asked Burton.

"Turned up in your girlfriend, there. Got up, threw up, dropped the first one came running in."

"Shit. Who?"

"Pigtail. Funeral suit."

"Ossian. Tell me you haven't fucked everything up."

"Ash doctored him. With something like a cross between a bull's balls and a jellyfish. Are those contacts she's got?"

"They're like a piercing or something. How much speed, intensity, and violence of action exactly did you whip on things?"

"He's pissed at me, not you."

"How long were you there?"

"About three hours."

"Doing what?"

"Getting set up. Getting my ass out of your girlfriend and into something that won't make me blush. Talking corporatization with four-eyes. Who's your girl supposed to be, anyway?"

"Nobody seems to know."

"Every time I'd pass a mirror, I'd jump. Does sort of look like you."

"Just the haircut."

"Wounded fucking warrior here!" cried Conner.

"Get up," said Flynne. "Let me by."

Burton stood. She stepped up and past him. Conner was propped up on the bed with Burton's pillow and one of Macon's blue duffels behind him, wearing one of his Polartec body socks. So much of him missing. She remembered him running, in the other peripheral.

"What?" he asked, looking up at her.

"Just remembered," she said, "didn't bring cups."

"Burton got cups," Edward said, from his seat in the Chinese chair. He bent over and fished a yellow resin mug out of a transparent Hefty gear box.

She put the Thermos jug down on the table beside the white cables leading to her phone. "I thought that thing was custom-made for my head."

"You have more hair," Edward said. "I padded it out in back with

251

Kleenex, keeps it pressed against his forehead. That and the saline, seems to do it."

"Print him his own. I don't want anybody using mine. Or my peripheral."

"Sorry," Edward said, unhappy.

"I know he made you."

"No way he's getting in my sweet golden boy either," said Conner, prissily, from the bed.

"They got him something," Edward said. "Came back here for a few minutes, then he went again."

"A peripheral?" she asked.

"Little Muppet-assed thing," said Burton, behind her.

She turned. He had some color back in his face. "Muppet?"

"Six inches tall. Put a kind of cockpit on this exoskeleton, where the head would go, put the Muppet in that. Synched 'em. I was doing backflips." He grinned.

She remembered the headless white machine. "You were in that exercise thing?"

"Ash didn't want me in your girl."

"Neither do I. Put your pants on."

He and Edward did a dance in the narrow space, Burton getting to his clothes rod and Edward getting to Conner, on the bed, with the yellow mug in his hand. Edward sat on the bed, holding the mug so Conner could slurp coffee. Burton pulled a brand-new pair of cammies off a hanger. "Come here a minute," he said to her, and went out, carrying his pants. She followed him. "Close the door behind you." He took one foot out of the unlaced boot, balancing, as he put his leg through the leg of his cammies, then his foot back into the boot, then repeated this with the other leg. "You go outside the house, when you were there?" He was buttoning the fly.

"Just in the back garden. And up in a quad, virtual."

"Hardly anybody," he said. "You get that? Biggest city in Europe. See many people?"

"No. Just in one place, but it's a kind of tourist attraction, and Netherton told me they mostly weren't real, after we got back. And it's too quiet, in the backyard. For a city."

"I got the quad ride too, with Ash, when she'd fixed the pigtail up, while he was getting my Muppet ready for the exo."

"Cheapside?"

"Nothing cheap about it, just lonely. We went out over the river, low. Floating islands, some kind of tidal generator. I might've seen fifty, a hundred people, the whole flight. If they were people. And hardly any vehicles, nothing really like traffic. It's the way heritage games looked, before they got updated. Before they could really do much in the way of crowds. If it's not a game, where is everybody?"

She remembered her own first view of the city, as she rose straight up, feeling that.

"Asked her," he said.

"So did I. What did she say?"

"Said there aren't as many people as we're used to. What did she tell you?"

"Changed the subject. She tell you why?"

"Said she'd explain when she had more time."

"What do you think?"

"You know she thinks it all sucks, up there?"

"She say that?"

"No, but you can feel it. That she does. Can't you?"

She nodded.

64.

STERILE

The bar was locked. He pressed his thumb against the oval of brushed steel again. Nothing happened.

But this seemed inconsequential, he noted, as he lowered his hand. Perhaps how it would feel to have had the laminates installed, in Putney. Sufficiently uncharacteristic a thought that he glanced around, as if to be sure that no one had seen him entertain it. He was, he judged, in some complex bio-pharmacological state, the Medici having toyed with his dopamine levels, receptor sites, something. Enjoy it, he advised himself, though perhaps it wasn't quite that simple.

From Ash, he'd understood that he'd fallen immediately and deeply asleep, on stretching out upstairs, before waking to Burton's arrival. The Medici, she'd said, had emulated the effect of much more REM sleep than he'd actually gotten, and done other things as well. But after he'd helped her get Ossian into the chair, to have his shoulder repaired, she'd insisted that Netherton go back to sleep. Which he had, after a second application of the Medici. Having just seen it do something very unpleasant looking to Ossian, not to mention bloody, this had seemed less than fastidious, though he knew that at its nanoscale of operation it was constantly sterile.

He'd awakened again, and descended the cheese-grater stairs, alone except for the peripherals in their respective cabins. Flynne's friend Conner had left his on Lev's grandfather's baronial bed, arms spread cruciform, ankles primly together.

Lowbeer's sigil appeared now, with its coronet, pulsing. He happened to be looking in the direction of the desk, its thronelike chair behind it, so that the sigil momentarily suggested the crown of some ghost executive of Milagros Coldiron, itself a sort of ghost corporation.

"Yes?"

It stopped pulsing. "You've slept," Lowbeer said.

"Flynne's brother arrived," he said, "unexpectedly."

"He was rigorously selected by the military," she said, "for an unusual integration of objective calculation and sheer impulsivity."

Netherton moved his head slightly, placing the sigil over the window, but then it looked as if a coronet-headed figure were outside, looking in. "I suppose," he said, "that he does seem more balanced than the other one."

"He wasn't, initially," she said. "Their service records have survived here, from before Lev touched their world. Both were damaged, to various extents."

Netherton moved to the window, thinking he'd seen a pulse of squidlight. "I didn't like him using her peripheral." Another arch pulsed and he saw Ossian, walking toward the Gobiwagen in a peculiar way, arms at his sides and slightly bent, hands held forward at the waist. "Ossian looks as though he's pushing something that isn't there," he said.

"A Russian pram. I'm having a technical in Lev's stub take it apart."

"A pram?" Then he remembered the cloaked buggy, in the entranceway.

"We make it very difficult to secure prohibited weapons. The ones extracted from that pram will be entirely sterile."

"Sterile?" Thinking of the Medici.

"Devoid of identification."

"Why would you want them?"

"Have you eaten?" she asked, ignoring his question.

"No." He realized that he was actually hungry.

"Best wait, then," said Lowbeer.

"Wait?"

But her sigil was gone.

65.
BACKDOOR TO NOW

ab was one end of the strip mall, the end nearest town, Sushi Barn the other, three empty stores in between. The one next to Fab had done pretty well when those little paintball robots were hot. One next to that had been nails and hair extensions. She couldn't remember the one between that and Sushi Barn ever having been anything but vacant.

Burton pulled the rental into the lot, parked in front of the former mini-paintball place, windows pasted over on the inside with sticky gray plastic, starting to peel at the corners. "This is ours now," he said.

"What is?"

"This." Pointing straight ahead.

"Rented it?"

"Bought it."

"Who did?"

"Coldiron."

"They bought that?"

"Bought the mall," he said. "Closed on it this morning."

"What's that mean, 'closed'?"

"Ours. Papers are going through right now."

She didn't know whether it was harder to imagine having the money to buy this place, or to imagine wanting to. "What for?"

"Macon needs a place to keep his printers, we need a place to work out of. Shaylene's back room won't cut it. She's already sold the business to Coldiron—"

"She has?"

"That meeting she had with you, then what she saw Macon fabbing.

Got herself right in. We can't be running our end out of a trailer down by the creek. So we centralize here. Gets the heat away from Mom, too."

"Guess it does that, anyway," she said.

"We've got drones over here, more on the way. Carlos is on that. It'll cut us out of that dumbfuck with lawyers driving over from Clanton, bags of cash. Might as well be builder money, that way. Can't put it in the bank, can't pay taxes on it, and we get a haircut every time any's laundered. If we're working for Coldiron USA, incorporated right here, that's a salary. Salary and shares. Corporate headquarters."

"So what does Coldiron USA do?"

"Property development," he said, "today. Lawyers have papers for you to sign."

"What lawyers?"

"Ours."

"What papers?"

"Incorporation stuff. Buying the mall. Your contract as CCO of Milagros Coldiron USA."

"I am fucking not. What's CCO?"

"Chief communications officer. You are. You just haven't signed yet."

"Who decided? Not me."

"London. Ash told me when I was up there with them."

"So what are you, if I'm CCO?"

"CEO," he said.

"Know how stupid that sounds?"

"Talk to Ash. You're CCO, communicate."

"We aren't doing that timely a job communicating ourselves, Burton," she said. "You keep agreeing to shit without asking me first."

"It's all moving that fast," he said.

Conner's Tarantula swung, growling, into the empty parking lot, to brake beside them, coughing the smell of fried chicken until he killed the engine. She looked down, saw him grinning up at her.

"What did they put him in?" Burton asked her.

"Cross between a ballet dancer and a meat cleaver," she said, as Conner squinted up at her. "Martial arts demonstrator."

"Bet he was loving that," said Burton.

"Too much," she said, and opened her door. Burton got out on his side, walked around front.

Conner twisted his head, to see her. "Let's get back where there's all the fingers," he said.

She rapped him with a knuckle, hard, on top of his stubbled head. "Don't go forgetting who took you up there. My brother's gone native there. Thinks we've got a startup going, that he's CEO of. Don't get like that."

"Fingers, legs 'n' shit, that's all I want. Brought my catheter. In a ziplock, on the back of the trike."

"Now that's exciting," she said.

Burton was unstrapping him.

"Lady, gents," said Macon, opening the blank gray glass door from inside, "our North American flagship and headquarters." He wore a blue business shirt, with a striped tie that was mostly black. Every button buttoned, but the crisp tails weren't tucked into his holey old jeans.

"Not casual Friday," Flynne said, seeing Shaylene, behind Burton, in a navy skirt-suit, still managing her big hair thing but looking surprisingly office-ready.

"Hey, Shaylene," Burton said. He bent over and picked up Conner, like you'd pick up a ten-year-old who couldn't walk. Conner slid his left arm, his only arm, around Burton's neck, like he was used to it.

"Conner," Shaylene said. "How're you doing?" She seemed different now, Flynne wasn't sure how.

"Hangin' in," said Conner, and used his crooked arm to pull himself up to where he could give Burton a big wet smack on the cheek.

"Could just drop an asshole on the concrete," Burton said, like he was thinking out loud.

"Let's get in out of the public eye," Conner said. Macon stepped back, out of the doorway. Burton carried Conner in, Flynne behind them. Then Shaylene, who closed the door behind her. One big room, lit by shiny new work-LEDs on clean yellow cables. Musty smell. Gyprock walls randomly patched with paint, showing where counters and dividers had been before. Someone had sawn a doorway through, just a raw door-shaped hole, from the back room of Fab. Covered with a blue tarp, on the Fab side. A couple of new electric saws lay beside it on the floor.

Further back, there were three new hospital beds, partially extracted from their factory bubble wrap, white mattresses bare, and three IV stands, plus a lot of white foam cartons, stacked high as Flynne's head. "What's all this?" she asked.

"Ash tells me what we'll need, I order it," Macon said.

"Looks like you're setting up a ward," Flynne said. "Smells, for a hospital."

"Plumber's on the way to fix that," Shaylene said. "Electrical's good to go, and the mini-paintball guys put in a shitload of outlets. Going to try to get it cleaned up, working around whatever we wind up doing here."

"Those beds are for us," Flynne said to Burton. "We're going back together, aren't we?"

"Conner first," Burton said, carrying him to the nearest bed and putting him down on it.

"Just finished printing him a new phone," said Macon. "Same as yours, Flynne. Ash wants him to acclimate more, work out. They can run training sequences for him through the peripheral's cloud AI."

Flynne looked at Macon. "You sound pretty well up on things there," she said.

"Biggest part of the job," Macon said. "It mostly makes its own kind of sense, then you hit something that seems impossible, or just completely wrong, and she either explains it or tells you to ignore it."

She looked back and saw Burton and Shaylene talking. Couldn't hear what they were saying, but Shaylene's thing about Burton looked to her to be gone. "She sell Fab, to them?" she asked Macon.

"Did," he said. "Don't know what she got for it, but they've totally got her attention. Which is good, because I'm too busy to wrangle stuff that's late, and she's a natural at that."

"She get along with Burton?"

"Just fine."

"Used to be awkward," Flynne said, "like a whole day or two ago."

"I know," Macon said. "But before this, she'd managed to feed herself, and a bunch of other people in this town, with a business that wasn't Hefty, wasn't building drugs, and was at least partly unfunny. That way, I'd say she hasn't actually changed much. Just gotten more focused."

"I wouldn't have expected she'd get over that, about Burton."

"What's changing here," he said, "is economics," and the look on his face reminded her of being in Civics with him, when they'd studied the electoral college. He'd been the only one who really got it. She remembered him sitting up straight, explaining it to them. Same look.

"How's that?"

"Economy," he said. "Macro and micro. Around here's micro. Pickett's not the biggest money in this county anymore." He raised his eyebrows. "Macro, though, that's mega weird. Markets all screwy everywhere, everybody's edgy, Badger's buzzing, crazy rumors. All just since Burton came back from Davisville. That's us, causing all that. Us and them."

"Them?" She remembered how good he'd been at math, better than anybody, but then they'd graduated and he'd had family needed taking care of, college no option. He was one of the smartest people she knew, good as he was at helping you forget it.

"Ash tells me there's somebody else, up there, able to reach back here. You know about that?"

She nodded. "Hiring people, to kill us."

"Uh-huh. Ash says there's two different anomalous proliferations of subsecond extreme events in the market, right now. Us and them. You understand subsecond financial shit?"

"No."

"Markets are full of predatory trading algorithms. They've evolved to hunt in packs. Ash has people with the tools to turn those packs to Coldiron's advantage, nobody the wiser. But whoever else is up there, with their own backdoor to now, they've got the same tools, or near enough."

"So what's it mean?"

"I think it's like an invisible two-party world war, but economic. So far, anyway."

"Macon, honey," called Conner, from his hospital bed, framed by a corona of ragged bubble-pack, "bring a wounded warrior his catheter. It's out on the back of my trike. Wouldn't want some dickbag stealing it."

"Or maybe I'm just crazy," said Macon, turning to go.

Flynne went to the very back of the room, behind the beds and the IV stands, and stood looking at the barred, unwashed windows, dusty cobwebs in their corners, dead flies and spider eggs dangling. Imagined, behind her, kids paintballing their little robots and tanks in the big sandbox they'd had in here. Seemed forever long ago. A couple of days seemed a long time, now. She imagined the spider eggs hatching, something other than spiders coming out, she had no idea what. "Predatory algorithms," she said.

"What?" Conner asked.

"Haven't got a clue," she said.

66.

DROP BEARS

he'll ring you," Ash said, passing Netherton a U-shaped piece of colorless transparent plastic, like something to hold back a young girl's hair. "Put it on."

Netherton looked at the thing, then at Ash. "On?"

"Your forehead. Haven't eaten, I hope?"

"She suggested I wait."

Ash had, ominously, come equipped with the polished-steel wastebasket he remembered from Flynne's initial arrival. It stood, now, beside the crow's nest's longest section of gray upholstery.

Lowbeer's sigil appeared. "Yes?" he asked, before it could pulse.

"The autonomic cutout, please," said Lowbeer.

He saw that Ash was descending the stairway, taut wires vibrating with her every step. He gingerly settled the flimsy yoke across his forehead, nearer hairline than brows.

"Best you fully recline," said Lowbeer, her tone reminding him of dental technicians.

Netherton did, reluctantly, the upholstered bench all too eagerly adjusting itself to more comfortably support his head.

"Eyes closed."

"I hate this," said Netherton, closing his eyes. Now there was nothing but the sigil.

"With your eyes closed," said Lowbeer, "count down from fifteen. Then open them."

Netherton closed his eyes, not bothering to count. Nothing happened. Then something did; he saw Lowbeer's sigil, just for an instant, as though it were some ancient photographic negative. Opened his eyes.

The world inverted, slammed him down.

He lay curled on his side in an entirely gray place. The light, what little there was, was gray as every visible thing. Beneath something very low. It would have been impossible to stand, or indeed to sit up.

"Here," said Lowbeer. Netherton craned his neck. Huddled, too near his face, was something unthinkable. A brief, whining sound, then he realized he'd made it himself. "The Australian military," Lowbeer said, "call these drop bears." The thing's blunt, koala-like muzzle, unmoving when she spoke, was held slightly open, displaying a nonmammalian profusion of tiny crystalline teeth. "Reconnaissance units," she said, "small, expendable. These two were haloed in, then guided here. How are you feeling?" Its blank gray eyes were round and featureless as buttons, the color of its hairless face. Mechanical-looking concave ears, if they were ears, swiveled fitfully, independent of one another.

"You didn't," said Netherton. "Not here. Please."

"I did," Lowbeer said. "You're not nauseous?"

"I'm too annoyed to be sick," Netherton said, realizing as he said it that it was true.

"Follow me." And the thing crawled quickly away from him, toward some source of light, head low to avoid the ceiling, if it were a ceiling. Terrified of being left behind, Netherton crawled after it, gagging slightly at glimpses of his forepaws, which had opposed thumbs.

Clearing the overhang, whatever it was, Lowbeer's peripheral rose on short hind legs. "On your feet."

Netherton found himself standing, without being certain how that had been accomplished. He glanced back, seeing that they'd apparently crawled from beneath a bench in an alcove. Everything was that milky translucent gray. The glow ahead, he guessed, was moonlight, filtering down through however many membranes of revolting architecture.

"These units," Lowbeer said, "are already being consumed by the island's assemblers, which devour anything not of their own making, from flecks of drifting polymer to more complex foreign objects. As we're currently being eaten, our time here is short."

"I don't want to be here at all."

"No," said Lowbeer, "but remember, please, that you were very recently employed in a scheme to monetize this place. You may dislike it intensely, but it's as real as you are. More so, perhaps, as there are presently no schemes to monetize you. Now follow me." And the koala-like form was suddenly bounding, partially on all fours, in the direction of further light. Netherton followed, immediately discovering an unexpected agility. Lowbeer led the way, across a blank, repulsive landscape, or perhaps floorscape, as they seemed to be within some enclosed structure larger than Daedra's hall of voice mail. Vast irregular columns lined either side, much nearer on their right. The surface over which they ran was uneven, slightly rippled.

"I hope you've some compelling reason for this," Netherton said, catching up with her, though he knew that people like Lowbeer didn't need reasons, whether to put Annie Courrèges on a moby for Brazil or to bring him here.

"Whim, quite likely," she said, confirming his thought. The bears' exertions didn't seem to affect her speech, or his. "Thought perhaps it will help you remember what I tell you here. For instance, that my investigation currently seems to hinge on a point of protocol."

"Protocol?"

"The corpse of al-Habib," she said, "if it wasn't touched in the attack, but rather lay where it fell, makes no sense whatever in terms of protocol. The protocols of a low-orbit American attack system most particularly."

"Why?" asked Netherton, clinging to the mere fact of conversation as to a life preserver.

"A system prioritizing her security would have immediately neutralized any possibility of his posing a posthumous threat."

"Who?" asked Netherton.

"Al-Habib," she said. "He might, for instance, have been implanted with a bomb. Considering his bulk, quite a powerful one. Or a swarm weapon, for that matter. The system saw to the others." Netherton remembered the silhouette of the flying hand. "Protocol required him to be dealt with in the same fashion. He wasn't. There must have been a strategic reason for that. Slow a bit, now." Her hard gray forepaw tapped his chest. Distinctly, claws. "They're nearby."

Music. Aside from the scuffing of his and Lowbeer's feet, the first local sound he'd heard since arriving here. Like the tones of the wind-walkers, but lower, more organized, ponderously rhythmic. "What's that?" Netherton asked, halting entirely.

"A dirge for al-Habib, perhaps." She'd stopped as well. Her ears rotated, searching. "This way." She steered him to the right, toward the long base of the nearest column, then forward again, alongside it. As they neared its corner, she dropped on all fours and crept forward, to peer around it, like something from a children's book, but gone appallingly wrong. "And here they are."

Netherton braced his right paw on the column and leaned over Lowbeer's bear, until he could see around the corner. A sizable throng of small, gray, predictably horrid figures squatted, around the upright corpse of the boss patcher. He was hollow now, Netherton saw, membrane thin, like the island's architecture. Eyeless, the cavern of his mouth agape, he appeared to be propped up with slender lengths of silvered driftwood.

"Incorporating him into the fabric of the place," Lowbeer said. "But not about myth so much as plastic. Each cell in his body replaced with a minim of recovered polymer. He's made his escape, you see."

"His escape?"

"To London," Lowbeer said. "Americans enabled that, by not destroying his apparent remains. Though he's always been a bit of an escape artist, our Hamed. Minor Gulf klept. Dubai. But a fifth son. Quickly the black sheep. Very black indeed. Had to flee in his late teens, under a death warrant. The Saudis particularly wanted him. The aunties knew where he was, of course, though I'd quite forgotten about him myself. And we wouldn't tell the Saudis, of course, unless it became worth our while. His mother's Swiss, by the way, a cultural anthropologist. Neoprimitives. That would be what he based his patchers on, I imagine."

"He faked his death?" The music, if it could be called that, was a largely subsonic auger, boring into Netherton's brain. He straightened, stepping back from Lowbeer and the column. "I can't do this," he said.

"Faked it most complexly. The peripheral's DNA is that of an imaginary individual, albeit with a now highly documented past. I imagine Hamed's own DNA is fairly imaginary by now, for that matter, by way of keeping a step ahead of the Saudis. But I'm taking mercy on you, Mr. Netherton. I can see how difficult this is for you. Close your eyes."

And Netherton did.

67.

BLACK BEAUTY

Their lawyers were from Klein Cruz Vermette, in Miami. One of the three who'd met them in the snack bar at Hefty was a Vermette, Brent, but not the one in the name. Son of the one in the name, not yet a full partner.

It had been Macon's idea to sign the papers there. Otherwise they'd have been doing it in Fab, or the space next door, or in Tommy's police car, Tommy having driven them over from the football field, where the helicopter they'd chartered in Clanton had landed. They'd flown in their own jet, from Miami to Clanton, and they were nice. So nice, she figured, that Coldiron must be paying them fuckloads of money not to show how weird they must think this all was, that she and Burton and Macon were being set up as a corporation that was buying a strip mall. But it did make it easier, the niceness. Brent, who had an even more expensive-looking tan than Pickett's, had put away a plate of pork nubbins, while the other two had Hefty lattes.

She'd only seen Tommy when he'd walked them in from the parking lot, hadn't had a chance to speak with him. She guessed driving and being security was part of his job now, or part of the part about Jackman's deal with Pickett. He'd given her a nod, when he went back to the car. She'd smiled at him.

She'd have thought having Tommy drive the lawyers to a meeting in Hefty Mart was too obvious, but now she figured his relationship with the town had always been funny. Plenty of people must know about Jackman and Pickett, and more than she wanted to imagine must be making money off building, though maybe not that directly.

So if you saw Tommy drive some people in business clothes to Hefty, then sit there in the parking lot while they had a meeting inside, maybe you'd ignore it. Or maybe you'd go over and say hello, and Tommy would give you something from the Coffee Jones machine, but you wouldn't ask him what he was doing.

Now it was just her and Macon there, Burton having gone with Tommy to take them back to their helicopter. She'd gotten herself a half-order of chicken nubbins, which she sometimes liked more than she'd admit.

"We could all have had two heads," Macon said, "and they wouldn't have mentioned it." He had his Viz in, and she guessed he was literally keeping an eye on news and the market.

"They were nice, though."

"You wouldn't want to be on their bad side."

"You're Chief Technical Officer, huh?" she asked him.

"Yep."

"Shaylene's not on the board? That Burton's idea?"

"I don't think it was his call. My guess is they're looking at who's essential to whatever makes this worthwhile to them. You're essential, Burton is, evidently I am, and Conner."

"Conner?"

"Not on the board either, but it looks like he's essential."

"Why does it?"

"He's already swallowed one of these." He took a small plastic box from the front pocket of his new blue shirt and put it on the table between them. Clear, flat, square. Inside, white foam with a single cutout, fitting a glossy black pill. "You'll want some water."

"What is it?" She looked at him.

"Tracker. That's not it. Gel cap around it, makes it less easy to lose, easier to swallow. Barely big enough to see, on its own. Ash ordered them from Belgium. Bonds to your stomach lining, good for six months, then it disassembles itself and nature takes its course. Company makes it has its own string of low-altitude satellites. Have to keep putting 'em up, but they make that a feature, not a bug, 'cause they get to keep changing their hardwired encryption."

"To keep track of where I'm at?"

"Pretty well anywhere, unless somebody sticks you in a Faraday cage, or way down in a mine. A little more robust than Badger"—he smiled—"and you could lose your phone. Want some water?"

She opened the box, shook the thing out. Didn't feel any different than any other pill. Tiny little reflections of the snack bar lights in the deep glossy black. "Don't bother," she said, putting it on her tongue and washing it down with half a short cup of black coffee Burton had left on the table. "Wish it meant somebody in Belgium could tell me where the fuck I am," she said. "In terms of all the rest of it, I mean."

"Know what 'collateral damage' means?"

"People get hurt because they happen to be near something that somebody needs to happen?"

"Think that's us," he said. "None of this is happening because any of us are who we are, what we are. Accident, or it started with one, and now we've got people who might as well be able to suspend basic laws of physics, or anyway finance, doing whatever it is they're doing, whatever reason they're doing it for. So we could get rich, or killed, and it would all still just be collateral."

"Sounds about right. What do you say we do, with that?"

"Try not to get damaged. Let it go where it's going, otherwise, because we can't stop it anyway. And because it's interesting. And I'm glad you swallowed that. You get lost, it'll tell us where to find you."

"But what if I wanted to get lost?"

"They aren't the ones trying to kill you, are they?" He took his Viz off, looked her in the eye. "You've met them. Think they'd be trying to kill you, if you stood to get them in some kind of very deep shit, or lose them a bunch of money?"

"No. Couldn't tell you exactly why. But they could still completely screw up the world, just by dicking around with it. Couldn't they?"

His fingers closed around the tangled, rigid, silvery filaments. She looked down and saw the lights of the projectors, moving in there. She looked up at him.

He nodded.

68.

ANTIBODY

etherton, eyes screwed shut, viscerally dreading the gray light of the patchers' island, became aware of a honeyed scent, warm yet faintly metallic.

"I'm sorry, Mr. Netherton," Lowbeer said, from nearby. "I suppose that was very unpleasant for you. Not to mention unnecessary."

"I'm not opening my eyes," he said, "until I'm sure we're no longer there." He opened his right, fractionally. She was seated opposite where he lay.

"We're in the cupola of the land-yacht," she said. "Not peripherally."

Opening both eyes, he saw that she'd lit her candle. "Were you here, before?"

"I was in Ash's tent," she said. "Had I come in earlier, you'd have asked where we were going. And refused, possibly."

"Revolting place," he said, meaning the island, though equally true of Ash's tent. He sat up, the cushion that had supported his head lowering itself as he did.

"Ash," said Lowbeer, fingers extended around the candle as if for warmth, "imagines you a conservative."

"Does she?"

"Or a romantic, perhaps. She sees your distaste for the present rooted in the sense of a fall from grace. That some prior order, or perhaps the lack of one, afforded a more authentic existence."

The autonomic cutout slid down Netherton's forehead, over his eyes. He plucked it off, resisted the urge to snap it in half, put it aside.

"She's the one mourning mass extinctions. I simply imagine things were less tedious generally."

"I personally recall that world, which you can only imagine was preferable to this one," she said. "Eras are conveniences, particularly for those who never experienced them. We carve history from totalities beyond our grasp. Bolt labels on the result. Handles. Then speak of the handles as though they were things in themselves."

"I've no idea how anything could be otherwise," he said. "I simply don't like the way things are. Neither does Ash, apparently."

"I know," she said. "It's in your dossier."

"What is?"

"That you're a chronic malcontent, albeit quite a purposeless one. Otherwise we might have met earlier." Periwinkles quite sharp, just then.

"And why, exactly, do you think al-Habib is here?" Netherton asked, a change of topic seeming suddenly welcome.

"That was a peripheral, that you saw her stick her thumb into," she said. "He'd been peripherally there for years, though not with the peri you and Rainey saw. Very expensively bespoke, the one you saw die. It had only been there for a few days. Complete genome, full complement of organs, fingerprints. The formal forensic signatures of a legal death, waiting to be ticked off. The island's history assigned to an imaginary figure. His previous peripheral, most likely, was weighted and dropped into the water column, to be consumed by their assemblers. None of his immediate cohort would have been privy to that, nor to his real identity, and now, conveniently, courtesy of the Americans, they're all dead. But we saw the survivors, didn't we? Mortaring him into the fabric of the place. Memorializing what he'd pretended to be."

"He hadn't actually been there, before?"

"Present at the start, certainly, for their initial flotilla and whatnot. Perhaps for the cannibalism as well. He isn't at all nice, Hamed. Good at pretending, though."

"What did he pretend to be?" he asked.

"A prophet. A shaman. Motivated extraordinarily, thus extraordinarily motivating. Taking the same drugs they took, which he himself provided. Though of course he didn't actually take them. If you fancy resenting the tedious, I recommend intentional communities, particularly those led by charismatics."

"You believe he was here, while he was doing that?"

"No, not here. Geneva."

"Geneva?"

"As a place to await an opportunity to optimally monetize the island, as good as any. And, of course, his mother is Swiss."

"With two penises and the head of a frog?"

"All easily reversible," said Lowbeer, pinching out the candle's flame. "He's made a mistake, though, in not staying there. London's his mistake. Premature."

"Why?"

"Because he's come to my attention again," she said, her expression just then making Netherton wish for another change of topic.

"What is it," Netherton asked, "since you're encouraging my curiosity, that you've offered Lev?"

"Assistance with his hobby."

"Would you lie to me?"

"If the need were sufficiently pressing," she said, "yes."

"You're telling me you're helping him manage his stub?"

"I've an overview of its history, after all. I've information which isn't generally available, here. Nor there either, or I should say, then. Where certain bodies are buried, you see. The nature of actual as opposed to ostensible policy, for any number of state and nonstate players. Fed the right bits of that, on a need-to-know basis, Ash and Ossian become considerably empowered. I'm surprised at just how engrossing I've started to find it."

"Who else is in there, trying to kill Flynne and her brother? Do you know that?"

"I don't," she said, "yet, though I've suspicions." Taking a crisp white handkerchief from an inside breast pocket, she wiped her thumb and forefinger. "This business with al-Habib is fully as dull as its pretentious exoticism, Mr. Netherton. We're on the same page, there. Real estate, recycled plastic, money. Whoever's gained entrance to Lev's stub is likely involved with that. A more interesting question, of course, being how they came to be admitted."

"Is it?"

"It is, since the very mysterious server enabling all of this remains a mystery," she said.

"May I ask you what it is that you actually do?"

"You pride yourself on not knowing who employs you. Rather behind the curve, in that. I might pride myself, were I so inclined, on not knowing what it is I do."

"Literally?"

"If one has a sufficiently open mind about it, certainly. I was an intelligence officer, early in my career. In a sense I suppose I still am, but today I find myself enabled to undertake investigations, as I see fit. Into, should I so deem them, matters of state security. Simultaneously, I'm a law enforcement officer, or whatever that means in as frank a kleptocracy as ours. I sometimes feel like an antibody, Mr. Netherton. One protecting a disease."

She offered him an uncharacteristically wan smile then, and he remembered her saying she'd had memories suppressed, as he and Rainey's rented Wu had sat with her in her car. She must have more, unsuppressed, he thought, because just then he was certain that he felt their weight.

69.
HOW IT SOUNDS

hen Reece tased her in the neck with what she'd thought was a flashlight, she'd just noticed how nothing on Burton's table was squared up straight. It hurt. Then she wasn't thinking, wasn't there.

After her talk with Macon, she'd ridden home, taking her time, trying not to notice where the dead men's car went into the ditch. Not looking out for drones. Pretending things were normal.

Her mother was asleep when she got there, Janice replaced by Lithonia, who said Leon had driven her out from Fab. Upstairs, she stretched out on her own bed, not meaning to sleep, and dreamed of London. From the air, every street was crowded as that Cheapside, but cars and trucks and buses instead of horses and carts. Full of people, except it wasn't London but her town, gotten huge, rich, with a river the size of the Thames because of that. Waking, she went downstairs. Her mother still sleeping, Lithonia watching something on her Viz. Then down to the trailer, wondering if Burton was there but too lazy to check on Badger.

"Fuck, Reece," she protested now, tugging at the zip ties around each of her wrists.

Reece, driving, didn't say anything, just looked over, and that made the fear come. Not because he'd tased her and fastened her to this car seat with zip ties, but because, when he looked over, she saw that he was scared shitless.

She had a zip tie around each wrist, one fastening those together, all looped through with a longer one that went down under the front of the seat. She could raise her hands high enough to rest them on her thighs, but that was it.

Didn't know what he was driving, but it wasn't cardboard, wasn't electric.

"Made me," he said. "No fucking choice."

"Who did?"

"Pickett."

"Slow down."

"He'll be after us," he said.

"Pickett?"

"Burton."

"Jesus . . ." Was this Gravely? She thought it was but then she didn't. Looked out at roadside bushes, whipping past.

"Said they'd kill my family," he said. "Would, too, 'cept I don't have any. Just be me. Dead."

"Why? What did you do?"

"Not a fucking thing. Kill me if I didn't get you for them. He's got people inside Homes. Homes can find anybody. So they'd find me, then somebody'd come and kill me."

"Could've told us."

"Sure, then they'd come and kill me. Kill me anyway, I don't get you over there right now."

She looked over and saw a muscle working, all on its own, at the hinge of his jaw. Like if you hooked it up to something, it could send his life story in code, all the parts of it he couldn't tell, maybe didn't know.

"Didn't want to," he said. "Not like I had a choice, to believe them or not. They're who they are, and that's what they do."

She felt both front pockets of her jeans. Phone wasn't there, wasn't on her wrist, she wasn't sitting on it. "Where's my phone?"

"Copper mesh they gave me."

She looked out the window. Then at the plastic chrome lettering on the glove compartment. "What's this you're driving?"

"Jeep Vindicator."

"Like it?"

"Are you crazy?"

"Helps to make conversation," she said.

"It's not cardboard," he said, "it's American."

"Don't they make most of it in Mexico?"

"You just want to shit on my damn car now?"

"That you're fucking kidnapping me in?"

"Don't say that!"

"Why not?"

"How it sounds," he said, between his teeth, and she knew he was just that far from crying.

70.

ASSET

The kitchen was fragrant with the blini Lev was making. "She's helping you with the stub," Netherton said. "She told me." Rain was falling in the garden, on the artificial-looking leaves of the hostas. Did thylacines dislike rain? Neither Gordon nor Tyenna was in sight.

Lev looked up from the segmented iron pan. "I don't expect you to understand."

"Understand what?"

"The appeal of continua. Or of collaborating with her. She's already gotten us into the White House."

"That would be what, then, the first Gonzales administration?"

"No direct contact. Yet. But we're close. No one I know of has ever penetrated a stub this efficiently. She knows where the pivots are, the moving parts. How it works."

"Is that what she offered you, after that first meeting?"

"It's reciprocal," Lev said, removing the pan from the element. "She assists me, we protect Burton and his sister, you help her with the Aelita business, Daedra, whatever that is." Using a spatula, he began to transfer the blini to two waiting plates. "Salmon, or caviar?"

"Is the caviar real?"

"You'd want my grandfather, for caviar from a sturgeon."

"I wouldn't, actually."

"I've had it," Lev said. "I couldn't tell the difference. This is entirely its equal."

"I will, thank you."

Lev tidily burdened each blintze with sour cream and caviar.

"Ossian's taken delivery of a Bentley," Netherton said. "Drove itself in from Richmond Hill. Like a silver-gray steam iron, windowless, six wheels. Hideous. Parked by Ash's tepee. What's that about?"

"Executive transport," Lev said. "Early jackpot. They need to disassemble something, so they'll do it inside. Assemblers might be released."

"The buggy?"

Lev looked up from the blini. "Who told you about that?"

"Ossian pointed it out to me, when we were waiting for your brother's peripheral. He didn't mention disassembling it. But later I saw him pushing it through the garage, and Lowbeer told me she wants its weapons."

"He didn't know, when you first saw it. She only asked for it when you'd returned from that club. Immediately after. Well, not for it, exactly. She asked if I had any weapons. I don't keep weapons. But then I remembered."

"Assemblers?"

"Short-acting," Lev said. "Decommission themselves. If there were an accident, the vehicle should be able to contain them."

"Dominika didn't want it, Ossian said."

"Neither did I. Grandfather means well, but he's of another generation. You haven't visited the Federation, have you?"

"No," said Netherton.

"I've somehow managed to avoid it myself."

"Dominika was born here?"

"Literally, in Notting Hill," said Lev.

Lev was one of those people whom marriage seemed basically to suit in some fundamental way, a state Netherton found unimaginable. The world seemed to consist increasingly of such states. "Why does Lowbeer want the buggy's weapons?" he asked, as Lev passed him a warm plate.

"She hasn't said. Given the quality of advice she's providing Ash and Ossian, I'm disinclined to second-guess her."

"You've no idea who else is in your stub?"

"No. But their quants are easily as good as Ash's." They were seated at the pine table now, Lev with his fork poised above his blini. He frowned. "Yes?" he said. "When? Do they know who?" He looked at Netherton, or rather through him. "Let me know, then." He put down his fork.

"What is it?"

"The signatures of Flynne's phone have vanished, about two miles from her home."

"You don't know where she is?"

"We do," said Lev. "She has a tracker in her stomach. The service alerts us if she leaves our specified perimeter, as it now has. Both her tracker and her phone drove together to the nearest town, which she does frequently, then both turned north. As they did, her phone was lost. Either she turned it off, which she never does, or someone blocked its signal. Shortly after that, she left the perimeter. The vehicle has since been exceeding speed limits, on very rough roads."

"She's in it now, this vehicle?"

"Yes, but nearing the base of operations of the drug synthesist who controls her county."

"She's been abducted?" asked Netherton.

"Lowbeer's cross, Ash says."

"What are you doing about it?"

"Lowbeer has her own asset, or assets, in the stub," Lev said. "Ash says they're on this too. As are her brother and Macon, of course."

"Who are they, these assets?"

"She isn't saying. Ash and Ossian don't like that. It would be whoever has access to the Gonzales White House, I imagine, not that she's ever suggested as much." He picked up his fork. "Eat these while they're still warm. Then we'll go down and see Ash."

71.

McMANSION

ickett's place, as much as she'd ever see of it, wasn't what she'd imagined at all.

Reece had driven her past a white gatehouse with window slits, but hadn't turned in. Further along, past a long stretch of white plastic fence, fabbed to look like somebody's idea of Old Plantation, he'd turned in to a less-important-looking gate, already open, where two men in cammies and helmets were waiting, beside a golf cart. They both had rifles. Reece got out and talked to one of them, while the other one spoke to somebody else on his headset, none of them looking at her.

She'd given up trying to talk to Reece a few miles back. She'd seen it made his driving worse, and there was no point getting killed, out on some back-ass county road in the dark, even in a situation like this. They'd kept passing old wrecks, left there because the state, let alone the county, couldn't afford to do anything about them. She'd wondered if people in those had been talking to somebody like Reece when the crash happened. Then she'd remembered swallowing the black pill in the Hefty snack bar, and wondered if it was doing what it was supposed to do. Reece didn't know about that, but he'd put her phone in a Faraday pouch.

Then Reece came back to the Jeep, opened the door on her side, took a pair of wire clippers out of his side pocket, snipped through the zip tie that fastened her to the seat, and told her to get out.

He put his hand on her head when she did, the way you saw cops do in shows, and it made her think how he'd never touched her before, that she could remember, not even shaken hands, and she'd known him to speak to for about three years.

"You see Burton," he said, "tell him wasn't anything I could do."

"I know there wasn't," she said, and it hurt her that it was true. That a man like Pickett, just by being what he was, could give Reece a choice of doing this or waiting for them to come and kill him.

He closed the Jeep's door, handed the pouch with her phone in it to the man standing nearest, walked around the back, got in on the driver's side, closed his door, pulled back out on the road, and drove away.

The man with her phone in the Faraday pouch snapped what she guessed was a dog's training leash onto the zip tie that held the ones around her wrists together. The other man was watching the gate close itself. Then they brought her over to the golf cart, which said CORBELL PICKETT TESLA on the side. The man who held the leash sat beside her, in the back, and the other man drove, and neither one of them said a word, as they drove her to Pickett's house, some back way, on single-lane gravel that hadn't been properly graded.

The house had floodlights trained on it, bright as day and ugly as shit, though this was just the back of it. They'd painted everything white, she guessed to tie it together, but it didn't. Looked like somebody had patched a factory, or maybe a car dealership, onto a McMansion, then stuck an Interstate chain restaurant and a couple of swimming pools on top of that. There were sheds scattered, beside the gravel and further back, and machinery too, under big tarps, and she wondered if he actually built drugs here. She'd figured he wouldn't, but maybe he didn't have to give a shit. But then maybe he didn't actually live here.

The cart rolled up to a corrugated white door in the factory-looking part, stopped, and the man beside her gave the leash a little tug, so she got off. He watched her, but didn't make eye contact. The other man touched something on his belt and the door clanked up. They led her into a big, mostly dark space, and then between rows of white plastic tanks taller than she was, like the ones for holding rainwater.

Came to a wall she guessed was the foundation of the original house, rough-cast concrete, with a door in it. Regular door from Hefty, but with an old-fashioned hasp bolted on it, a big rusty bolt stuck down through the U-shaped part. More tree fort than builder baron, but then she guessed he didn't have to give a shit about that either. She waited, like she saw you did if somebody had you on a leash, while the other one pulled out the bolt, opened the door, and turned on too many lights all at once, hanging low from a rough concrete ceiling that was already none too high. They led her over to a table in the middle, the only furniture in the room aside from two chairs, one on either long side of it, like the ones in the Hefty snack bar. The table, bolted to the floor with galvanized L-brackets, had a stainless-steel top that had seen a lot of wear, like in a cafeteria kitchen. Some dents and dings there that she didn't want to imagine how they'd been made, and someone had drilled a hole exactly in the center, put in a big screw eye, the kind you'd use to hang a porch swing. The man with the leash walked her around to the chair behind the table facing the door, pointed at it, and she sat down. Then he tugged her wrists over to the eye bolt, fastened Reece's white zip ties to it with a much more serious-looking zip tie, this one in that official Homes blue, unclipped the leash, and they both just turned and walked out, leaving the lights on and closing the door behind them. She heard them drop the bolt into place.

"Fuck a duck," she said, then realized she sounded five years old and was probably being recorded. She looked around for cams, didn't see any. Probably there, though, because they didn't cost anything, and maybe your prisoner would say or do something you'd like to know about. The lights were too bright, the kind of totally white LEDs that made your skin look really bad. She guessed she could stand up, but she might knock the chair over doing it, and then have nowhere to sit.

She heard the bolt come out of the hasp.

Corbell Pickett opened the door. He was wearing black wraparound sunglasses. Came over to the table, leaving the door open behind him. His watch looked like a clock out of an old airplane, but gold, on a leather strap.

"Well?" he asked.

"Well what?"

"Ever dislocate your jaw?"

She looked up at him.

"I could do it for you," he said, looking her in the eye, "if you don't tell me more about your people in bullshit Colombia."

She nodded, just a little.

"How much more do you know than you told me at the house?"

She was about to open her mouth but he raised his hand, the one with the big gold watch. She froze.

"Your Colombians," he said, lowering his hand, "bullshit or not, aren't necessarily the ones in this with the most money. Could be somebody else. Could be I've been talking with them. About you. All the lawyers in Miami don't mean shit to them. I'd say you're out of your depth, but that doesn't do it justice."

She waited for him to hit her.

"Don't tell me any shell story." His suntan looked weirder, under the light, than her skin did, but more even.

"They don't tell us much."

"People I'm talking to want me to kill you. Right now. They see proof you're dead, they give me more money than you can imagine. So you aren't just some random-ass poor, much as you look to me like one. What makes you that valuable?"

"I don't have clue one, why anybody would give a shit about me. Or why Coldiron hooked up with us. If I did, I'd be telling you." And then that crazy thing that had first come to her in Operation Northwind chimed in: "Where'd they say they're from, these people of yours?"

"They don't," he said, pissed that it was true, then pissed at himself for answering the question.

"If I'm worth more dead than alive," said the crazy thing, "how come I'm alive?"

"Difference between a cashed check and leverage," he said. He leaned a little closer. "Aren't stupid, are you?"

"Wilf Netherton," she said, the crazy thing gone as suddenly as it had come. "At Coldiron. He'd want a chance to outbid them."

Pickett smiled, maybe, just a tiny little change at the corners of his mouth. "We use your phone from here," he said, stepping back, "they'll know exactly where it is, where you are. We wait another few hours, till it gets somewhere else, we'll patch a call through, you and I, to your Mr. Coldiron. Meantime, you sit here."

"Any chance you could turn the lights down?"

"No," he said, and she saw the micro-smile again, and then he turned and went back out, closing the door behind him.

She heard the bolt rattle.

72.

HALFWAY POSH

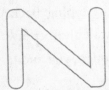etherton watched as Ossian transformed the de-cloaked baby buggy, glossy as a wet peppermint toffee, red and cream, into something surprisingly if only vaguely anthropomorphic.

The two rear pairs of wheels, now flat on the garage's floor, had formed figure-eight feet, from which sprouted candy-striped legs. Its gleaming armor, around the actual baby seat, had flattened laterally, widening at the top, emulating a muscular dynamism. The tires at the ends of each arm suggested clenched fists. Netherton could actually imagine this having some appeal, for a child. It didn't look as though it were armed, particularly, but cocky, certainly, belligerent.

Thumbing its cream-and-red controller, Ossian guided it to the open door of the Bentley executive-hauler, into which it climbed, wheel-paws gripping the silver-gray bodywork. It sat on a backward-facing seat, freezing as Ossian gave the controller a final tap.

Ash had insisted Netherton remain with Ossian while she and Lev dealt with Flynne's apparent abduction. She and Ossian were in contact, but Netherton could only hear Ossian's side of any exchange, and that in their morphing gibberish.

Netherton had watched Ossian put a pair of grotesque gloves, or rather hands, on the white exoskeleton. These had far too many fingers, black and unsettlingly limp, like oversized, anatomically incorrect rubber spiders. The second one had given Ossian some unspecified trouble, so he'd left it for the meantime, choosing instead to decloak and transform the buggy.

"When will they reach Flynne?" Netherton asked.

"As you know," Ossian said, "I don't know." He dropped the controller into the wide pocket on the front of his apron, bent to adjust the yellow kneepads he wore over his black trousers, then knelt before the white exoskeleton.

"Is there anything I can do?"

"You might try buggering off," Ossian suggested, without looking up.

"Burton's gone to bring her back?"

"Seems likeliest."

"I'd think him competent," Netherton said.

"Tendency to fly violently off the handle aside." Ossian prodded a black, penlike instrument into the recalcitrant glove's jiggly black digits, causing a small red light to strobe briefly.

"He was disoriented," Netherton said. "Understandably. When you came barging in, he reacted."

"I might disorient you," Ossian said, "if Zubov didn't need you to lie to your girlfriend's face. Is it true, that she periodically has herself flayed, her entire epidermis, to hang in whatever establishment might be willing to display such a thing?"

"If you want to put it that way," said Netherton.

"Kinky, are we?"

"She's an artist," said Netherton. "I wouldn't expect you to understand."

"My hairy arse," said Ossian, as if naming the root precept of a long-held philosophy, then pressed the penlike tool repeatedly into the black spider, managing to briefly produce a steady green light.

"Why are you putting those on?"

"For Macon's technical. Field manipulators, military. Anything from stone masonry to nanosurgery. Once he's locked in, can't have him coming up short the right size spanner."

"Locked in?"

"There," indicating the windowless silver vehicle. "Put them both in, seal it, depressurize it, partial vacuum. Should anything escape, it stays inside. Really, though, this is all to satisfy Zubov. Those assemblers are self-terminating. If they weren't, nothing in this vehicle would stop them."

Netherton looked at the exoskeleton. Ossian had bodged a domed, transparent cylinder onto the thing's shoulders, during Burton's visit. Within this, immobile, legs akimbo, stood the homunculus that had driven him, along with Lev, to the house of love. Though really, he knew, Ash had been the driver.

Ossian got to his feet, dropping the black tool into the pocket with the controller. "Lowbeer," he said, "has someone in the stub. You wouldn't know anything about that, would you?"

"No," Netherton lied. "Who?"

"If I knew, would I be asking? Whoever it is, they aren't being paid. Not by us. Ash signs off on all monies spent, there. Lowbeer has someone at her beck and call, apparently able to get in anywhere, learn anything."

"I'd think that would be exactly what you'd want."

"Not if it means someone on our team who's an entirely unknown quantity. Becomes Lowbeer's game, then."

"She's an unknown quantity as it is. And it's quite obviously been her game since she had that private talk with Lev."

"He doesn't see that," said Ossian. "She's leveled his game up for him. That's all he sees now. He might listen to you, though. You're halfway posh." He blinked, then, distracted. Looked away, listening. Said something in that moment's Esperanto. Listened again. "Closer to her, now," he said to Netherton.

"She's safe?"

"Alive. Tracker in her stomach's giving them basic vitals."

"Tracker?"

"We'd have had no way to find her, otherwise."

The exoskeleton's new hands, with an unexpected dry rustle,

sprang suddenly to a state of bristling attention, hyper-manipulative readiness.

"Hold your horses," Ossian said, neither to Netherton nor, evidently, to Ash. "I'll need to get you inside first, then depressurize."

Netherton saw the homunculus, under the transparent dome, lower its own hands and the exo's simultaneously, black digits drooping.

73.
RED GREEN BLUE

The only good thing you could say for this toilet was it had a seat. No door on it, and dog-leash man was about six feet away, keeping track of her out of the corner of his eye. He'd replaced his rifle with a pistol, worn on one of those nylon harnesses slung down from his belt and strapped across his thigh, like where a gorilla would wear his gun.

She was glad she just had to pee, seeing as she had company. She'd gotten them to take her here by explaining that she really needed to, that if she didn't she'd eventually wet her pants, and that that wouldn't be nice for Pickett, assuming he was coming back, which she told them he definitely intended to, but not for hours. So she'd been right about there being cams, and she must've struck some right tone with her prisoner's assisted urination pitch. Nothing angry, not too urgent. Just sitting there, addressing the door, because she had no idea where any cams might be. She'd gone through it twice, giving it a few minutes in between, careful not to escalate the second time. The two of them had come in, not that much later, put her on the leash, snipped the blue Homes zip tie fastening her to the table, and led her out. About thirty feet to the left, away from the roll-up door they'd first brought her in through, was this doorless single stall.

Sitting there, she thought this could've been the place where the heroine of the Resistance, in Operation Northwind, took out dog-leash with an OSS thumb-dagger she'd hidden in her underwear. She didn't have any thumb-dagger, but then they hadn't searched her, and maybe Reece hadn't either. Which meant they were slacker than a lot of game AI she'd played against, and didn't know she had a tube of lip gloss, which might be poison or an explosive gel. But then that was all she did have, and it wasn't either. To dog-leash's credit as a jailer, though, he'd zip-tied the nylon ring on the handle of the leash to a vertical, paint-flaking pipe, just right of the toilet, which would've made it hard for her to take anybody out with anything, short of a gun. When she pulled up her jeans and stood, he came in and snipped the tie. Then they took her back to the bright room.

That was probably when she first noticed the bug, though she barely did. Just a gnat. Fast, close, then gone.

But back in her chair, fastened to the table with a fresh Homes-blue zip tie, both men gone, something whined past her ear. If those tanks outside were standing water, there'd be mosquitos in here. With her hands tied, she wouldn't be able to do much about them.

She was looking in the direction of the closed door, given that was easiest and she hadn't much choice, when three bright small points of light moved horizontally across her vision, dead level, one after another, right to left, and vanished. Red, then green, then blue. They'd seemed to be either square or rectangular, and she'd barely had a chance to wonder whether she might be having a stroke, a seizure or something, when they were back, right to left again, same order, closer together, then collapsing into a single longer one. Aquamarine.

Unmoving now, in the middle of Pickett's white, finger-smudged door.

She moved her head, expecting the pixel-thing to move. But it stayed put, above the tabletop, closer than she'd first taken it to be. Like it was really there, an object, aquamarine, impossible.

"Huh," she said, mind filling with those things she'd seen kill and eat the woman, then with however many episodes of *Ciencia Loca* she'd watched about UFOs. Hadn't mentioned any tiny ones. This one descending, now, as she watched, to the tabletop, between her tethered wrists. Straight down, like a little elevator. Its length doubling, on the dull steel, it began to rotate on a central axis, revving to become a slightly blurry aquamarine disk, size of an antique dime, flat on the table. And she heard it do that, faintly buzzing. Couldn't get her wrists any further apart than they already were.

Aquamarine to bright yellow, then a stylized red nubbin, dead center. Thing still spinning, because she could hear it. A kind of animation. "Macon?"

The disk flared red.

She'd done something wrong.

Aquamarine again. Then a graphic of an ear, drawn with one black line, like a PSA warning. Becoming a housefly, in the same style. Then both, side by side, the fly shrinking to vanish into the ear. Then yellow again, Edward's two nubbins instead of Macon's one. The yellow background went cream, the two nubbins becoming Lowbeer's emblem, that pale gold crown. Then the disk was gone, leaving an actual bug, much smaller, in its place. Not a housefly. Translucent, waxy looking.

"No way," she said, under her breath. She leaned forward.

Too fast to see. Into her left ear. Buzzing. Deeper. "Don't speak," the buzz became Macon's voice. "You're miked, on cam. Pretend nothing's happening. Do exactly what I say."

She made herself look at the door. It sounded like him, but she could see the woman's clothing fluttering down, over that empty street.

"Click your teeth together twice, one-two, without opening your mouth. Quiet as possible."

She looked down. Clicked her teeth, twice. Loudest thing in the world.

"Need a minute of you not moving much. How you are now, but not moving. Not too still, 'cause I'm going to capture, then loop that back to them, so they'll see that loop and not what's happening next. Got it?"

Click-click.

"No major head or body movement. Move too much, it highlights repetition in the loop. I say done, be ready to go. Earplugs first, then the suit."

Suit?

"You good?" he asked.

Click-click.

"Capturing now," he said.

She stared at the door. The knob, the smears above it. Hoped her mother was okay, Lithonia still there.

"Done," said Macon, finally. "Looping. Stand up."

She put her palms flat on the steel, stood, pushing back the Hefty chair. She heard the bolt rattle.

The door opened. Weirdness came in. Like her retinas were melting. A kind of roiling blob.

"Squidsuit," said Macon, in her ear. Cuttlefish camo, like Burton and Conner used in the war.

The suit was reading whatever was nearest, emulating that, but part of it looked sprayed with blood. Like a chunk of broken game code, walking in. Then a squidstuff glove, with the head of Burton's tomahawk, darting toward her, under her hands, to hook and sever the blue zip tie In the bottom curve of the head was a special notch, sharper even than the rest of it, crazy sharp. For ropes, webbing, harness. It nipped back in, between her wrists, to cut the tie that held them together. His other glove a steel-gray paw, offering two orange blobs on an orange string, like low-end Hefty candy. Then she had them in her ears, like Macon had told her to, but had he meant her to trap the bug in there?

Burton dropped to the floor, scooted under the table, popped up beside her. Velcro ripping, glimpse of his eyes. Squidstuff unfolding, shaken out in front of her, instantly going what must be the color of her face under these lights, plus two big smears, the brown of her eyes, trying to emulate her, and then she had her head in it, her arms, was pulling it down, oversized and loose, dark inside but then she could see, the lights mercifully dimmer. Burton closing his own suit, then bending to close hers, starting at her feet.

"Out," said Macon, the earplugs changing his voice.

Burton picked her up, swung her over the table, came over it himself like a gymnast clearing a pommel horse, pulled her to the door and out. She stumbled. Her foot a concrete blur beside dog-leash's holster, pistol still in it, splotched with blood.

Stepped over him.

"Door," said Macon, close to her ear, "move." The roll-up door they'd brought her in through, open, the night beyond it darker now. The big loose pajama feet of the suit scuffing, threatening to trip her up.

Not game blood, some other part of her said, from some distant sideline.

74.

THAT FIRST GENTLE TOUCH

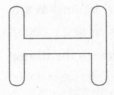as her now," said Ossian.

The exoskeleton's operator, in the stub, had just positioned it in the executive-hauler, in a rear seat facing the inert buggy, black manipulators drooping.

"Who does?"

"The hot-head brother. Commencing exfiltration. Ash says she's overreacting."

"Flynne?"

"Lowbeer. Seal the door." This last, evidently, to the Bentley, its open door obediently shrinking to nothing at all, an unbroken expanse of silver-gray bodywork, Netherton finding the very last bit of closure peculiarly unpleasant, somehow octopoid. "Full hermetic. Vent one third captive atmosphere."

Netherton heard a sharp outrush of air.

"Take it apart," Ossian said, Netherton assumed to the operator. "If the tutorials aren't adequate, ask us for help."

"Overreacting?"

"She's about to make a point. Quite a sharp one, irreversible."

"She needs to get Flynne out first."

"Shall I get her for you? Couldn't possibly mind being interrupted just now, by our resident bullshit artist."

Netherton ignored this. "What's it doing in there?"

"Attempting to relieve a pram of two autonomously targeting, self-limiting swarm weapons. Shouldn't be too terribly difficult, you might suppose, having just seen me shut the bastard down cold. Not that the sadistic shits who engineered it would let life be that simple. And now our technical is broaching the matter . . ." Ossian was listening to something Netherton couldn't hear. "And there you have it. I was right."

"Have what?" Netherton asked.

Ossian seemed quite satisfied now. "It didn't fancy that first gentle touch, did it? Projected assemblers. Ate the better part of Zubov's father's leather upholstery, and the biological elements of our left manipulator. They wouldn't believe me, that the bugger never sleeps. Has no off switch. Waiting all this time to kill anyone who tried to get it out of the pram. We'll have them both, though, now, in short order. And the one that triggered expended no more than a few thousand bugs. Millions yet to go. Can't be reloaded, you know, not this side of Novosibirsk Oblast."

The gilt coronet appeared.

"Is she safe?" Netherton asked.

"Told you I don't know," said Ossian.

Netherton moved away from the Bentley.

"Apparently, yes," said Lowbeer.

"Ossian tells me that Ash thinks you're overreacting. That was his word."

"She's bright, Ash, but unaccustomed to operating from strength. Pickett is entirely unlikely to find his place in our scheme of things. And someone did recently attempt to kill you, Mr. Netherton. Pickett, we can assume, already has some relationship, at whatever remove, with whoever ordered that. Would you like to go there?"

"Go where?"

"Lev's stub."

"That's impossible. Isn't it?"

"Physically, yes. Virtually, however crudely? Child's play."

"It is?"

"A bit too literally in this case," she said, "but yes."

75.

PRECURSORS

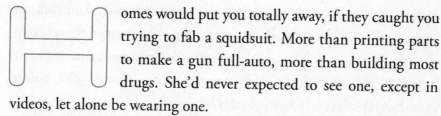 omes would put you totally away, if they caught you trying to fab a squidsuit. More than printing parts to make a gun full-auto, more than building most drugs. She'd never expected to see one, except in videos, let alone be wearing one.

The night out back of Pickett's seemed impossibly quiet, what little she could see of it from the suit. She kept expecting somebody to yell, start shooting, set off an alarm. Nothing. Just the wheels of this ATV, crunching over gravel. Electric, so new she could smell it. Paid for with some of Leon's lottery win, she guessed, or that Clanton money. She could feel it had major torque, like if you put a blade on it you could grade this road up right. They'd run rappelling rope through the factory gear-anchors, to make it easier to hold on. Had those skeleton wheels, nonpneumatic. On the gravel they shaped themselves like mountain bike tires, but when Burton swung right, off the gravel, she saw them widen out. Even quieter on the grass.

"Macon?" Not sure he could hear her.

"Here," said the gnat in her ear. "Getting you gone. Talk later."

She couldn't see where they were going. Burton's suit was too close to the part of hers she was supposed to see through, so they were doing that mutual feedback thing, trying to emulate each other, ramping them both up into a headachy swarm of distorted hexagons. *Ciencia Loca* had had that on. Now Burton braked, cut the motor. She felt him swing his leg over, get off the ATV. Heard him rip his suit's Velcro, then he reached over and ripped hers, near her neck. Night air on her face. He reached in, squeezed her upper arm. "Easy Ice," he said. She could barely hear him, with the earplugs. She pulled the left one out, on the orange string. "Keep 'em in," he said, "might get loud." So she pressed it back in, turning her head to do that, and there was Conner, in his anime-ankled VA prosthesis, behind Burton, in the shadow of a metal shed.

Then she saw it couldn't be him, because the torso and both limbs were all wrong. Lumpy, like someone had stuffed one of his black Polartec unitards full of modeling clay, too much of it. And had put, in dreamlike randomness, she saw, stepping closer, one of those shitty-looking Gonzales masks on it, the president's iconic acne scars rendered as stylized craters across exaggerated cheekbones. She looked into the empty eyes. Blank paleness.

Carlos stepped around it, bullpup under his arm. All in black. Burton too, under the open squidsuit. Carlos wore a black beanie pulled down over his brows, his eyes solid black with night-vision contacts. "Need your suit for our guy," Carlos said. She let it fall around her ankles, stepped out of it. Hex-swarm gone, it instantly did grass. Carlos picked it up and started undoing zips, more Velcro. Draped it over the big tall backpack she now saw the prosthesis wore. Burton was putting his own suit on it from the front, the Gonzales mask poking out through an unzipped slit. They worked on this, making little Velcro noises, joining the suits. If you did it right, the two suits wouldn't do that feedback thing and hex out. The black of their clothes swirled on the squidstuff. When they were done, they both stepped back, and it became the shadow it stood in.

"Outfit's go," Burton said, to somebody who wasn't there.

The thing took a first step, out of shadow. The mask was all you could really see of it, except for the ankles and feet. Like a glitch in a buggy game. The dog-leash man's blood would still be on it somewhere. She couldn't remember his face. It took another step, another. That gait she remembered, Conner going to the fridge, but leaning forward, here, under the weight of the pack. Tramping out, flat-footed, thick-ankled, to the gravel. She couldn't see the mask now. It was headed back, toward Pickett's ugly, flood-lit house. "What are you doing?" she asked Burton.

He raised an index finger to his lips, mounted the ATV, motioning for her to get on behind him. Carlos climbed on behind her, reaching around to grab a stretch of rappelling rope, and Burton took off, across the grass, away from the gravel road.

Pickett had a golf course, she saw, as Burton drove further from the house, the sheds and machinery. The moon was coming up. Smoothness of the turf, polymer or GM grass. She saw a raccoon freeze, seeing them, its head turning as they passed.

Beyond the green, the land slanted up, into uncut pasture with a few paths through it, maybe made by cattle or horses. She could see white up ahead, and then she saw it was that same ugly fence, but along a different stretch of road. Two figures in black rose up, as they drew closer, running to the fence, lifting a length of it between them and moving it aside. Burton drove through the gap without slowing, out onto blacktop Pickett must have paid the county to keep in such good shape, then they were on that, speeding up.

About half a mile on, Tommy was waiting by his big white car, in a Sheriff's Department helmet and his black jacket. Burton slowed, pulling up beside him. "Flynne," Tommy said, "you okay?"

"I guess so."

"Anybody hurt you?" Tommy was looking at her like he could see inside her.

"No."

Still looking inside her. "We'll take you home."

Burton got off the ATV, walked across the road, and stood with his back to them, peeing. She climbed off. Carlos scooted himself forward, to the driver's part of the saddle, took the handlebars, started the engine, swinging around. He was gone into the dark before Burton could cross the road again, headed back the way they'd come, she guessed to pick up the other two.

Tommy opened the passenger-side door for her and she got in. He went around, opened the driver-side passenger door, then his own, got in. Burton got in behind him and they both closed their doors.

"You okay, Flynne?" Tommy asked, again, looking over at her.

She closed her door.

He started the car, and they drove for a while in the dark, opposite direction to the one Carlos had gone in. He put the headlights on.

"Pickett's a dick," she said

"Knew that," Burton said. "Was it Reece?"

"Pickett said they'd kill him if he didn't bring me. Said Homes could find him anywhere."

"Figured," Burton said.

But she didn't want to talk about Reece, or whatever else it was that they were doing. She didn't feel like she could talk to Macon through the bug, because they'd hear her, and Tommy was concentrating on the road. So it felt like a long ride back to town, and everything that had happened before felt kind of like a dream, but still going on.

They were almost to town when Burton said, to whoever it was that wasn't there, "Do it."

They saw the light from it, the fireball, behind them, throwing the cruiser's shadow ahead of it on the road. Then they heard it, and later she'd think she could've counted off the miles, like after a lightning strike.

"Goddamn," Tommy said, slowing. "What the hell did you do?"

"Builders," Burton, said, behind her, "still managing to blow their own asses up."

Tommy said nothing. Got back up to speed. Just looking at the road.

She hoped Reece hadn't stopped at all, had got out of the county, headed someplace interstate, gone. She didn't want to ask Burton about that.

"You feel like a coffee, Flynne?" Tommy asked her, finally.

"Too late for me, thanks," she said, her voice like somebody else's, someone none of this ever happened to, and then she just cried.

76.
EMULATION APP

The headband Ash was extending looked like the one Lowbeer had used to take him back to the patchers' island, but with the addition of a clear bendable cam, its milkily transparent head like a very large sperm. "I'm not going back there," he said, grateful for the expanse of Lev's grandfather's desk.

"You aren't being asked. You'll be visiting Flynne. At very low resolution."

"I will?"

"We've already installed the emulation app in your phone."

He leaned forward, took the thing from her. It weighed no more than the other one, but the spermlike cam lent it something at once Egyptianate and cartoonish. "They have peripherals?"

"I'll let you find that out for yourself."

77.

WHEELIE BOY

"Y ou got a bug in your stomach?" Janice finally asked, from the dark at the foot of the bed. "And one in your ear?"

Flynne was sitting up against her pillows, in her underpants and the USMC sweatshirt, moonlight streaming in her window. "One in my stomach's a tracker," she said, "from a Belgian satellite security service. Me, Macon, Burton, Conner, we all got one, that I know of."

"One in your ear?"

"Burton took it."

"How'd he get it out?"

"Macon flew it out. Into a pill bottle. I thought it was some future-ass thing they showed Macon how to fab, but he says it's from here, last season's military."

"The one you swallowed showed them where you were?"

"Or I wouldn't be here now. Reece bagged my phone."

"Macon's made you a new one. Got it right here. How hard would it be to get that thing out of your stomach?"

"Six months, it just lets go, Macon said."

"And?"

"You shit it out, Janice."

"In the toilet?"

"On your friend's head."

"Happens daily," said Janice, from the dark, "kind of people I know. But you'd just trust Belgians, telling you you'd pooped out their tracker bug?"

"Macon would. Where's Madison?"

"Building a fort. Over at your new world headquarters, next to Fab."

"Why?"

"Burton told him to. Gave him a Hefty charge card. Said improvise."

"Out of what?"

"About two hundred pallets of those faux-asphalt roof tiles, mostly. The kind made of shredded bottles, old tires and shit. Leaves 'em in their bags, has Burton's guys stack 'em like bricks, seven feet high, two bags deep. Stop some serious ammunition, that stuff."

"Why?"

"Ask Burton. Madison says if it's about Homes coming after us, won't be any help at all. And Homes is all over what's left of Pickett's place. Got Tommy over helping them."

"Must be getting sick of driving, there and back."

"You didn't get raped or anything, did you?"

"No. Pickett just mentioned maybe dislocating my jaw. Not like his heart was in it, though. I think he mainly just wanted the most money he could get for me."

"That's it in a nutshell," said Janice.

"What is?"

"Why I hope the fucker's dead."

"If you'd seen how they delivered that bomb, you'd know it wasn't liable to be sneaking up on anybody, even with a squidsuit on."

"Here's hoping anyway," said Janice.

"How'd they get squidsuits?"

"That Griff."

"Who?"

"Griff. Ironside people sent him, right away."

"Coldiron."

"He was here almost as soon as Burton knew you were off the reservation. Jet helicopter, landed over in the pasture there." Janice pointed, hand emerging into moonlight. "I never got a look at him. Madison did. Sounded English, Madison said. Probably where they got that micro-drone too."

"What is he?"

"No idea. Madison says that copter came from D.C. Says it was Homes."

"Homes?"

"The copter."

Pickett had people in Homes, Flynne remembered Reece saying. "Guess I'm behind the curve again." If she wasn't in the future, she thought, she was getting kidnapped and rescued.

"With Pickett's place all blown to shit, we get to wake up tomorrow and see who looks like their main source of income's gone tits up. Here's the phone Macon made you." She passed it to Flynne, out of the dark.

"I'd rather have mine back." Pissed her off, all the hours she'd put in at Fab to pay for that.

"Yours got flown to Nassau."

"Nassau?"

"Somebody in a lawyer's office there. They took it out of a Faraday bag, a little after Burton and them broke you out of Pickett's. Macon bricked it."

Flynne remembered Pickett saying he'd have her call Netherton, try to get more money for her than the others were offering.

"Macon said Pickett has fancy lawyers, in Nassau," Janice said, "but not as fancy as yours, and not as many."

"All of three, that I know of."

"Lots more now, in town. Housing and feeding them's a growth industry. Timely one, too."

"He put my apps and stuff on it?" Flynne raised her new phone, sniffed. Fresh.

"Yeah, plus some major encryption, runs in background. He says to change your passwords on everything. And don't just use your birthday or your name backwards. And there's a Hefty Wheelie Boy for you, in that tote there, on your desk."

"A what?"

"Wheelie Boy."

"The fuck?"

"Macon got it off eBay. New old stock. Mint in box."

"Huh?"

"Back in grade school. Like a tablet on a stick? Bottom's like a little Segway. Remember those things? Motors, two wheels, gyros to keep 'em upright."

"Looked stupid," Flynne said, remembering them now.

Janice's phone chimed. She checked it, the screen lighting her face. "Ella needs me."

"If it's anything serious, get me. Otherwise, I'm going to try to sleep."

"I'm glad they got you back okay. You know that?"

"I love you, Janice," Flynne said.

When Janice had gone downstairs, she got up, put on her bedside light, brought the tote back to the bed. There was a box inside with a picture of a Hefty Wheelie Boy on the lid. Like a red plastic flyswatter stuck into a softball the same color, two fat black toy tractor tires on either side of that. Swatter part was a mini-tablet with a cam, on a stick. Marketed as toys, baby monitors, long-distance friendship or sad romance platforms, or even a kind of low-rent virtual vacation. You could buy or rent one in Vegas or Paris, say, drive it around a casino or a museum, see what it saw. And while you did, and this was the part that had put her off, it showed your face on the tablet. You wore a headpiece with a camera on a little boom, which captured your reaction as you saw things through the Wheelie, and people who were looking at it saw you seeing that, or them, and you could have conversations with them. She remembered Leon trying to gross her out, telling her how people were getting sexy with them, all of which she'd hoped he'd made up.

Back on the bed, opening the box, she thought this must have been part of where peripherals were going to come from. Wheelie Boy, in its cheap-ass way, had been one.

There was a yellow sheet from a Forever Fab notepad inside. DR's ORDERS, FULLY CHARGED + HARDASS NCRYPT—M in thick flu-pink marker.

She lifted the thing out and tried to stand it up, but it fell over backward, tablet in the moonlight like a black hand mirror. On the bottom of the red ball, a white button. She pressed it. Gyros spun themselves up with a little squawk, the red plastic rod with the tablet on the end suddenly upright on the bed, black wheels moving independently in the sheets, turning it left, then right.

She poked the black screen with her finger, knocking it back, the gyros righting it.

Then it lit, Netherton's face on it, too close to the cam, eyes wide, nose too big. "Flynne?" he said, through a cheap little speaker.

"Shit the living fuck," she said, almost laughing, then had to yank the sheet over her legs because she just had her underpants and the sweatshirt on.

78.

FRONTIERLAND

eed from the thing's cam, in full binocular, reminded him of still images from an era prior to hers, though he couldn't remember the platform's name. She looked down at him, over knees draped in pale fabric.

"It's me," he said.

"No shit," she said, reaching out, fingertip becoming enormous, to flick him, the cam platform, whatever it was, backward. To be arrested by whatever it stood on. Briefly showing him a low, artisanal-looking surface he assumed must be the ceiling. A horizontal seam, as if glued paper were starting to peel. Then it righted itself, with an audible whirr.

"Don't," he said.

"Know what you look like?" Leaning over her knees.

"No," he said, though the emulation software's sigil depicted something spherical, two-wheeled, with a topmost rectangle upright on a thin projection. She reached past him, arm growing huge, and the feed filled with a promotional image of the thing on the sigil, rectangular screen tightly framing an eager child's face.

"No hot synthetic bods, back here in Frontierland," she said, "but we got Wheelie Boy. Where are you?"

"In the Gobiwagen."

"The RV?"

"At my desk," he said.

"That really your desk?"

"No."

"Ugly-ass desk. Never was really any Coldiron?"

"There are companies, registered in that name, in your Colombia, your Panama," he said. "And now in your United States of America. You're an executive of that one."

"But not there."

"No."

"Just Lev's hobby? With your fuck-up and Lowbeer's murder investigation on top of it?"

"To my knowledge."

"Why are you here?"

"Lowbeer suggested it," he said. "And I wanted to see. Is it day? Is there a window? Where are we?"

"Night," she said. "My room. Bright moon." She reached to the side, turning off a light source. Instantly, she was differently beautiful. Dark eyes larger. Daguerreotype, he remembered. "Turn around," she said, doing it for him. "I have to put my jeans on."

Her room, rotating the cam as far as he could, was like the interior of some nomadic yurt. Nondescript furniture, tumuli of clothing, printed matter. This actual moment in the past, decades before his birth. A world he'd imagined, but now, somehow, in its reality, unimaginable. "Have you always lived here?"

She bent, plucked him up, carrying him toward the window, into moonlight. "Sure."

And then the moon. "I know this is real," he said, "it must be, but I can't believe it."

"I can believe in yours, Wilf. Have to. You should try stretching a little."

"Before the jackpot," he said, instantly regretting it.

She turned him around then, away from the moon. Stood staring, moonlit, grave, into his eyes. "What's that, Wilf, the jackpot?"

Something stilled the part of him that knitted narrative, that grew the underbrush of lies in which he lived.

79.

THE JACKPOT

She sat with him on her lap, in the old wooden chair under the oak in the front yard.

Ben Carter, the youngest of Burton's soldiers, who looked like he should still be in high school, sat on the front porch steps, bullpup across his lap, Viz in his eye, drinking coffee from a Thermos. She wanted some, but knew she'd never sleep at all if she had it, and Wilf Netherton was explaining the end of the world, or anyway of hers, this one, which seemed to have been the beginning of his.

Wilf's face, on the Wheelie's tablet, had lit her way downstairs. She'd found Ben on the porch steps, guarding the house, and he'd been all embarrassed, getting up with his rifle and trying to remember where not to point it, and she'd seen he had a cap like Reece had had, with the pixilated camo that moved around. He hadn't known whether to say hello to Wilf or not. She told him they were going to sit out under the tree and talk. He told her he'd let the others know where she was, but please not to go anywhere else, and not to mind any drones. So she'd gone out to the chair and sat in it with Wilf in the Wheelie Boy, and he'd started to explain what he called the jackpot.

And first of all that it was no one thing. That it was multicausal, with no particular beginning and no end. More a climate than an event, so not the way apocalypse stories liked to have a big event, after which everybody ran around with guns, looking like Burton and his posse, or else were eaten alive by something caused by the big event. Not like that.

It was androgenic, he said, and she knew from *Ciencia Loca* and *National Geographic* that that meant because of people. Not that they'd known what they were doing, had meant to make problems, but they'd caused it anyway. And in fact the actual climate, the weather, caused by there being too much carbon, had been the driver for a lot of other things. How that got worse and never better, and was just expected to, ongoing. Because people in the past, clueless as to how that worked, had fucked it all up, then not been able to get it together to do anything about it, even after they knew, and now it was too late.

So now, in her day, he said, they were headed into androgenic, systemic, multiplex, seriously bad shit, like she sort of already knew, figured everybody did, except for people who still said it wasn't happening, and those people were mostly expecting the Second Coming anyway. She'd looked across the silver lawn, that Leon had cut with the push-mower whose cast-iron frame was held together with actual baling wire, to where moon shadows lay, past stunted boxwoods and the stump of a concrete birdbath they'd pretended was a dragon's castle, while Wilf told her it killed 80 percent of every last person alive, over about forty years.

And hearing that, she just wondered if it could mean anything, really, when somebody told you something like that. When it was his past and your future.

What had they done, she'd asked him, her first question since he'd started, with all the bodies?

The usual things, he'd said, because it was never all at once. Then, later, for a while, nothing, and then the assemblers. The assemblers, nanobots, had come later. The assemblers had also done things like excavating and cleaning the buried rivers of London, after they'd finished tidying the die-off. Had done everything she'd seen on her way to Cheapside. Had built the tower where she'd seen the woman prepare for her party and then be killed, built all the others in the grid of what he called shards, and cared for it all, constantly, in his time after the jackpot.

It hurt him to talk about it, she felt, but she guessed he didn't know how much, or how. She could tell he didn't unpack this, much, or maybe ever. He said that people like Ash made their whole lives about it. Dressed in black and marked themselves, but for them it was more about other species, the other great dying, than the 80 percent.

No comets crashing, nothing you could really call a nuclear war. Just everything else, tangled in the changing climate: droughts, water shortages, crop failures, honeybees gone like they almost were now, collapse of other keystone species, every last alpha predator gone, antibiotics doing even less than they already did, diseases that were never quite the one big pandemic but big enough to be historic events in themselves. And all of it around people: how people were, how many of them there were, how they'd changed things just by being there.

The shadows on the lawn were black holes, bottomless, or like velvet had been spread, perfectly flat.

But science, he said, had been the wild card, the twist. With everything stumbling deeper into a ditch of shit, history itself become a slaughterhouse, science had started popping. Not all at once, no one big heroic thing, but there were cleaner, cheaper energy sources, more effective ways to get carbon out of the air, new drugs that did what antibiotics had done before, nanotechnology that was more than just car paint that healed itself or camo crawling on a ball cap. Ways to print food that required much less in the way of actual food to begin with. So everything, however deeply fucked in general, was lit increasingly by the new, by things that made people blink and sit up, but then the rest of it would just go on, deeper into the ditch. A progress accompanied by constant violence, he said, by sufferings unimaginable. She felt him stretch past that, to the future where he lived, then pull himself there, quick, unwilling to describe the worst of what had happened, would happen.

She looked at the moon. It would look the same, she guessed, through the decades he'd sketched for her.

None of that, he said, had necessarily been as bad for very rich people. The richest had gotten richer, there being fewer to own whatever there was. Constant crisis had provided constant opportunity. That was where his world had come from, he said. At the deepest point of everything going to shit, population radically reduced, the survivors saw less carbon being dumped into the system, with what was still being produced eaten by these towers they'd built, which was the other thing the one she'd patrolled was there for, not just housing rich folks. And seeing that, for them, the survivors, was like seeing the bullet dodged.

"The bullet was the eighty percent, who died?"

And he just nodded, on the Wheelie's screen, and went on, about how London, long since the natural home of everyone who owned the world but didn't live in China, rose first, never entirely having fallen.

"What about China?"

The Wheelie Boy's tablet creaked faintly, raising the angle of its camera. "They'd had a head start," he said.

"At what?"

"At how the world would work, after the jackpot. This," and the tablet creaked again, surveying her mother's lawn, "is still ostensibly a democracy. A majority of empowered survivors, considering the jackpot, and no doubt their own positions, wanted none of that. Blamed it, in fact."

"Who runs it, then?"

"Oligarchs, corporations, neomonarchists. Hereditary monarchies provided conveniently familiar armatures. Essentially feudal, according to its critics. Such as they are."

"The King of England?"

"The City of London," he said. "The Guilds of the City. In alliance with people like Lev's father. Enabled by people like Lowbeer."

"The whole world's funny?" She remembered Lowbeer saying that.

"The klept," he said, misunderstanding her, "isn't funny at all."

80.
THE CLOVIS LIMIT

lovis Fearing, introduced by Lowbeer as a very old friend, most spectacularly and evidently was: as old or older than Lowbeer herself, and very deliberately looking it. With her head likely hairless under a black knit cloche, atop a display of Victorian mourning so fustily correct as to make Ash's outfits seem racily burlesque, she resembled some crumbling relict saint, one with acute and highly mobile black eyes, their whites yellowed and bloodshot. The Clovis Limit, her shop in Portobello Road, dealt exclusively in Americana.

He was here, Lowbeer had explained on their short ride over, because Daedra had now invited him to her party on Tuesday evening, though Lowbeer hadn't yet permitted him to open the message. That, along with his RSVP, must be done from a location that didn't involve Lev. One, he understood, that wouldn't introduce the architecture of the Zubov family's security to whatever architectures Daedra herself might be involved with, something Lowbeer regarded as messiness, and very much to be avoided.

"This young man, Clovis, is Wilf Netherton," she said now, looking mildly around at the barbaric clutter of the crowded shop. "He's a publicist."

Mrs. Fearing, for such was her title on the shop front, eyed him, lizard-like, out of perhaps the densest matrix of wrinkles and mottle he'd ever encountered. Her skull was worryingly visible, seemingly mere microns behind what time had left of her face. "I don't suppose we should blame him," she said, her voice surprisingly firm, accent American but more pronounced than Flynne's. "Wouldn't think you'd need one." Her hands, atop the counter's glass, were like the claws of a bird, the back of one marked with an utterly illegible blot of subcutaneous ink, ancient and totally unmoving.

"His friends are continua enthusiasts," Lowbeer said. "Are you familiar with that?"

"I've had a run of them, these past few years. They'll buy anything from the twenty thirties, twenty forties. Seem to try to get as far back from the jackpot proper as they can. About twenty twenty-eight, latest. What can I do you for, then, hon?"

"Wilf," said Lowbeer, "if you wouldn't mind, I need to catch up with Clovis. You could open your mail and make that call from the pavement, if you like. Do stay near the car. Should you stray, it will retrieve you."

"Of course," said Netherton. "A pleasure, Mrs. Fearing."

Ignoring him, Clovis Fearing was peering sharply at Lowbeer.

"I need my memory refreshed, dear," he heard Lowbeer say, as he went out.

Saturday's crowd had considerably thinned, this late in the evening, the barrow sellers mostly packed up and gone, though shops like Fearing's remained open. Lowbeer's car was parked there, cloaked but steaming slightly, an odd effect, though passersby studiously ignored it. A pair of theatrically professorial Italians, deep in conversation, were passing as he emerged. They crossed to an horologer's shop, diagonally opposite. The car was making random ticking sounds, as of metal cooling, contracting. He remembered Flynne's face, luminous in the moonlight, stricken. He hadn't liked having to tell her about the jackpot. He disliked the narrative aspects of history, particularly that part of it. People were so boringly deformed by it, like Ash, or else, like Lev, scarcely aware of it.

He turned to face Mrs. Fearing's display window, pretending to study a shallow glass-topped tray of stone arrow points, enigmatic symbols of a prior order. In Flynne's moonlit garden, he felt, he'd glimpsed some other order. He tried to recall what Lowbeer had said

Ash thought about him, in that regard, but couldn't. He tapped the roof of his mouth, selected Daedra's invitation, studied its particulars. The event was to be held in Farringdon, Edenmere Mansions, fifty-sixth floor, and that would be Aelita's residence, the place Burton had been assigned to watch, where Flynne had apparently seen her murdered. He was invited, as was Dr. Annie Courrèges, though she was expected peripherally. The evening was described only as "a gathering," no hint as to purpose or tone.

Tongue back to palate. Gyre on her sigil. No towering granite hall, this time. An indeterminate space, crepuscular, intimate, slightly boudoirlike in affect. "Mr. Netherton!" Her posh-girl module, startled but delighted.

"Responding to Daedra's very kind invitation, thank you," he said. "Dr. Courrèges will accompany me peripherally."

"Daedra will be so sorry to have missed you, Mr. Netherton. Shall I have her try to phone you?"

"That won't be necessary, thank you. Goodbye."

"Goodbye, Mr. Netherton! Have a lovely evening!"

"Thank you. Goodbye."

Daedra's sigil vanished, Lowbeer's replacing it. "You appear to be in quite good odor," she said.

"You were listening."

"As the pope remains Catholic, I trust. Please come back in for a moment."

He reentered the shop, avoiding a stuffed, top-hatted alligator, or perhaps crocodile, upright and waist-high, which wore a matched and holstered set of what he took to be a child's toy pistols, their cast-metal handles decorated with steer heads. Lowbeer and Fearing were still at the counter. Between them now, a rectangular tray of off-white plastic.

"Recognize this?" asked Lowbeer, indicating the tray.

"No," he said. He saw the words CLANTON BICENTENNIAL in a clumsy font, a pair of years two centuries apart, small drawings or vignettes, the printing faded, worn.

"Your peripheral happened to record one of these in her house," Lowbeer said. "We compared the various objects there to the catalogs of Clovis's cooperative of dealers. This one was under Ladbroke Grove. Assemblers brought it up."

"Just now?"

"While you were out."

"I don't recognize it." He vaguely knew that former tube tunnels in the vicinity were packed with artifacts, the combined stock of many dealers, minutely cataloged and instantly accessible to assemblers. It struck him as sad, somehow, that this thing had been down there, just moments before. He hoped it wasn't literally the one from Flynne's house.

"Hers was on a mantelpiece," Lowbeer said, "pride of place."

"Been to Clanton," said Mrs. Fearing. "Shot a man there. Lounge of the Ramada Inn. In the ankle. I was always a decent shot, at the range, but it's how you do when you aren't that counts."

"Why?" asked Netherton.

"He was trying to leave," said Mrs. Fearing.

"You were a piece of work, Clovis," said Lowbeer.

"You were a British spy," said Mrs. Fearing.

"So were you," said Lowbeer, "though on a freelance basis."

Mrs. Fearing's extraordinary topography of wrinkles readjusted slightly. A smile, possibly.

"Why did you say she'd been a British spy?" he asked Lowbeer, a few minutes later, in her car. Two small children, tended by a Michikoid nanny, had been passing as the door decloaked, and had applauded, delighted. Lowbeer had wiggled the fingers of one hand at them as she'd climbed in, after Netherton.

"She was," said Lowbeer, "at the time." She gazed at the flame of her candle, on the table between them. "I ran her, out of the embassy in Washington. It led to her marrying Clement Fearing, as it happened, one of the last Tory MPs." She frowned. "I never shared her enthusiasm for Clement, at all, but there was no denying the convenience of an influential husband. Not that she wasn't inexplicably fond of him. Terrible days."

"I told Flynne, about the jackpot."

"I listened, I'm afraid," said Lowbeer, obviously neither afraid nor in the least regretful. "You made a good job of it, considering."

"She demanded I tell her. Now I worry that I've made her sad, frightened her." And he actually did, he realized.

"It is," said Lowbeer, "as people used to say, to my unending annoyance, what it is. I'm going to have Ash sedate you, when we get back."

"You are?"

"It's like alcoholic oblivion, but without the bother of the run-up or the subsequent mess. I need you rested. I must have you and Flynne ready for Daedra's party, Tuesday evening."

"You had so little time with her, back there," Netherton said. "I thought you needed information."

"I do," she said, "but she'll need time to retrieve and decrypt it. It's nothing she literally remembers."

"I was going to phone Flynne," Netherton said.

"She's asleep," said Lowbeer. "She had a brutally long day. Kidnapped, held prisoner, rescued, then you gave her the whole of the jackpot to absorb."

"How do you know that she's asleep?"

"We had Macon add a feature to her new phone. Not only do I know that she's asleep, just now, but that she's dreaming."

Netherton looked at her. "Do you know what she's dreaming?"

Lowbeer looked at her candle. Looked up at him. "No. Not that it can't be done, of course, though our connection in the stub is slightly makeshift, perhaps not entirely up to it. I've seldom found the results particularly useful, myself, as thematically interesting as primary oneirics can be. Though mainly in how visually banal they generally are, as opposed to the considerable glamor we all seem to imagine they had, as we remember them."

81.

ALAMO

ow?" Flynne asked, surprised, around a mouthful of banana, as the rental crested the high point of Porter, not very high but she knew it from cycling. A perfect day, to look at. Sunny, eleven thirty, headed into town with Janice driving a rented cardboard. Except for Netherton, the night before, telling her the world was ending. Or that it always had been, or something.

"Nope," Janice said. "Burton put it up there, yesterday."

Flynne squinted back at it, up in what had been a hay lot, before developers bought it and then didn't build anything. She thought she saw the head move. "No shit? A drone?"

"More like a satellite," Janice said. "Serious-ass sensing capabilities. But drones can come and charge off it, too."

Flynne finished the last of the banana. "Guess he didn't get it at Hefty," she said, when she'd swallowed.

"Got it off Griff, maybe. Or one of your many lawyers."

"How many's that?"

"Enough to buy out all the chili dogs from Jimmy's, noon and night. They preorder, send drones to pick 'em up. Danny went to Commercial Kitchen Warehouse for new chili pots." Danny was the man who ran Jimmy's, a grandnephew of the actual Jimmy, who her mother remembered from when she was little. "He wanted to put his price up, but Burton had Tommy tell him not to. So I think you're subsidizing the chili dogs, kinda."

"Why?"

"So's not to put the town off Coldiron. They already think it's about Leon. Conspiracy theory's that he won a lot more in that lottery than the state let on."

"No sense in that."

"Conspiracy theory's got to be simple. Sense doesn't come into it. People are more scared of how complicated shit actually is than they ever are about whatever's supposed to be behind the conspiracy."

"What's the theory?"

"Not that firmed up, yet. Inquiring minds, now, on the steps outside Jimmy's, say Pickett was on Homes' payroll all along."

"They think Homes was building drugs?"

"How else do you finance the United Nations taking over?"

"There's hardly any UN left, Janice. Rotary or Kiwanis would be more like it."

"UN's got deep roots in the demonology." Janice slowed to let a feral orange tabby slink, belly down, across the road, giving them the stinkeye. "Madison says not letting Danny raise prices came down from your friends in the future."

"Micromanaging." Flynne was watching the beginning of town come into sight.

"If they'd just slow the changes down, I wouldn't mind a little micromanagement. Town's not the way you left it."

"I subbed for Burton last Tuesday night, first time. Sunday morning, now."

"And us not in church. Little while, big difference. I've been watching it, watching the news too. Looks the same, but it's not."

They were pulling into the mall. Flynne saw cell towers and antennas, on top of Sushi Barn, that hadn't been there before, and shiny German cars in most of the spaces, with go-faster folds and Florida plates. "Whoa," she said.

"Or doesn't look the same, depending." Janice parked in a space in front of Sushi Barn. "Hong's doing fine. Sushi Barn's the lawyers' other favorite, plus it's open all night. They're even buying his t-shirts. And he got some compensation for you sticking all those antennas up there."

"Not from me."

"Far as Hong's concerned, you. You're CCO, your sig's on all that correspondence."

"Is that legal?"

"Talk to the future. Burton's got his hands full with the paramilitary side." Janice got out, so Flynne did too, the Wheelie Boy tucked under her arm like a bottle of wine.

Macon and Carlos were coming along the mall-front sidewalk toward them, Macon in his old jeans and a Sushi Barn t-shirt, red on white, with a fake Japanese font and a bad drawing of a barn with a single huge slice of maki roll in front of it. Carlos, in cammies and that soft body armor, had his bullpup under his arm. She knew that was legal, constitutionally and everything, but it still looked wrong here. The week before, none of them would've worn camo to town, let alone carried a rifle. So now Carlos was in body armor, even if it was the kind that looked like skater clothes. They each had a Viz on. Macon gave her a big smile, Carlos a smaller one, but Carlos was looking around. It dawned on her that he was entirely ready, right then, to shoot somebody. "You put all that shit up on top of Hong's?" she asked Macon.

"Klein Cruz Vermette," he said.

"Janice says there's more of them here now."

"Lawyers and paper is what Coldiron mostly consists of, still. That and equity."

"They're not all in that stinky storefront, are they?"

"Hardly any. Rented smaller spaces all over town. Better for us if they're distributed, and mostly away from what we do here."

"Which would be, exactly?"

"Got Conner up the line, currently, training on something."

"In his peripheral?"

"Something less intuitive to operate, seems like, but you ask him. Been there about six hours straight. They just told us he'll be back soon. Then he gets to meet his hot nurse."

"What hot nurse?"

"Griff sent her," said Janice.

"Nurse," said Carlos, "my ass."

"Carlos thinks she's an operator," Macon said. "She says she's a paramedic. No reason she can't be both."

"Stone killer," said Carlos, like that might be his favorite flavor of pie.

"Griff," Flynne said. "Name keeps coming up."

"Let's talk inside," said Macon, and led the way back toward the space next to Fab. It didn't look very different, just that the outside of the windows and door had been washed.

Inside, it was different. Those interior barricades of Tyvek-bagged roofing shingles, to start with, that she remembered Janice telling her about. And she saw that Madison had sprayed about three inches of Burton's Hefty polymer on the inside of the windows, which wouldn't keep a bullet out, but would stop glass flying, and then this internal Alamo, the bags stacked like giant bricks, in walls about three feet thick, maybe seven feet tall. She guessed it went straight around the inside, with an opening for the front door, probably one for the hole cut through into Fab, and maybe one in back. The front door had been pasted over, inside, with layers of what Carlos's vest was lined with, like thin sheets of greenish-purple cotton candy. She'd never understood the physics, just that it somehow translated the kinetic energy of a bullet into momentary steely rigidity, and could sometimes break your arm, doing that, depending on various things. There was a lot of the bland Homes blue of the zip ties they'd used to fasten her to the table at Pickett's, mostly all these tarps, hung from rafters the acoustic tile ceiling had covered before. She saw a gray wasp nest up there, from however many summers ago. But that dead plumbing smell she'd noticed before was gone too, and she was glad of that.

"Departments," Macon said. "That's our legal, there." He pointed into a space where she could see Brent Vermette, who'd come to the meeting at Hefty, in pressed khakis and a Sushi Barn t-shirt like Macon's, talking to a girl with short red hair. "You like your Wheelie?" Macon asked. "See you brought it with you."

"Talked to Netherton on it, last night."

"How was that?"

"Either depressing and scared the fuck out of me, or sort of how I'd always figured things are?"

He looked at her.

"Complicated," she said. "Conner in the back?" She started that way, Janice behind her.

He caught up with them. "Lowbeer wants you up there in about an hour. You can do it from here."

"Burton here?"

"Over at Pickett's."

She stopped. "Why?"

"Tommy deputized him. Homes found Jackman."

"You didn't tell me," she said to Janice.

"Getting harder to prioritize," Janice said. "Homes found enough of him at Pickett's to make the identification. Would've been dental records and a belt buckle, before they invented DNA."

"How's he taking that, Tommy?"

"He's acting sheriff, with Jackman gone," Macon said. "Sheriff Tommy. Busy man."

"How about you?"

"Wakey," he said. "Haven't been sleeping."

"That shit makes me too crazy, Macon. Don't do it."

"Not builder's wakey," he said. "Government wakey. From Griff." He hitched up his Sushi Barn shirt, showing her a little one-inch yellow triangular patch on his stomach, a vertical green line running from base to apex.

"Who's this Griff?"

"From England. Diplomatic or something. D.C. Has access to things."

"What kind of things?"

"Funniest things I've run across, myself."

"What do they tell you about him?"

"Nothing. They sent him, from D.C. Reece grabbed you, Lowbeer took over from Ash. Felt like she already had him in place, in case of whatever. If you hadn't had that pill in you, I'd guess Griff would have called down all manner of government funniness to find you. He got Clovis in to mind Conner, when he's under the crown." He looked back, where Carlos had stayed put by the door. "Carlos thinks she's a ninja."

"Clovis is a boy's name," Flynne said. "Some king, back in France."

"From Austin. Says she's named after the town in New Mexico."

"What's she like?"

"Easier to introduce you." He pulled a tarp aside. There were the three hospital beds, in a row, with Conner in one of them, in his Polartec but under a white sheet, eyes closed, wearing a Snow White crown.

"Clovis," Macon said, "Flynne Fisher. Flynne, Clovis Raeburn."

The woman beside the bed was a little older than Flynne, taller, and looked like she'd be good on a skateboard. Lanky, black-eyed, black hair cut short on the sides and up in a little fin on top. "Wheelie Boy," Clovis said. "Had one in high school. You into collectibles?"

"Macon gave it to me. You born in Clovis?"

"Conceived. Mom figured it was really Portales, but she didn't want Dad naming me that."

"Getting along with Conner?"

"Hasn't opened his eyes since I got here." Clovis wore narrow stretch cammies and one of those shirts they'd worn under the old rigid plate armor, sleeves like a combat jacket but the torso like a clingy jersey top. She had a big first-aid pouch slung in front of her crotch, the red cross suppressed, two shades of coyote brown. She came over and shook hands.

"My friend Janice," Flynne said, and watched them shake.

"Vermette's got about three hundred documents he needs signed and notarized," Macon said. "We'll set a table up in here and you can talk while you do that."

"Ladies," Conner said, from the bed, "which one of you wants to help me with this catheter?"

Clovis looked at Flynne. "Who's the douche-canoe?"

"No idea," said Flynne.

"Me neither," said Janice.

Flynne went over to the bed. "What were you in, up there? Macon says you're training."

"Kind of like a washing machine, inertial propulsion. Big-ass flywheels inside."

"Washing machine?"

"About three hundred pounds. Big red cube. I'd just learned to balance it on one corner, then rotate, when they made me come back."

"What's it for?"

"Fuck if I know. Wouldn't want to meet one in a dark alley." He lowered his voice. "Macon's high on a government stimulant. Like builders' best, but minus the jitters. None of that dys-fucking-functional kind of paranoia."

"Not like your own super-functional kind?"

He looked from her to Macon. "Won't give me any," he said.

"Doctor's orders," Macon said. "And anyway they engineered every last thing out of it that people do drugs for. Except staying awake."

"You quit being so whiny-assed special," Clovis advised Conner, having stepped closer to his bed, "like every other butt-hurt Haptic Recon pussy it's been my misfortune to meet, and maybe I'll get you a nice cup of coffee."

Conner looked up at her like he'd discovered a kindred spirit.

82.

THE NASTINESS

T *he lawn in Flynne's garden stretched to the edges of the world. The moon was a floodlight, too bright. Carbon-black seas, flat as paper. He couldn't find her. He rolled forward, on ridiculous wheels, head bobbing. Lowbeer was monitoring this dream, he knew, and wondered how he knew. The craters of the moon becoming the coronet—*

Her sigil. "Yes?" Expecting the Gobiwagen's dome as he opened his eyes, but a different dome, moving, rain, streaks of sunlight through cloud, wet gray masonry, black-painted mullions, the branches of plane trees. He was slumped back in a chair, something cradling his neck and head, but now that withdrew.

"Sorry to wake you," Lowbeer said. "Or not to wake you, actually. That would be the Medici's dosing, scheduled to rouse you now."

He was in her car again, seated at the table, opposite Flynne's peripheral, which, though it smiled at him now in AI reflex, wasn't Flynne. The upper part of the vehicle, previously windowless, was now completely transparent, raindrops seeming to roll across some invisible bubble of force. "Can anyone see in?" he asked.

"Of course not. You were asleep. It seemed an unnecessarily boring journey for the peripheral. Difficult not to anthropomorphize something that looks so entirely human."

Netherton rubbed his neck, where some temporary extrusion from the chairback had propped his head at what the car had deemed a comfortable angle. "Who put me in here?" he asked.

"Ossian and Ash, after you'd had a good long sleep in the Mercedes. Ash operated the exoskeleton, via a homunculus, in order not to leave Mr. Murphy with all of the heavy lifting."

Netherton peered out through the rain, trying to recognize the street. "Where am I going?"

"Soho Square. Flynne will join you there. Before she meets Daedra, I want you to explain the role she'll be playing, your neoprimitive curator. Her theory about Daedra's artistic evolution."

"I haven't made it up yet, entirely."

"You need to do that, and to share it with Flynne. She must be able to make conversation about that, convincingly. Coffee."

A circular opening expanded on the tabletop, a steaming cup emerging, as on a tiny stage elevator. He saw the peripheral looking at the cup, restrained an urge to offer her one. It. Her. "I never fail to impressed with Ash's medicine," he said.

"That in itself is probably not a good sign," said Lowbeer, "though otherwise I'm pleased to hear it."

"Where are you?"

"With Clovis," she said, "virtually. She's refreshing my memory. Her own as well, of course. That really was quite a vile period, Flynne's day. We tend to forget, all that came after having so overshadowed it. I scarcely grasped its nastiness, then, even with my resources at the time."

The car turned a corner. He still had no idea where they were. Lifting the steaming cup, he admired the steadiness of his hand. The peripheral was watching. He winked. It smiled. He smiled back, feeling obscurely guilty, and sipped his coffee.

83.
ALL THE KINGDOMS OF
THE WORLD IN A MOMENT
OF TIME

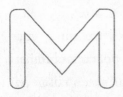acon had been kidding, about the three hundred signatures, but she'd quit counting after about thirty. She was almost through the stack now, the red-haired girl notarizing each one, with a stamp and a signature of her own and a spring-loaded seal, after Flynne had signed.

They'd set up a card table for her in the space with the beds. Janice and Clovis were propped on the edge of the bed nearest Conner's, facing him, legs out straight, and Macon was seated beside Flynne on a folding chair.

"I should be reading these," Flynne said, "but I wouldn't understand them anyway."

"The way things are going," Macon said, "you don't have a lot of choice."

"How are they going?"

"Well," leaning back to briefly consult something in his Viz, "there haven't been any catastrophic market imbalances yet, but it's early days. It's a race to the top, and the way we're doing it, the way our competitor's doing it, is seriously stressing the system."

"What's the top?"

"Won't know until we get there, and if we aren't on it, we'll likely be dead."

"Who's the competitor?"

"They don't have a name. More the numbered account school of funny. Shells within shells. That's us too, mainly, but if you get through all of our shells, there's Milagros Coldiron. Just a name, and nobody knows what it means, but at least we got one. With Pickett gone, we lost our governor for a while, but then Griff went back to D.C. and fixed that up from there, so in a way we're already up to federal."

Flynne thought of fists stacking up around the handle of a softball bat. The girl passed her another contract, sliding the signed one out of the way, stamping and signing it herself, smacking her seal.

"I think we're pretty close to somebody coming after us here," Macon said. "If it's unemployed vets, like those last two out at your place, Burton might be able to handle it. If it's state police, or Homes, some other federal agency, or for that matter the Marines, no use even fighting. Why we've got lawyers out the ass." He looked at the red-haired notary. "Pardon the expression," he said, but she just kept signing and sealing. "Homes has its funny side," he said to Flynne. "Look where they are right now."

"Pickett's?"

"First time, ever. Pickett was building when we were kids. His place hadn't looked anything like a house for twenty years. Looked like what it was. Took the scale of that explosion to get Homes over there."

"Don't tell me Homes is behind all the drug building. That's a conspiracy theory."

"Not behind, but there can be accommodation. Wait and see who has a quiet word with Tommy, now Jackman's gone."

Flynne had signed three more contracts while he spoke. "My hand's starting to hurt," she said to the girl.

"Only four more," the girl said. "You might consider simplifying your signature. You'll be doing a lot of this."

Flynne looked over at Conner. Clovis had mounted a Thermos cup on one of the bed's articulated equipment stands. Conner was sucking black coffee through a transparent tube. Flynne signed the last four contracts and passed them to the girl. Stood up. "Back in a few minutes," she said. "Macon." She ducked around a blue tarp, hearing the thump of the notary's seal, Macon behind her. "Where can we have a private conversation?" she asked him.

"Fab," he said, pointing at another tarp.

Fab's back room looked the same as ever, aside from a few more printers and the hole sawn in the wall. She looked into the front of the store, saw a girl she didn't know behind the counter, looking down at her phone. "Where's Shaylene?"

"Clanton," Macon said.

"Doing what?"

"More lawyers. She's opening two new Fabs there."

"I just get bits and pieces. What's been happening here?"

"All anybody gets." He took out his Viz, put it in his pocket, rubbed his eye. She saw his tiredness, propped up by the government wakey.

"Why's there a fort made out of building supplies, next door?"

"Coldiron's global valuation's billions, now."

"Billions?"

"Lots of 'em, but I don't want to give you a nosebleed. Kind of try to ignore it, myself. It'll be more, tomorrow. Shit's exponential. Not all that obviously, because we need to avoid that, as long as we can. Burton's getting constant advice from up the line, and having Madison build those walls was their idea."

"How come not in here?"

"They wouldn't want you over on this side. Wall's there to protect you from some kind of drive-by. Not that any amount of fort-building would make a difference, if somebody big enough decided to hit us. Smart munitions make any thickness of anything a joke, and the roof here might as well be cardboard. But they must've figured it needed doing, in case somebody sees an opportunity to lowball the job, and just sends more assholes from Memphis."

"Robot cow up in the pasture, driving in. Janice said Burton put it there."

"Part of our system upgrade. I voted for it looking like a zebra, myself."

"Tommy still over at Pickett's?"

"Burton too. Better them than me."

"What do you think's going to happen?"

"You and Conner and Burton are doing something soon, right? Up there."

"I'm supposed to go to a party with Wilf. See if I recognize anybody. Conner's going as our bodyguard. Not sure about Burton."

"That'll be it, then."

"Be what?"

"Some kind of move. A gamble. That that'll change things, whatever it is. Otherwise, what's happening here's unsustainable. Something'll give, blow out. Could be local, could be the national economy, could be the world's."

"If what Wilf told me was right, that could be the least of our worries."

"What's that?"

"Said everything fucks up here, pretty soon. Goes down the tubes for decades. Most everybody dies."

He looked at her. "Why there's hardly any people, up there?"

"They get you there yet?"

"No, but Edward and I read between the lines. In the tech stuff they show us. Kind of inherent history, if you read it right. But they did get themselves some super-fresh tech, whatever else was going on."

"Didn't get it fast enough, according to Wilf."

"They want you back. Just about now. You and Conner. Clovis'll mind you."

"What's she about, anyway?"

"Carlos might be right. That EMT bag of hers is mainly full of gun. Once you've met Griff, she makes more sense. I think he's the same as her, but management."

She looked around at the room. Remembered trimming the afterbirth off Christmas ornaments, toys, smoothing and putting the pieces together, eating takeout from Sushi Barn and bullshitting with Shaylene. It suddenly seemed like all of that had been so easy. When the sun came up, you just got on your bike, rode home, and not past a place where Conner had put bullets into the heads of four men, who'd have killed you and your mother and Burton, probably Leon too, for the money somebody promised them for doing it.

"Leon saw two boys from Luke 4:5 on Main Street last night, outside the old Farmer's Bank," he said.

"How'd he know? They have signs?"

"No signs. Said he knows because he'd happened to have a long look at both of them, in Davisville, while Homes had Burton. They were holding up a sign in front of the VA hospital and he was sitting on a bench there, just the other side of the police tape."

"They recognize him?"

"Didn't think so."

"Why would they be here?"

"Leon figured they were looking for Burton. Who did cause some sharp discomfort to their boy in Davisville. Why Homes sat him to chill in the middle of the high school track. Why they call it that, anyway, Luke 4:5?"

"'Cause that's one spooky-ass Bible verse, probably."

"It's a white people thing, Luke 4:5? Never paid 'em any attention."

"'And the devil, taking him up into a high mountain, showed unto him all the kingdoms of the world in a moment of time.'"

"Know scripture?"

"Know that one. Burton's prone to recite it if he hears they plan a protest. He's got some fucked-up thing going about them. Or maybe just an excuse to go and kick somebody's ass."

"We've got people keeping an eye out around town," Macon said, digging in a front jeans pocket for his Viz. He blew on it, put it over his eye. She saw him blink, behind it. "They're ready for you up the line, about now."

84.

SOHO SQUARE

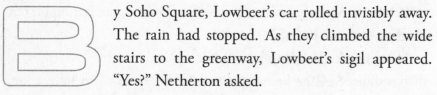y Soho Square, Lowbeer's car rolled invisibly away. The rain had stopped. As they climbed the wide stairs to the greenway, Lowbeer's sigil appeared. "Yes?" Netherton asked.

"They're ready," Lowbeer said. "Find a seat for her."

Netherton took the peripheral's hand, guided it to the nearest bench, one facing the forest that led, along what had been a length of Oxford Street, to Hyde Park. He gestured for it to sit. The bench vibrated briefly in anticipation, shedding drops of rain. The peripheral sat. Looked up at him. He was, he realized, waiting for it to drop this elaborate pretext of being an automaton, driven by AI. Not that she'd then be Flynne, but somehow the woman whose face this must be. "Have you learned who it was modeled after?" he asked Lowbeer.

"Hermès has a privacy policy, regarding bespoke peripherals. I could bypass that, but in this case I prefer not to. It might tip our hand."

The peripheral wore black tights, black walking boots with large silver buckles, and a narrow knee-length cape the color of graphite. "What exactly am I to do, here?" Netherton asked.

"Have an outing. Stroll to Hyde Park. Then we'll see. Answer her questions as best you can. I'm not expecting her to be terribly convincing as a neoprimitive curator, but do what you can. She'll be there to make an identification. Assuming she doesn't make it on walking in the door, I want the masquerade to remain viable for as long as possible."

"I've told Daedra that Annie's very shy in her presence, out of an excess of admiration. That may help."

"It may. Please ask the peripheral to close its eyes."

"Close your eyes," he said.

The peripheral did. Watching its face, he thought he actually saw Flynne arrive, a second's confusion in facial micro-musculature and then the eyes sprang open. "Holy shit," she said, "is that a house, or trees?"

He looked over his shoulder, toward the greenway. "A house grown from trees. A sort of playhouse, actually. Public."

"Those trees look old."

"They aren't. Their growth was augmented by assemblers. Sped up, then stabilized. They were that size when I was a child."

"Doors, windows—"

"They grew that way, directed by assemblers."

She stood, seemed to test the pavement. "Where are we?"

"Soho. Soho Square. Lowbeer suggests we walk along this greenway, to Hyde Park."

"Greenway?"

"A forest, but linear. Oxford Street was ruined here, variously, in the jackpot. Mainly department stores. The architect had assemblers eat their ruins back. Carved them into what amounts to a very long planter for the trees, with a central pathway elevated above the original level of the street—"

"Department stores? Like Hefty Mart?"

"I don't know."

"Why did they want a forest instead?"

"It wasn't a very beautiful street to begin with, and hadn't fared well in the jackpot. The buildings didn't lend themselves to repurposing. Selfridges had actually been a single private residence, briefly—"

"Fridges?"

"A department store. But the vogue for residences on that scale was brief, limited to a final desperate wave of offshore capital. I don't think we have department stores, actually."

"Malls?"

"What about them?" he asked, puzzled, but then remembered the difference in usage. "You saw Cheapside. That's one, of sorts. A destination, select associational retail. Portobello, Burlington Arcade . . ."

She looked around. Kept turning. "We're in the biggest city in Europe. Aside from you, I haven't seen one living soul."

"There's a man, right there." Netherton pointed. "Sitting on a bench. I think he's brought his dog."

"No traffic. Dead quiet."

"Prior to regreening, the majority of public transport was via trains, in tunnels."

"The tube."

"Yes. And that's all still there, and more, though it's generally not used for public transport. It can configure a train, should you want one. People generally go to Cheapside by period train." That had been how he and his mother had gone.

"Seen a few big trucks."

"Moving goods from the underground to where they're ultimately needed. We've fewer private vehicles. Cabs. Otherwise, walking or cycling."

"Those are the tallest trees I've ever seen."

"Come and see. It's more impressive from the greenway proper." He led the way, trying to remember when he'd last been here. When they reached the greenway, between the trees, he indicated the direction of Hyde Park.

"You say they aren't real, the trees?"

"They're real, but their growth was augmented, engineered. A few are quasi-biological megavolume carbon collectors that look like trees." Something chinged, behind them. A goggled rider shot past, pedaling hard on a black bicycle, a mud-spattered beige trench coat flapping out behind.

"How did they make this?"

The trees, many of them taller than the buildings they'd replaced, were still dripping; larger, more widely distributed drops. One went down the back of Netherton's jacket. Toward Hyde Park, in the high canopy of branches, there was a suggestion of cloud. "I can open a feed for you, and show you, if you like."

"WN?" she asked, evidently seeing his sigil as their phones connected. "That's you?"

"It is. Let's go along to Hyde Park, and I'll show you feeds, how they did it." Without thinking, having led the peripheral to and from Lowbeer's car, he took her hand, instantly aware of his mistake.

Her eyes met his, alarmed perhaps. He felt her hand tense, as if she were about to withdraw it, or perhaps to shake his. "Okay," she said. "Show me."

And then they were walking, hand in hand.

"You looked ridiculous," she said, "on the Wheelie Boy."

"I assumed as much."

85.
FUTURE PEOPLE

He said they built all this with what he called assemblers, which she guessed were what she'd seen kill his ex's sister.

What he called a feed was a window in her vision, not so big that she couldn't see to walk, but watching it and looking where she was going could be tricky. Like a Viz would be, she guessed, but without having to wear it.

Architects had told the assemblers to cut a cross-section, down the length of the original street, in the shape of a big circle, a long central tubular emptiness. The buildings had been ruins to begin with, only partly standing, so the profile the assemblers cut away had mostly been less than the bottom half of that circle. Where the cut had gone through, regardless of the material encountered, the surface it left was slick as glass. What you'd expect with marble, or metal, but weird with old red brick, or wood. Assembler-cut brick looked like fresh-cut liver, assembler-cut wood slick as the paneling in Lev's RV. Not that you saw much of that now, because the next step had been to overgrow the length of the cut with these fairy-tale trees, trunks too wide to be real, roots running everywhere, down into the ruins behind the edge of the cut, with their canopy so far above that you couldn't see the highest branches at all.

Hybrid, Wilf said. Something Amazonian, something Indian, and the assemblers to push it all. The bark was like the skin of elephants, finer-textured on the twisted roots.

He used his hands when he talked. He'd had to let go of hers to explain the feed of how they built this, but she'd found holding hands comforting, just to touch something alive here, even if it wasn't her own hand she was doing it with. She had a different feeling about him, since he'd told her about the jackpot. She thought that that was about how she'd seen he was fucked up by the story, how he didn't know he was. He put a lot of energy into convincing people, and that was his job, or why he had that job, but really he was always convincing himself, maybe just that he was there, whatever he was trying to convince you. "The one whose party we're going to, she's your ex?" she asked. The feed had ended, the window had closed, his badge had blinked out.

"I don't think of her that way," he said. "It was quite brief, extremely ill-advised."

"Who advised you?"

"No one."

"She some kind of artist?"

"Yes."

"What kind?"

"She has herself tattooed," he said. "But it's more complicated than that."

"Like with rings and things?"

"No. The tattoos aren't the product. She herself is the product. Her life."

"What they used to call reality shows?"

"I don't know. Why did they stop calling them that?"

"Because it got to be all there is, except *Ciencia Loca* and anime, and those Brazilian serials. Old-fashioned, to call it that."

He stopped, reading something she couldn't see. "Yes. She's descended from that, in a sense. Reality television. It merged with politics. Then with performance art."

They walked on. "I think that already happened, back home," she said. It smelled amazing, in here. The wet trees, she guessed. "Doesn't she run out of skin?"

"Each of her pieces is a complete epidermis, toes to the base of the neck. Reflecting her life experience during the period of the work. She has that removed, preserved, and manufactures facsimiles, miniatures, which people subscribe to. Annie Courrèges, who you'll be pretending to be, has a complete set, though she can't afford them on her salary."

"Why does she?"

"She doesn't," he said. "I made that up, to tell Daedra."

"Why?"

"To get her to put her clothes back on."

She side-eyed him. "She has herself skinned?"

"While having a fresh epidermis grown. Removal and replacement are conterminous, virtually a single operation."

"She sore, after?"

"I've not been around her when she's done that. She'd done it recently, though, before I was hired. Clean epidermal slate. She'd agreed, after meeting with you, or rather with Annie Courrèges and two other neoprimitivist curators, not to be tattooed till completion of our project."

"What are they?"

"Who?"

"Neoprimitivists."

"Neoprimitivist curators. Neoprimitives either survived the jackpot on their own or have opted out of the global system. The ones our project hinged on were volunteers. An ecology cult. Curators study neoprimitives, experience and collect their culture."

Three cyclists were approaching from the opposite direction, brightly dressed. Children, she supposed, as they sped past, in what she took to be superhero costumes. "You don't seem to like it up here," she said.

"The greenway?"

"The future. Neither does Ash."

"Ash makes an avocation of not liking it," he said.

"Know her before she got that done to her eyes?"

"I've known Lev since before he hired the two of them. She came that way. You take what you can get, in good technicals."

"What's he do, Lev?" She wasn't sure that rich people necessarily did anything.

"Family's powerful. Old klept. Russian. His two older brothers seem likely to sustain that. He's a sort of scout for the family. Looks for things they might invest in. Not about profit so much as keeping fresh. Sources of novelty."

She looked up into the branches, which seemed to be dripping less now. Something with red wings went flopping there, the size of a large bird but the wings were a butterfly's. "This isn't novelty to you, is it?"

"No," he said, "it isn't. That's why there are neoprimitivist curators. To scoop up any random bits of novelty the neoprimitives might produce, vile as they are. That was why we were working with Daedra. Technological novelty in that case, more easily commodified than usual. Three million tons of recycled polymer, in the form of a single piece of floating real estate. That's Hyde Park there, ahead."

And she saw they were nearing the end of the greenway, the trees less tall, more thinly planted, opening out. She could hear a squawking, like a loudspeaker. "What's that?"

"Speaker's Corner," he said. "They're all mad. It's allowed."

"What's that white thing, like part of a building?"

"Marble Arch."

"Has a couple of arches. Like they took it off something else and sort of left it there."

"They did," he said. "But then it probably made more sense, visually, with traffic going through it."

They were out of the greenway now, descending widening stairs to the level of the park.

"The one who's talking," she said, "he's got to be on stilts, but it doesn't look like it." The spidery figure, she guessed, would be close to ten feet tall.

"A peripheral," he said. The tall thing's round pink head was fronted with a sort of squared-off trumpet, that same pink, through which it blared down, incomprehensibly, at the small crowd of figures surrounding it, at least one of which seemed to be a penguin, though as tall as she was. The tall speaker wore a tight black suit, its arms and legs very narrow. She couldn't understand what it was saying, but thought she made out the word "nomenclature." "They're all mad," he said. "They might all be peripherals. Harmless, though. This way."

"Where are we going?"

"I thought we could walk to the Serpentine. See the ships. Small replicas. They sometime enact historic battles. The *Graf Spee* is particularly good."

"Is that speaker making any sense at all?"

"It's a tradition," he said, and led her along a smooth gravel path, beige. And there were people here, walking in the park, sitting on benches, pushing buggies. They didn't look particularly like future people to her. She guessed Ash did, more than anyone else she'd seen here, if you didn't count the ten-foot trumpet-head Wilf said was a peripheral. She could still hear him ranting, behind them.

"What will it be like, when we go to your ex's party?"

"I wish you wouldn't call her that. Daedra West. I don't know, exactly. Powerful people will be there, according to Lev and Lowbeer. The Remembrancer himself, possibly."

"Who's that?"

"An official of the City. I don't think I could explain to you what his traditional function was. Originally, I think, to remind royalty of an ancient debt. Later, entirely symbolic. Since the jackpot, best not spoken of."

"Does he know Daedra?"

"I've no idea. I've not been to that sort of occasion, and glad of it."

"You scared?"

He stopped on the path, looked at her. "I suppose I'm anxious, yes. This whole business is entirely outside my experience."

"Mine too," she said. She took his hand. Squeezed it.

"I'm sorry we've invaded your life," he said. "It was lovely, where you were."

"It was? I mean, is?"

"Your mother's garden, in the moonlight . . ."

"Compared to this?"

"Yes. I've always dreamed about it, in a way, the past. I didn't fully realize that, somehow. Now I can't believe I've actually seen it."

"You can see it more," she said. "I've got the Wheelie Boy, at Fab."

"At what?"

"Forever Fab. I work there. Did. Before this all started."

"That's what I mean," he said, his hand tensing. "We're changing it all."

"We're all poor, except Pickett, who's maybe dead now, and one or two others. Not like here. Not a lot to do. I would've joined the Army when Burton went in the Marines, but our mom needed taking care of. Still does." She looked around at the wide flat park, the lawns, paths like something in a geometry class. "This is the biggest park I've ever seen. Bigger than the one by the river in Clanton, with the Civil War fort. And that greenway's probably the craziest thing I've really ever seen, that people built. That the only one?"

"From here, we could walk greenways to Richmond Park, Hampstead Heath, and on, from either. Fourteen in all. And the hundred rivers, all recovered . . ."

"Glassed over, lit up?"

"Some of the largest, yes." He smiled, but stopped when it seemed to surprise him. She hadn't seen him smile much, not that way. He let go of her hand, but not all at once.

He started walking again. She walked beside him.

Macon's red nubbin badge appeared. "I'm seeing Macon's badge," she said.

"Say hello," he said.

"Hello? Macon?"

"Hey," said Macon, "got this situation getting going. Clovis wants you back."

"What?"

"Luke 4:5's outside with the signs and shit, here. You and your brother and your mother, you're on the signs. Cousin Leon too."

"The fuck?"

"Looks like Coldiron is their new thing they've decided God hates."

"Where's Burton?"

"On his way back from Pickett's. Just started."

"Shit," Flynne said.

86.

CHATELAINE

L ooking up from the battle taking place on the Serpentine, he saw Ash approaching, in various tones of black and darkest sepia, along the pathway's beige gravel, as if on hidden casters.

He'd been regretting Flynne missing the miniatures, though he himself preferred steam to sail, and the drama of long-range guns to these sparkings of tiny cannon. But the water in the region of the battle had scaled waves, and miniature cloud, and something about that always delighted him. The peripheral, seated on the bench beside him, seemed to be following it as well, though he knew attention to moving objects was just a way of emulating sentience.

"Lowbeer wants you back at Lev's," said Ash, coming to a halt in front of their bench. Her skirts and narrow jacket were a baroquely complicated patchwork of raw-edged fragments, some of which, though no doubt flexible, resembled darkened tin. She wore a more ornate reticule than usual, covered in mourning beads and hung with a sterling affair he knew to be a chatelaine, the organizer for a set of Victorian ladies' household accessories. Or not so Victorian, he saw, as a sterling spider with a faceted jet abdomen, on one of the chatelaine's fine chain retainers, picked its agile way up from the jacket's waist, its multiple eyes tiny rhinestones.

"Flynne seemed worried, to be called back," he said, looking up at her. "The timing was unfortunate. I was about to explain the framing narrative for Annie."

"I've explained to her that you're a publicist," she said. "She seemed to understand it in terms of some already very degraded paradigm of celebrity, so it was relatively easy."

"Public relations isn't one of your areas of expertise," he said. "I hope you haven't left her with misconceptions."

Ash reached out, brushed the peripheral's bangs aside. It looked up at her, eyes calm and bright. "She does bring something to it, doesn't she?" she said to him. "I've seen you noticing."

"Is she in more danger now, there?"

"I suppose so, though it's difficult to quantify. Some apparently powerful entity, based here, wants her dead, there, and brings increasingly massive resources to the task, there. We're there to counter that, but in our competition with them, we've stressed her world's economy. That stress is problematic, as it can and probably soon will produce more chaotic change."

A sudden sharp crack from the battle in the Serpentine. Children cheered, nearby. He saw that one of the ships had lost its central mast to a cannonball, as had happened long ago, he'd no idea where, according to whatever account was being reenacted. He stood, extended his hand to the peripheral, which took it. He helped it to rise, which it did gracefully.

"I don't like it, that she's sending you to Daedra's," said Ash, fixing him with her vertically bifurcated gaze. It occurred to him that he'd now been around her so much that he scarcely noticed her eyes. "It's almost certain that Daedra, or one of her associates, is our competitor in the stub. They may be unable to do more to Flynne, here, than destroy her peripheral, in which case she finds herself back in the stub, however painful the experience may have been. The same for Conner, in brother Anton's dancing master. But you'll attend in person. Physically present, entirely vulnerable."

"Tactically," he said, "I don't see what other choice she has." He looked at her, struck with the idea that she might be genuinely concerned for him.

"You haven't considered the danger you'll be placing yourself in?"

"I suppose I've tried not to consider it too closely. But then what would happen to Flynne, if I were to refuse? To her brother, mother? Her whole world?"

Her four pupils bored into his, her white face perfectly immobile. "Altruism? What's happening to you?"

"I don't know," he said.

87.

THE ANTIDOTE FOR
PARTY TIME

lovis Raeburn had beautiful skin. When Flynne opened her eyes, Clovis was right there, up close, like she was looking at Flynne's autonomic cutout, or its cable. Easiest transition yet, from sitting on a bench beside a path in that Hyde Park to propped on pillows in a brand-new hospital bed. Like somersaulting backward, but not in a bad way. "Hey," Clovis said, straightening up as she saw Flynne's eyes were open.

"What's going on?"

Clovis was pulling the two halves of something apart, packaging of some kind. "Griff says the competition's hired Luke to make us look bad. I say anybody they protest just looks better."

"Macon said Burton's on his way back from Pickett's."

"In a deputized car," said Clovis. "Been an orgy of car deputizing, over there. Pickett's employees, the ones still being shoveled out of the pile, had their cars on the lot there." She extracted something small from the packaging: circular, flat, bright pink. She peeled its backing off, reached under the hem of Flynne's t-shirt, and pressed the adhesive down, just left of Flynne's navel.

"What's that?" Flynne asked, raising her head off the pillow, against the weight of the crown, trying to see it. Clovis hiked up the bottom of her own combat shirt. On abs you could do laundry on, the pink dot, with two sharp red lines crossing in the center.

"The antidote for party time," Clovis said, "but I'll let Griff explain that. Just you keep yours on." She lifted the crown from Flynne's head and put it carefully down on what looked like an open disposable diaper, on the table to the left of the bed.

Flynne looked from the crown to Conner, in the next bed, under his own crown.

"Better he's still up there," said Clovis, "considering the situation. He does have a proven potential to make things crazier."

Flynne sat up. A hospital bed made you feel like you needed someone's permission to do that. Then Hong walked into her line of sight, a plastic sack of takeout dangling from either hand. He wore a Viz and a dark green t-shirt with COLDIRON USA on it in white, the logo she'd seen on the envelope in Burton's trailer, that first night. She realized he'd come in through a narrow vertical gap, in the wall of shingles, to the left of her bed. "Hey," he said.

"There's a secret passage from Sushi Barn, now?" she asked.

"Part of the deal for the antennas. Weren't those e-mails from you?"

"Guess I've got secretaries and shit."

"Have to be able to get food over here," Clovis said. "Always have a few of Burton's boys sitting in there, watching out."

"Getting fat," said Hong, grinning, and went out, past a blue tarp.

"Food's for Burton and whoever," Clovis said. "You hungry?"

"Might be," Flynne said, picking up her Wheelie Boy from the chair where she'd left it.

"I'm here with sleeping beauty, you need me," Clovis said. "True that you've got your own whole other body, up there?"

"More or less. Somebody built it, but you couldn't tell."

"Look like you?"

"No," Flynne said, "prettier and tittier."

"Go on," Clovis said, "pull the other one."

Flynne followed the smell of Sushi Barn. The bags were on the card table, the one she'd signed the contracts on, which was now back behind the blue tarp of what Macon had said was their legal department, but Hong wasn't there.

"You're Flynne," the man said. Brown hair, gray eyes, pale, cheeks pink. Another Englishman, by his accent, but here in what she was starting to try not to think of as the past. "I'm Griff," putting out his hand over the foam containers and three bottles of Hefty water, "Holdsworth." She shook it. Broad shouldered but light framed, maybe not quite as old as she was, he had on a beat-up, waxy-looking jacket, the color of fresh horse poop.

"Sounds American," she said, but really it sounded more like a character in a kids' anime.

"It's Gryffyd, actually," he said, then spelled it for her, watching like he wanted to see exactly when she'd laugh.

"You Homes, Griff?"

"Not even slightly."

"Madison thought you came in a Homes copter, that first time."

"I did. I'd access to one."

"Hear you've got a lot. Access."

"He does," Burton said, moving the tarp aside with an index finger. He looked tired, and like he needed a shower. His cammies and black t-shirt were dusty. "Handy for fixing things." He stepped in.

"Sheriff Tommy been wearing you out?" she asked him.

He put his tomahawk down on the card table, its edges clipped into orthopedic Kydex.

"Punishment detail, but he won't admit it. Doesn't like what we did over there. Way of rubbing my nose in it. Not that it wasn't more than we intended, Jackman aside. Wouldn't have minded finding a little bit of Pickett while I was at it, though. Then I heard Luke's bringing us the Lord's own sweet judgement, here." He looked at her. "Thought you were in London."

"Lowbeer got me back," she said. "Whoever wants us dead has Luke down here to psych you out. Get you to fuck up, like you tend to do when they protest shit."

"You seen the animations on those signs?"

"Looks delicious," said Griff, who'd opened the foam boxes. "Where is Hong from?"

"Philadelphia," Flynne said.

"I'll wash up," said Burton, picking up his tomahawk.

"Now you've got me feeling like following him," she said to Griff, when Burton was out of earshot.

"Carlos is on the front entrance, to discourage him leaving," he said, unscrewing the caps on the three bottles of water. "Clovis on the rear and the inside route to Hong's." He began to transfer the food to the three compostable plates Hong had brought with it, using two pairs of plastic chopsticks like a fork. Then he used a single pair to quickly reposition everything, so that it suddenly looked better than she would've guessed it was possible for Hong's food to ever look. If she'd done it, she knew, she'd have wound up with three approximately same-sized messes of noodles and rolls. Watching him use the chopsticks to redistribute those little salty fake fish eggs, she remembered the robot girls prepping the snacks for the dead woman's party. "Consider ignoring the placards our rent-a-zealots are displaying," he said. "They were designed by an agency that specializes in political attack ads, and are specifically intended to upset you personally, while turning the community against you."

"The other guys put them up to it?"

"Luke 4:5 are as much a business as a cult. As tends to be the case."

"You're from the Chef Channel or something?"

"Only with authentic Philadelphian cuisine," he said. He tilted his head. "Give me the best northern Italian and I'll have it looking like rubbish."

"Let's eat," said Burton, coming back in and putting his tomahawk down on the table again, beside one of the plates. Seeing it, this time, Flynne remembered stumbling over the dog-leash man in Pickett's basement.

She put the Wheelie Boy in the middle of the table, like it was flowers or something, then sat down on one of the folding chairs.

"What's that?" Burton asked, looking at the Wheelie Boy.

"Wheelie Boy," she said.

Griff put the empty boxes in one of the plastic bags, then put that in the other plastic bag, put it on the floor, seemed to consider the way the table was set, then sat. She almost wondered if he was about to say grace, but then he picked up his plastic chopsticks and gestured. "Please," he said.

The going back and forth between her body and the peripheral was confusing. Was she hungry or not? She'd had a banana and coffee, but she felt like the walk through the greenway had been real. Which it had, but her body hadn't done it. Smell of the food made her miss the week before, when none of this had happened, plus there was how Griff had made the plates look. "What's party time?" she asked him.

"Where'd you hear that?" Burton asked.

"Clovis gave me the antidote," she said.

"Party time around here?" Burton was looking at Griff, hard.

"Let's discuss it after we eat," Griff said.

"What is it, Burton?"

"On a war crimes dial stops at ten? About a twelve." Burton put a slice of roll in his mouth, chewed, looking at Griff.

88

PARLIAMENT OF BIRDS

sh's tepee smelled of dust, though nothing there seemed actually to be dusty. Perhaps there was a candle for that, he thought, taking a seat. The peripheral regarded him levelly, from around the ostentatious intricacy of Ash's faux-antique display, then lowered its eyes, as if tracing the patterns carved in the tabletop. Ash was to his left, nearer the peripheral. She'd unpinned her threatening little hat, which resembled a black leather toad, and placed it before her on the table. "You're being given a ticket for the parliament of birds," she'd said to him, and when he'd started to ask what that might mean, she'd touched a finger to her black lips, silencing him.

Now he saw the jet-and-sterling spider from her chatelaine, untethered, crawl down from her left jacket cuff, to pick its rapid, needle-footed way across the carving, toward him, rhinestone eyes glinting.

It climbed onto the back of his left hand. Entirely painlessly. Indeed, he couldn't feel it there. He thought of the Medici, dropping tendrils imperceptibly between the cells of his skin.

Ash spoke at length then, in birdsong, and he understood.

"Don't do that," he said, horrified, when she'd stopped, but what he actually produced was birdsong, shrill and urgent. But then he realized that what she'd told him was that the "ticket," which they could only use here, and the one time, admitted him to their morphing encryption, hers and Ossian's, which was as impenetrable as anything in the world, so that even Lowbeer and her omnipotent aunties were unlikely to learn what was said. And then she began to tell him more.

That Lowbeer (and he did his best to ignore birdsong gradually be coming something characterized by harsh glottal clicks) had become very interested in continua and their enthusiasts. There were, for in stance, Ash said, continua enthusiasts who'd been at it for severa years longer than Lev, some of whom had conducted deliberate exper iments on multiple continua, testing them sometimes to destruction insofar as their human populations were concerned. One of these early enthusiasts, in Berlin, known to the community only as "Vespa sian," was a weapons fetishist, famously sadistic in his treatment of the inhabitants of his continua, whom he set against one another in grind ing, interminable, essentially pointless combat, harvesting the weap onry evolved, though some too specialized to be of use outside whatever baroque scenario had produced it.

Netherton glanced at the peripheral, which could have understood none of this in any language, but was watching Ash as she said that Lowbeer had obtained from this Vespasian plans and specifications for something that Conner Penske was being trained to operate.

"What?" Netherton asked, hearing the query emerge instead as two mewling, long-voweled syllables.

She'd no idea, Ash said, her own vowels lengthening, but given Vespasian's fetishism and Conner's evident delight in his first lesson, it was most certainly a weapon of some kind. Lowbeer, she pointed out, would have resources for having things rapidly and secretly fabricated.

But why, Netherton asked, their shared tongue growing more Ger manic, was Ash telling him this now? He didn't tell her that he found it increased his anxiety, or that this costume jewelry perched on the back of his hand made him want to scream, but he wished that those feelings could somehow be inadvertently conveyed through whatever mutant Low Dutch he might momentarily be mouthing.

Because, Ash said (swinging off into something that reminded him of no language whatever, nor birdsong), Lowbeer had herself, virtually overnight, become a continua enthusiast. And because she, Ash, had come to see, while facilitating Lowbeer's strategies in Lev's stub, that Lowbeer was playing a longer game there than made sense for her to play. And because, and here her eyes narrowed to a single pupil per, having delivered the plans for whatever system or device to Lowbeer, Vespasian had gone uncharacteristically off to Rotterdam and died there, on Friday, suddenly and unexpectedly, but of apparently natural causes, a circumstance in which Lowbeer, in Ash's opinion, had seemed remarkably uninterested.

And this had all occurred since they'd met Lowbeer, she continued, so really rather a busy week. But now, she said, the period of Netherton's ticket, necessarily quite brief, was nearing its end. Once it ended, she expected Netherton not to mention these things at all. She had been motivated in sharing, she said, out of a degree of self-concern, but also by concern for him, and for Lev, and for Flynne and her family as well, whom she viewed as relative innocents, inadvertently abroad.

But what, Netherton asked, only now managing to ignore the constant unfamiliarity of his own verbal production, had she hoped thereby to accomplish?

She didn't know, he understood her to say, but had felt she had to do something. And Lowbeer's means of knowing who said what, via the aunties of the klept, were inestimable. And here it ended, with the spider springing from his hand and scrambling back to her.

Then the three of them sat there for a long moment, Netherton taking the peripheral's hand beneath the table, and wondering how a sadistic continua enthusiast might die unexpectedly but seemingly naturally, in Rotterdam, and how he himself might best remember not to ask Lowbeer that, as he wasn't supposed to know. But then, he thought, what if she'd heard them conversing in birdsong and gibberish? What wouldn't she make of that?

89.
STROBE

riff had made her put on armor for the ride, a black-magic cotton candy jacket. Burton wore one too, and in a way that was what nearly killed him, how the lining flash-hardened with the energy of the bullet. Fired into the concrete between Burton's feet, by a man who was probably already dead when his finger pulled the trigger, the bullet had ricocheted up, hit the jacket's sleeve around Burton's left wrist. The bullet had disintegrated then, something about the physics of the cotton candy tending to cause that, and one fragment headed back down, into Burton's right thigh, nicking the femoral artery.

It all seemed to happen at once, making no more sense than Tommy said any gunfight ever did, when you were in it. She'd been walking a little behind Burton, to his left, Clovis on her right, and afterward she remembered having sensed Clovis go up a notch, when they'd stepped out into the alley. They were going to get into Tommy's car, to go and see her mother and try to talk her into letting them move her. Griff hadn't mentioned the party time yet, whatever it might be, but if he didn't, she was going to bring it up on the ride out. Mainly he'd talked about her mother, who refused to hear of moving. He wanted to move her to northern Virginia, where he said he had a safe house. Lithonia had agreed to go with her. Sweet as her mother was on Lithonia, she still wasn't having any. Then Tommy had arrived to drive them, so she'd been looking forward to seeing her mother, even though she didn't have much hope for her buying the idea of any safe house, and to sitting beside Tommy, if the way things were didn't mean Carlos had to be sitting there instead, with his bullpup between his knees.

It had been so quiet outside, in spite of the forty-seven protesters the drones had been able to count, over on the far side of the building, across the street in front of the parking lot. But Burton must've had his tomahawk head in his right hand, arm down at his side, the handle straight up, against the inside of his arm, and when he'd seen whatever gave the man in the squidsuit away, he'd popped the Kydex sheath off and dropped the tomahawk's head, because she'd distinctly heard the sheath hit the concrete, just by where she'd locked her bike so many times. He'd caught the handle by its very end, how he did, before the head could hit the concrete, and wrist-snapped it, somehow, smack up into the man's still-invisible head, making a sound like whacking an unripe pumpkin, and that had been the last thing she heard for a while, because then the guns were too loud to understand as sound at all.

It seemed like separate gifs to her now. The front of Clovis's paramedic crotch pack open like a clamshell. The fat plastic pistol clipped in it, same color as the pack. Clovis, who'd shoved her to the side so hard that it really hurt, the pistol in both her hands, arms out shoulder-high, leaning into recoil, the muzzle flash continual, until the magazine was empty, and no more expression on her face than if she'd just been driving, paying serious attention to the road. Another was ejected brass, from Carlos's rifle, weightless cartridges, floating, like they were frozen by a strobe, but one bounced off the back of her hand, burning her. Another was the thing the squidsuits did as bullets hit them, how whatever stolen color and texture flared, whited out, died, as whoever wore it fell. And Burton on the ground, eyes open, blank, nothing moving but the blood pumping from his thigh with every heartbeat.

Her ears ringing, so bad she never expected them to stop. Tommy holding her back, as Clovis, the reloaded pistol in its open clamshell now, pulled things from pockets behind it. Homes blue latex gloves. A flat white ceramic hook. Crouched beside Burton, she used the hook to slit his cammies back in blood-soaked flaps, exposing his right thigh. Pushed the full length of her bright blue index finger straight into the spurting hole, frowned, moved it a little. The spurting stopped. She looked up. "Walter fucking Reed," she demanded, "stat."

90.
METRIC OF CAUTION

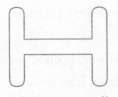e was in the shower, off the Gobiwagen's master bedroom, when Rainey's sigil appeared. "Hello," he said, eyes closed against shampoo.

"Is it still true," she asked, "that you don't know who you actually work for?"

"I'm unemployed."

"I do," she said. "More or less."

"Do what?"

"Know who you work for."

"What do you mean?"

"Our last date, so to speak."

"Yes?"

"Your friend."

"Lev?"

"The one I met."

"I don't work for her."

"But you do what she tells you to."

"I suppose I do," he said. "For obvious reasons."

"So would I, if I were in your situation."

"Which is?"

"I don't want to know. I made a few discreet inquiries. Now anyone I asked about her, however privately, no longer knows me. Retroactively. Never have. Some have gone to the trouble of scrubbing me from group images. As metrics of caution go, that one's telling."

"It isn't something I can discuss now. Not this way."

"No need. I'm calling to tell you that I've tendered my resignation."

"From whatever new version of the project?"

"From the Ministry. I'll be looking at the private sector."

"Really?"

"Whatever it is you're doing, Wilf, it isn't good to know about. But I don't, so I'll keep it that way."

"Then why call me?"

"Because in spite of myself I still give a shit about you. I have to go now. Whatever it is, consider getting out of it. Goodbye." Her sigil vanished.

He waved his hand, stopping the shower, stepped out, groped for one of Lev's grandfather's thin black linen towels, dried his eyes and face.

He looked into the bedroom, where Penske had left the dancing master lying perfectly straight on the huge bed, like the carved lid of a knight's sarcophagus, hands crossed upon its chest.

"'Whatever it is,'" he said, quoting Rainey. Surprised to discover that he missed her, and that now he supposed he would have cause to continue to.

91.

ISOPOD

ith Burton on the middle bed, blood on the sheets, under a drone surgical unit like the carapace of a giant pill bug, made of that same color plastic as Clovis's pistol, the back room of Coldiron looked like a field hospital. The drone, controlled by a team at Walter Reed National Military Medical Center, was sucked down tight around him, navel to just above his knees, and making a surprising amount of noise, as it did whatever they were making it do. Clunks and clicks as it worked on him. Extracting the shapeless bullet fragment, which it extruded on a little tray, patching the artery, closing up the hole in his leg. That was the plan, anyway. Hydrostatic shock hadn't been that bad, Griff had told her, the ricochet off concrete having spilled a lot of energy. Otherwise, at that range, the impact itself might have killed him, in spite of the armor stopping the bullet.

The drone was somewhere else peripherals might come from, she thought, reminding her she had the Wheelie Boy on her lap, on the edge of the bed furthest from Conner. When she couldn't look at Burton anymore, because he was unconscious, with a clear tube up his nose, sticky monitor-dots on his forehead and bare chest, and a couple of different tubes in his arm, she'd look over at Conner, face smooth and quiet, running something seventy years in the future, or at Griff, phone to his ear, nodding, talking but too low for her to hear. Then, when she could again, she'd look back at Burton.

The drone kept clunking. A pill bug was an isopod, not an insect.

The biggest ones lived in the ocean. Was that high school or *National Geographic*? She couldn't remember.

Clovis had gone to take a shower. Cold to start, she'd said, and fully dressed, because that would probably get most of Burton's blood out of her clothes. Flynne hadn't even known there was a shower. Clovis said it was on a hose, in a janitorial closet, with a drain in the floor, and right then it didn't seem particularly strange, Clovis explaining that, standing there with Burton's blood all over her. He'd needed a transfusion, but they'd had plenty of blood, his type. Which meant they had Flynne's type too, because they were the same. And they'd had this drone, that Clovis said was what the Secret Service kept handy in case the president got shot, and was maybe even being run by the same surgeons.

If Conner hadn't been under the crown, she'd have had to explain it all to him. Not that she knew anything about it, other than what she'd seen. Tommy had phoned for some deputies to clean things up in the alley, after, get whoever had been waiting in those squidsuits out of there, and there hadn't been one single siren. Shooters hadn't been local, or the deputies would've let Tommy know who they were by now. And it was like nobody in town had heard the shooting.

There was something wrong with her now, she decided, looking over at her brother's face while the drone clicked and whirred, all those little pill-bug legs doing whatever they were doing. She'd seen them glittering, as Carlos and Griff lifted it and put it down over him, Clovis kneeling by the bed with her bloody bright blue finger still stuck in his thigh, pressing on the artery, and then she'd pulled her finger out as the drone came to life, making its noises.

The thing that was wrong was that she'd gone to where she'd been that time in Operation Northwind, but now she couldn't scream on the couch, or walk out on Janice's porch to puke on the grass. Just sit here, on the edge of the bed she guessed would be hers, with the ringing in her ears, and beyond it the edges of Griff's accent, talking softly on his phone. She felt like Burton would be okay, but it worried her that she couldn't feel more about it.

"You don't look so good," Tommy said, sitting down beside her and taking her hand, just like that was natural.

And she remembered Wilf's hand, in that Oxford Street greenway, and the thing with floppy red wings, high up in the wet gray branches. "My ears are ringing," she said.

"Be lucky if you don't get any permanent loss," he said. "Part of what you're feeling now's just decibel level. Affects your nervous system."

"They were like the first four in that car," she said. "Then those two down below the trailer. Dozen people dead, because of us."

"You aren't making them come after you."

"I can't tell anymore."

"Not a good time to try to figure it out. But I've got something I have to run by you, while our man here's on the phone. Not a good time for that either, but I have to do it." He was looking at Griff.

"What?"

"I don't want them using that shit on Luke 4:5. Not on anybody."

"Party time?"

"You wouldn't call it that, if you had any better idea what it does."

"Burton said it's a war crime."

"It is," he said, "and good reason. It's an aerosol. They'd have a single little bird go down the line, painted black, tonight, spray 'em all."

"What's it do?"

"Stimulant, aphrodisiac, and, I have trouble pronouncing this, psychotomimetic."

"What's it mean?"

"It duplicates the condition of being totally serial-killer sadist bugfuck."

"Fuck . . ."

"You wouldn't want it on your conscience. Don't want it on mine."

He looked over at Burton. "Now I feel like shit for riding his ass, for what they did at Pickett's."

"He told me you were unhappy. Didn't seem to hold it against you."

"They didn't know they'd set off those tanks of precursor. What they put on Conner's gobot might've been fine just for Pickett and a few of his posse, which is frankly something I couldn't hold against anybody. But they did blow up some poor assholes with no better way to make a living, on my watch, some of whom I knew to say hello to." He gave her hand a squeeze, then let go of it.

She wondered who it was, up the line, had given Ash those crazy eyes, and whether they could do the same to somebody here, with the isopodal drone? Or if they might know how to fix whatever it was about Burton's haptics that glitched him? Crazy things to wonder, but she felt a little better now. She reached over for Tommy's hand again, because holding it and hearing his voice was making that Operation Northwind thing go away.

92.
YOU GUYS

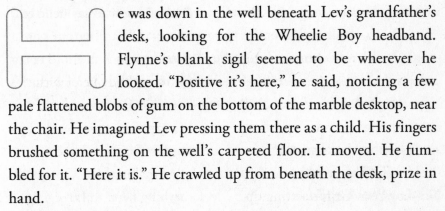e was down in the well beneath Lev's grandfather's desk, looking for the Wheelie Boy headband. Flynne's blank sigil seemed to be wherever he looked. "Positive it's here," he said, noticing a few pale flattened blobs of gum on the bottom of the marble desktop, near the chair. He imagined Lev pressing them there as a child. His fingers brushed something on the well's carpeted floor. It moved. He fumbled for it. "Here it is." He crawled up from beneath the desk, prize in hand.

"Fiddle with the cam," she said. "You had it too close to your nose, last time."

He sat in the chair, put the band on, tried to center the cam, and tongued the roof of his mouth. The sigil of the Wheelie Boy emulation app appeared, the feed opened, her blank sigil disappearing. She was seated at a table, against a backdrop of dull blue. The unit seemed to be on the table in front of her, but he didn't try to move it, or change the angle or direction of its cam. "Hello?"

"Get it a little higher, more in line with your eyes."

He tried to do that.

"Better," she said. "Your nose is smaller." She looked tired, he thought.

"How are you?"

"They fucking shot my brother."

"Who did?"

"Guys in squidsuits. Clovis and Carlos killed 'em."

"And your brother?"

"He's asleep. They gave him something. Government drone gave him a long-distance operation. Got the bullet out, patched a hole in his artery, cleaned everything, stitched him up."

"Were you hurt?"

"No. Feel fucked, but that's not the problem."

"What problem?"

"Lowbeer's English boy. Back here. Griff. Gryffyd. Holdsworth. Tommy thinks Griff's what he calls an intelligence liaison. Has diplomatic cover or some shit, out of their embassy in Washington. Lots of connections, government stuff. Our government, I mean. He got squidsuits and a micro-drone for Burton, to get me out of Pickett's. Got the pill bug they used on Burton—"

"Pill bug?"

"No time. Just listen."

"Griff is the problem?"

"Lowbeer. Griff's setting up to do something here, to Luke 4:5—"

"Who?"

"They're just assholes. You listen to me, okay?"

He nodded, then imagined that on the Wheelie Boy's tablet.

"The competition's using them to embarrass us, and probably hoping to get Burton out there so somebody can shoot him. He doesn't like 'em to begin with, so they're good bait. But Griff's got this chemical weapon, called party time. Like every really bad builder drug rolled into one, but worse. If what it makes you do doesn't kill you in the process, you're liable to commit suicide from remembering what you did. Tommy says builders can't find a survivable recreational dose. Go homeopathic on it, it monsters you out just as bad. Clovis already put me on the antidote. Griff's planning to use it on Luke 4:5, and I'd bet tonight."

"Then how is Lowbeer your problem?"

"She calls the shots. Either it's her idea or his, but if it's his, she signed off on it. Using that shit on anybody is just too crazy. Too mean. It's your world."

"My world?"

"Different way of doing things. Stone cold. But I'm not letting it happen, neither is Tommy, and if Burton were conscious, neither would he."

"How would you stop it?"

"By letting her know I'm not going to the party with you, if they do that. They use it, we smash up the crowns, print new phones with different numbers, and pretend you guys don't exist. Whatever shit comes down, we deal with it. And fuck you. Not you personally. You guys."

"Seriously?"

"Shit yes."

He looked at her.

"So?" she asked.

"So what?"

"You in?"

"In?"

"You tell her. She wants to talk to me, I'm right here. But they put any party time on those sorry assholes across the road, you're going to that party alone. Me and my family, we'll be out of the future business."

He opened his mouth. Closed it.

"Call her," she said. "I'm going to go talk to Griff."

"Why would you do this? Without her, you'll be in a desperate position. So might we, for that matter. And you're doing it for the sake of . . . assholes?"

"They're assholes. We're not. But we're only not assholes if we won't do shit like that. You calling her?"

"Yes. But I don't know why."

"Because you're not an asshole."

"I wish I believed that."

"Everybody's got one. And an opinion to go with it, my mother says. It's how you behave makes the difference. Now I'm going to turn you off and go tell Griff." And she did.

93.

MISSION STATEMENT

S he was three steps into the back before she realized she was carrying the Wheelie Boy like a teddy bear. Not hugging it, but sort of in her arms. Fuck it.

They turned and looked at her. The red-haired notary from Klein Cruz Vermette, in cammies now and a Clovis-style crotch pouch. Blue surgical gloves. Seemed like she'd just finished putting clean sheets on Burton's bed. Someone must've had to help her, because the pill bug was still all over him. She'd spread one relatively unstained sheet on the floor, between Burton's bed and Conner's, which was empty, and had a big ball of blood-stiff sheets on top of that. Clovis was beside Conner's bed, in fresh clothes, doing something to the white crown on the table there. Griff was at the foot of Burton's bed, phone to his ear, and as she came in, just his eyes moved.

"Where's Conner?" she asked.

"Shower," Clovis said. "Macon took him."

"How's Burton?"

"Vitals look good, Walter Reed says. They want him to sleep longer, so it's still sedating him."

"I will," said Griff, to his phone, "thank you." He lowered it.

"Need to talk," she said, wishing she hadn't brought the Wheelie.

"Yes, but not about what you assume we do."

"The fuck we don't."

"Herself." Holding up his phone. "Wiping party time off the mission statement."

"You won't do it?"

"Absolutely not."

"Huh." All pissed off, she wondered, and nowhere to go? "Was that shit her idea in the first place?"

"It was," he said. "I didn't feel it was appropriate, or advisable. She told me I was unaccustomed to operating from a position of strength." With that, he gave her a look she couldn't read. "Could we have a moment, Clovis, please?" The KCV girl, bloody sheet ball folded in the cleaner one, was on her way out. Clovis turned and followed her.

"Now she says she won't do it?" She watched Clovis's back vanish around the blue tarp. "Why?"

"Your conversation with the publicist."

"She listened?"

"Assume she can access anything, any platform, always."

"So she sits, and listens?"

"She has global intelligence feeds, analytical tools of tremendous functionality. The systems I work with here would surprise you, I imagine, but I have to take her word for what hers are capable of. She doubts anyone fully comprehends them, herself included, as they've become largely self-organizing. Having had to evolve from the sort I use today, I suppose. Which means that if you mention anything that concerns her, over or within reach of any platform whatsoever, she learns of it immediately. And at this point, I suppose, anything you speak of concerns her."

"No party time?"

"Canceled."

"But you couldn't convince her yourself, that it sucked?"

"It's a literally atrocious idea. Using it would constitute, morally and legally, an atrocity. Coldiron's brand would be attached to something horrific, no matter how effectively we were able to spin the blame. Coldiron is concerned about the townspeople not being priced out of chili dogs, but willing to condone dosing religious protesters, however repellant, with something that turns them into homicidal erotomaniacs?"

"Coldiron knew? Who?"

"No. I knew. And Clovis."

"She told me. But not what it was. Tommy told me what it does."

"I had to bring him in. He needed to be prepared, to be ready to tidy up. I'm delighted you've put a stop to it."

She looked at him. "I still don't see why you couldn't talk her out of it."

"Because there's a way in which I lack agency, in all of this. By virtue of more pressing concerns."

"What's that mean?"

"Lowbeer knows the history of her world, and the secret history of ours. The history that produced Lowbeer's world includes the assassination of the president."

"Gonzales? You shitting me?"

"She never finished her second term."

"She gets elected again?"

"Exactly. And in Lowbeer's view, Gonzales's assassination was pivotal, a tipping point into the deeper jackpot."

"Shit—"

"We may be able to change that."

"Lowbeer knows how to fix history?"

"It isn't history yet, here. She knows, in large part, what really happened here. But now the two have diverged, will continue to. The divergence can be steered, to some extent, but only very broadly. No guarantee of what we'll ultimately produce."

"She's trying to stop the jackpot?"

"Ameliorate it, at best. We are, very much, already in it, here. She hopes, as do I, that the system in which she operates can be avoided in this continuum. She believes, and I agree, that a necessary step in that is the prevention of the assassination of Felicia Gonzales."

She stared at him. Was this the loopiest bullshit ever, even after the past week? His pale gray eyes were wide, serious. "Who kills the president?"

"The vice president, not to put too fine a point on it."

"Ambrose? Wally fucking Ambrose? He kills Gonzales?"

"What Coldiron and your competitor are doing could affect that outcome, but by crashing the global economy, which is a danger in itself. But I can't know all of what she knows. It isn't as though she could brief me, and in any case she's far more experienced than I am. Were she to tell me the use of party time was necessary to prevent the assassination, I'd use it."

"Why?"

"Because she's explained her world to me. She's shared the course of her career, her life. I don't want it to go that way here."

"Cute sister," bellowed Conner, "where's hot nurse?" His surviving arm, tattooed down its length with "FIRST IN, LAST OUT" in gang-style lettering, was pale around Macon's neck. Macon himself was bare-chested, in wet shorts, hair matted from carrying Conner under the shower. He'd managed to get Conner mostly back into his Polartec. Now he carried him to his bed, put him down, helped him get his arm into the sole sleeve.

"Going back for my clothes," Macon said, then looked at Flynne and Griff. "You two okay?"

"Fine," said Flynne.

"Burton good?" Conner asked, squinting at her unconscious brother.

"Hospital says," she said.

"Head office canceled the distribution," Griff said to Macon.

"Okay," said Macon. "You going to tell me what it would have been?"

"Another time," Griff said.

Macon raised his eyebrows. "I'll get my clothes." He went out.

"Hot nurse said squidsuit fuckers popped a cap in his ass," Conner said. "Girl's a baller. Macon says she took down half of them. Fucking Carlos, he only got two."

"Why aren't you up in the future," Flynne asked him, "flying your washing machine?"

"Man's got to eat."

Hong stepped sideways through the narrow vertical slit in the barricade, a foam box in one hand. "Shrimp bowl?"

"That's me," said Conner.

Hong saw Burton, raised his eyebrows. "He okay?"

"Wasn't your cooking did it," Conner said, "it was Jimmy's. Nearly died of the runs."

Flynne looked at Griff, who widened his eyes slightly, as if to say their real conversation was over, for a while at least.

Gonzales? Was he shitting her? Was Lowbeer shitting him?

94.
APOLLINARIS WATER

T he bar was still locked, just as it had been some minutes before. He looked at his thumb on the oval of brushed steel, inset into the glassine veneer. He was, minus a drink, as ready as he ever expected to be to confront Lowbeer with the news of Flynne's unwillingness to attend Daedra's event. It wasn't, after all, his decision, or his idea. Though he had, somehow, it seemed, become party to it.

He'd indicated to Flynne that he'd contact Lowbeer immediately, and shortly he would, certainly, but he wasn't happy about it. He supposed he understood Flynne's reason for taking this course, but it wasn't his. Though perhaps it sprang from that strata of archaic self-determination he found so exciting in her. Exciting and problematic. Why did the two seem so often to be inextricably linked, he wondered? And wondered, remembering Ash's parliament of birds, whether Lowbeer might have in any case been privy to his conversation with Flynne? He paced nervously to the window, peered out into the dark garage.

Saw squidlight pulse, as Lowbeer stepped beneath an arch, headed his way. He backed away from the window. Definitely her broad shoulders, white hair, the ladylike take on a City suit. He sighed. Found the panel that brought the armchairs up, selected two and raised them. Looked at the closed bar. Sighed again. Went to the door, opened it, stepped out. She was at the bottom of the gangway, smiling pinkly. "I was nearby," she said, "for a chat with Clovis. You don't mind my dropping in?"

"Do you know?" he asked her.

"About what?"

"Flynne's decision."

"I do," she said. "After all these years, I still find it vaguely embarrassing. Though it wasn't that I specifically asked to hear it. The aunties fetched it."

He wondered if that was true, that she could still be embarrassed by her own acts of surveillance? Perhaps it was akin to his own unease at knowing she'd listened, when of course one did assume that the klept was entirely able to do that. Just as one assumed, to whatever extent, that that was always being done. "Then you heard me agree to convey Flynne's terms."

"I did," she said, starting up, "and your bafflement at doing so."

"Then you know that she won't go, unless this so-called party time is removed from the equation."

She paused, midway. "And how do you feel about that yourself, Wilf?"

"It's awkward. I'm prepared to attend, as you know. But you've proposed to do something, in the stub, that she finds very offensive."

"She doesn't find it offensive," she said, starting up again. "She finds it evil. As it would have been, had I followed through."

"Did you intend to?"

She'd reached the top. Netherton stepped back. "I field-test operatives," she said. "A part of my basic skill set."

"You wouldn't have done it?"

"I would have infected them with a mild strain of Norwalk virus, had she not protested, having made her and the others immune. And been disappointed, I suppose. Though I never felt there was much chance of that, really." She entered the cabin.

"It was a trick?"

"A test. You've passed it yourself. You made the right decision, though without quite knowing why. I assume you did it because you like her, though, and that counts for something. I think I might like a drink."

"You do?"

"Yes, thank you."

"I can't open it. But you might be able to. There. Touch the oval with your thumb."

She crossed to the bar, did as suggested. The door slid up, into the ceiling. "A gin and tonic, please," she said. He watched as her drink rose, startling in its seemingly Socratic perfection, up out of the marble counter. "And you?" she asked.

He tried to speak. Couldn't. Coughed. Lowbeer picked up her drink. He caught the scent of juniper. "Perrier," he said, in what seemed a stranger's voice, as alien an utterance as any in Ash's parliament of birds.

"I'm sorry, sir," said the bar, young, male, German, "but we have no Perrier. May I suggest Apollinaris water?"

"Fine," said Netherton, his voice his own now.

"Ice?" the bar asked.

"Please." His water emerged. "I don't understand why you'd test her," he said. "If it was her you were testing."

"It was," she said, gesturing toward the armchairs. He picked up his scentless water and followed her. "I've a further role in mind, for her," she continued, when they were both seated, "should we be successful at Daedra's soiree. And perhaps one for you as well. I imagine you're actually rather good at what you do, in spite of certain disadvantages. Disadvantage and peculiar competence can go hand in hand, I find."

Netherton sipped the German mineral water, tasting faintly of what he supposed might be limestone. "What exactly are you proposing, if I may ask?"

"I can't tell you, I'm afraid. In sending you to Daedra, I send you beyond the reach of my protection, and of Lev's. It's best that you know no more than you do now."

"Do you," Netherton asked, "know literally everything, about everyone?"

"I most certainly don't. I feel hindered by a surfeit of information, oceanic to the point of meaninglessness. The shortcomings of the system are best understood as the result of taking this ocean of data, and the decision points produced by our algorithms, as a near enough substitute for perfect certainty. My own best results are often due to pretending I know relatively little, and acting accordingly, though it's easier said than done. Far easier."

"Do you know who that was, the man Flynne saw, when Aelita was killed?"

"I imagine I do," she said, "but that isn't good enough. The state requires proof, paradoxically, however much it may be built on secrets and lies. Were there no burden of proof, this all would be boneless, mere protoplasm." She sipped her gin. "As it can all too often seem to be. Waking, I find I must remind myself how the world is now, how it became that way, the role I played in what it became and the role I play today. That I've lived on, absurdly long, in the ever-increasing recognition of my mistakes."

"Mistakes?"

"I suppose I shouldn't call them that, realistically. Tactically, strategically, in terms of available outcomes, I did the best I could. Rather better, sometimes, it can feel, even today. Civilization was dying, of its own discontents. We live today in the result of what I and so many others did to prevent that. You yourself have known nothing else."

"Well hey," said Lev's brother's peripheral, the dancing master, from the entrance to the master bedroom, "didn't expect you."

"Mr. Penske," said Lowbeer, "delighted. How goes it with the cube?"

"Who thought that thing up?" asked the peripheral, now very clearly Flynne's brother's friend, Conner, lounging against the jamb in a way Pavel would never have done.

"A tortured nation," said Lowbeer, "in the sole service of a pervert."

"Sounds about right," said Conner.

"And how is Mr. Fisher?" asked Lowbeer.

"You'd think he got his ass blown off," said Conner, an oblique little smile misplaced amid the dancing master's facial bone, "the way everybody goes on about it."

95.

WHOLE WORLDS FALLING

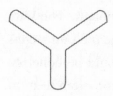ou work for Klein Cruz Vermette?" she asked the red-haired girl, who was making up a bed for her in a smaller tarped-off section behind the one they'd eaten in. There was a bare slab of beige foam on the floor, nothing else. The girl had just popped a new sleeping bag out of a stuff sack, was unzipping it.

"I do." She unrolled the bag and spread it on the foam. "Pillows haven't come, sorry."

"How long?"

The girl looked at her. "The pillows?"

"When'd you start, at KCV?"

"Four days ago."

"Got a gun in that pouch?"

The girl looked at her.

"You work for Griff? Like Clovis?"

"I'm at KCV."

"Keeping track of them?"

Same look, no answer.

"So what do you ordinarily do?"

"I'm not just trying to be some kind of hard-ass," the girl said, "but I can't tell you. I'm under constraint, and that's aside from just basic opsec. Ask Griff." She smiled, to take the edge off.

"Okay," said Flynne.

"Want a fast-acting sedative with a really short half-life?"

"No, thanks."

"Sleep tight, then." When she was gone, it struck Flynne that she'd changed from her cammies into really bad mom jeans and a man's blue tank top with the mascot of the Clanton Wildcats on the front. On the way in here, they'd passed Brent Vermette, wearing a boonie hat that Leon wouldn't have minded, and some kind of cheap black plastic watch.

She stood the Wheelie Boy on the open sleeping bag, took off the soft armor jacket, rolled it, put it against the wall of Tyvek-bagged shingles at the head of the foam. Sat down on the foam and undid her laces. Needed new shoes. Took them off, leaving her socks on, stood up, took off her jeans, sat back down, picked up the Wheelie, pulled the top of the open sleeping bag across her legs. It wasn't dark in here, or light either. Just sort of blue. Like being in the middle of a clear block of Homes blue plastic. There was light up by the rafters, leaking from tarped-off sections where people were working. They might all be keeping it down, so she and Burton could sleep. Lowered voices. She was in here because Clovis needed the other bed, now they'd lifted the pill bug off Burton. Clovis had put on a helmet and examined the sutured hole in his thigh, doing what a surgeon in D.C. told her to, while seeing what she saw. Like Edward working long distance with a Viz in each eye, but the helmet was older, the way government stuff could be, sometimes way ahead, sometimes way behind. Burton had been conscious, but woozy, and Flynne had kissed his scratchy cheek and told him she'd see him in the morning.

"Hello?"

She looked at the Wheelie Boy. Netherton, big-eyed and big-nosed. "You got the cam too close again," she told him. He adjusted it. Not that much better.

"Why are you whispering?"

"Quiet time, in here."

"I spoke with Lowbeer," he said. "In person. She isn't going to do it."

"I know," she said. "Griff told me."

He looked disappointed.

"I should've called you when I found out," she said, "but they were doing things to Burton's leg. She with you now?"

"She's upstairs, with Conner."

"Listening now?"

"Her modules," he said, "but they always are. She says she never intended to use that weapon."

"Macon was set to. Didn't know what it was, but he was ready."

"She would have been disappointed, she said, if you hadn't objected. Then given them all stomach flu, having made you immune."

"Maybe she should do that anyway. Why would she have been disappointed?"

"In you," he said.

"Me?"

"It was a test."

"Of what?"

"Evidently she wanted to determine whether, as you might put it, you are an asshole."

"I'm just the only one who happened to see what happened. I could be an asshole and still ID the guy I saw. What would it matter?"

"I don't know," he said. "How is your brother?"

"Not bad, considering. They're mainly worried about infection."

"Why?"

"Because antibiotics don't work for shit."

He gave her a look.

"What?" she asked.

"You're still relying on antibiotics."

"Not that much. They only work about a third of the time."

"Do you get cold?" he asked.

"When?"

"'Colds.' 'Common cold'?"

She looked at him. "Don't you?"

"No."

"Why not?"

"Induced immunity. Only neoprimitives forgo it."

"They don't want to be immune from colds?"

"Ostentatiously perverse."

"I don't get that about you," she said.

"About what?"

"How you don't seem to like your own tech-level, but you don't like people who opt out of it either."

"They don't opt out of it. They volunteer for another manifestation of it, but with heritage diseases. Which they then believe make them more authentic."

"Nostalgic for catching colds?"

"If they could look as though they catch them, but avoid any discomfort, they would. But others, insisting on the real thing, would mock them for their inauthenticity." The Wheelie's tablet rotated, creaking slightly. "Everything's blue."

"They hung tarps, to break up the space. This blue's Homes surplus. Cheapest stuff at Hefty is always Homes blue."

"Homes?" he asked.

"Homeland Security. Question for you, different topic. Are the people brought in to work here trying to look local? I just saw a girl wearing jeans I'd figure she'd gnaw her legs off to get out of."

"Ash brought in wardrobe stylists. And less demonstrative vehicles."

"The parking lot out front looks like a BMW dealership."

"It probably doesn't, now."

"Luke still across the street?"

"I think so, but Ossian's exploring buying them out."

"Buying a church?"

"You may already own several. Coldiron's acquisition strategy is entirely situational. If buying a church facilitates the next takeover, they buy the church."

"Why's it called that? Coldiron?"

"Spell-correct. Ash chose 'milagros' because she likes them. Not miracles but small metal charms, offerings to the saints, representing various suffering body parts. Calderón is a partner in a Panama City law firm Lev nearly hired, but didn't. Ash liked the sound of it, then liked the look of the accidental result."

"You don't hang out a lot with artists?"

"I don't, no."

"I would, if I could. What kind of music do you like?"

"Classical, I suppose," he said. "What kind do you like?"

"Kissing Cranes."

"Cranes?"

"Like storks."

"Kissing?"

"It's an old German trademark, knives and razors. You have Badger?"

"Music?"

"A site. Keeps track of your friends and stuff."

"'Social media'?"

"I guess so."

"It was an artifact of relatively low connectivity. If I remember correctly, you already have less of it than there was previously."

"Now there's mostly just Badger. And darknet boards, if you're into that. I'm not. Hefty owns Badger. My peripheral there?"

"Back cabin."

"Can I see her?"

He reached up, giant fingers fumbling, and did something to his cam. She saw the room with the tacky marble desk, the little round leather armchairs. On the Wheelie screen it looked like a grifter bank, but for puppets. He got up, went into the back, along the skinny passage of slick wood, to where her peripheral, in a silky-looking black sweatshirt and black tights, lay on the ledgelike bunk, eyes closed.

"Totally looks like somebody," she said. It really did. It was the opposite of something they'd build to meet some general idea of beauty. And if she understood correctly, nobody knew who it looked like. It was like the pictures in a box at a yard sale, nobody remembering who those people were, or even whose family, let alone how they came to be there. It gave her a sense of things falling, down some hole that had no bottom. Whole worlds falling, and maybe hers too, and it made her want to phone Janice, who was out at the house, and see how her mother was doing.

96.
DISANTHROPOMORPHIZED

s he left the rear cabin, the Wheelie window vanished, taking the sigil of the emulation software with it. She'd gone to phone about her mother, and perhaps to sleep. He'd heard it in her voice, that she needed that. The attack, her brother's wound, the business with the party time. But still she had that way of simply going forward.

He pictured the peripheral's upturned face, eyes closed. It wasn't sleeping, but where was it, within itself? But then it didn't, as he understood it, possess a self to be within. Not sentient, yet as Lowbeer had pointed out, effortlessly anthropomorphized. An anthropomorph, really, to be disanthropomorphized. Though when she was present in it, or perhaps through it, was it not some version of her?

He saw the two glasses on the desk before he realized that the bar was still open. Enrobed in a sudden ponderous nonchalance, he moved to pick them up, returning as casually to the open bar, a glass in either hand. As he put them down, the bar's door slid down. Lev's sigil appeared. He fought the urge to block the door with his arms, palms flat on the gold-veined marble, fingers spread. Surely it wouldn't crush his hands.

"What are you doing?" asked Lev, as Netherton heard the door's lock click.

"I was with Flynne," he said, "in that toy peripheral. But she had to phone her mother." He pressed both hands against pale glassy veneer, feeling the German solidity, the complete lack of movement.

"I'm grilling sandwiches," Lev said. "Sardines on Italian bread, pickled jalapeño. Looking tasty."

"Is Lowbeer there?"

"She suggested the sardines."

"I'll be right up."

As he was going out the door, he remembered that he was still wearing the headband, with its vaguely Egyptianate, milkily translucent giant sperm of a cam. He took it off and put it in his jacket pocket.

When he'd crossed the garage, taken the bronze elevator, and made his way to the kitchen, he saw through the mullioned doors that Conner was in the garden, on hands and knees, snarling at Gordon and Tyenna. The peripheral's features lent themselves terrifyingly to this, seeming to expose more teeth than the two creatures possessed between them, in spite of their peculiarly long jaws. They were facing him, side by side, as if ready to spring, their musculature looking even less canine than usual, their stiff tails in particular. Carnivorous kangaroos, in wolf outfits with Cubist stripes. Netherton felt an oddly intense gratitude, just then, for their not having, as the drop bears had, hands.

The kitchen smelled smokily of grilled sardines. "What's he doing out there?" Netherton asked.

"I don't know," said Lev, at the stove, "but they love it."

Now the two creatures lunged at Conner simultaneously. He fell between them, flailing, wrestling with them. They were making a high-pitched, repetitious coughing sound.

"Dominika's gone to Richmond Hill, with the children," Lev said, checking flattened panini in a sandwich press.

"How is she?" Netherton asked, as unable as ever to read the domestic temperature of Chez Lev.

"Rather annoyed with the time I've been devoting to all of this, but her taking the children there was my idea. And Lowbeer's." He nodded in her direction.

"Lev's father's house," Lowbeer said, seated at the pine table, "is literally untouchable. Should we earn the enmity of anyone of genuine consequence, in the next forty-eight hours or so, Lev's family will be secure."

"Whom would you expect to anger?" Netherton asked.

"Americans, primarily, though I wouldn't be so worried about them. They are likely, though, to currently have allies in the City. It's beginning to look as though my assumption was correct, that the motive in Aelita's death will prove to have been sadly quotidian."

"Why is that?"

"The aunties, continually mulling it over. A process akin to repetitious dreaming, or the protracted spinning of a given fiction. Not that they're invariably correct, but over a sufficient course they do tend to find the likely suspects."

Conner was on his feet now, walking toward them, Gordon and Tyenna hopping in unison after him on their hind legs. He entered, closing the door behind him. Outside, still upright, they followed him with their eyes.

"Infatuated with you," said Lev, taking the first of the sandwiches from the press.

"Like you crossed possums with coyotes," Conner said. "Smell a little like possums. They get TB?"

"Get what?" Lev asked.

"Tuberculosis," Lowbeer said.

"No," Lev said, looking up from the press. "Why should they?"

"Possums mostly do," said Conner. "Not many left. People like 'em even less, they get TB. Sandwich smells good. Why don't you build these things so they can eat?"

"We do," Lev said, "but it's much more expensive. Unnecessary in a martial arts instructor."

"Sit with us," said Lowbeer. "You do rather loom."

Conner pulled out the chair opposite her, reversed it, and sat, forearms crossed atop its back.

"Is Flynne sleeping now?" Netherton asked, taking the chair beside

Conner. To be seated with Lowbeer and not face her, he thought, wouldn't have occurred to him.

"She is," said Lowbeer, "after speaking with her mother's caregiver. She'll visit, tomorrow. There's an increasing risk involved, but we want her able to give her full attention to her evening with you and Daedra. And whoever else may be present." Lev placed a white plate with her sandwich in front of her. "That looks absolutely delicious, Lev. Thank you."

97.
CONVOY

The inside of the truck they took her home in was like the Hummer limo her class had all chipped in on for the senior prom, but no stink of air freshener and the seats were nicer. The outside had been made to look like shit, but she didn't think it really worked that well, because if anybody in town had an American car that new, they'd wash it. And the dirt looked sprayed on. It was an American-looking truck, but not quite any particular make or model. Carlos loved that about it, said it was "gray man," what he called things he'd've called tactical otherwise, except for it having been styled down to not attract attention. But he wouldn't have liked it, she guessed, if it hadn't been no make in particular, had a brutal profile, and been armored all to shit. The red-haired girl was driving, in her same bad jeans and Wildcats tank top, but now she had one of the soft-armor jackets on over that. Her name was Tacoma.

Griff and Tommy wouldn't let Flynne just take a car out to the house. Had to be this whole procession. First, a little remote-control three-quarter-scale SUV rigged to set off mines and roadside bombs, that Leon, to her amazement, was actually piloting, from the front seat of the SUV in front of the gray man truck. Loving it, apparently. No figuring Leon, sometimes, what he'd really like. They'd even gotten him to put on one of the black jackets, over his jean jacket, a weirdly businesslike look for him, except that he was also wearing a headscarf in old-fashioned deer-hunter camo, like a life-sized photograph of tree bark, and he wasn't somebody who should ever wear that, if anybody was. He was in the SUV with five of Burton's boys, all with bullpups and soft armor. Four more in a second SUV taking up the rear, plus some unspecified number of drones, recharging themselves off a pack on the top of the second SUV. She supposed the drones all still had a piece of aquamarine duct tape on them, because she could see a two-foot length of it across the rear bumper of the front SUV. Burton's aquamarine army, and him hors de combat, in the back of Coldiron's tarp maze. If he was conscious now, he must think that that really sucked.

But he probably wouldn't have gotten a look yet at how much dress-up was going on, or maybe dress-down. While she'd slept, it seemed, all the Klein Cruz Vermette people had started competing to look like a stylist's idea of county, a few even sporting tattoos she hoped were fake, or anyway the kind that faded to nothing after a year or so. Way too into it. Tommy, this morning, had said that was because they weren't just getting paid shitloads of money, but potential shares in Coldiron too. Said that even the ones who weren't very qualified were getting some of the highest salaries in the state, period, right then, and it made them giddy and determined and paranoid all at once, not to mention way too nice to her. Tacoma wasn't, though, because she wasn't just KCV. Griff had said she was with him, when Flynne had asked him, but that was all he'd say. It looked to Tommy, though, like Clovis and Tacoma were both "acronym," but no telling which agency. Too smart to be Homes, he said, and not asshole enough for the really big ones. Where that fit with Griff being English, Flynne didn't know.

Tommy and Griff were both needed in town today. They were only letting her go out alone because Griff still wanted her to talk her mother into the safe house in Virginia. Clovis would stay with Burton, and to do the helmet thing for the surgeons in D.C. Macon and Edward were sleeping, after their run on government wakey. She'd seen them curled up together on a foam, under a sleeping bag, Macon snoring, Edward in his arms. She guessed that not having to dose

Luke 4:5 with party time, or what Griff would have thought was party time, had cut the two of them some much-needed slack.

So here she was, just her and the Wheelie Boy, in the back of this stealth-limo truck, two rows of seats behind the front seats, then the back window, then the pickup bed with a flat hardshell cover. For all she knew, they might have a rocket launcher under there.

"Air con good?" Tacoma asked her.

"Fine," she said. Tacoma had told her the truck could drive under water if it had to, popping up a breather tube for the engine. There weren't any bodies of water around to seriously do that in, that Flynne knew of, and just as well. She looked up now and saw the cow-drone, more or less where she'd last seen it, but pretending to graze. She'd seen bullet streaks on the concrete wall back of Coldiron and Fab, thinking how lucky it was that Burton had been the only one to catch a ricochet. The way they'd gone out to the truck this morning, they'd been out of Luke 4:5's sight, at least until they got on Porter, and by then they were far enough away that it didn't matter. And anyway Luke were mostly still sleeping, in identical black pup tents they'd pitched in the lot opposite the mall, in tight rows, like insect eggs, Leon said, or slime mold. Now she knew that they hadn't really been targeted with a drug that turned you into a homicidal sex maniac, she found herself feeling less kindly disposed toward them. Like why couldn't Griff and Tommy, between them, figure out some relatively low-impact, legally nonatrocious way to get them the fuck out of town? Made a mental note to ask about that. "Any chance we could get the breakfast burrito and some coffee, at Jimmy's?" she asked Tacoma.

"Pretty serious dog and pony with security here," Tacoma said, "but say I call them, they bring it out to you?"

"Fine by me."

"Well, not to you directly. Lead car, up front. Then we get it droned back to us, don't have to stop."

"Complicated."

"Protocol. Jimmy's brings it directly to us, I've got to stop, unseal, even if it's just the window."

"Unseal?"

"Vehicle's hermetic, except for filtered intakes."

"Lot of trouble, for a burrito."

"They're spending as much money as they can on keeping your ass intact and present. You've already been kidnapped once. Those shooters last night could've been more interested in you than your brother."

Flynne hadn't thought of that. "You as good with a gun as Clovis?"

"No," said Tacoma. "Better."

"Am I alone back here to reduce the chance of one of Burton's boys trying to do what Reece did?"

"Or worse. What kind of burrito? Want milk and sugar in your coffee?"

"They just have the one burrito. Milk and sugar." She looked over at the Wheelie Boy, on the seat beside her, and wondered where Wilf was. She'd fallen asleep on the foam, after phoning Janice at the house.

Tacoma was talking to someone on her earbud. She slowed, Jimmy's parking lot up ahead, and Flynne saw a boy in a white t-shirt come running out across the gravel, something in his hands. He passed it, through an open window, to someone in the SUV, which had almost but not quite stopped. The SUV pulled out again. Tacoma sped up, matching its speed, maintaining a fixed distance.

When Jimmy's was out of sight, Flynne saw something lift out of the SUV, headed back toward them. It became a small quadcopter, toting a fabbed cornstarch travel tray with a silver-foil bundle and a paper cup clipped in it.

"Watch this with the bed," Tacoma said, without looking back.

Flynne turned in time to see a rectangular hatch in the bed cover sliding open. The drone matched their speed, then lowered itself through the opening. Then came right back up, minus the tray with the burrito and coffee, climbing out of sight as the hatch closed beneath it. "How do we get it?"

"Doing an airlock thing now," Tacoma said.

A hatch slid up, in the back of the passenger cab. Flynne undid her seatbelt, got down on hands and knees and crawled back. With her head through the opening, she saw the tray, pulled it out. The foil was warm. They kept their breakfast burritos ready to go, at Jimmy's, under a heat lamp.

She managed to get back into the seat with the tray on her lap, hearing the hatch close behind her, refastened her seatbelt, and peeled the foil off one end of the burrito. "Thanks."

"We aim to please."

Jimmy's breakfast burritos were gross. Scrambled eggs and chopped-up bacon, green onions. Exactly what she wanted right now.

"Good morning," said Netherton, from the Wheelie.

She had her mouth full of burrito. Nodded.

"I hope you had a good night's sleep," he said. The Wheelie's tablet whined, turning, then tilted back, so he could see out the window. Nothing but sky, unless there were drones there.

She swallowed, drank some coffee. "Slept okay. You?"

"I slept in the Gobiwagen's jacuzzi," he said.

"Were you wet?"

"When it's not a bath, it's an observation cupola. Conner's peripheral has the master bedroom. He was here peripherally, earlier. He played with Lev's analogs in the garden. Watched us have sandwiches, in Lev's kitchen. Then I came back down with him. He put his peri to bed, off for more of whatever it is she has him training on. Where are we going?"

"My house."

The tablet straightened up, panned left to right, back again.

"This is kind of a limo, disguised as a truck," Flynne said. "Bomb-proof. That's Tacoma."

"Hey," said Tacoma, keeping her eyes on the road.

"Hello," said Netherton.

"Tacoma works for Griff," Flynne said. "Or with him."

"Or for you, if it comes to that," Tacoma said.

"I still don't get that."

"Look at it this way," Tacoma said. "Everything you can see outside of this vehicle, except for the sky and the road, you own. Bought it all in the meantime. Everything, a good twenty miles back, from either side of the road."

"You're shitting me," Flynne said.

"Coldiron owns most of the county now," Tacoma said, "hard as it might be to prove it in court. KCV's gone full matryoshka on that."

"What's that?" Flynne asked.

"Know those Russian dolls, nest inside each other? Matryoshka. Shells within shells. So it isn't that obvious that you own all this land."

"Not me. Coldiron."

"You and your brother," Tacoma said, "own the majority of Coldiron between you."

"Why do they?" asked Netherton.

"And who exactly is this talking head on the toy?" asked Tacoma, and Flynne realized that she was watching them, as she drove, on cams Flynne hadn't known were there.

"Wilf Netherton," said Flynne. "He's Coldiron, from London."

"You're on the list, then, Mr. Netherton," Tacoma said. "Sorry. Had to ask. Tacoma Raeburn."

"Raeburn?" Flynne asked. "You her sister?"

"Yep."

"And you're named Tacoma because—"

"Didn't want me called Snoqualmie. You from the future, Mr. Netherton?"

"Not exactly," he said. "I'm in the future that would result from my not being there. But since I am, it isn't your future. Here."

"What do you do, in the future, Mr. Netherton, if you don't mind my asking? What do people do there generally?"

"Wilf," he said. "Publicity."

"That's what people do?"

"That would be one way of looking at it," he said, after a pause, which seemed to satisfy Tacoma, or maybe she just didn't want to be too pushy.

Flynne finished her burrito. When they passed the spot where Conner had killed the men in the stolen cardboard, it felt more like a story than something that had happened at that particular place, and she was okay with that.

98.

BICENTENNIAL

y daylight her house was different. He reminded himself that none of this was about assemblers. Natural processes only. He associated untidiness with klept privilege. Lev's house, for instance: its absence of cleaners, as opposed to the corridor beneath Impostor Syndrome, its spotless sameness uniform through every uninhabited room in London.

The vehicle in front of them had continued on, beyond the house, then halted. In front of it, a smaller version had already stopped. Flynne had said that the smaller one was a bomb sniffer, operated by her cousin, who must be among the six who now emerged from the larger vehicle, all in identical black jackets. Four held stubby rifles. The fifth, who didn't, might be Flynne's cousin, who also wore some odd headpiece. Tacoma, the driver, had parked near the largest tree, the one he and Flynne had sat under in the moonlight. He recognized their bench, which he now saw was made of sawn lengths of graying wood, their once-white protective coating worn with use.

Out of the car now, tucked under her arm, he couldn't adjust the Wheelie Boy's camera quickly enough to compensate for her movement. He glimpsed the vehicle that had been following them, identical to the one in front, and four more black-coated men, each with a black rifle.

Then Flynne was striding toward the house, Tacoma evidently beside her. "Get them out of sight," Flynne said to Tacoma, whom he couldn't see. "Bullpups and jackets'll worry my mother."

"Got it," he heard Tacoma say, and wondered what bull pups were. "Says your cousin's coming in."

"You stay here," Flynne said, stepping up onto the planked veranda. "Keep Leon here. Don't let him inside while I'm with my mother. No such thing as a serious conversation, him around."

"Got it," Tacoma said, stepping into the frame of the Wheelie's camera. "We'll be right here." She indicated a sort of settee, in the same style as the bench under the tree, but with frayed fabric cushions.

Still carrying him, Flynne opened a curiously skeletal door, its thin frame tautly stretched with some sort of fine dark mesh, and stepped into the shade of the house. "I have to talk with my mother," she said, and set him down on something, a table or sideboard, level with her waist.

"Not here," he said. "On the floor."

"Okay," she said, "but stick around." She put the Wheelie down on the floor, then turned and was gone.

He activated the thing's tires, in opposite directions, slowly, the camera rotating with the spherical chassis. The room looked very tall, but wasn't. The camera was quite close to the wooden floor.

There was the mantelpiece, the one with the commemorative plastic tray whose duplicate he'd seen in Clovis Fearing's shop in Portobello Road, a pale oblong propped against the wall. He rolled forward, the camera bobbing annoyingly, until he could make out "Clanton Bicentennial," and the dates. And seventy-some years on from the year of celebration, he sat at Lev's grandfather's desk in the Gobiwagen, the band of the Wheelie-emulator across his forehead, looking back through this clumsy toy at this strange world, in which worn things weren't meticulously distressed, but actually worn, abraded by their passage through time. A fly buzzed heavily past, above the Wheelie Boy. Anxiously, he tried to track it, then remembered that here it was more likely a fly than a drone, and that the mesh on the weirdly fragile auxiliary door was meant to keep it out.

He turned the camera, studying the shabby, shadowy tableau of lost domestic calm. At the end of its arc, he discovered a cat glaring at him, on its haunches. As he saw it, it rushed the Wheelie, hissing, batting it fiercely back, the rear of the tablet striking the wooden floor. As the gyro whined, righting the Wheelie, he heard the cat push the mesh door far enough open to escape, and then the sound of it closing.

The fly, if it was the same one, could be heard buzzing, somewhere deeper in the house.

99.

AMERICAN ANTIQUITIES

'm not going anywhere," her mother said, propped on pillows against the chipped varnish of the bedstead, the prongs of the oxygen tube in her nose.

"Where's Janice?"

"Picking peas. I'm not going."

"Dark in here." The roller blind was down, drapes drawn together over it.

"Janice wanted me to sleep."

"Didn't you sleep last night?"

"I won't go."

"Who wants you to go?"

"Leon. Lithonia. Janice too, but she won't admit to it."

"Go where?"

"Northern fucking Virginia," her mother said, "as you know perfectly well."

"I just recently heard about that idea myself," Flynne said, sitting down on the white candlewick bedspread.

"Is Corbell dead?"

"Missing."

"You kill him?"

"No."

"Try to?"

"No."

"Not like I'd blame you. All I know is what I see on the news, and lately what little I can pry out of Janice and Lithonia. Is all of this happening because of whatever it is you and Burton are doing, that landed Corbell Pickett in my living room?"

"I guess so, Mom."

"Then what the hell is it?"

"I'm not even sure. Burton thought he was moonlighting for some company in Colombia. Turns out they're in London. Sort of. They've got a lot of money. To invest. One thing and another, they set up a branch office here and hired Burton and me to run it, or at least act like we do." She looked at her mother. "I know it doesn't make a lot of sense."

"Kind of sense the world makes," her mother said, drawing the candlewick up under her chin, "there's death and taxes and foreign wars. There's men like Corbell Pickett doing evil shit for a dollar, only real money anybody local and civilian makes here now, and there's decent-enough people having to work for their own little bit of that. Whatever you and Burton are doing, you aren't going to be changing any of that. Just more of the same. I've been here all my life. So have you. Your father was born where Porter meets Main, when they still had a hospital. I'm not going anywhere. Particularly not anywhere Leon tells me I'm going to like."

"Man in our company suggested that. He's from London."

"I don't give two shits, where he's from."

"Remember how hard you tried to get me not to talk like that?"

"Nobody was trying to make you move to northern Virginia. And I wouldn't have let them, either."

"You're not going anywhere. You're staying right here. I thought Virginia was a nonstarter the minute I heard it."

Her mother peered at her over the clenched bedspread. "You and Burton aren't making the economy about to crash, are you?"

"Who said that?"

"Lithonia. Smart girl. Gets it off one of those things they wear over one eye."

"Lithonia said we were making the economy crash?"

"Not you. Just that it might. Or anyway that the stock market's weirder than anybody's ever seen it."

"I hope not." She stood up, went and kissed her mother. "I've got to call them now," she said. "Tell 'em you're not going anywhere. They'll need to get you more help around the place. Friends of Burton's."

"Playing soldier?"

"They were all in the service, before."

"Think they'd've got their fill of it," her mother said.

Flynne went out and found Janice in the living room, in plaid flannel pajama bottoms and a black Magpul t-shirt, her hair in four stumpy pigtails. She was holding an old ceramic bowl with most of the edge chipped off, full of fresh-picked peas. "Ella's not going anywhere," Flynne said. "They're just going to have to make her safer out here."

"I figured," said Janice. "Why I didn't try to push it."

"Where's Netherton?"

"Guy on the Wheelie Boy?"

"Here," said Netherton, wheeling out of the kitchen.

"In the kitchen if you need me," said Janice, stepping past the Wheelie.

"Did you speak with your mother?" Netherton asked.

"She's definitely not going anywhere. I have to call and sort that with Griff and Burton and Tommy. They'll have to protect her out here, whatever happens."

The Wheelie had kept going. Was across the room now, in front of the fireplace. She watched the tablet tilt back. "This tray," he said, voice tiny at that distance, on the little speakers.

"What?"

"On the mantelpiece. Where did you get it?"

"Clanton. Mom took us all over for the bicentennial, when we were kids."

"Lowbeer found one like it, recently, in London. Her modules had recorded this one the night I was here. Her friend searched for it. She deals in American antiquities. She's American herself. Clovis Fearing."

"Clovis?"

"Fearing," he said.

"Not Raeburn?" It didn't make any sense. "How old is she?"

"No older than Lowbeer, I suppose, though she chooses to be more obvious about it. Ah. Looked it up. Raeburn. Mrs. Clovis Fearing's maiden name."

"She's an old lady? In London?"

"They knew one another, when they were younger. Lowbeer said she was visiting her to have her own memory refreshed. Mrs. Fearing said something about Lowbeer having been a British spy, and Lowbeer said that that had made Fearing one herself."

"But she was Raeburn then," said Flynne. "Now." She was looking at the white tray but not seeing it. Seeing Lowbeer's hand instead, holding her hat against their quadcopter's downdraft in the Cheapside street, and Griff's hands, arranging the Sushi Barn food. "Shit," she said, then said it again, more softly.

100.

BACK HERE

omething about the mention of Clovis Fearing had caused Flynne to abruptly change the subject. She'd taken him out on the veranda, placed him on the love seat between Tacoma Raeburn and the man Flynne had introduced as her cousin Leon, and gone out to stand beneath the largest tree, having a conversation on her phone. Netherton had panned from Tacoma, whom he found attractive in an obliquely threatening way, to Leon, who wore a strange elasticated headscarf, its fabric abstractly patterned in shades Netherton associated with the droppings of birds, before cleaners tidied them away. He had pale, bushy eyebrows and the start of an equally pale beard.

"Mr. Netherton's in the future," Tacoma said to Leon, whose mouth was slightly open.

"Wilf," said Netherton.

Leon tilted his head to one side. "You in the future, Wilf?"

"In a sense."

"How's the weather?"

"Less sunny, last I looked."

"You should be a weatherman," Leon said, "you're in the future and you know the weather."

"You're someone who only pretends to be unintelligent," Netherton said. "It serves you simultaneously as protective coloration and a medium for passive aggression. It won't work with me."

"Future's fucking snippy," said Leon, to Tacoma. "I didn't come out here to be abused by vintage product from the Hefty toy department."

"I think you might be stuck with that," said Tacoma. "Wilf's paying your salary, or close enough."

"Well shit," said Leon, "I guess I should remove my hat."

"I don't think he cares about that, but you could always take it off just because it's butt-ugly," Tacoma said.

Leon sighed, and pulled off the scarf. His hair, what there was of it, was only a slight improvement. "Do I have you to thank for winning the lottery, Wilf?"

"Not really," Netherton said.

"Future's going to be a huge pain in the ass," Leon said, but then Flynne was there, picking up the Wheelie.

"Time for your visit with Mom, Leon," she said. "You're here to cheer her up, relax her. Way you do that, you start by telling her I got them to promise me she can stay here."

"They're scared of somebody getting ahold of her," Leon said, "having that over you."

"So now they get to throw money at it," Flynne said. "They're good at that. Go on, get in there with your aunt Ella. Make her feel good. You make her any more worried, I'll tear you a new one."

"I'm going," said Leon, "I'm going," but Netherton saw that he was neither frightened nor angry. Leon got to his feet, making the love seat creak.

"I'm taking Wilf down to the trailer," Flynne said to Tacoma.

"That on the property?" Tacoma asked.

"Bottom of the hill behind the house. Near the creek. Burton lives there."

"I'll just walk along with you," Tacoma said, getting up, the love seat not creaking at all.

"Wilf and I need to have a talk. It's a small trailer."

"I won't come in," Tacoma said. "Sorry, but you go outside the house, or this front yard, I have to move boys around, and drones."

"That's okay," Flynne said. "I appreciate it."

And then they were off the porch, Flynne striding across the lawn he'd seen as moonlit silver. It looked nothing like that now. Thinly, unevenly green, starting to brown in places. She rounded the corner of the house. Tacoma was murmuring to her earbud, he supposed telling boys and drones what she needed done.

"Tomorrow night's the party," Flynne said to him. "I need you to tell me about Daedra, explain who this woman is I'm supposed to be, what she does."

"I can't see," he said. The camera side of the tablet was trapped under her upper arm. When she freed it, and turned him around, he saw trees, smaller ones, and a trampled earthen trail, descending. "Where are we going?"

"Burton's trailer. Down by the creek. He's lived there since he got out of the Marines."

"Is he there?"

"He's back at Coldiron. Or in town somewhere. He won't mind."

"Where's Tacoma?"

She swung the Wheelie around. He saw Tacoma on the trail behind them. Swung it back, started down. "Daedra," she said. "How'd you meet her, anyway?"

"I was hired to be a publicist on a project she was central to. Its resident celebrity. Rainey brought me on. She's a publicist as well. Or was. She's just resigned." Trees on either side, the trail crooked.

"Envy her that," Flynne said, "having the option."

"But you do. You used it when you thought Lowbeer's agent would use the party time on those religionists."

"That was bullshit. Well, not bullshit, 'cause I'd have done what I said. But then, pretty soon, we'd all be dead. Us back here, anyway."

"What's that?"

"Burton's trailer. It's an Airstream. Nineteen seventy-seven."

The year, from the century previous even to this one she carried him through, struck him as incredible. "Did they all look like that?"

"Like what?"

"An assembler malfunction."

"That's the foam. Uncle who hauled it down here put that on to stop it leaking, and for insulation. Shiny streamline thing, under that."

"I'll be out here if you need me," said Tacoma, behind them.

"Thanks," said Flynne, reaching for the handle on a battered metal door, set back in the weathered larval bulge of whatever the thing had been covered with. She opened it, stepped up, into a space he recognized from first having interviewed her. Tiny lights came on, in strings, embedded in some slightly yellowish transparent material. A small space, as small as the rear cabin of the Gobiwagen, lower. A narrow metal-framed bed, table, a chair. The chair moved.

"The chair moved," he said.

"Wants me to sit in it. Man, I forget how hot this sucker gets . . ."

" 'Sucker'?"

"Trailer. Here." She put him down on the table. "Got to crack a window." The window creaked, opening. Then she opened a squat white cabinet that stood on the floor, took out a blue-and-silver metallic-looking container, closing the cabinet. "My turn to not be able to offer you a drink." She pulled a ring atop the container. Drank from the resulting opening. The chair was moving again. She sat in it, facing him. It hummed, creaked, was silent, unmoving. "Okay," she said, "she your girlfriend?"

"Who?"

"Daedra."

"No," he said.

"But was she?"

"No."

She looked at him. "You two were doing it?"

"Yes."

"Girlfriend. Unless you're an asshole."

He considered this. "I was quite taken with her," he said, then paused.

"Taken?"

"She's very striking. Physically. But . . ."

"But?"

"I'm almost certainly an asshole."

She looked at him. Or rather, he remembered, at part of his face on the Wheelie Boy's tablet. "Well," she said, "if you really know that, you're ahead of most of the dating stock around here."

"Dating stock?"

"Men," she said. "Ella, my mother, she says the odds are good around here, but the goods are odd. 'Cept they aren't odd, usually. More like too ordinary."

"I might be odd," he said. "I like to imagine I am. Here. I mean there. In London."

"But you weren't supposed to get involved with her that way, because it was business?"

"That's correct."

"Tell me about it."

"About . . . ?"

"What happened. And when you get to a part that I can't understand, or I don't know what you're talking about, I'll stop you and ask you questions until I understand it."

She looked very serious, but not unfriendly.

"I will, then," said Netherton.

101.

ORDINARY SAD-ASS HUMANNESS

Her time in the trailer with Wilf had kept her mind off what she couldn't quite believe she'd decided about Lowbeer and Griff. The ordinary sad-ass humanness of his story with Daedra, in spite of big lumps of future-stuff, had been weirdly comforting.

She still wasn't sure how Daedra made her living, or what her relationship with the United States government was. Seemed like a cross between a slightly porny media star and what sophomore year Art History called a performance artist, plus maybe a kind of diplomat. But she still didn't get what the United States did either, in Wilf's world. He made it sound like the nation-state equivalent of Conner, minus the sense of humor, but she supposed that might not be so far off, even today.

After the trailer, the three of them had gone up to the house and had the peas Janice had stir-fried with some bacon and onions, sitting around the kitchen table with Leon and her mother. Her mother had asked Tacoma about her name, and her job, and Tacoma had been good at not seeming like she wasn't explaining what she did, and Flynne had seen her mother seeing that, but not minding. Her mother was in a better mood, and Flynne took that to mean she'd accepted that she wouldn't be sent off to northern Virginia with Lithonia.

Driving back, it was the same convoy, and no other traffic on the road at all. "Should be more people driving out here, this time of day," she said to Tacoma.

"That's because it's shorter to list what Coldiron doesn't own in this county. You own both sides of this road. In the rest of the county, Hefty still owns the bulk of what you don't. What's left either belongs to individuals, or Matryoshka."

"The dolls?"

"The competition. It's what we call them in KCV. Out of Nassau, so that's probably where they first came through from the future, the way Coldiron did in Colombia."

They were at the edge of town now, and Tacoma started talking to her earbud, making the convoy take unexpected turns, or as unexpected as you could manage anywhere this size. Flynne figured they were angling to get into the back without attracting the attention of Luke 4:5, on the other side of Tommy's yellow Sheriff's Department tape. They knew how to obey police tape, because that could help them in court, when they eventually sued the municipality, like they always did, most of them having gone to law school for that express purpose. They always protested in silence, and that was deliberate too, some legal strategy she'd never understood. They'd hold their signs up and stinkeye everybody, never say a word. You could see the mean glee they took in it, and she just thought it was sorry, that people could be like that.

At least there was some traffic in town, mostly KCV employees trying to look local. Not a single German car. Anyone who made a living selling secondhand Jeeps should be hosting a big fiesta about now, for the workers at the factory in Mexico.

"Always been a redhead?" Flynne asked Tacoma, to get her mind off Luke 4:5.

"A day longer than I've been with KCV," Tacoma said. "They have to bleach it almost white, before they dye it."

"I like it."

"I don't think my hair does."

"You get contacts at the same time?"

"I did."

"Otherwise, you'd look enough like your sister that people would put it together."

"We drew straws," Tacoma said. "She would've gone blond, but I lost. She was blond when she was younger. Brings out her risk-taking tendencies, so this is probably better."

Flynne looked over at the blank screen of the Wheelie's tablet, wondered where he was now. "Are you really a notary?"

"Hell yes. And a CPA. And I've got paper for you to sign when we get back, taking your brother's little militia from cult of personality to state-registered private security firm."

"I have to talk with Griff, first thing. Has to be private. You help me with that?"

"Sure. Your best bet's Hong's. That one table, off in an alcove? I'll have him hold that for you. Otherwise, you can't know who's on the other side of the nearest tarp."

"Thanks."

And then the truck was in the alley behind Fab, sandwiched between the two SUVs as they disgorged black-jacketed Burton boys, everybody with a bullpup except Leon.

"Ready?" Tacoma asked, killing the engine.

Flynne hadn't been ready for any of it, she thought, not since that night she went to the trailer to sub for him. It wasn't stuff you could be ready for. Like life, maybe, that way.

102.

TRANSPLANT

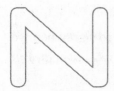etherton found Ossian waiting, a narrow rosewood case tucked beneath one arm, beside Ash's tent, the unpleasant profile of the six-wheeled Bentley nowhere to be seen.

"Is Ash inside?" Netherton asked, Flynne's peripheral beside him, watching him speak. He'd awakened it, if that was the term, after Ash had phoned, asking him to bring it along to the tent, for a meeting.

"She's been delayed," Ossian said. "She'll be along shortly."

"What's that?" Netherton asked, eyeing the rectangular wooden box.

"Case for a pair of Regency dueling pistols, originally. Come in." The tent smelled, familiarly now, of the dust that wasn't there. Ash's displays, the agate spheres, were the sole source of light. Netherton held a chair for the peripheral, which then sat, looking up at Ossian. Ossian put the rosewood box down on the table. Like a shopman, employing a certain constrained drama, he undid two small brass latches, paused briefly for effect, then opened the hinged lid.

"Temporarily deactivated," he said, "and for the first time since they left the pram factory." The case was lined with green felt. In identical fitted recesses nested a pair of what Netherton assumed to be guns. Like toys, really, given the glossy candy-cane cream-and-scarlet twisted around their short barrels.

"How is it that they fit the box so perfectly?"

"Rejigged the interior. Wanted something to carry them in. Wouldn't want one tucked in my pocket, however positive I am that they're disabled. Took some serious doing, to turn them off, but we managed to only release assemblers the one time, when you were there. Zubov has the Bentley with a specialist now, having five meters of leather cloned, to repair the upholstery."

"Lowbeer values these things because they're difficult to trace?"

"Because they're terror weapons, more likely," said Ossian. "They aren't guns in any ballistic sense. Not about the force of a projectile. They're directed swarm weapons. Flesh-eaters, in the trade."

"What trade would that be?"

"They project self-limiting, single-purpose assemblers. Range a little under ten meters. Do nothing whatever but disintegrate soft animal tissue, including, apparently, your finer Italian leathers. But more or less instantly, and then they disassemble themselves. That way, they're of no danger to the user, or rather to the infant, as their only user was intended to be the pram."

"But they have handles," Netherton observed. The handles were shaped something like the profile of a parrot's head. They were the same cream shade as the barrels, minus the scarlet, but matte, bonelike.

"Grips and manual triggers are your Edward's, to Lowbeer's specifications. He isn't bad at all."

"I don't understand why a pram would have been equipped with these in the first place."

"Aren't Russian then, are you? Effect of one of these on a human body will absolutely get your attention, foremost. Quite the spectacular exit. See a fellow kidnapper go that way, the thinking runs, you'll flee. Or try to. Self-targeting. Once the system acquires a target, it sends the assemblers where they're needed."

"But you've entirely disabled them?"

"Not permanently. Lowbeer has the key to that."

"Why does she want them?"

"Discuss it with her," said Ash, ducking in, something fleeing cumbrously, on four legs from her cheek, across her neck, as she entered.

"When are we expecting Flynne?" Netherton asked, glancing at the peripheral.

"I'd assumed she'd be here by now," Ash said, "but we've just been told she's unavailable. And that we'll wait." Briefly, she cawed to Ossian, in some coarser birdsong. He lowered the lid over the peppermint pistols. "In the meantime," Ash said, "we think we've solved the problem of Flynne's lacking the gift of neoprimitivist curatorial gab."

"How is that?" Netherton asked.

"I suppose you could call it fecal transplant therapy."

"Really?" Netherton looked at her.

"A synthetic bullshit implant," Ash said, and smiled. "A procedure I don't imagine you'll ever be in need of."

103.

SUSHI BARN

The tunnel to Sushi Barn was less a tunnel than a giant hamster run. Madison had built two seven-foot walls of shingle bags, with a walkway in between, from a hole in the wall in the back of Coldiron, across the vacant store next door, through another hole in its far wall, across the next empty store, and finally through another hole, into Hong's kitchen.

Coming in from the alley, Flynne had seen Burton, looking pale, under one of the white crowns. Conner was under another. "Want to switch jobs?" Clovis asked Tacoma, seeing her. "Neither of these guys are home much."

"They're making Burton work?" Flynne asked.

"Nobody's twisting his arm," Clovis said. "Glad to get out of his body. Conner just comes back to be fed and sleep."

Griff didn't seem to have any idea what Flynne might have on her mind. She wasn't sure what Lowbeer might have heard, or what Griff might know. She wanted to look at his hands now, but he had them in his jacket pockets.

Hong's kitchen was humid with cooking rice. He led them out to the front room, where the seating was at secondhand picnic tables, painted red, and over to an alcove, a sheet of red-painted plywood forming one of its walls. The alcove had its own picnic table, and a framed poster of the Highbinders on the inside of the red wall, a San Francisco band she'd liked in high school. She put the Wheelie Boy down on the scuffed, red-painted concrete floor, under the seat, and sat, facing the Highbinders poster. Griff took the seat opposite. A kid she recognized as a cousin of Madison's brought them glasses of tea.

"You need food, just let somebody know," Hong said.

"Thanks, Hong," she said, as he turned back to the kitchen. She looked at Griff.

He smiled, raised a tablet, consulted it, looked up from it, met her eyes. "Now that we know that a safe house elsewhere isn't an option for your mother, we're looked into maximizing security for your family home. With a view to keeping it as low key, as transparent really, as we possibly can. We don't want to disturb your mother. We think a compound might be in order."

"Pickett had a compound," she said. "Don't want that."

"Exactly the opposite. Stealth architecture. Everything remains apparently the same. Any new structures will appear to always have been there. We're speaking with specialist architects. We need it done yesterday, largely at night, silently, invisibly." He scrolled something with a fingertip.

"Can you do that?"

"With sufficient money, absolutely. Which your firm most certainly has."

"Not my firm."

"Partially yours." He smiled.

"On paper."

"This building," he said, "isn't paper."

She looked out at the front room of Sushi Barn. Noticed four members of Burton's posse, men whose names she didn't know, seated two-by-two at different tables, black Cordura rifle bags tucked under their seats. The rest of the customers were in KCV county outfits. "Doesn't feel real to me," she said. She looked back at him. "Been a lot lately that doesn't." She looked down at his hands.

"What doesn't?"

"You're her," she said, looking up, meeting his pale eyes. Not that crazy cartoon blue. Not blue at all, but widening now. A woman laughed, tables away. His hand lowered the tablet, came to rest on the table, and for the first time since the end of the ride back from Pickett's, she thought she might be about to cry.

He swallowed. Blinked. "Really, I'll be someone else."

"You don't become her?"

"Our lives were identical, until Lev's first communication was received here. But this is no longer their past, so she isn't who I'll become. We diverged, however imperceptibly at first, when that message was received. By the time she first contacted me, there were already bits of my life she was unfamiliar with."

"She mailed you?"

"Phoned me," he said. "I was at a reception in Washington."

"Did she tell you she was you?"

"No. She told me that the woman I'd just been speaking with, a moment before, was a mole, a deep-cover agent, for the Russian Federation. She, the woman, was my American equivalent, in many ways. Then she, Ainsley, this stranger on the phone, told me something that proved it. Or would, when I'd used classified search engines. So it was rather a gradual revelation, over about forty-eight hours. I did guess," he said. "During our third call. She told me, then, that she'd made a wager with herself, that I would. And won." He smiled slightly. "But I'd seen that she had knowledge not only of the world, but of my exact and most secret situation in it. Knowledge no one else could possess, not even my superiors. And she'd continued to identify other foreign and domestic agents in my own agency, and in the American agency I liaise with. In her time, they'd gone undetected for years, one for over a decade, and at very serious strategic cost. I'm unable to act on most of them, else I attract too much attention, become suspect myself. But possession of that information has already had a very beneficial effect on my career."

"When was this?"

"Thursday," he said.

"It hasn't been very long."

"I've barely slept. But it was nothing professional that convinced me. It was that she knew me as no one else could. Thoughts and feelings I've had constantly, all my life, but had never expressed, not to anyone." He looked away, then back, shyly.

"I can see her now," Flynne said, "but it didn't strike me until Wilf told me about the tray, this morning."

"The tray?"

"Like the one at my house. Clovis has one, in London. She's an old lady there. Has a store that sells American antiques. Lowbeer's friend. Took Wilf there when she needed Clovis to refresh her memory about something. When he told me, I remembered your hands, hers. Saw it."

"How utterly peculiar it all is," he said, and looked down at his hands.

"You're not named Lowbeer?"

"Ainsley James Gryffyd Lowbeer Holdsworth," he said. "My mother's maiden name. She was allergic to hyphenation." He took a blue handkerchief from a jacket pocket. Not Homes blue but darker, almost black. Dabbed his eyes. "Pardon me," he said. "A bit emotional." He looked at her. "You're the first person I've discussed this with, other than Ainsley."

"It's okay," she said, not sure what that even meant now. "Can she hear us? Right now?"

"Not unless we're in range of a device of some kind."

"You'll tell her? That I know?"

"What would you prefer?" He tilted his head then, reminding her more than ever of Lowbeer.

"I'd like to tell her myself."

"Then you will. Ash just messaged me that they need you back, as soon as possible."

104.

THE RED MEDICI

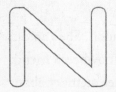etherton, just then looking at the peripheral, saw Flynne arrive. It was like seeing someone jarred out of a reverie, the peripheral suddenly informed, present. She took in the faces around the table. "Where's Lowbeer?" she asked.

"You'll be meeting with her," Ash said, "but you're here now for equipment, for tomorrow's event."

"What kind of equipment?"

"Two kinds," Ash said.

Ossian opened the rosewood pistol case.

"These are weapons," Ash said.

"Why do they look like that?" Flynne raised an eyebrow at Netherton.

"They were built into a high-security pram," Netherton said, "as an antikidnapping measure."

"Are they guns?"

"Best think of them as that," Ash said. "Never point one at anyone you don't want to kill. There's a relationship between what happens when you depress this stud," she indicated a point on the inner curve of the parrot-head handle, "and the position of the barrel. Though not exclusively, so not entirely like a gun in that regard. Once the system acquires a biological target, on being triggered, it dispatches assemblers, which seek and find the target regardless. Pick one up."

The peripheral leaned forward, tapped the gun nearest her with the nail of her index finger. "Like an old derringer, but made of peppermint." She used both hands to lift it from its recess, neatly managing,

Netherton noted, to not point it at any of them. It lay on her open palm.

"It's deactivated, currently," said Ossian, "after considerable effort. You can try the grip."

She closed her hand around the parrot's head, extended the thing, its festive barrel pointing at a palm-sized bald patch on Ash's velour tent. "I'm taking these to Wilf's ex's party?"

"You certainly aren't," said Ash. "Weapons of any sort are proscribed, and you'll be scanned thoroughly, prior to admission. In any case, these happen to be as blatantly illegal as anything in London today."

"Then why are you showing them to me?" She returned the thing to its fitted recess, sat back.

"Under certain conditions," Ash said, "as I understand it, one of these may be delivered to you. We're showing them to you now so you'll recognize them, if necessary, and know how to use them."

"Point and click," Ossian said. "Has absolutely no effect on inorganic material. Soft tissue only." He lowered the lid.

"Second order of business," said Ash, opening her hand, palm up, to reveal what Netherton assumed was a Medici, but red. "This will install a cognitive bundle that will enable you to sound something like a neoprimitivist curator. If not to another neoprimitivist curator, though I'd imagine that's debatable."

"It will?" Flynne asked, eyeing the thing. "How?"

"Think of it as a disguise. You no more need to operate it than you need to operate a mask. Certain specific sorts of query will trigger it."

"And?"

"You'll spout a reasonably high grade of facile nonsense."

"Will I know what it means?"

"It won't mean anything," said Ash. "Were you to keep it up, you'd shortly repeat yourself."

"Bullshit baffles brains?"

"One hopes. I'll need to install it in your peripheral now."

"Where did you get it?" Flynne asked.

"Lowbeer," said Ossian.

"The back of your hand, please," said Ash.

Flynne placed the peripheral's hand palm down on the table, beside the corroded base of Ash's display, spread its fingers. Ash pressed the red Medici gently against the back of the peripheral's hand, where it remained, seeming to do nothing at all.

"Well?" Flynne asked, looking up at Ash.

"It's loading," Ash said.

Flynne looked at Netherton. "What have you been doing?" she asked.

"Waiting for you. Admiring your guns. Yourself?"

"Talking with Griff." He couldn't read her expression. "They're talking about defenses for our house. Stuff that's supposed to not bother my mother."

"The mystery man," said Ossian. "So you've actually met him."

Flynne looked at him. "Sure."

"Any idea how she recruited him?" Ossian asked.

"No," Flynne said, "but wouldn't it figure that she'd be good at that?"

"No doubt," said Ossian. "But we seem to be increasingly following his orders, with next to no idea of who he might be."

"No idea who she is, either," Flynne said. "Maybe he's like that."

Ash leaned forward to remove the Medici, then tucked it into her reticule. "We'll just test it," she said to Flynne. "Tell us, please, why you think Daedra West's art is important today."

Flynne looked at her. "West's oeuvre obliquely propels the viewer through an elaborately finite set of iterations, skeins of carnal memory manifesting an exquisite tenderness, but delimited by our mythologies of the real, of body. It isn't about who we are now, but about who we would be, the other." She blinked. "Fucking hell." The peripheral's eyes were wide.

"I'd hoped for something in a more colloquial register," said Ash, "but I suppose that's a contradiction in terms. Try not to let it run on. The thinness will show."

"I can interpret, for Daedra," Netherton suggested.

"Quite," said Ash.

105.

STATIC IN YOUR BONES

n the elevator, she tried thinking about what Wilf had told her about Daedra's art, wondering if she might hear that bullshit voice in her head, but she didn't. "What is that thing that talks?" she asked him.

"Cognitive bundle," he said, as the doors opened. She smelled Lev's cooking from the kitchen. "It constructs essentially meaningless statements out of a given jargon, around whatever chosen topic. I won't walk you up. You've been there before." He'd stopped at the foot of the stairs.

"I said it," she said, "but I didn't think it."

"Exactly. But that isn't evident to anyone else. And it wasn't bad, for a collage from rote."

"Creeps me out."

"I think it's actually a good idea, in our situation. Best you get upstairs."

"Try the Wheelie, when I get back."

"Where is it?"

"On a chair in the back of Coldiron. By the beds."

"Good luck," he said.

She turned and climbed the stairs, with their runner of patterned carpet, to turn at the landing, up again. At the top, furniture gleamed softly, glass sparkled. She wished she could've stopped to look at the things, but here was Lowbeer, at the double doors, only one of them partially open, her hand on the knob. "Hello," she said. "Please come in." Into that green again, gilt trim. A single lamp, incandescent element behind glass cut like diamonds. "Griff is sorting out protection for your mother, I understand."

Flynne looked at the long table, its dark top perfectly smooth but not too glossy. It no longer felt to her like Santa's Headquarters here. She wished it did. A very business-y room, almost an office. She looked at Lowbeer, who was wearing another one of her suits. Saw Griff there, more strongly than she'd expected. "He's you," she said. "He's you when you were younger."

Lowbeer's head tilted. "Did you guess, or did he confide in you?"

"You have the same hands. Netherton saw the tray on our mantel. Said he'd seen one in Clovis's store here. That she's an old woman. I guess once I thought of her being there, and here, at the same time . . ." She stopped. "But it isn't the same time. I guessed you might be there too."

"Exactly," said Lowbeer, closing the door.

"Am I here, that way?" Flynne asked.

"Not that we've been able to determine. Your birth record survives. No death record. But things became messy, as I understand Netherton's explained to you. Records, during the deeper jackpot, are incomplete to nonexistent, and more so in the United States. There was a military government there, briefly, that erased huge swathes of data, seemingly at random, no one seems to know why. If you were alive today, you'd be about my age, and that would mean either that you were wealthy or very well connected, which tend to be the same thing, here. Which should mean that I'd be able to have found you."

"You don't mind, that I know?"

"Not at all. Why would you think I might?"

"Because it's a secret?"

"Not from you. Come, sit here." She went to the tall, mossy-green armchairs, at the head of the table. She waited until Flynne was settled in one, then sat in the other. "I understand that Netherton is pleased with the cognitive bundle."

"Glad somebody is."

"And you've been shown the guns."

"Why do I need them?"

"Only one," she said. "The other's either for Conner or your brother, depending. I hope none of you need them, but there's a crudeness of mind behind this business. Best we have our own options for crudeness."

The tall windows were hidden behind green curtains. Flynne imagined a maze behind them, more green curtains, like the blue tarps in Coldiron. "What about President Gonzales? Griff says they killed her."

"They did. It set the tone."

"You're going to change that?"

"That depends. It's less like a conspiracy than a climate, at this point."

"What does it depend on?"

"Daedra's party, it seems."

"How?"

"Coldiron and Matryoshka, as your people are calling it, are racing for ownership of your world. Competing tides of subsecond financial events. We are not winning. We are not losing, by that much, but we are not winning. Lev is employing a brilliant but makeshift apparatus on Coldiron's behalf. Matryoshka, which exists in order to kill you, and for no other reason, appears to be employing some more powerful state financial apparatus, here. I need to stop that, in order to enable Coldiron's dominance, which may then enable the prevention of Gonzales's assassination. But the politics here are such that I'm unable to do that without first having proof, or some reasonable facsimile thereof, of who murdered Aelita. I can't begin to explain how power works, here, but someone powerful must have an interest in Matryoshka. Invariably, they will have stepped on someone else's toes, or stand to. I can leverage that, offer that other party a fulcrum with which to crush them. But in order for any of that to happen, you and Netherton must succeed at Daedra's event."

Flynne looked at the cut glass and silver on the sideboard. She looked at Lowbeer. "It all hangs on me identifying the asshole on that balcony?"

"Yes."

"That's fucked."

"It is that, yes. But here we are. Should you recognize him, you'll alert me, and things will be set in motion."

"What if I don't? Can't?"

"Best not dwell on that. But if you do succeed, we face another level of difficulty, in that Daedra's gathering operates under a protocol that strictly bans the use of personal communication devices. As peripherals, telepresent devices, you and Mr. Penske become exceptions of a sort, but you'll be very tightly monitored. So it then becomes a question of how, should you identify our murderer, you will then communicate that to me."

"So how do I?"

"Your peripheral's newly installed cognitive bundle is, literally, a bundle. Within it is a communications platform the security bubble around Daedra's event will be unable to detect. You will hear me, when you do, as, and I quote, 'static in your bones.' I understand it's peculiarly unsettling, but it's our safest option."

"And if he's there?"

"Far the more interesting fork to consider. And why I was pleased by your complete unwillingness to allow the use of that peculiarly vile chemical weapon."

"Why did you do that?"

"Because I may need you, going forward, to be exactly the person who won't do that."

"You always want to know a lot," she said, "but you won't tell me much at all."

"We need you focused on the moment."

" 'We' who?"

"You and I, my dear," said Lowbeer, and reached across to pat her hand.

106.
BUTTHOLEVILLE

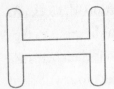ello?" he said, settled in the Gobiwagen's cupola, as the Wheelie's window opened. "Flynne?"

"She's not back yet," said a voice, a woman's, the accent familiar. The window's contents looked abstract, white verticals against that same blue.

"Tacoma?"

"Clovis," she said. "You're Netherton." And she picked the Wheelie up, turned it.

Unflattering angle, from below, of what he nonetheless took to be a very attractive face. Short black hair. He tried to see the face of the proprietor of The Clovis Limit there, but only saw her ancient, waiting skull. Terrifying. God's view of humanity, perhaps, were there one. "Wilf," he said, "hello."

"Here she is," she said, turning, and he was looking down on Flynne, her head in a strange, awkward, glitteringly white construct of some kind, cushioned with white pillows. Her eyes were closed. It was like looking down at the peripheral in the back cabin, except that this was Flynne herself. Absent.

"Can she hear us?" he asked.

"No. The crown's an autonomic cutout. So I'm told. I thought you had all this tech, up there."

"We do," he said. "I'm not technical, myself. But our version of this looks like a transparent plastic hairband."

"They were made up to your specs, but we had to improvise." She turned him again. Flynne's brother was in the next bed, under an identical crown. In the third bed, a face he didn't recognize. The two of them under blue blankets. What he'd first seen were white bars at the foot of Burton's bed, against blanket. The second man's body mass seemed child like.

"Who's that?" he asked.

"Conner."

"Penske. I've only seen him in the dancing master."

"The who?"

"Lev's brother's martial arts instructor. Peripheral. Excellent dancer, apparently."

"I'd give my left nut to get up there, see all that," she said, turning him to face her again. "What can I do for you, Wilf?"

"Is there a window?"

"Not really. On the other side of this stupid wall," and she turned him, to view an improvised surface that seemed to be made of stacked white envelopes, perhaps containing paper files. "But they've sprayed it with polymer, so you can't see out. Even if you could, you'd just be seeing the alley behind a strip mall in Buttholeville."

"Is that the town's name?"

"Nickname. Mine. My sister's too, I guess. We're awful."

"I've met her," he said. "She's not awful."

"Told me she met you."

"Do you know when Flynne will be back?"

"No. Want to wait? Watch the news? I've got a tablet here."

"The news?"

"Local's interesting, today. We've got Luke 4:5 pulling out, nobody's sure why. Griff actually doesn't like it. He's had two PR firms keeping them from getting media coverage, and that's been working. Now that they're leaving, for no apparent reason, there's some national interest. Basically because it's not what they usually do. You won't be able to change the channel."

"I'll try it, then," he said. "It fascinates me, here."

"Takes all kinds."

107.
LITTLE BUDDY

Flynne opened her eyes.

"Your little buddy's here," said Clovis.

"Wilf?"

"Got any others?"

"Where is he?"

"Watching the news." She lifted the crown off Flynne's head, put it down on the bedside table.

Flynne rolled on her side, sat up slowly, lowered her legs over the side. She'd been standing with Lowbeer in Lev's kitchen, looking out at the garden. She felt like she could still see it, if she closed her eyes. She did. Didn't see it. Opened them.

"You okay?" asked Clovis, eyeing her narrowly.

"Jet lag, maybe," Flynne said. Standing up. Clovis was obviously ready to catch her if she fell. "I'm okay. Burton okay?"

"Fine. Been back to pee, again to have dinner and hydrate. Walter Reed's happy with him."

Flynne went over to the chair where she'd left the Wheelie. Clovis had collapsed the telescoping rod the tablet rode on, and propped a tablet of her own against the back of the chair, on a wadded sweatshirt. The Wheelie was watching the *Ciencia Loca* episode about spontaneous human combustion. "Hey," she said, "hi."

"Wah!" said Netherton, startled. The Wheelie's spherical body rotated backward on fixed wheels, tilting its tablet and camera up at her. "That was frightening me," he said. "I kept imagining my body igniting, in the Gobiwagen's observation cupola. It came on after the news and I couldn't change it."

"Want to watch the rest? Second half's scuba stuff, the old tip of lower Manhattan."

"No! I came to see you."

"I've got to eat. I'll take you to Sushi Barn."

"What's that?"

"Hong's restaurant. It's at the other end of the mall. Madison's cut holes through and built a hamster run with shingle bags." She checked her reflection in a plastic-framed mirror that someone, probably Clovis, had taped to a blue tarp with aquamarine duct tape. "That crown is hell on my hair." She sat down on the chair, put the Wheelie on the floor, and put her sneakers on. The Wheelie extended its tablet, whirred, and wheeled across the floor, tablet swiveling. "Stay there," she said, getting up. She crossed to it, picked it up, and ducked through the slit.

"This is bizarre," he said, on the other side. "It looks like some primitive game."

"Boring game."

"They all are. What is it for?"

"If we're under attack, we can walk through this to Sushi Barn and get the shrimp special."

"Does that make sense?"

"It's a guy thing. But I think it was Lowbeer's idea, as interpreted through Burton and my friend Madison."

"Who is Madison?"

She stepped through the hole in the central wall. "My friend's husband, nice guy. Plays Sukhoi Flankers."

"What's that?"

"Flight sim game. Old Russian planes. Lowbeer is Griff."

He didn't say anything. She stopped, between the shingle-bag walls, raised the Wheelie Boy. "'Is Griff'?" he asked.

"Griff. Becomes her. But not exactly. Like this isn't her past anymore, so he won't have her life, because none of this happened to her when she was him." She started walking.

"You somehow seem," he said, "to simply accept all these things."

"You're the one living in the future, with nanobots eating people, spare bodies, government run by kings and gangsters and shit. You accept all that, right?"

"No," he said, just before she ducked through, into Hong's kitchen, "I don't. I hate it."

108.
COLDIRON MORNING

Tommy came in and squatted down on his haunches at the foot of her foam, hat in his hand. She was groggy from the pill she'd let Tacoma give her, but she'd had her best sleep in about a week. "Sit on the foam, Tommy, you'll wreck your knees."

"Best they got for you in here?" he asked, swiveling on his heels and dropping his butt on the corner of the slab.

"Hospital beds feel like hospital. And Burton and Conner both fart a lot. What's that with Luke 4:5 packing up? Are we sure we didn't buy them?"

"You sure shit didn't buy 'em," he said. "Why I'm waking you up before anybody wants me to. To tell you about that."

"What?" She got up on her elbows.

"I think the other guys pulled them out because they're a media magnet. Not that much on their own, anymore, but you add something else to the mix, media'll be all over it. Or even if they just do something off-script, like leaving here now, they're more interesting, maybe just for a news cycle. Like your PR operation's been dialing them down, keeping your face pretty much out of it, but there's still been a blip from them leaving."

"So why would someone want them to leave?"

"So they won't be an add-on draw when something else hits town," he said. "Something they really don't want any spare attention on, if they can help it."

"Like what?"

"Homes. A strategic shitload of Homes. Vehicles, personnel. Grif's connections are showing two big convoys headed this way. Serious lot of white trucks. Meanwhile, over at what's left of Pickett's, Ben Carter's cousin's in that quite sizable detachment of Homes, right there. And he's telling Ben that the rumor's they're headed here, today, to mop up the armed remnants of the evil Cordell Pickett's multicounty drug empire. Which incidentally they're now behaving as though they put a stop to, as opposed to your vigilante brother, his best friend, and a prosthesis from the Veterans Administration."

"They're coming here?"

"Don't doubt it."

"And we're the evil remnants?"

"You got it."

"They're that corrupt?"

"In today's modern world, yeah, at least as of maybe twenty-four hours ago. They sure are. But you're probably holding too big a stake in one of the prime corrupters to want to have too much of an attitude about that."

"And when they get here?"

"We'll resist arrest. Regardless what we might actually do, we'll have resisted arrest. Those stacks of shingles won't stop smart munitions. This is exactly the kind of improv urban fortress they were designed to be used against. The roof on this building might as well not be there, and Homes has real attack drones anyway. Wouldn't matter if we were in bunkers. Plus your brother's boys are constitutionally disinclined to go peacefully, in spite of odds."

"Why's it happening now?"

"Griff's best bet is that both the two hands are slap up to the top of the handle of the bat, and there's no room for another. Just worked out that way. They bought whatever it took to get Homes in their pocket, and there's nothing left for us to buy to get 'em into our ours."

"What if Griff got tight with Gonzales?"

"I think he already is, though you can probably still see some daylight between them. But there's politics, and Homes isn't on her side of the table, president or no."

"When do they get here?"

"This evening. But they tend to operate after midnight."

"You could just meet 'em as they come in and help keep order, Tommy. I don't see that this has to be your fight."

"Fuck that," he said, perfectly pleasantly. "You want a breakfast burrito? Brought you one."

"How come I can't smell it?"

"Had 'em double-bag it, so it wouldn't ruin my uniform," he said, reaching into one of his jacket's big side pockets.

109.
BLACK SILK FROGS

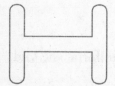e was trying to sleep on a granite bench in the tall cold hall of Daedra's voice mail, while trains, or perhaps mobies departed, dimly announced by gravely incomprehensible voices. Light pulsed.

He opened his eyes. He lay on the leather cushions in the cupola. Out in the darkness of the garage, another pulse. He sat up, rubbed his eyes, peered out.

Squidlight again, on Ossian, upholding, in one hand, on a hanger, dark clothing. Beside him Ash, grim-faced, though no more than usual, dressed in what seemed a chauffeur's uniform, black, the breast of its stiff tunic crossed with frogs of black silk cord. She wore a large hat, like some Soviet commodore, its gleaming patent bill obscuring her eyes.

Now he remembered what Flynne had said, about Lowbeer and Griff. The mind reels, he thought, struck by the phrase itself, and how seldom, if ever, his seemed to. And how it didn't, now, at the thought of Lowbeer and Griff being in some sense the same person. He was glad, though, to be too young to have some earlier self abroad, in Flynne's day.

Pulse.

110.
NOTHING FANCY

They'd given the peripheral a shower, before she'd arrived, done its hair, and put on makeup. The dress Ash had chosen fit it better than anything Flynne had worn in her life. Nothing fancy, Ash explained, because Annie Courrèges wasn't wealthy. But Ash's idea of not too fancy was a little black dress, made of something that felt like velour but looked like fresh black carbide sandpaper, supple as silk. Her jewelry was a heavy round bangle made from antique plastic dentures and something that looked like black licorice, and a necklace that was a rigid loop of black titanium wire, strung with lots of different zipper pulls, like they'd been buried somewhere, the paint or plating corroded away. Ash said both of these were real neoprimitive, the bracelet from Ireland and the necklace from Detroit. The black shoes were made of the same stuff as the dress, had wedge heels, and were more comfortable than her sneakers at home. She wished they'd waited until she got there, so she could've put it all on, herself. But that familiar pang, when she looked into the tall mirror: Who was that? She was starting to feel like the peripheral looked like somebody she'd known, but she knew it didn't.

The badge with the gold crown appeared in the mirror, and she thought for a second of the bull in the mirror at Jimmy's, but it was just Lowbeer calling.

"Tommy thinks Homes is coming after us," she said.

"Assume as much."

"Can't Grif do anything?"

"Not yet. In spite of being able to prove, should the opportunity arise, that the head of their Private Sector Office is in Chinese pay.

But we do seem to have reached an impasse. Basically, we need to be able to command them to stop. Rescind the order."

"What if he tells the president she's going to be assassinated, but you can stop it, if she orders them to turn around?"

"It isn't that simple," said Lowbeer. "We've not yet established sufficient trust. Her office is riddled with those aligned with the people who'll soon be plotting to kill her. And the rest is simply politics."

"Seriously? There's nothing we can do?"

"Clovis," Lowbeer said, "my Clovis, here, is allowing the aunties to root about in her documents. She managed to extract an archipelago of data, before her flight to the U.K. I'd no idea how much, at the time. More a hoarder than a spy, Clovis. If there's anything of use there, in our present situation, they'll find it. In the meantime, if you're successful tonight, it should be a game changer. Though how, exactly, is impossible to predict."

She bit her lip, then stopped, not wanting to mess up the peripheral's makeup.

"You look marvelous," Lowbeer said, reminding her that she could see what the peripheral was seeing. "Have you said hello to Burton yet?"

"No," she said.

"You should. He's in the lounge, with Conner. You'll be unable to see him, once you're on the way to Farringdon. He'll be in the trunk. I'm delighted he's able, after his injury."

"The trunk?"

"Folds quite flat. Like a piece of old-fashioned Swedish drain-cleaning machinery, folded. Say hello to your brother for me." The crown was gone.

She went to the door, opened it.

They were sparring, the two of them. She remembered this from before Conner's injury, even from before they'd enlisted. They had rules of their own. They'd hardly move, shifting weight from foot to foot, watching each other, and when they did move, mainly their hands, it was too fast to follow, and then they were back, the way they were before, shifting their weight, but one of them had won. She saw that it was the same, now, except that Conner was in Lev's brother's peripheral and Burton was in the white exoskeleton workout thing, with a bell jar glued where its head would be if it had one, and a pair of creepily real-looking human hands where she remembered it having white cartoon robot hands before. There was a little robot in the bell jar that did everything the exoskeleton did, but actually the other way around, because Burton was in that. Homunculus, they called it. The new hands on Burton's exoskeleton were tanned a color that reminded her of Pickett. Then their hands moved, blurring, but Conner was faster, she thought.

"I break a finger on your Tin Woodman ass, you're in deep shit," said Conner. His peripheral was in a skinny black suit that looked about as restrictive as karate pajamas.

Now the little figure in the dome turned, the exoskeleton turning with it. "Flynne," said a stranger's voice, like a voice from an infomercial, "hey."

"Shit, Burton," she said, "I thought we'd lost you, back in that alley." She sort of felt like hugging it, but then that seemed crazy. Plus it had those creepy-ass hands.

"Guess you did, for a while," the voice said. "I don't recall chopping that client, or anything really, until I woke up and saw the real-world version of handsome, here."

"If you'd got yourself that piddling wound in the service," said Conner, his peripheral holstering its large hands in the pockets of its black suit trousers, "I guess it still might count as wounded fucking warrior."

The exoskeleton feinted at him, cat-quick, but Conner somehow wasn't where the tan hands went, fast as they were.

"Lowbeer says say hello," she said to Burton. "She's glad you can come with us. So am I."

"Cross between a trunk monkey and a fancy jack," said his infomercial voice. "What I joined the Marines for."

111.

ZIL

etherton walked around the black limousine, their transport to Farringdon and the reason Ash was dressed that way. Built in 2029, she'd informed him, the ZIL, the last off the assembly line, had never been a part of Lev's father's collection, but his grandfather's personal vehicle, dating from when he'd lived in this house. Lowbeer, apparently, had opted to use it now.

Its bodywork reminded him of Flynne's new dress, at once dull and very faintly lustrous. What few bits weren't that peculiar black were stainless steel, beadblasted to nonreflectivity: the oversized wheels, and the broad and utterly minimalist grille, looking as though it had been laser-sliced off a loaf of ZIL grille-stuff. The hood was only fractionally longer than the rear deck, both of which could easily be imagined as tennis courts for the use of rather large homunculi. It had no rear window whatever, which gave him the sense that it had turned up its collar. The gravitas of its imminently thuggish presentation was remarkable, he thought. Perhaps that was why Lowbeer had chosen it, though he couldn't see the sense in that, particularly. Curious about the interior, he leaned forward.

"Don't touch it," Ash said, behind him. "You'd be electrocuted."

He turned. Met her double stare from beneath the patent bill. "Seriously?"

"It's like the pram. They had trust issues. Still do."

He took a step back. "Why did she want this one? Hardly in character for me, and certainly not for Annie. If I were really attending, this evening, I'd arrive in a cab."

"You are attending, this evening. Otherwise I wouldn't be gotten up this way."

"Without an agenda, I mean."

"When was it you were last without one?"

Netherton sighed.

"I imagine," said Ash, "that she's decided to make a point. This will be recognized, absolutely, as belonging to Lev's grandfather. Daedra's security, whatever that may consist of, will certainly know that it emerged from this address. Any pretext that you aren't associated with the Zubovs will end, upon our arrival. Possibly she sees advantage in that. There's usually some degree of advantage in underlining one's association with klept. Disadvantages too, of course." She considered him. "Suit's not bad."

Netherton looked down at the black suit she'd had made for him. Looked back up. "Is it black because the occasion requires it, or because you ordered it?"

"Both," said Ash, a distant herd of something or other choosing that instant to transit her forehead, what was visible of it below the bill, making it appear as though a cloud of restless foreboding were lodged beneath her hat.

"Will you wait for us, there?"

"We aren't allowed to park within two kilometers," she said. "When you're ready to go, they'll call us. Though Lowbeer will already have done, I'm sure."

"When do we leave?" He glanced up at the Gobiwagen.

"Ten minutes. Need to put Burton in the trunk."

"I'll use the toilet," he said, starting for the gangway. And check to see that the bar's still locked, he thought, certain as he was that it would be.

112.

TO FARRINGDON

It wasn't far, Ash said.

The interior of this car felt larger than the lounge in the Mercedes RV. It wasn't, but it felt it. The way grown-up furniture felt when you were little. And everything in here was this black that made her like her dress less. It must be a thing, that black.

And the light outside was rainy, silvery, pink, the way it was when she'd first come here, lifting out of that launch bay in the white van.

Netherton, seated beside her, was almost too far away to reach, and if they'd been closer, it would've felt too much like a date. Conner was up front with Ash, room enough between them for two other people.

She wished it had a coffee machine, but that made her think of Tommy and Carlos and everybody back there, with Homes convoying in from three different directions. "Can I still phone home?" she asked Ash, assuming she could hear her through the partition.

"Yes, but do it now. We'll be there soon."

Ash had helped her set up the peripheral's phone for dialing, while they waited for Burton to get into the trunk and fold up, transferring the numbers from her own phone. Now she brought the badges up, scrolled to Macon's yellow one with the single red nubbin, and tapped the roof of her mouth.

"Hey," said Macon.

"What's happening?"

"Guests still on the way," he said.

"Shit . . ."

"Putting it mildly."

"Who's with my mother?"

"Janice. And Carlos and his friends, some of them."

Flynne saw herself in the white bed, under the white crown, Burton and Conner beside her in their own beds. What would happen here if she died there, she wondered for the first time? Nothing, except that her peripheral would go on automatic pilot, that cloud thing. Would it still bullshit, then, if you asked it about Daedra's art? Would that be the only remaining evidence that she'd been here?

"Better wrap it up," Ash said. "We're driving into their protocol now."

Faintly at first, she heard the whispers of those fairy police dispatchers, around the base of Aelita's building.

113

BOUNCY CASTLE

Michikoid with a luminous wand waved their ZIL to the curb, behind something more on the order of the six-wheeled silver Bentley steam iron, though the color of Lowbeer's car when uncloaked. A couple with shaven heads and Maori facial tattoos were briefly visible, between the sleek graphite wedge of the vehicle and a solemn-looking bouncy castle affair that obviously wasn't a routine architectural feature of Edenmere Mansions or any other shard. The various scanners would be in there, he assumed. The entrance seemed staffed entirely with Michikoids, in identical gray, vaguely quasi-military uniforms. He remembered the one on Daedra's moby, just before it flung itself over the rail, bristling with weapons, and what Rainey had said about how she'd seen them move like spiders, down on the patchers' island.

Ash and Conner each opened a door, as if on cue. The ZIL's doors were so massive that they must be servo-powered, though silently. Simultaneously, Ash on Netherton's side and Conner on Flynne's, they opened the passenger doors.

Without thinking, Netherton leaned toward Flynne, squeezed her hand. "We'll lie like champs," he said, not knowing where that had come from. She gave him an odd, startled smile, and then they were out, on either side, the air damp, colder than he expected, but fresh. A Michikoid scanned Conner with a nonluminous wand, another doing the same to Ash, and then he and Flynne were waved into the bulging gray inflatable, as between the thighs of some oversized toy elephant.

A field of some kind induced a moderately dissociative state, as they were scanned and prodded, by a variety of unpleasantly robotic portals, for perhaps the next fifteen minutes, and then they were being greeted by an artfully distressed Michikoid in an ancient kimono.

"Thank you for honoring our celebration of the life of Aelita West. Your personal security attendant has been admitted separately. You will find him awaiting you. The elevator is third from the left."

"Thank you," said Netherton, taking the peripheral's hand. The tattooed couple was nowhere in sight. Nor was anyone else, the lobby as welcoming as Daedra's voice mail, though typical in that.

"Celebration of life?" Flynne asked, as he led her toward the elevator.

"So it said."

"Byron Burchardt's parents had one of those."

"Who?"

"Byron Burchardt. Manager at the Coffee Jones. Got run over by a robot eighteen-wheeler, Valentine's Day. I felt guilty because I'd been pissed at him, for firing me. But I went anyway."

"They seem to have accepted that she's gone."

"I don't see how they could be sure she is. But I wish we'd known. Could've brought some flowers."

"Daedra never suggested this. It seems to be a surprise."

"A surprise funeral? You do that, here?"

"A first, for me."

"Fifty-sixth floor," she said, indicating the bank of buttons.

The doors opened as he touched the button. They stepped in. The doors closed behind them. The ascent was perfectly silent, rapid, slightly dizzying. He was sure that drink would be served.

114

CELEBRATION OF LIFE

hen they came out of the elevator, she saw, between two knots of people in black, the view from her first time here, that curve in the river. All the windows were unfrosted and the interior walls had been removed. Not so much removed but like they'd never been there. One big space now, like Lev's dad's gallery. Conner stood near the elevator, scoping everything. He looked completely on his game, and she guessed he was finally back to some version of what she imagined he'd been, before whatever it was had blown him up. He wasn't quite smiling, because he was in full bodyguard mode, but he almost was.

"No way up or down except this elevator," he said, as they reached him. "Stairs to the floor above and below. Some seriously ugly mofos in here. They'd be like me, security. Mofo-ettes too. Like a bad-ass convention sprinkled on a small town's worth of rich folks."

"More people than I've ever seen here in one place before," she said, and then something howled, deep in every bone in the peripheral's body. "Testing the entanglement," the nastiest voice she'd ever heard said, a kind of modulated ache, but she knew it was Lowbeer. "Please acknowledge."

Twin taps of the tongue's tiny magnet, left forward palate-quarter.

"Good," said the bones, horribly. "Circulate. Tell Wilf."

"Let's circulate," she said to Wilf, as a crowd of tattooed New Zealanders passed them. Tā moko, she remembered, from *Ciencia Loca*. Technically not tattoos. Carved in. Grooved. The skin lightly sculpted. The boss, she guessed, was the blonde with the profile like something on a war canoe. They definitely didn't look like they were here to party, or for that matter to celebrate life. Something had happened, around the blonde's face as she'd passed them, a stutter of image-capture, barely visible. She remembered what Lowbeer had said, about artifacts in her field of vision.

"Keep a minimum of two meters distance," Wilf said, to Conner. "When we engage in conversation, double that."

"I'm housebroken," Conner said. "She had me taught that in a virtual coronation ball, king of fucking Spain. This is like poolside casual."

A Michikoid with a tray of glasses, pale yellow wine, offered her one. "No thanks," she said. She saw Wilf reach for one, smiling, then freeze. Like seeing the haptics glitch Burton. Then his hand changed course, for one with fizzy water, near the edge of the tray. He winced, picking it up. "Follow me," he said.

"Where?"

"This way, Annie." He took her hand, led her toward the center, away from the windows, the glass of water held near his chest.

She remembered how long it had taken her to fly a circuit around this space. Wondered if the bugs were out there now, and what they'd really been.

There was an entirely black screen, square, floor-to-ceiling, near the middle of the space, people around it, talking, holding drinks. It looked like a giant version of one of those old flat displays that Wilf had on his desk, the first time she'd seen him. Wilf kept moving, looking as though he knew where he was going, but she assumed he didn't. From a slightly different angle, now, she saw the black screen wasn't entirely blank, but showed, very dimly, a woman's face. "What's that?" she asked Wilf, nodding in its direction.

"Aelita," he said.

"Is that something you do, here?"

"Nothing I've ever seen before. And I—" He broke off. "And here's Daedra," he said.

Daedra was smaller than she'd expected, Tacoma's size. She looked like somebody in a video, or an ad. At home that was something, even just to see someone like that. Pickett had had a little of it, sort of by osmosis, but not like he'd ever really tried. He was local. Brent Vermette had a lot of the guy version, via Miami and wherever else, and if he had a wife she'd have a lot of it too. But Daedra had it all, and tattoos on top of that, squared-off black spirals, up over her collarbones, out of the top of her black dress. Flynne realized she was waiting for the tattoos to move, and no reason to assume they wouldn't, except she thought Wilf would have mentioned it, if they did.

"Annie," Wilf said, "you've met Daedra before, at the Connaught. I know you weren't expecting this, but I've told her about your sense of her art, her career. She's very interested."

Daedra was staring at her flatly. "Neoprimitives," she said, as if she didn't entirely like the word. "What do you do with them?"

Did she have to be asked directly about Daedra's art for the bullshit implant to kick in? She guessed she did. "I study them," she said, some part of her reaching back to the ragged yellow-spined wall of *National Geographic*, to *Ciencia Loca*, anything. "Study the things they make."

"What do they make?"

The only thing she could think of was Carlos and the others making things out of Kydex. "Sheaths, holsters. Jewelry." Jewelry wasn't true, but it didn't matter.

"What does that have to do with my art?"

"Attempts to encompass the real, outside of hegemony," said the implant. "The other. Heroically. A boundless curiosity, informed by your essential humanity. Your warmth." Flynne felt like her eyes were bugging. She forced herself to smile.

Daedra looked at Wilf. "My warmth?"

"Exactly," said Wilf. "Annie sees your essential humanity as the least appreciated aspect of your work. Her analysis seeks to remedy that. I've found her arguments to be extraordinarily revelatory."

"Really," said Daedra, staring at him.

"Annie's quite shy, in your presence," he said. "Your work means everything to her."

"Really?"

"I'm so grateful to meet you," Flynne said. "Again."

"That peripheral looks nothing like you," Daedra said. "You're on a moby, headed for Brazil?"

"She's supposed to be meditating," Wilf said, "but she's cheating now, in order to be here. The group she'll be embedding with insists on visitors having all of their implants removed. Remarkable dedication, on her part."

"Who's it supposed to be?" Still staring at Flynne.

"I don't know," said Flynne.

"A rental," said Wilf. "I found it through Impostor Syndrome."

"I'm sorry about your sister," Flynne said. "I didn't know that this was about her, until we got here. Must be so sad."

"My father was on the fence about it until yesterday afternoon," Daedra said, not sounding sad at all.

"Is he here?" Flynne asked.

"Baltimore," Daedra said. "He doesn't travel." And behind her, through the crowd, came the man from the balcony, not in a dark brown robe now but a black suit, his dark beard grown in a little, trimmed. Smiling.

"Fuck," Flynne said, under her breath.

Daedra's eyes narrowed. "What?"

Tongue to palate. That shiver of frames, around him.

"Sorry," said Flynne. "I'm so awkward. You're my favorite artist in the whole world. I keep feeling like hyperventilating or something. And asking you about your dad when you've just lost your sister . . ."

Daedra stared at her. "I thought she was English," she said to Wilf.

"The neoprims she's embedding with in Brazil are American," said Wilf. "Working on fitting in."

The man from the balcony walked right past, didn't glance at them, but Flynne wondered who wouldn't take a second look at Daedra?

"But we've come at the wrong time," said Wilf, who as far as Flynne knew would have no idea that she'd just tagged their man. They should have worked out a signal. He was bluffing now. She could tell. "At least the two of you have been reintroduced—"

"Downstairs," Daedra said. "Easier to talk there."

"Go with her," said the bone-voice. It made dragging your fingernails across a chalkboard seem like stroking a kitten.

"This way," said Daedra, and led them toward the windows facing the river, around a low wall and down a wide flight of white stone stairs. Flynne looked back, saw Conner following them, flanked by two of the china-white robot girls, with their identical featureless faces, in loose black tunics and pants that zipped tight at their ankles, their feet white and toeless. They'd been standing at the head of the stairs, she guessed guarding it. Wilf walked beside her, still carrying his glass of water, which he didn't seem to be drinking.

The floor below was more like what she'd seen from the quadcopter. Like a more modern version of the ground floor at Lev's, rooms in every direction. Daedra led them into one with windows on the river, but Flynne saw them frost over as they walked in. Another Daedra, in the same dress, was standing there. She seemed to see them but didn't react. A brunette in exercise clothes was sitting in an armchair that looked uncomfortable but probably wasn't, a few white papers in her hand. She looked up. "You're on in ten," Daedra said to her, Flynne getting it that this woman wasn't a guest at the party.

"Is that a peripheral of you?" Flynne asked, looking at the other Daedra.

"What does it look like?" Daedra asked. "It's giving my talk. Or Mary is, with it. She's a voice actress."

Mary had gotten to her feet, the white paper in her hand.

"Take it somewhere," Daedra said. "We're having a talk."

Mary took the Daedra-peripheral's hand and led it away, around a corner. Flynne watched her go, feeling embarrassed.

"You think you're safe here," Daedra said.

"Yes," said Flynne, all she could think of to say.

"You aren't, at all. Whoever you are, you've let this idiot bring you here." She was looking at Wilf, who put his glass of water down on the piece of furniture nearest him, looking pained. "Take that apart," Daedra said, apparently to the two robot girls, pointing at Conner. And one of them, instantly, too quick to follow, was squatting upside down on the ceiling, white mantis-arms lengthening.

Flynne saw Conner smile, but then he was gone, a blank curved wall surrounding Flynne, Wilf, Daedra. It was just there, or seemed to be. Flynne reached over and rapped it with the peripheral's knuckles. Hurt.

"It's real," Daedra said. "And whoever was operating your guard is now wherever you started from, whenever, telling whoever is there that you're in trouble." She was right about Conner. If the robots wrecked Lev's brother's peri, Conner woke up in the back of Coldiron, beside Burton. "But not understanding how much."

The man from the balcony stepped through the wall, then. Just stepped through it, like it wasn't there, or like he and it could temporarily occupy the same space and time.

"How'd you do that?" she asked, because you couldn't see that and not ask.

"Assemblers," he said. "It's what we do here. We're protean." He smiled.

"Protein?"

"Without fixed form." He waved his hand through the wall, a demonstration. He crossed to the side she thought Conner would be behind, stuck his face into it, instantly withdrew it. "Get them some help," he said to Daedra.

"I can't move," said Netherton.

"Of course you can't," said the man. He looked at Flynne. "Neither can she."

And he was right.

Two more robot girls ran out of the wall, where he'd come through, and back into it, where he'd stuck his head in, and then they were gone.

115.

DISSOCIATIVE STATE

robably they were using something akin to whatever they'd used during the security scans, Netherton thought, as the elevator descended. Something that induced a dissociative state. It was difficult to complain about a dissociative state. It even seemed to take the place of a drink.

But there was something else in effect, something that reduced his freedom of movement. He could move his eyes, and walk when Daedra or this friend of hers told him to, stand where they indicated he should, but he couldn't, for instance, raise his hands, or—he'd tried—clench a fist. Not that he felt particularly like clenching a fist.

The elevator doors had appeared in the circular wall. Quite a lot of assemblers, to do that. He vaguely recalled there being restrictions, on too wholesale a use of assemblers, but they didn't seem to apply here, or were perhaps being ignored.

Flynne, beside him, seemed much the same, her peripheral reminding him of when she wasn't using it.

"Out," said Daedra, and pushed him, when they reached the bottom.

The lobby now. Daedra's friend led the way, and when he happened to glance to the left, Netherton found that he did too, without having meant to. Then they were both looking ahead again, through the glass, out to where the gray bouncy castle had been, but no longer was. There was a black car waiting, not as long as the ZIL. The gray-clad Michikoids from the bouncy castle were arranged in two lines, facing one another, two-by-two, and as the glass doors sighed open and he stepped out between them, he felt a faint celebratory elation, at the formality of it all.

Halfway to the car he heard, or perhaps felt, a single, extended, uncomfortably low bass-note, seemingly from somewhere above them. Daedra's friend, evidently hearing it too, began to run, toward the car, whose rear door was open now. Netherton running with him, of course. Through a confetti storm of what Netherton supposed might once have been a window, though the glittering, slightly golden bits seemed soft as mulch, and as harmless.

Something white, round and smooth, arced down into the street, beyond the waiting car. Bouncing back up, well above the car's roof.

The head of a Michikoid.

Then a white arm, bent at the elbow, fingers clawed, struck the roof of the car, reminding him of the frozen silhouette of a severed hand he and Rainey had seen, on the feed from the patchers' island.

Someone, he supposed Daedra's friend, shoved him, painfully, into the waiting, pearl-gray interior. And screamed, very close to his ear, amid an explosion of what he assumed must be blood.

116.

CANNONBALL

ummers they'd all go to the town pool, which was beside the Sheriff's Department and the town jail, and Burton and Conner would do cannonballs off the high board, curled up with their heads on their bent knees, hands holding their ankles in, against their haunches, to come up, laughing, to cheers, or sometimes just to Leon, executing a massive belly flop off the same board, making fun of how hard they tried.

And that was what she thought of, when Daedra looked up at the weird sound. Which made her look up too, that copycat thing they had. Artifacts of image-capture strobing, in a descending line, around Conner's peripheral, in its black suit, coming down cannonball on the balcony man and the Michikoid behind him, trying to get him into the car. So that mostly he took out that Michikoid. Blood like some gross-out anime, the Michikoid and Conner's peripheral exploding two feet from her, like bugs on a windshield.

Someone, Daedra, grabbed her by the top of the back of her dress, hauling her in, kicking her hard in the ankle, probably just out of how pissed she was. And balcony man screaming, hugging his right arm, covered with blood, Flynne wasn't sure whose, as another Michikoid bundled him into the car, the door closing behind it.

"Newgate," Daedra said, over the man's sobs of pain, and they pulled away.

117.

ITS GRANITE FACE,
BRISTLING WITH IRON

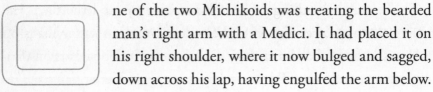

ne of the two Michikoids was treating the bearded man's right arm with a Medici. It had placed it on his right shoulder, where it now bulged and sagged, down across his lap, having engulfed the arm below. Blood swirled, through the yellowish fluid that filled the thing. The man's eyes were closed, his face relaxed, and Netherton envied him whatever dissociative state he might be enjoying.

Netherton himself was feeling entirely too associative, whatever had been used to induce his prior state having been abruptly shut off, possibly by the impact of Penske's peripheral. Either that or the dissociative field had been local to Edenmere Mansions, already some distance behind them. Whichever, he was now also free of the compulsion to imitative movement, or so he assumed, else wouldn't his eyes be closed?

He turned his head to look at Flynne, beside him on the wide rear seat. She seemed to be very definitely present in the peripheral now. There was a smear of Penske's blood across her cheek, or rather the blood from his ruined peripheral. Her dress was spattered with blood as well, but it scarcely showed on the black fabric. She gave him a look he couldn't read, if indeed there was anything to be read.

The Michikoid, squatting in front of the bearded man, removed the Medici. It shrank, dwindled, the fluid within it darkening. Cleaners were at work on the compartment's gray carpet, perfectly ordinary beige hexapods, removing the blood. Daedra and the bearded man sat at opposite ends of a backward-facing banquette, a second Michikoid between them, this watching Netherton and Flynne, having produced several pairs of shiny black spider-eyes for the purpose. Its arms had lengthened, both ahead and behind the elbow, and its hands were now knifelike white china fins, like the blades of two elegantly threatening spatulas.

Daedra looked from the bearded man to Netherton. "If I'd known how you'd fuck things up, I'd have killed you myself, the day I met you."

This wasn't something he'd ever had to respond to, before. He maintained his expression, which he hoped was neutral.

"I wish I had," Daedra said. "If I'd known more about your stupid gift, what a stub was, I'd never have accepted. But you knew the Zubovs, or their one useless son, and I thought they'd be good to know. And Aelita hadn't become a problem yet."

"Be quiet," said the bearded man, opening his eyes. "This isn't secure. We'll be there shortly, and you can say whatever you like."

Daedra frowned, never liking to be told what to do. She adjusted the top of her dress. "Feeling better?" she asked him.

"Considerably. That was a broken collarbone, three broken ribs, and mild concussion." He looked at Netherton. "We'll start with those for you, shall we? Upon arrival."

The windows depolarized, Netherton assuming the man had done that. He saw that they were turning onto Cheapside, and his immediate impulse was to warn them that they were violating a cosplay zone. But then he saw how utterly empty the street was. No carts, no cabs, no drays, no horses to pull them. They were headed west, past the shops vending shawls and feathers, scent and silver, all the fancy goods he'd strolled past with his mother, surreptitiously capturing the magic of the painted signs. He wondered where those images were today. He had no idea. The sidewalks were virtually empty, yet shouldn't have been. They should have been bustling still, the day just ending. Yet the few lone walkers looked lost, confused, anxious. They were people, it struck him, so were unable to have followed whatever signal had gone out, to all those cloud-driven peripherals enacting the visible lives of cabmen, piecework tailors, gentlemen of leisure, street boys. As the car passed, they turned away, as he'd seen people turn away in Covent Garden, at the first glimpse of Lowbeer's tipstaff.

"It's empty," said Flynne, sounding simply disappointed.

Netherton leaned to the side, peering around the tall back of the gray banquette, and saw, through the windscreen, the glowering bulk of Newgate. He'd only walked that far with his mother once, and she'd quickly turned around, repelled by the structure's pitted granite flanks, spiked with iron.

At the City's westernmost gate, she'd told him, for more than a thousand years, had stood a jail, and this its ultimate and final expression. Or had been, rather, as it had been torn down in 1902, at the start of that oddly optimistic age before the jackpot. To be rebuilt, then, by the assemblers, a few years before his birth. The klept (she would never have called it that in front of him) having deemed its return a wise and necessary thing.

Before them now, the very iron-bound wicket gate, of nail-studded oak, that he'd stared up at as a child. The one his mother told him had frightened Dickens, though he'd confused that with the Dickens being frightened out of someone.

It had frightened him then. And did now.

118.

BALCONY MAN

I t wasn't Conner. Not Conner. It was the peripheral. Lev's brother's. Pavel. Wilf called it Pavel. Called it the dancing master. And Conner had meant to do that. Had tried to kill this asshole with it. Was okay. Was back in his white bed, beside Burton, totally pissed that he'd missed. Even so, fifty-five floors, straight down, he'd come that close. No way he'd been aiming for the robot girl.

She knew she'd seen it, could tell you what had happened, but she couldn't remember seeing it. That might be whatever the robot girls used to do the searches and scans, in that inflatable security tent, going into the party. Like the stuff they gave you for surgery. You didn't sleep, exactly, but you didn't remember.

Now it looked like they'd shut that Cheapside down.

And then she saw what Wilf was craning his neck at. Like a huge squashed stone pineapple, prickly with black iron spikes. Built to scare the shit out of people. So weird that she wondered why she'd never seen it in *National Geographic*. You'd figure it would be a big tourist thing.

Then the cardoor was open and the robot girls were getting them out, making sure they didn't try to run.

Nobody to meet them. Just her, Wilf, Daedra, balcony man, and the two robot girls, their white faces flecked with the peripheral's blood, like a robot skin disease. She had a robot girl's white hand around her upper arm, guiding her from behind. The other one had Wilf.

In through a gate that reminded her of a Baptist anime of hell she'd seen. Burton and Leon had thought the fallen women were hot.

Into this thing's shade, its coldness. Iron-barred doors, painted white but rust still coming through. Flagstone floors like paths in some very wrong garden. Dull lamps, like the eyes of big sick animals. Little windows, looking like they didn't go anywhere. Up a narrow stone stairway, where they had to go one at a time. It was like the intro segment for a *Ciencia Loca* episode, paranormal investigators, going someplace where a lot of people had suffered and died, or maybe just where the feng shui was so totally fucked that it sucked in bad vibes like a black hole. But she'd probably have to go with suffered and died, by the look of it.

When they got to the top of the stairway, she looked back at her robot girl, saw that it had sprouted extra eyes on that side of its face, just to keep better track of her. Neither Daedra nor the balcony man were saying anything at all. Daedra was looking around like she was bored. Now they crossed a court, open to the cloudy glow of sky, and entered something like a narrow, prehistoric Hefty Inn atrium, four floors of what looked to be cells, up to a glass roof, little panes set in dark metal. Lights flickered on, thin bright strips beneath the railings on the floors of cells. She guessed that wouldn't have been original. The robot girls marched them to a pair of whitewashed stone chairs, really simple, like a kid would build from blocks of wood, but much bigger, and sat them both down, side by side and about six feet apart. Something rough moved, against each of her wrists, and she looked down to see that she was fastened to the tops of the slabs that formed the chair's arms, her wrists in thick rusted cuffs of iron, polished brown with use, like they'd been there a hundred years. It made her expect Pickett might walk in, and for all she knew, given the way things were going, she felt like he might.

The stone seat was cold, through the fabric of her dress.

"We're waiting for someone." Balcony man was talking to her. He seemed to have gotten over what Conner had tried to do to him, physically anyway.

"Why?" she asked him, like he'd tell her.

"He wants to be here when you die," he said, watching her. "Not your peripheral. You. And you will, where you really are, in your own body, in a drone attack. Your headquarters is surrounded by government security forces. It's about to be leveled."

"So who is it?" All she could think to say.

"The City Remembrancer," said Daedra. "He had to stay to hear my appreciation."

"Of what?"

"Of Aelita," Daedra said. Flynne remembered the peripheral, the embarrassed actress. "You didn't manage to ruin our celebration, if that was what you had in mind."

"We just wanted to meet you."

"Really?" Daedra took a step closer.

Flynne looked at the man instead. He looked back, hard, and then it was like she was up by the fifty-seventh floor again, seeing him kiss the woman's ear. Surprise, he'd said. She fucking knew he'd said that. And she saw the SS officer's head pop, the red mist blown with the horizontal snow. But those had just been pixels, and it wasn't really France. The man from the balcony was looking back at her like there was nothing else in his entire world, right then, and he wasn't some accountant in Florida.

"Be calm," said the scratchy thing, not words so much as wind across some cold dry ridge, making her flinch.

He smiled, thinking he'd caused that.

She looked at Wilf, not knowing what to say, but then she looked back at the man from the balcony. "You don't have to kill everybody," she said.

"Really? No?" He thought that was funny.

"It's about me. It's because I saw you lock her out on the balcony."

"You did," he said.

"Nobody else did."

He raised his eyebrows.

"Say I go back. Say I go outside. In the parking lot. Then you don't need to kill everybody."

He looked surprised. Frowned. Then like he was considering it. He raised his eyebrows. Smiled. "No," he said.

"Why not?"

"Because we have you. Here, and there. Shortly you'll be dead, there, and that very expensive toy you're wearing will become my souvenir of this ridiculous episode."

"You're a horrible piece of shit," said Wilf, not sounding angry, but like he'd just come to that conclusion, and was still a little surprised by it.

"You," the man said to Wilf, cheerfully, "forget that you aren't present virtually. So you, unlike your friend, can die right here. And will. I'll leave you with these units, instructing them to beat you very nearly to death, restore you with their Medicis, then beat you again. Rinse. Repeat. For as long as that lasts."

And she saw how Wilf couldn't help but look at the robot girls then, and how they both grew extra sets of spider-eyes, looking back at him.

119

SIR HENRY

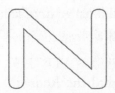etherton moved his wrists slightly in the metal cuffs, having decided that looking at the Michi-koids wasn't a good idea. The restraints appeared to have been embedded in the chair's granite arm for several centuries, but he assumed that assemblers had made them, and that his wrists were in them now because assemblers had made them temporarily flexible, and had briefly animated them. But they were, at the moment, solid.

The bearded man had just promised to have him repeatedly beaten almost to death by Michikoids, he noted, and he was thinking about assemblers, about faux antiques. Perhaps he was finding his own dissociative state. Or perhaps he was about to start screaming. He looked at Daedra. She looked back, without seeming to see him, then up, apparently at the glass roof, four floors above. And yawned. He didn't think the yawn was for his benefit. He looked up at the roof himself. It reminded him of a dress Ash had worn, it seemed years ago. Ash seemed so utterly normal, from this vantage, this moment. The girl next door.

"I do hope you have this quite entirely sorted out, Hamed," said a mellow but rather tired voice.

Netherton, lowering his gaze, saw a tall, very sturdy-looking older man, in perfect Cheapside cosplay, his coat long and caped, a top hat in his hands.

"New Zealand looked slightly pushy, I thought," the bearded man said, as the other crossed from the top of the stairway.

"Good evening, Daedra," the stranger said. "You gave a most moving testimony to your late sister's many sterling qualities, I thought."

"Thank you, Sir Henry," Daedra said.

"Sir Henry Fishbourne," Netherton said, remembering the City Remembrancer's name, and immediately regretted having said it.

The Remembrancer peered at him.

"I won't introduce you," said the bearded man.

"Quite," said the Remembrancer, and turned to look at Flynne. "And this is the young lady in question, albeit virtually physical?"

"It is," said the man.

"She looks rather the worse for wear, Hamed," said the Remembrancer. "It's been a long day for us all. I should be getting along. I need to be able to confirm the successful result to our investors."

"You're al-Habib," Netherton said to the bearded man, not quite believing it. "You're the boss patcher."

The Remembrancer looked at him. "I don't like this one at all. Can't say you seem very organized tonight, Hamed."

"I'm killing him as well."

The Remembrancer sighed. "Forgive my impatience. I'm quite tired." He turned to Daedra. "A very nice chat with your father, earlier. Always a pleasure."

"If you can look like the boss patcher, and then look like that," said Netherton, to the bearded man, "why didn't you simply change your appearance again, after you realized that you'd been seen?"

"Branding," said the bearded man. "Investment in persona. I represent the product. I'm known to the investors." He smiled.

"What product?"

"The monetization, variously, of the island I created."

"Doesn't it belong to the patchers as well?"

"They have endemic health issues," said Hamed al-Habib, bright-eyed, smiling, "of which they aren't yet aware."

120.

VESPASIAN'S CUBE

ir Henry's involvement surprises me," said Lowbeer's bone-static, like a full-body migraine that could talk. "He must have suffered some well-concealed setback in his affairs. That's usually the way."

"What way?" she asked, forgetting they weren't alone, and that even when she was, tonight, she wasn't supposed to speak to Lowbeer.

"Way?" asked al-Habib, sharply.

Faint warmth at her wrists. She looked down, seeing the iron cuffs crumble, collapse, like they'd only been pressed from dry, rust-brown talc. Beneath her right hand, the granite was going to talc too, spurting up between her fingers, drifting like smoke. And up from within what had been the chair arm's surface rose something hard and smooth. The candy-cane gun, its parrot-head handle pressing back against the base of her thumb, like it was alive, eager.

"Finish it," the balcony man said to the man with the hat, as if he sensed something, and she knew he meant the Homes drones hitting Coldiron. "Tell your people. Now."

"Surprise," Flynne said, and she was back on Janice's couch, full of the wakey Burton had given her, but now she was standing up, raising the gun, and the white bump that was the trigger didn't even seem to move. Not a sound. Nothing happened.

Then the balcony man's head fell off, having somehow become a skull, perfectly dry and brown, like you'd see in almost any issue of *National Geographic*, and then the top of his body caved in, inside his clothes, collapsed with a dry clatter of bone, every bit of softer tissue gone, as his knees gave way, so that the last parts of him in her field of vision, just for a second, were his hands, untouched by whatever had happened. She looked at the gun, its barrel slick as candy a kid had just licked, then down at the brown skull, on the stone floor in front of what was left of him, his legs and lower torso. It must seal the blood in, she thought, remembering the gloss of sliced red brick, like raw sliced liver, in the shadows of the Oxford Street greenway. A brown bone was poking out of the front of his black suit, like a dry stick. "Just as well," said the static, "that you don't legally exist here. Death by misadventure."

The robot girls started for her, then, but the whitewashed stone wall to her right was smoking, a big square of it falling down, dust, and out of the black hole shot this big red block. Cube, cuboid, thing. A nursery red. Cheerful. She heard the ceramic-looking shells of the robot girls shatter, between it and the far wall. Just hung, shivering, a few feet off the ground, like it was glued there, making a faint revving sound, like internal combustion motorcycles but really far away. Then it flipped, up and off the wall, the robots dropping to the stone floor in pieces, and came down on one of its eight corners without making a sound. And just stayed there, balanced, red, impossible.

"Security," said the man with the black hat, softly. "Red. Red."

Was he warning someone about the red thing?

Out of the corner of her eye, she saw Wilf, who must have discovered that his cuffs had crumbled too, starting to stand up too. "Sit the fuck down, Wilf," she said. He did.

"Hey, Henry," said a smoothly upbeat male voice, from the head of the stairwell, "sorry I broke your car." The exoskeleton stepped through the arch, the homunculus on its massive shoulders, under the bell jar. It stopped, seemed to look at the man in the hat, except it didn't have any eyes you could see.

"Red," said the man, softly.

"Sorry I killed your driver and your security detail," said the infomercial voice, like it was apologizing for not having 2-percent milk.

The cube rotated slightly, on the corner it was balanced on. Lowbeer appeared, on a square panel covering most of the nearest face. "You'll be unhappy to learn, Sir Henry," Lowbeer said, but not in that bone-static voice, "that your successor is your longtime rival and chief thorn-in-side, Marchmont-Sememov. It's an inherently awkward position, City Remembrancer, but I'd thought, until this, that you'd done rather well, considering."

The tall man said nothing.

"A real estate and development scheme, with resource extraction?" Lowbeer said. "And for that you'd see fit to deal with someone on the order of al-Habib?"

The tall man was silent.

Lowbeer sighed. "Burton," she said, and nodded.

The exoskeleton raised both its arms. The creepily tanned hands were gone, or else in black robotic gloves, both of them in fists now. A little hatch flipped open, on top of the exoskeleton's right wrist, and the other candy-cane gun popped out. From a second, slightly larger hatch, on the left wrist, emerged Lowbeer's tipstaff, gilt and fluted ivory. Burton had a better idea of how to aim it, because the tall man just blinked to bone entirely, his empty clothes falling straight down, with a rattle, and his tall hat rolling in a circle on the floor.

"So who do I have to kill," Flynne said, showing them she still had her own candy-cane gun, "to get somebody to fucking do something, back in the stub, about stopping fucking Homes from killing us all with drones, like right fucking now? Please?"

"Sir Henry's death has deprived your competitor of the sort of advantage that Lev and I afford you now. I took the liberty of effecting that immediately, upon Sir Henry's arrival here, this evening, assuming he would prove guilty. Which has resulted in a shift of influence, allowing for Homeland Security's withdrawal, their orders rescinded."

"Shit," said Flynne, lowering the gun, "what did we have to buy to do that?"

"A sufficient share of Hefty Mart's parent corporation, I gather," said Lowbeer, "though I haven't had the details yet."

"We bought Hefty?"

"Some considerable share of it, yes."

"How can you buy Hefty?" It was like buying the moon.

"May I stand up?" Wilf asked.

"I want to go home now," said Daedra.

"I imagine you do," said Lowbeer.

"My father's going to be very angry with you."

"Your father and I," said Lowbeer, "have known one another for a long time, I'm sad to say."

Now Ash was in the doorway, in her chauffeur outfit, Ossian behind her, in a black leather coat, the wooden pistol-box under his arm. He crossed to Flynne, eyes on the candy-cane barrel, keeping out of its way. He put the box down on the arm of her chair, where the iron cuff had been, lifted its lid, carefully took the gun from her hand, placed it in its felted recess, and closed the box.

"Goodnight, Miss West," said Lowbeer, and the screen went blank.

"We'll be going now," said Ash. She looked at Daedra. "Except for you."

Daedra sneered at her.

"And that," said Ash, gesturing with her thumb at the red cube. Which flung itself, somehow, straight up and then to the side, crashing with a big clang into the white-barred cell doors of the second level, a few lights going out. Then it threw itself to the far side just as loudly. Then somersaulted, fell, to land again on a single point. And began to spin, its corners blurring past, inches from Daedra's chin. She didn't move at all.

"Out," said Ash, "now."

And then they were single-filing the stairway, Ossian behind her. "What's Conner doing to her?" she asked, over her shoulder.

"Reminding her of the potential of consequences, at least," said Ossian, "or attempting to. Won't harm a hair on her head, of course. Or do a bit of good. Father's a big American."

Above them, the sound of crashing iron.

121.

NOTTING HILL

There was a park where the assemblers had long since collected, from beneath the deeper oligarchic burrowings in Notting Hill, the various excavating machines which the pre-jackpot wealthy had entombed in situ, back when removing them from whatever deepest point would have cost more than abandoning them beneath concrete. Mechanical sacrifices, like cats walled up in the foundations of bridges. The assemblers, going everywhere, had found them, bringing them to a certain park, their method having been exactly that by which Lowbeer had introduced the Russian pram's gun to the arm of the peripheral's interrogation chair, or brought Conner's terrible cube straight up through the granite foundations of Newgate, astronomical numbers of the microscopic units being employed in shifting particles of whatever intervening matter from front to back, or top to bottom, of the object being moved, solids seeming thereby to migrate through other solids, the way al-Habib had stepped through the curved wall, in Edenmere Mansions.

The rescued excavators, perfectly restored, had been arranged in a circle, their blades and scoops uplifted, paint and windscreens gleaming, to become a favorite of the area's children, Lev's among them.

Passing this now in the ZIL, on the way back to Lev's, the streets quite empty, he saw the moon catch the edge of a digger's upraised scoop.

He looked at Flynne's peripheral. She was gone now, back to Coldiron to check on everyone, and he was anxious to reach the Gobiwagen, to access the Wheelie, to see her there, to see what was going on.

Lowbeer's sigil appeared. "You did very well, Mr. Netherton," she said.

"I scarcely did anything."

"Opportunities to do very badly were manifold. You avoided them. The major part in any success."

"You were right about al-Habib. And the real estate. Why did he kill her?"

"It's still unclear. She'd been involved with him for some time, apparently was instrumental in bringing her sister aboard. She may have been jealous of his relationship with Daedra, which was largely simultaneous with your own. The aunties' latest iterations suggest she may have been considering shopping him to the Saudis, or perhaps was merely toying with the thought. They're a fantastically unpleasant family. I've known her father since I was Griff's age. A co-conspirator in the Gonzalez assassination, so I expect Griff will soon be dealing with him in that light. In our own continuum, however, he's far too well-connected ever to be troubled by any of this. She'll need a good publicist, now."

They were turning into Lev's street.

"Daedra?"

"Flynne," said Lowbeer. "That Hefty Mart buyout has attracted another magnitude of media attention in the stub. We'll speak tomorrow, shall we?"

"Certainly," said Netherton, and then the coronet was gone.

122.
COLDIRON MIRACLES

onner was under his crown, when she opened her eyes, nobody waiting to help her out of hers, and Burton's bed was empty. There was background noise that made no sense, but then she heard Leon's loudest jackass laugh, so she guessed it was a party. She left her crown there on the pillow, sat up, got her shoes on, and went to look around the edge of a blue tarp.

Most of the other blue tarps, except the ones walling off the ward space, were gone, taken down, making the former mini-paintballer franchise the single room it originally was, or at least the part inside the shingle wall. All the lights were on, bright, and people were sitting on desks, standing around, drinking beers, talking. Carlos had his arm around Tacoma, who was looking like she was about to laugh. Most of Burton's vets that she remembered were there, some she didn't, some still wearing the black armored jackets, but nobody carrying a bullpup, just open beers. And Brent Vermette, in jeans and a Sushi Barn t-shirt with SO FUCKING KILL ME across Hong's artwork, in that fat drippy graffiti marker (because, it turned out, he'd taped a protest video before Homes had even reached the town limits, and doing that would be a factor in what got him on the board as chief council a week later). Madison was talking to him, grinning like Teddy Roosevelt's teeth, vest full of pens and flashlights, Janice beside him. Janice saw Flynne and came right over, gave her a big hug. "Don't know what you did, but you saved everybody's ass."

"I didn't," Flynne said, "it was Lowbeer and them. Where's Griff?"

"D.C. Doing business with Homes. Or to them, more like it. Getting them a new director, Tommy told Madison."

"Where's Tommy?"

"Here somewhere. Just saw him with Macon and Edward." Janice looked around, didn't see any of them, looked back to Flynne. "They found Pickett."

"His body?"

"His builder ass, unfortunately."

"Where?"

"Nassau."

"He's in Nassau?"

"He's on Homes' dirtiest no-fly list, is where he is, since Griff got on the phone." Janice took a swig of her beer. "Meanwhile, looks like your brother's finally falling for Shaylene."

Flynne followed the direction of her glance, and saw Burton, on one of those little mobility cart things, a beer in his hand, saying something to Shaylene, who was sitting on the edge of a desk, leaning toward him.

"Hasn't happened in the biblical sense," Janice said, "because she wouldn't want him popping any stitches. Matter of time, though, looks to me."

"Burton's cute sister," said Conner, behind her, and she turned to find him propped in a wheelchair, Clovis holding its handles.

"How's Daedra?" she asked Conner.

"Getting new tattoos to commemorate it all? Sent her home in a cab."

"What did you do to her?"

"Berated her ass. Made loud noises. Don't think it actually impressed her that much." He looked at Janice. "Beer for a wounded warrior?"

"You got it," said Janice, and was gone.

"Harsh on Pavel, though," Flynne said.

"Lowbeer told me to go for it, if I got the chance. That suit had some wingsuit capabilities built in, so I wasn't just diving blind. Idea was, we'd take Hamed out before he had a chance to pull the trigger on Homes' drones, back here. Didn't happen, though. Why I wasn't Air Force, I guess. Lowbeer's ordered a brand-new one to replace it. Plus one for me."

"Easy Ice," Macon greeted her. He was holding hands with Edward, a beer in his other hand.

"Gimme a pull on that beer, Macon," Conner said, so Macon held his out, tipping it so Conner could get a drink. Conner wiped his mouth with the back of what was left of his hand.

And then she saw Tommy coming, from the front of the building, right through where the big sandbox for the paintball tanks had been, beaming at her, like she was some kind of miracle.

123.

COMPOUND

Back from her Wednesday afternoon walk with Ainsley, along the Embankment, she put on Tommy's oldest Sheriff's Department shirt, one that still had a Deputy Sheriff's patch on it. It was the most comfortable thing to wear over her bump, and it felt like him. Maybe they were getting like Janice and Madison, that way, but he basically wore the same thing every day, in uniform or out, and she had Coldiron's stylists for anything public. She just had to keep them from making her wear some new designer thing, which could feel like a job in itself.

She went into the kitchen, to get a glass of juice from the fridge, and stood there drinking it, wondering, the way she still did, how they could've built something like this without assemblers. They'd built it about a hundred yards from the old house, in what had been disused pasture before, and there was no way to tell it hadn't been built in the nineteen-eighties, then kept up, and gradually remodelled a little, by someone who could afford that but not much else. And they'd done it all without ever making a sound, and really fast. Tommy said they'd used a lot of different adhesives, none of them toxic. So that if you saw a nail head, that wasn't really a nail, but just there to look like one. But having so much money for a project that it just didn't matter, she'd learned, was a lot like having assemblers.

They'd built the barn that way too, but to look as old as the old house, or anyway on the outside. Macon and Edward lived there, and did all their really special printing there, stuff Coldiron needed to make sure didn't get out too soon. Industrial espionage had been identified as a major concern from the get-go, because Coldiron was really about knowing how to do things that nobody else knew how to do, back here. And they were just at the beginning, really, of mining that jackpot tech-surge. Too much at once, Ainsley said, and everything would go batshit on them, so a big part of the program was trying to pace that. Sometimes, particularly since she'd been pregnant, she wished she knew where it was all going. Ainsley said they couldn't know, but at least they knew one place where it wasn't going if they could help it, so hold on to that.

It kept her centered, living here. She thought it kept them all centered. They had an unspoken agreement never to call it a compound, probably because they didn't want anybody to think of it as one, but it was, really. Conner and Clovis had their own house another hundred or so yards away. Burton and Shaylene lived in town, in the residential wing of the Coldiron USA building. That stood, the whole block of it, where the strip mall with Fab and Sushi Barn had been. Hong had a new flagship Sushi Barn, just across the street, on the corner, looking kind of like the original but shinier, and there was a branch of Hefty Fab beside it. Flynne hadn't wanted them to call it that, but Shaylene said Forever Fab wasn't a name with good global legs, plus she'd just absorbed Fabbit in the merger, so she also needed something to call all the former Fabbit outlets. And now there was a Sushi Barn in every Hefty Mart, even if it was just the opposite end of the nubbins counter.

She didn't really like the business part of it. She guessed she disliked it about as much as Shaylene liked it. Coldiron actually had less money now, way less, because as soon as Matryoshka had stumbled, then collapsed, cut off from Sir Henry's financial modules, Coldiron had started to divest, to get the economy back to something more normal, whatever that meant now. But they still had more money than anyone could understand, or really keep track of. And Griff said that that was good, because they had plenty that needed to be done with it, more than they could know.

She took the empty juice glass over to the sink, washed it out, put it in the drying rack, and looked out the window, up the hill to where they'd built the pad that Marine One landed on, when Felicia came to see her. You couldn't see that there was anything there at all, even when you were standing on it. Satellites couldn't even tell it was there, because it was built with Coldiron science, emulating tech from up the line.

They'd talk in the kitchen, usually, when Felicia came, while Tommy sat out in the living room and shot the shit with the Secret Service, or anyway the ones he liked. Sometimes Brent came out from town, usually with Griff, when Felicia was there, and then it was more structured, about stockpiling vaccines against diseases they wouldn't even have known were out there, or what countries to best put the phage factories in, or climate stuff. She'd met Felicia a little after Vice President Ambrose had had his embolism, and that had been awkward, both because Felicia only ever spoke of Wally, as she called him, with what seemed like a real and painful fondness, and because Flynne knew that he'd died after Griff had shown her footage of her own state funeral, and explained to her exactly what had led up to that.

There was a jelly jar beside the drying rack, full of some of Conner's old toes, fingers, a thumb. He'd given them to Flora, Lithonia's daughter. They were some early iterations that Macon had printed back at the old Fab, with machines he'd had printed somewhere else, before they'd built the barn. Flora had forgotten them, that morning, when she'd been up to visit. She'd painted their nails sloppily pink, and Flynne saw that the thumb was moving a little, which had been the problem with the first few batches they'd printed. Watching Conner play squash, sometimes, she'd remember how fast Macon and Ash and Ossian had been able to get him up to speed. Now he never took the composite prosthesis off, the various parts of it, just wore them constantly, but up the line he still had his version of Pavel. She couldn't imagine using a different peripheral herself. "Hell no," Leon had said, at dinner once, when she'd said that, "that would be like having a whole other body." And then he'd made Flora scream, by telling her that if Flynne had a boy, she'd name him Fauna.

Now it was time to go down and have lunch with them. Her mother, Lithonia, Flora, and Leon, who was living in her old room now. Lithonia, it had turned out, was an amazing cook, so now Madison was sandblasting the inside of the old Farmer's Bank, for a restaurant Lithonia and her cousin would start there, nothing too fancy but a break from Sushi Barn and Jimmy's. Jimmy's wasn't likely to become a chain, and if it did, Leon said, it would be a sign that the jackpot was coming anyway, in spite of everything they were doing.

Her mother, now that all her medications were being made by Coldiron, and custom-made at that, no longer needed the oxygen. In the meantime, if anyone else needed anything, they'd bought Pharma Jon, whose profit margin, on Flynne's suggestion, they'd slashed by half, instantly making it the single most beloved chain in the country, if not the world.

Picking up the jelly jar, she went out, without bothering to lock the door, and down along to the path they'd been wearing between the two houses, which was starting to look as though it had always been there.

She'd told Ainsley, earlier, walking on the Embankment, how she sometimes worried that they weren't really doing more than just building their own version of the klept. Which Ainsley had said was not just a good thing but an essential thing, for all of them to keep in mind. Because people who couldn't imagine themselves capable of evil were at a major disadvantage in dealing with people who didn't need to imagine, because they already were. She'd said it was always a mistake, to believe those people were different, special, infected with something that was inhuman, subhuman, fundamentally other. Which had reminded her of what her mother had said about Corbell Picket. That evil wasn't glamorous, but just the result of ordinary half-assed badness, high school badness, given enough room, however that might happen, to become its bigger self. Bigger, with more horrible results, but never more than the cumulative weight of ordinary human baseness. And this was true, Ainsley had said, of the very worst monsters, among whom she herself had so long moved. Her job in London, she'd said, might seem to Flynne to be a patient caretaker amid large and specially venomous animals, but that wasn't the case.

"All too human, dear," Ainsley had said, her blue old eyes looking at the Thames, "and the moment we forget it, we're lost."

124.
PUTNEY

Living with Rainey was a little like having a cognitive implant, he thought, getting out of bed and looking down at her, but nicer in so many ways. He'd scarcely been aware that she had freckles, for instance, or that they were so widely distributed, or, indeed, that he liked freckles. Now he covered some of his favorites with the corner of the duvet and went to clean his teeth.

Her sigil appeared, before he could start. "Yes?"

"Coffee," she said, and he could hear her from the bedroom as well as on his phone.

"I'll use the machine as soon as I've brushed my teeth."

"No," she said, "that's a real Italian downstairs, in that fake news agent's. I want his espresso." She made it sound pornographic. "His crema."

"Phone him."

"You ruined my career, put me in a position that forced me to re- sign from an enviable government position, and ultimately resulted in my being threatened by assassins in the pay of New Zealand's secret state, and you won't bring me a decent human-made coffee? And a croissant, from that place across the street."

"All right," said Netherton. "Let me brush my teeth. I did rescue you from those darknet kiwis, who were hardly state assassins, and bring you here, under the protection of the British secret state. So to speak."

"Crema," she said, sleepily.

He brushed his teeth, remembering how Lowbeer had had to get her out of Canada, then into England, and how they'd wound up in bed together, not for the first time but definitely the first time he hadn't been drunk. And how he'd confessed, in possibly the single most awkward morning-after moment of what seemed a long career of them, his feelings for Flynne, or possibly her peripheral, or both, with Rainey pointing out that she, Flynne, had recently become his client. And hadn't he, she asked, had ample proof of what could come of having it off with clients? But Flynne wasn't Daedra, he'd protested. But what he was, most definitely, Rainey had said, was someone so immature as to believe that his own erotic projections should have actual weight in the world. And then she'd pulled him back into bed and argued it differently, though from the same position, and he'd begun, he supposed, to see it her way. And soon it had become apparent that Flynne and Sheriff Tommy were a couple, and here he was dressing, in their newly shared flat, to go down to the street, on a sunny Soho afternoon, grateful as ever that plans to implement a Cheapside-style cosplay zone here had never been implemented.

He was coming out of the baker's when Macon's sigil appeared. "Yes?"

"If we fly your boy to Frankfurt, will you be able to brief the German PR team, tomorrow morning, ten your time?"

"Where is it, now?"

"On the runaway in Cairo, cleared for takeoff. We've got Flynne's peri, the one for this hemisphere, in Paris, so if she's available then, you could brief them together."

"Sounds good. Anything else?"

"Nope. You coming to the barbecue, Sunday?"

"Wheelie, yes."

"You're weird, Wilf. I heard you got your girlfriend one."

"We'll both be there."

"You want to fetishize an extremely narrow-bandwidth experience," Macon said, "that's your business."

"If you spent more time up here," said Wilf, "you might start to appreciate that sort of thing. It's relaxing."

"Too rich for my blood," said Macon, cheerfully, and his sigil was gone.

Putney tomorrow, Netherton reminded himself, after ordering a pair of double espressos to take away. Two in the afternoon. His second follow-up appointment. If it was sunny, they'd ride bicycles. He doubted the German PR business would take that long.

Always nice to see Flynne.

ACKNOWLEDGMENTS AND THANKS

The idea of "third-worlding" the past of alternate continua owes everything to "Mozart in Mirrorshades" (1985) by Bruce Sterling and Lewis Shiner, though there the travel is physical, with extraction of natural resources the focus of exploitation. Filtered through simulation gaming, telepresence, and drones, that became something I mumbled about to James Gleick, on first meeting him, just when whatever became this book was getting started. (Later, he drew my attention to that Wells quote.)

The descriptions of Cheapside and Newgate owe much to Kate Colquhoun's *Mr. Briggs' Hat* (2011), a wonderfully vivid account of Britain's first railway murder.

Several landscape features of Wilf's London are from John Foxx's interview, by Etienne Gilfillan, in the March 2011 issue of *Fortean Times*.

Nick Harkaway, in his Hampstead garden, told me spooky things about the inner workings of the guilds of the City of London, any merely literal truth of which I have scrupulously avoided prying into.

"Buttholeville" is the title of a song with lyrics (and, I assume, title) by Patterson Hood.

The longer I write novels, the more I appreciate first readers. This one had quite a few, aside of course from my wife Deborah and daughter Claire. Paul McAuley and Jack Womack weathered countless near-identical iterations of the first hundred pages or so. Ned Bauman and Chris Nakashima-Brown both waded through cold reads of the book at midpoint, always valuable but tricky work. James Gleick and Michael St. John Smith did the same, but toward the conclusion. Sean Crawford, Louis Lapprend, and the enigmatic V. Harnell ran a sort of tag team. Meredith Yayanos kept a careful eye on Inspector Lowbeer throughout, an acute and articulate tunnel canary amid some issues I know little about. Sophia Al-Maria read the first completed version, helping mightily with Hamed in terms of Gulf Futurism.

Martin Simmons suggested the use of bagged roofing shingles for impromptu fortification.

Mr. Robert Graham very generously provided essential writing hardware.

My editor and literary agent were wonderful, as ever.

Thank you all.

—*Vancouver, 23 July 2014*